BOONE COUNTY LIBRARY

2040 9101 031 607 2

S0-AJA-360

WITHDRAWN

Ray Fawkes

intersect

HARMTEMPO
OARMTEMPH
MAROTEMPH
MERATOMPH
METAROMPH
METAMORPH

METAMORPH

JUN 1 4 2016

BOONE COUNTY PUBLIC LIBRARY
BURLINGTON, KY 41005
www.bcpl.org

IMAGE COMICS, INC.
Robert Kirkman – Chief Operating Officer
Erik Larsen – Chief Financial Officer
Todd McFarlane – President
Marc Silvestri – Chief Executive Officer
Jim Valentino – Vice-President

Eric Stephenson – Publisher
Kat Salazar – Director of PR & Marketing
Corey Murphy – Director of Retail Sales
Jeremy Sullivan – Director of Digital Sales
Randy Okamura – Marketing Production Designer
Emilio Bautista – Sales Assistant
Branwyn Bigglestone – Senior Accounts Manager
Emily Miller – Accounts Manager
Jessica Ambriz – Administrative Assistant
David Brothers – Content Manager
Jonathan Chan – Production Manager
Drew Gill – Art Director
Meredith Wallace – Print Manager
Addison Duke – Production Artist
Vincent Kukua – Production Artist
Sasha Head – Production Artist
Tricia Ramos – Production Assistant
IMAGECOMICS.COM

Intersect, volume 1. First printing. May 2015. Copyright © 2015 Ray Fawkes. All rights reserved. Published by Image Comics, Inc. Office of publication: 2001 Center Street, Sixth Floor, Berkeley, CA 94704. Originally published in single magazine form as INTERSECT #1-6. "Intersect," its logos, and the likenesses of all characters herein are trademarks of Ray Fawkes, unless otherwise noted. "Image" and the Image Comics logos are registered trademarks of Image Comics, Inc. No part of this publication may be reproduced or transmitted, in any form or by any means (except for short excerpts for journalistic or review purposes), without the express written permission of Ray Fawkes or Image Comics, Inc. All names, characters, events, and locales in this publication are entirely fictional. Any resemblance to actual persons (living or dead), events, or places, without satiric intent, is coincidental. Printed in the USA. For information regarding the CPSIA on this printed material call: 203-595-3636 and provide reference #RICH–619366.
For international rights, contact: foreignlicensing@imagecomics.com. ISBN: 978-1-63215-279-4

Part One

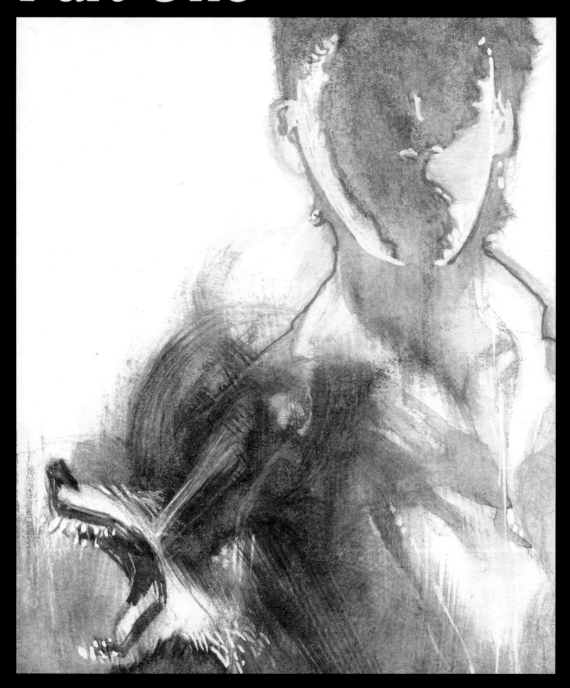

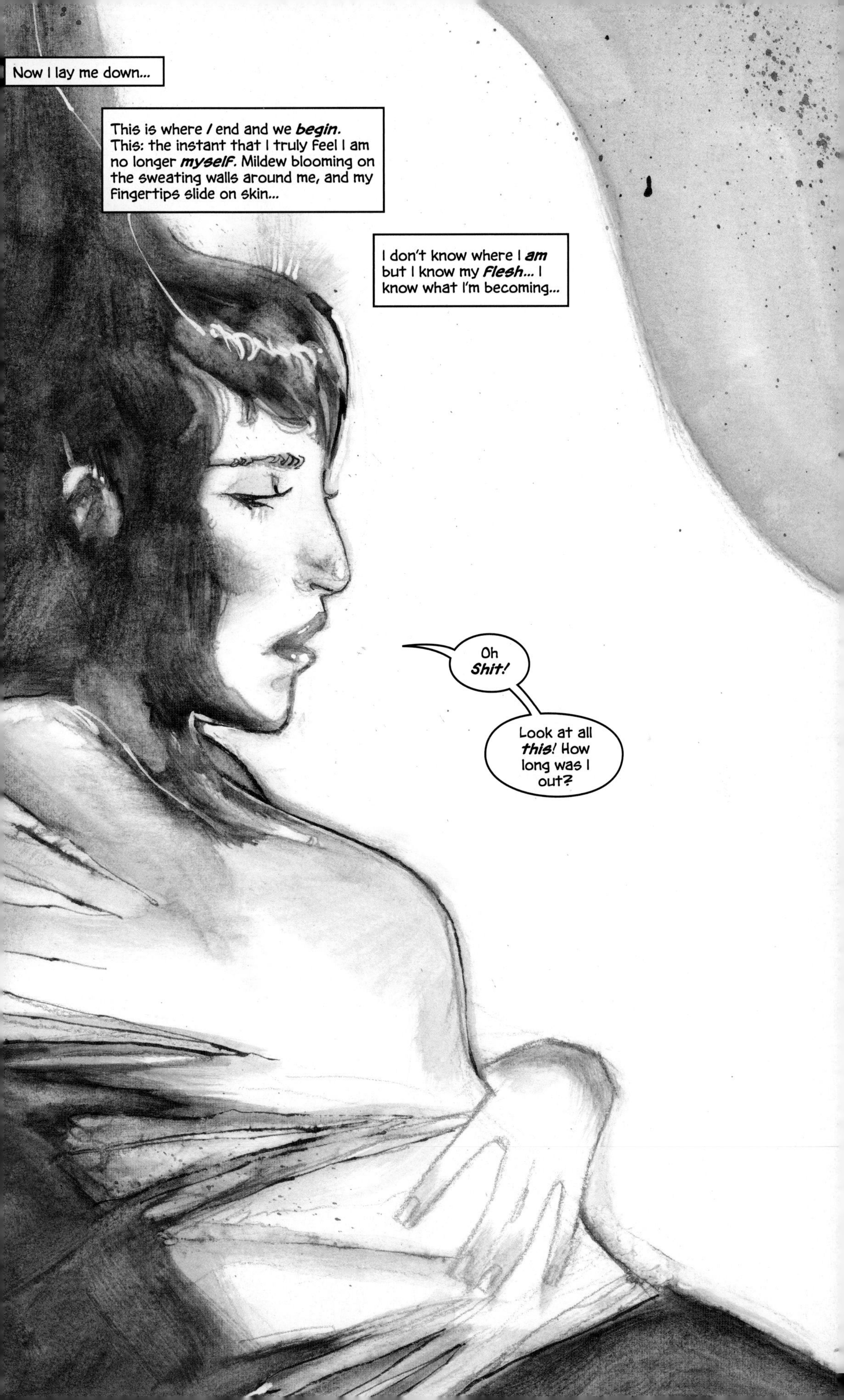
Now I lay me down...
This is where *I* end and we *begin*. This: the instant that I truly feel I am no longer *myself*. Mildew blooming on the sweating walls around me, and my fingertips slide on skin...
I don't know where I *am* but I know my *flesh*... I know what I'm becoming...
Oh *Shit!*
Look at all *this!* How long was I out?

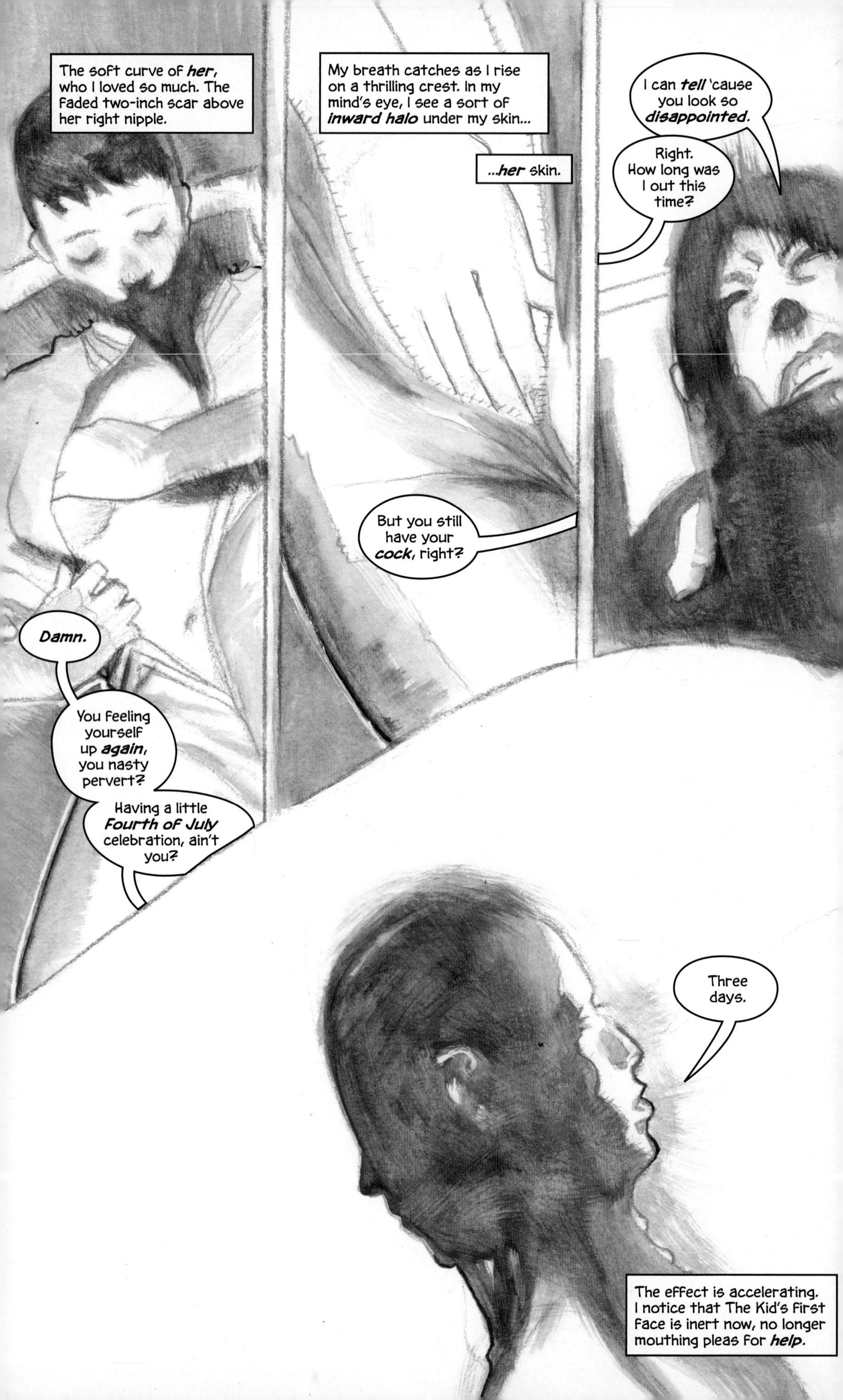

The soft curve of *her*, who I loved so much. The faded two-inch scar above her right nipple.
My breath catches as I rise on a thrilling crest. In my mind's eye, I see a sort of *inward halo* under my skin...
...*her* skin.
I can *tell* 'cause you look so *disappointed*.
Right. How long was I out this time?
But you still have your *cock*, right?
Damn.
You feeling yourself up *again*, you nasty pervert?
Having a little *Fourth of July* celebration, ain't you?
Three days.
The effect is accelerating. I notice that The Kid's First Face is inert now, no longer mouthing pleas for *help*.

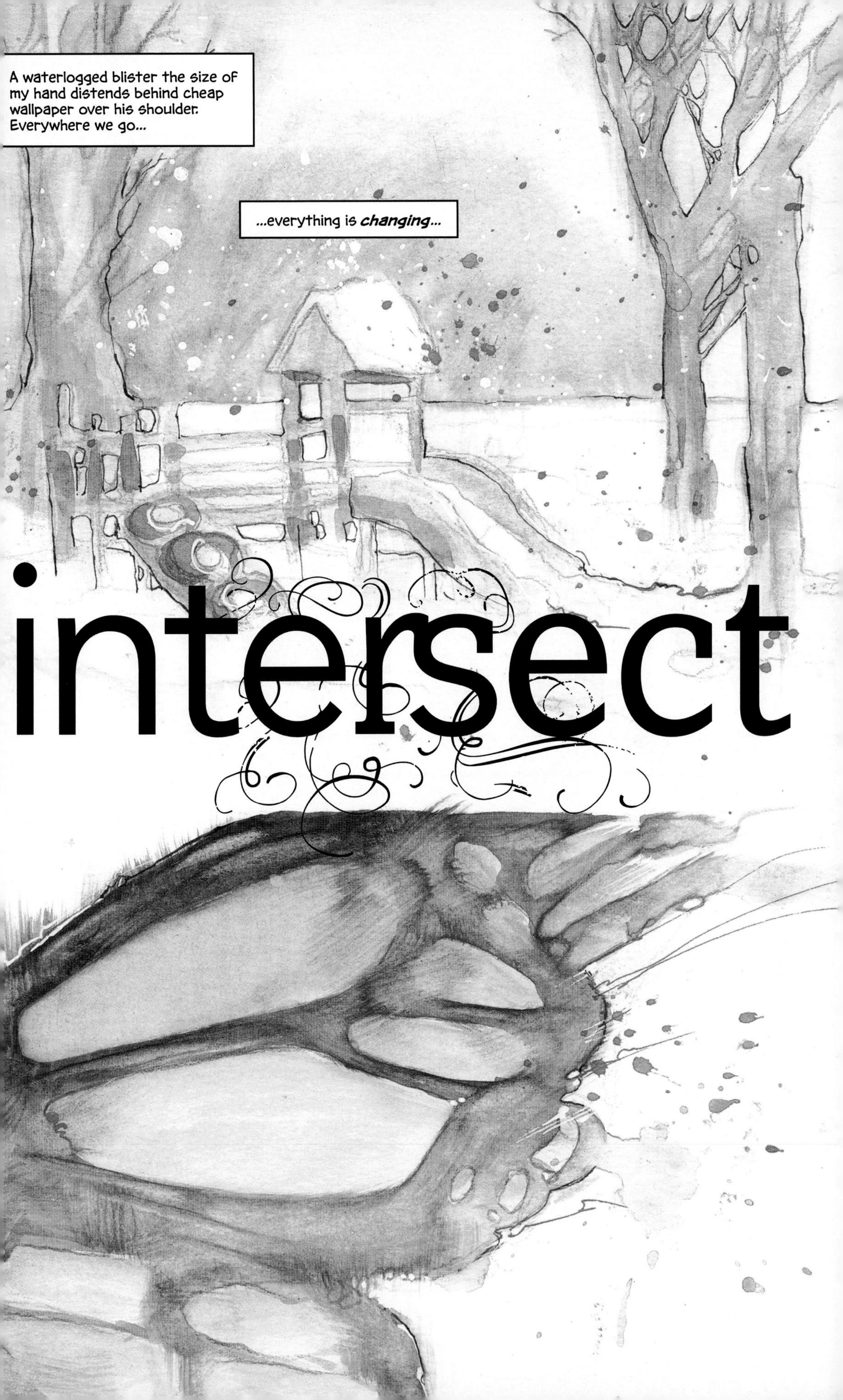
A waterlogged blister the size of my hand distends behind cheap wallpaper over his shoulder. Everywhere we go...
...everything is *changing*...
intersect

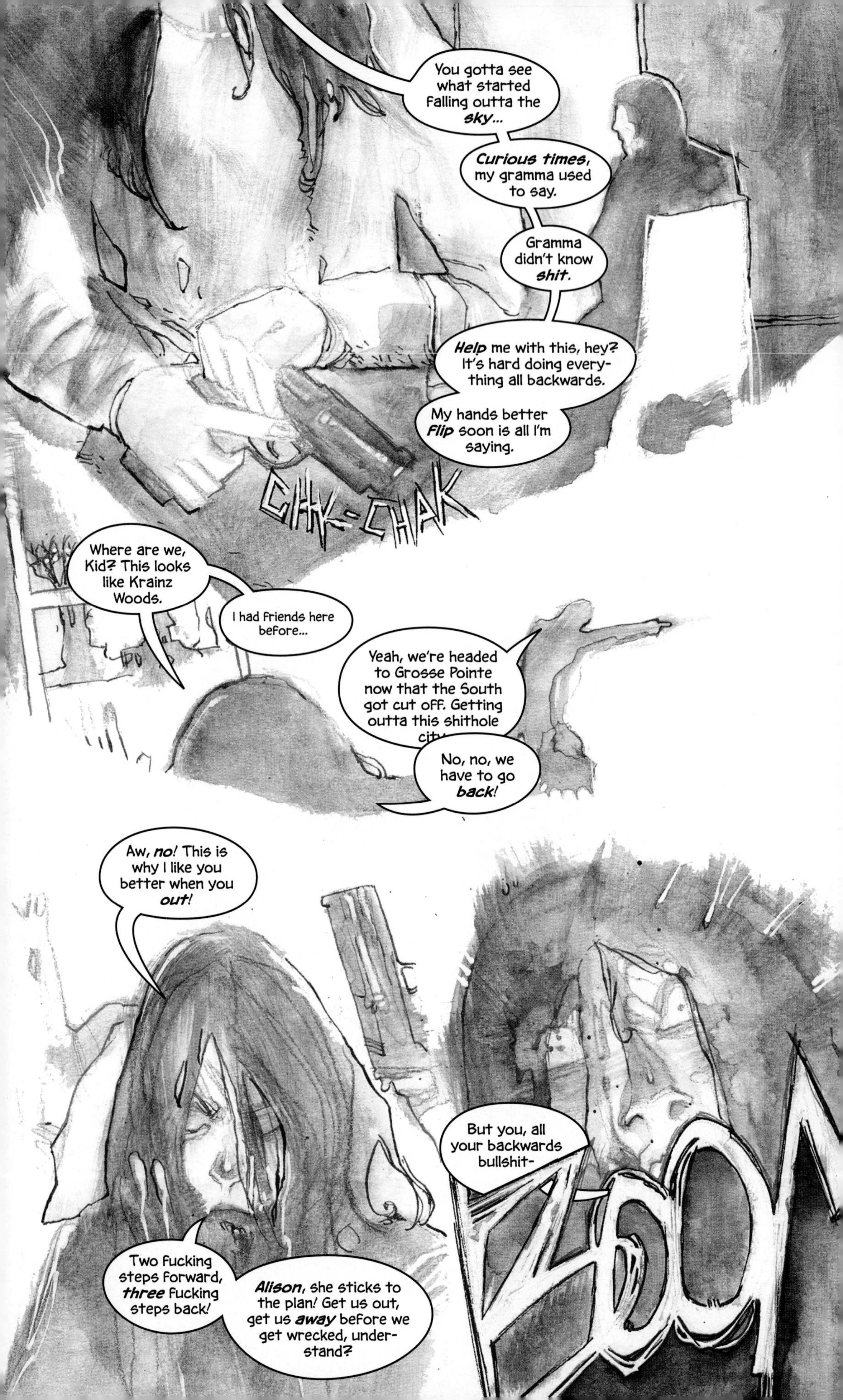

You gotta see what started falling outta the *sky*...
Curious times, my gramma used to say.
Gramma didn't know *shit*.
Help me with this, hey? It's hard doing everything all backwards.
My hands better *flip* soon is all I'm saying.
CHK-CHAK
Where are we, Kid? This looks like Krainz Woods.
I had friends here before...
Yeah, we're headed to Grosse Pointe now that the South got cut off. Getting outta this shithole city.
No, no, we have to go *back*!
Aw, *no*! This is why I like you better when you *out*!
But you, all your backwards bullshit-
Two fucking steps forward, *three* fucking steps back!
Alison, she sticks to the plan! Get us out, get us *away* before we get wrecked, understand?

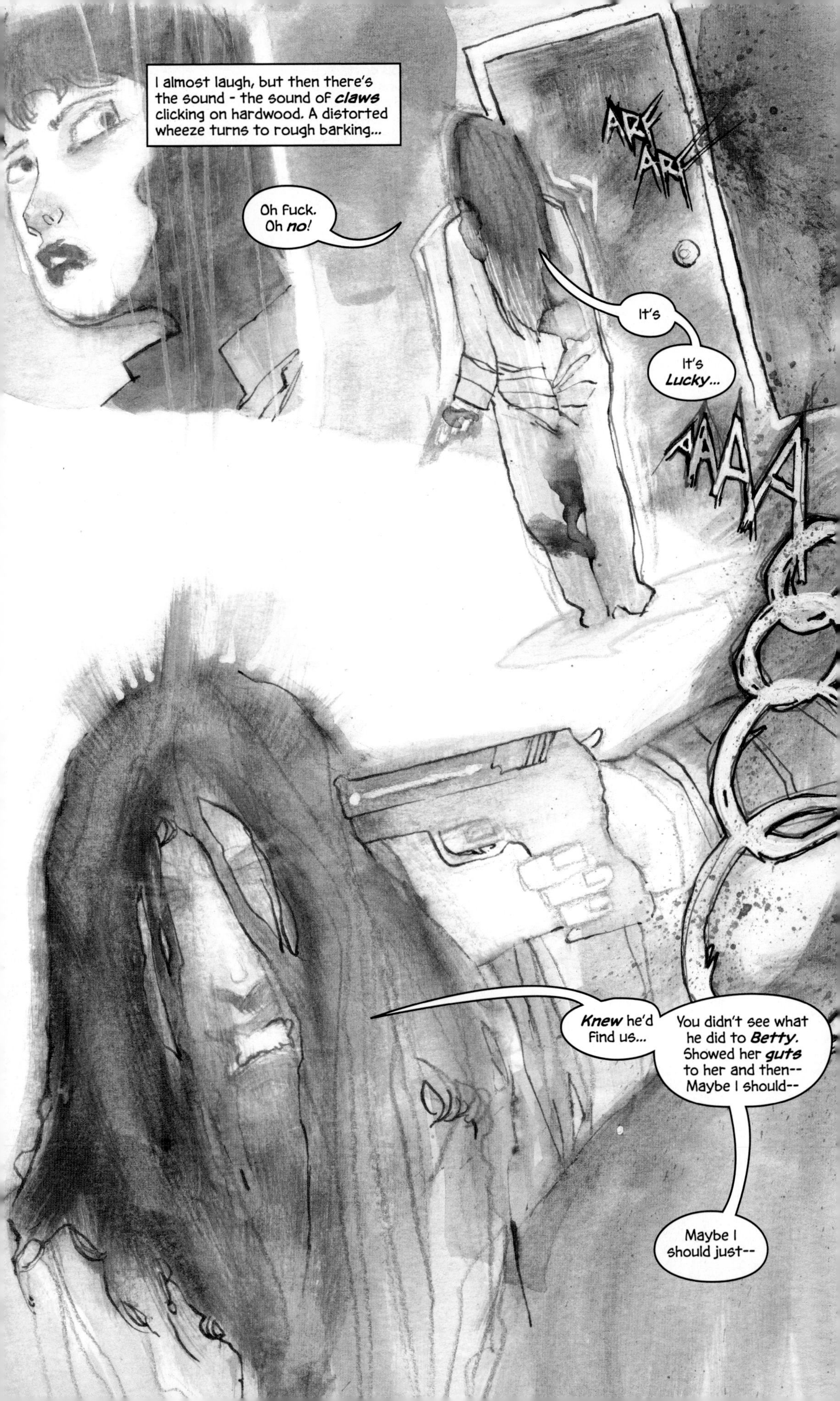
I almost laugh, but then there's the sound - the sound of *claws* clicking on hardwood. A distorted wheeze turns to rough barking...
Oh fuck. Oh *no!*
ARF ARF
It's
It's *Lucky*...
AAAA
Knew he'd Find us...
You didn't see what he did to *Betty*. Showed her *guts* to her and then-- Maybe I should--
Maybe I should just--

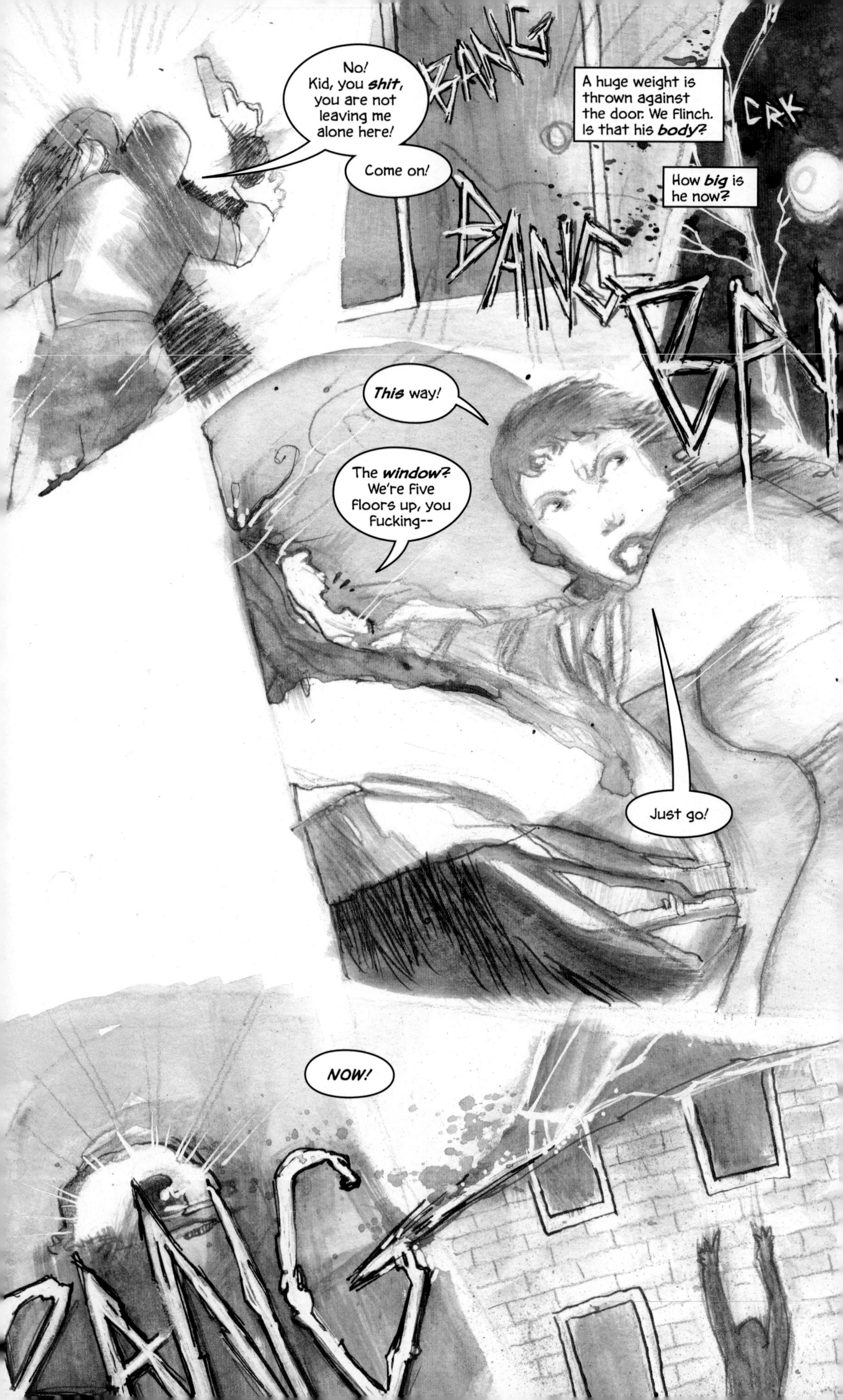
No! Kid, you shit, you are not leaving me alone here!
Come on!
BANG
A huge weight is thrown against the door. We flinch. Is that his body?
CRK
How big is he now?
BANG
This way!
The window? We're five floors up, you fucking--
Just go!
NOW!

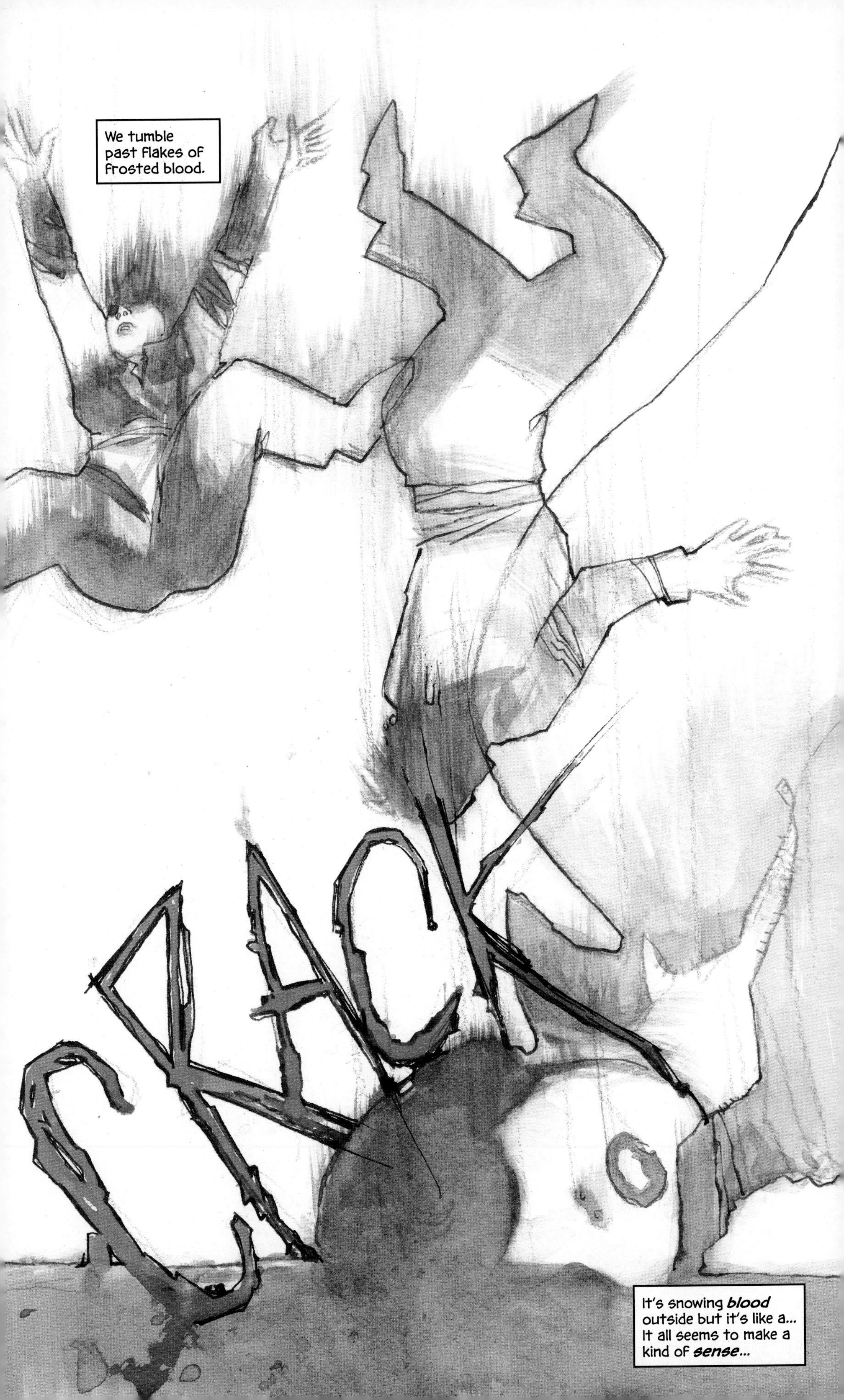
We tumble past flakes of frosted blood.
CRACK
It's snowing *blood* outside but it's like a... It all seems to make a kind of *sense*...

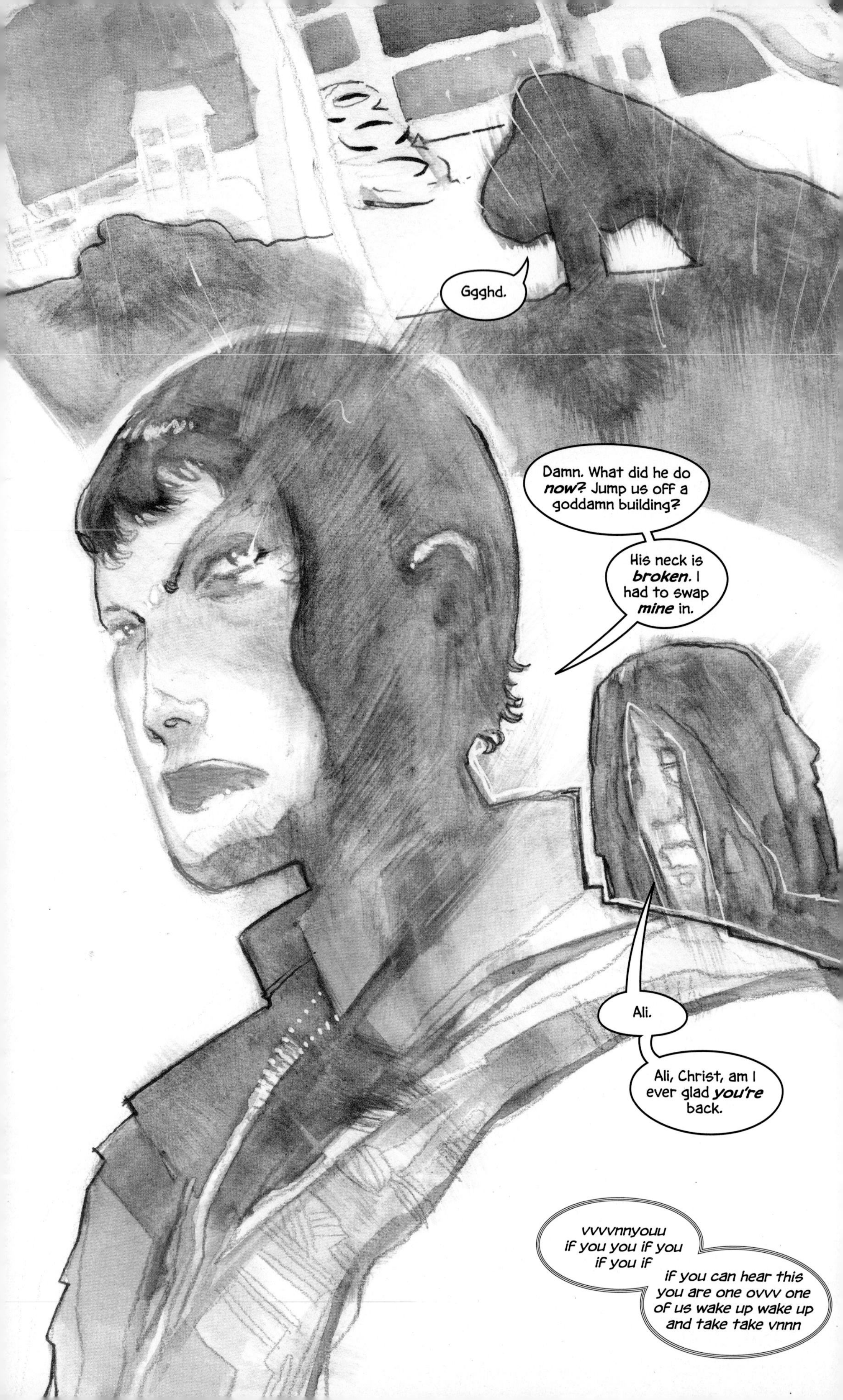
Ggghd.
Damn. What did he do *now?* Jump us off a goddamn building?
His neck is *broken*. I had to swap *mine* in.
Ali.
Ali, Christ, am I ever glad *you're* back.
vvvvnnyouu if you you if you if you if
if you can hear this you are one ovvv one of us wake up wake up and take take vnnn

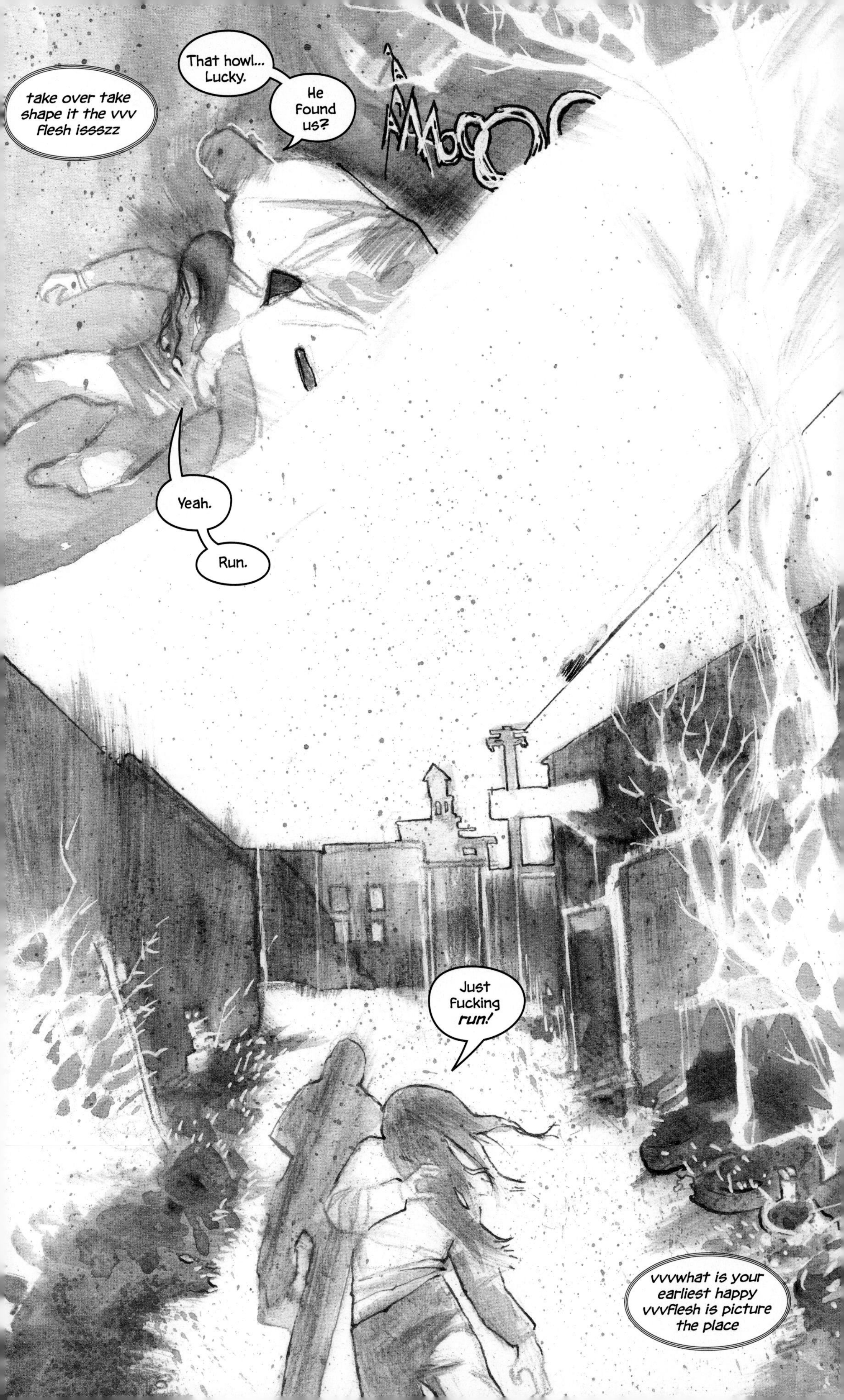
take over take shape it the vvv Flesh issszz
That howl... Lucky.
He found us?
AAAOOOO
Yeah.
Run.
Just fucking *run!*
vvvwhat is your earliest happy vvvflesh is picture the place

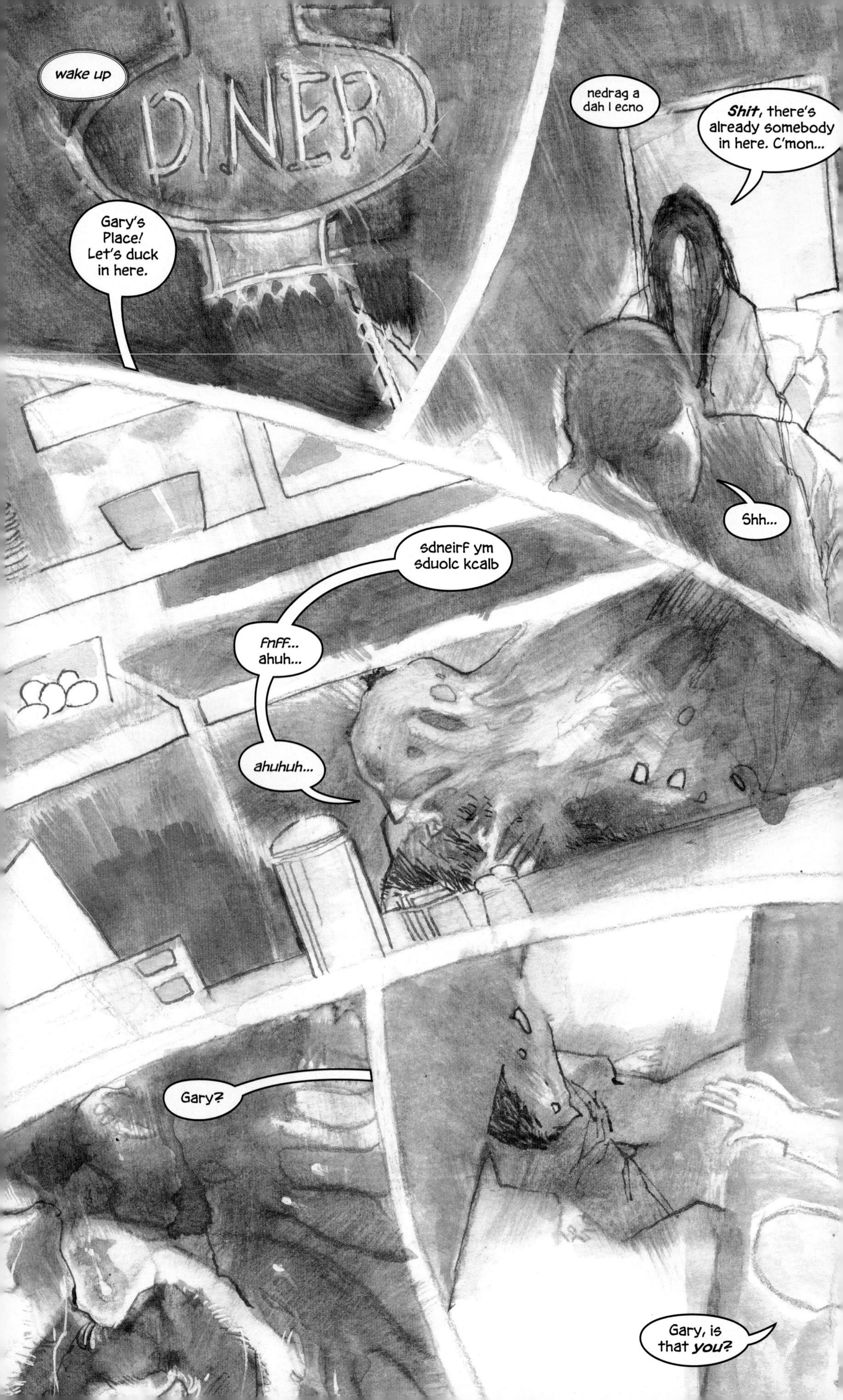
wake up
DINER
Gary's Place! Let's duck in here.
nedrag a dah I ecno
Shit, there's already somebody in here. C'mon...
Shh...
sdneirf ym sduolc kcalb
fnff... ahuh...
ahuhuh...
Gary?
Gary, is that *you?*

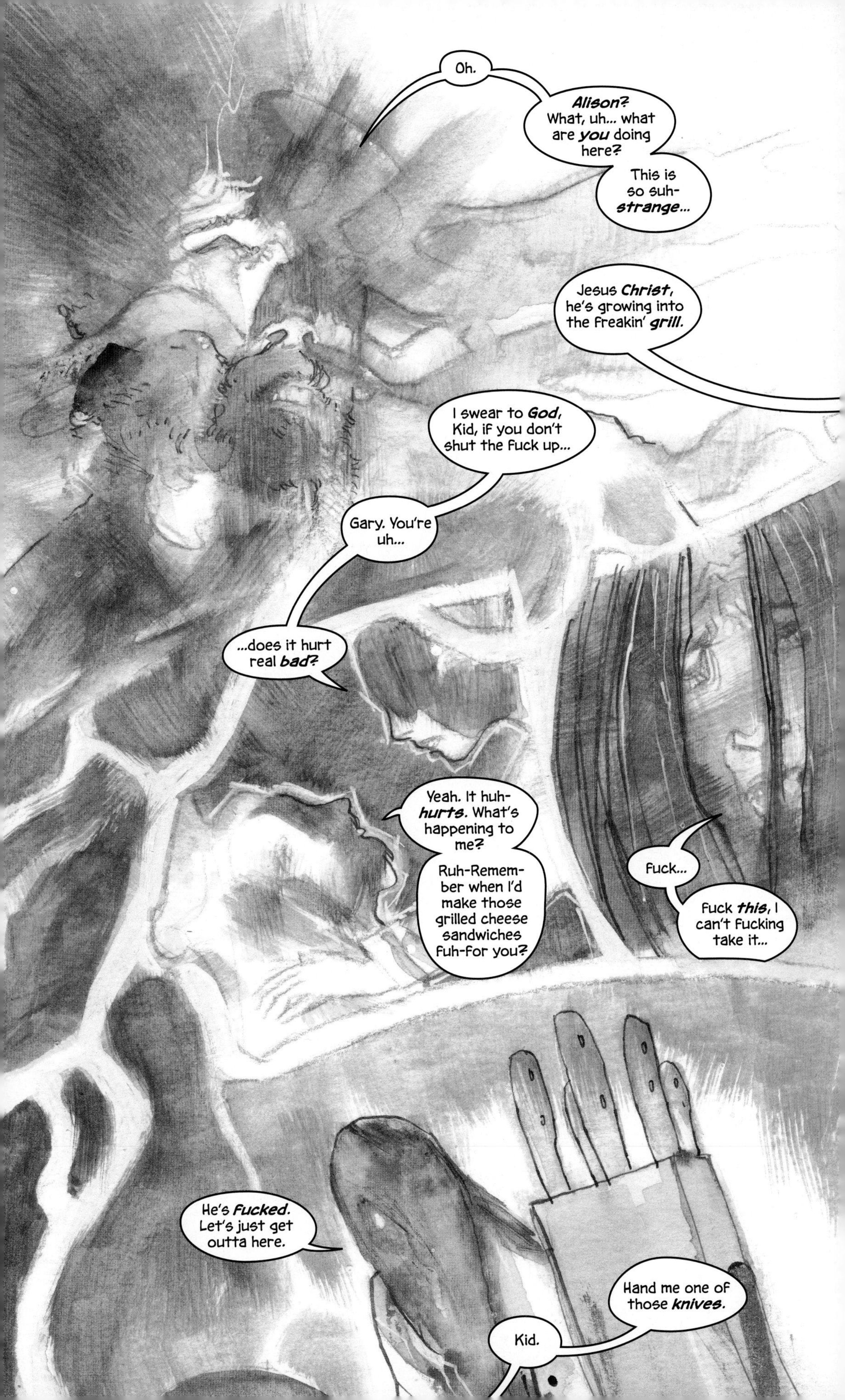
Oh.
Alisone? What, uh... what are you doing here?
This is so suh-strange...
Jesus Christ, he's growing into the freakin' grill.
I swear to God, Kid, if you don't shut the fuck up...
Gary. You're uh...
...does it hurt real bad?
Yeah. It huh-hurts. What's happening to me?
Ruh-Remember when I'd make those grilled cheese sandwiches fuh-for you?
Fuck...
Fuck this, I can't fucking take it...
He's Fucked. Let's just get outta here.
Hand me one of those knives.
Kid.

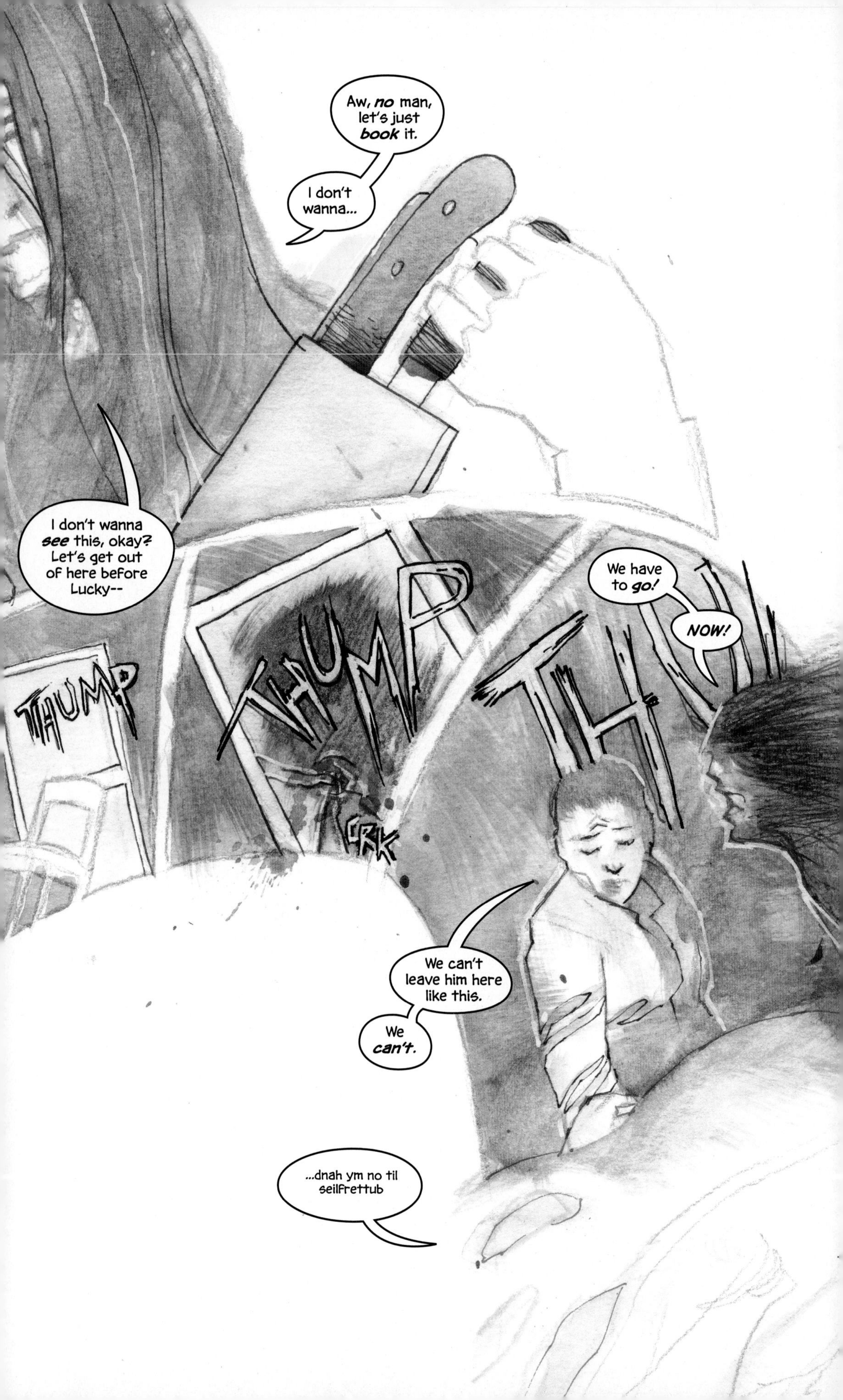

Aw, *no* man, let's just *book* it.
I don't wanna...
I don't wanna *see* this, okay? Let's get out of here before Lucky--
THUMP
THUMP
CRK
TH
We have to *go!*
NOW!
We can't leave him here like this.
We *can't.*
...dnah ym no til seilfrettub

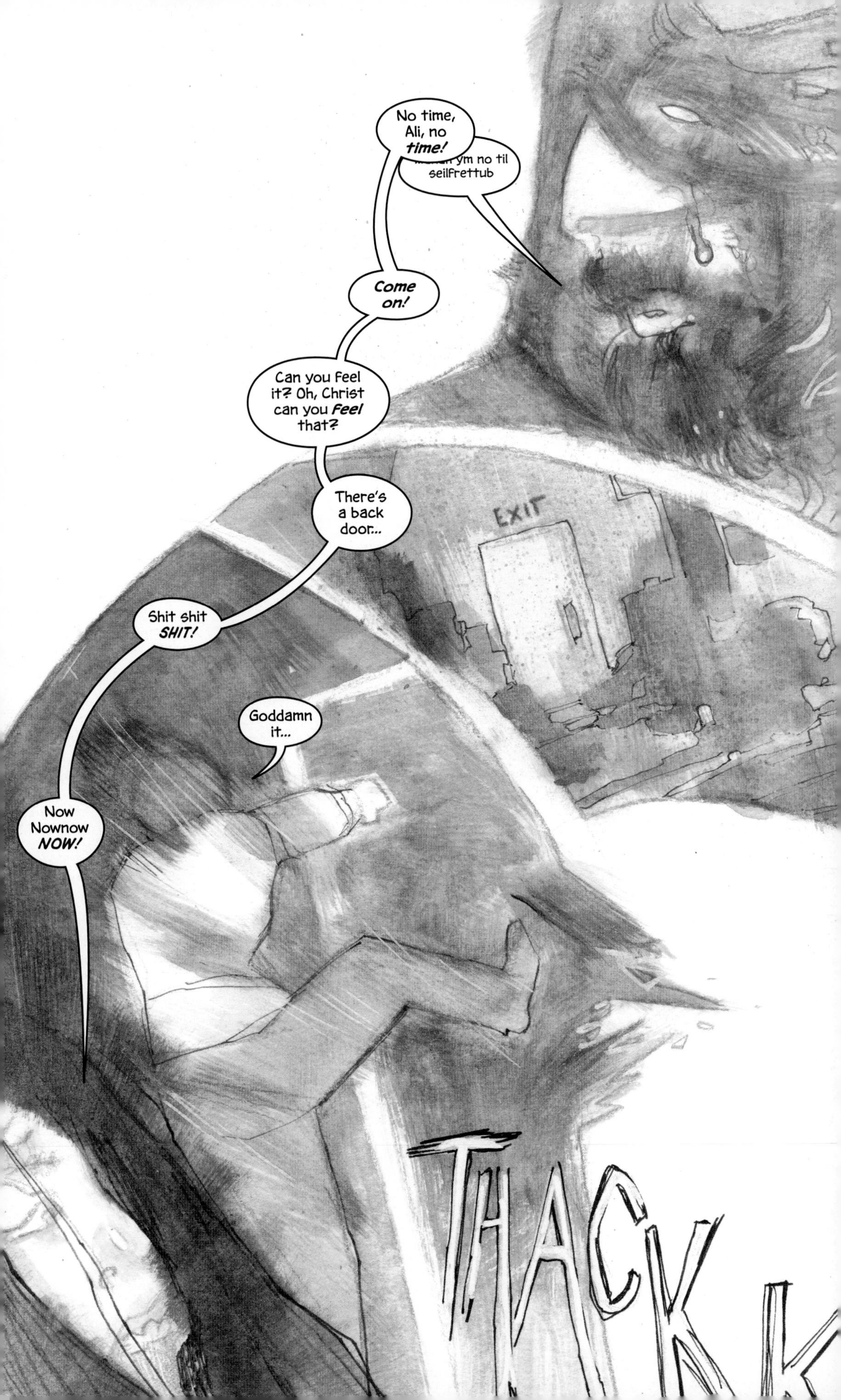
No time, Ali, no *time!*
ym no til seilfrettub
Come on!
Can you feel it? Oh, Christ can you *feel* that?
There's a back door...
Shit shit *SHIT!*
Goddamn it...
Now Nownow *NOW!*
THACK K

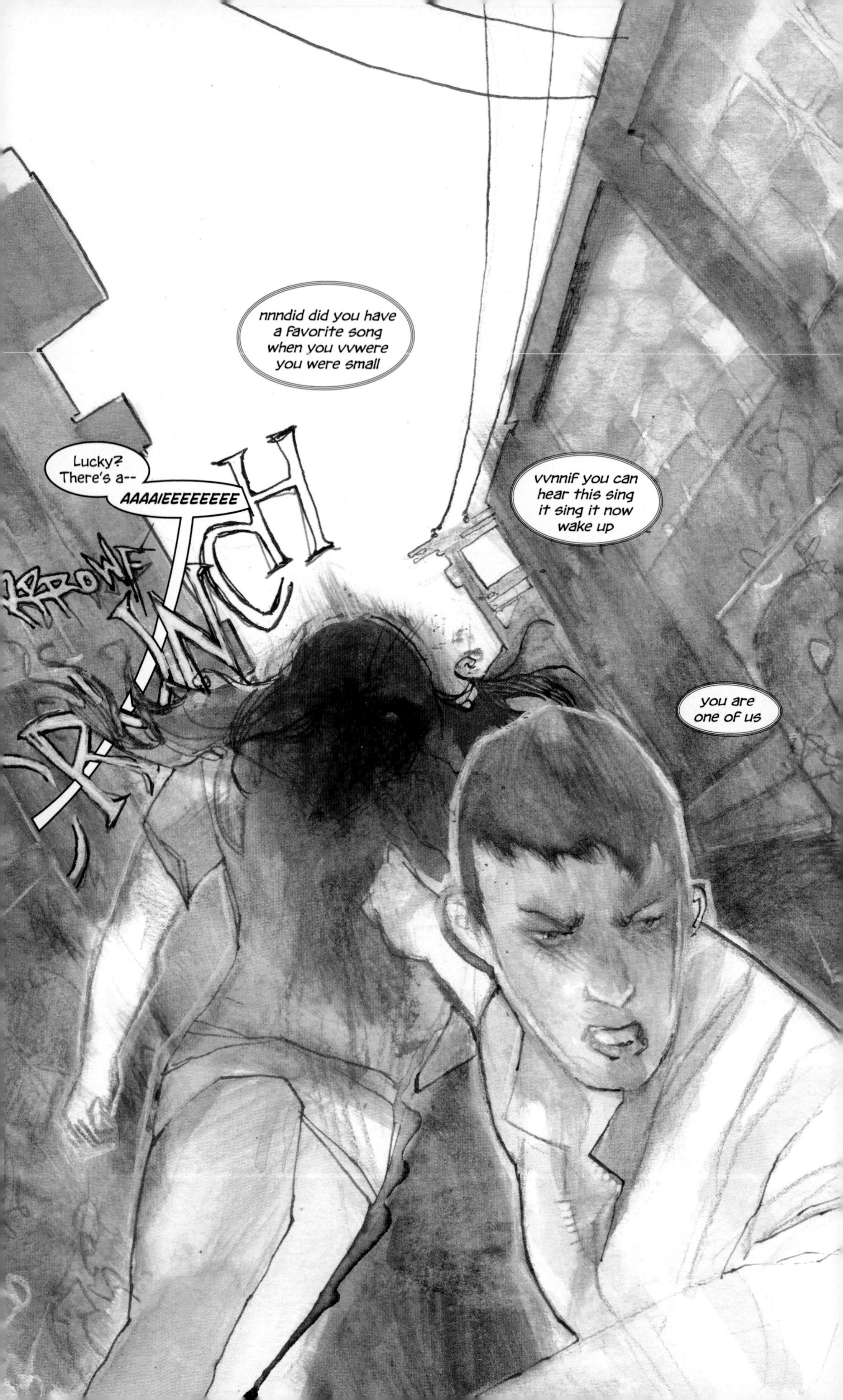
nnndid did you have a favorite song when you vvwere you were small
Lucky? There's a--
AAAAIEEEEEEEEE
vvnnif you can hear this sing it sing it now wake up
you are one of us

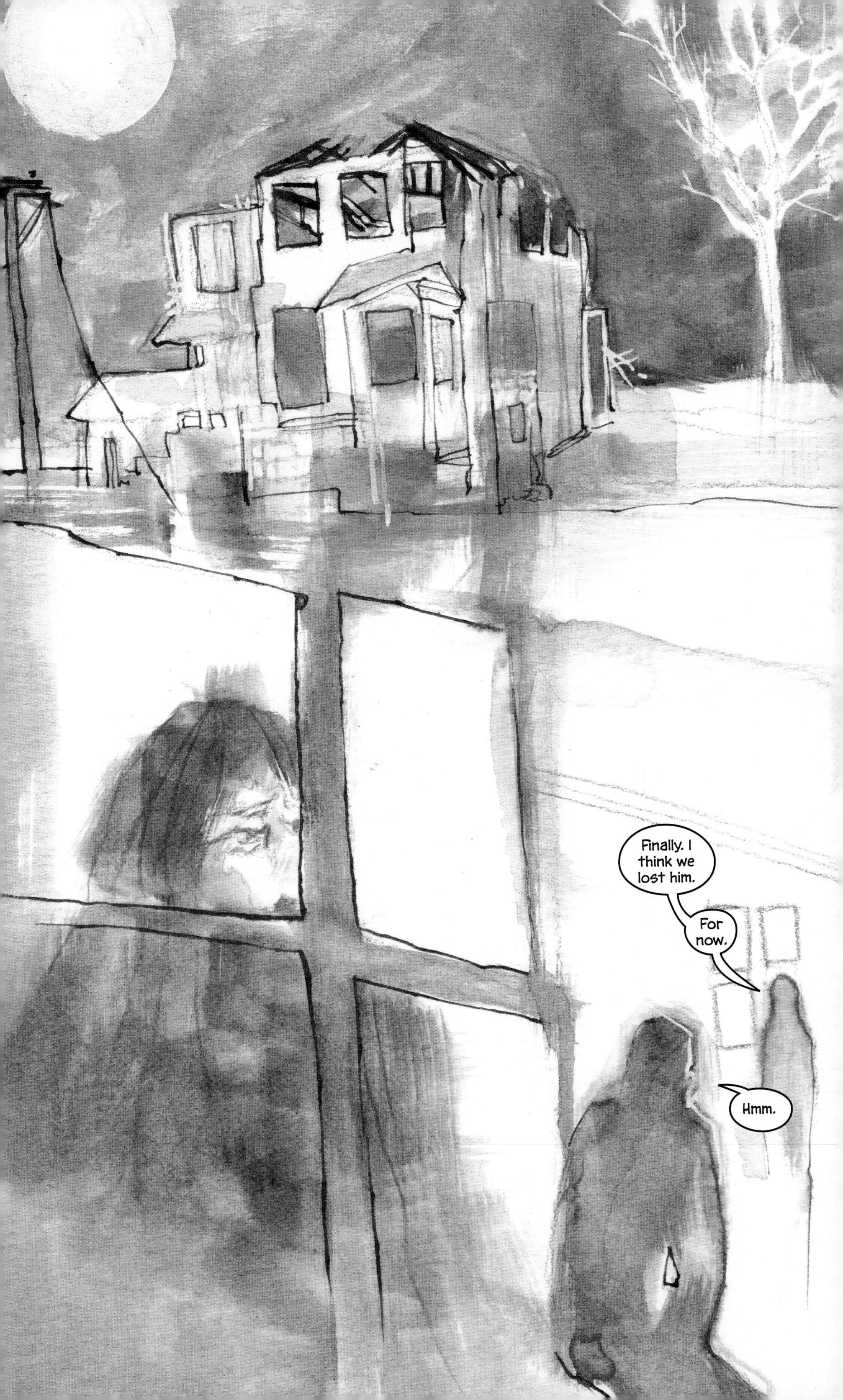
Finally. I think we lost him.
For now.
Hmm.

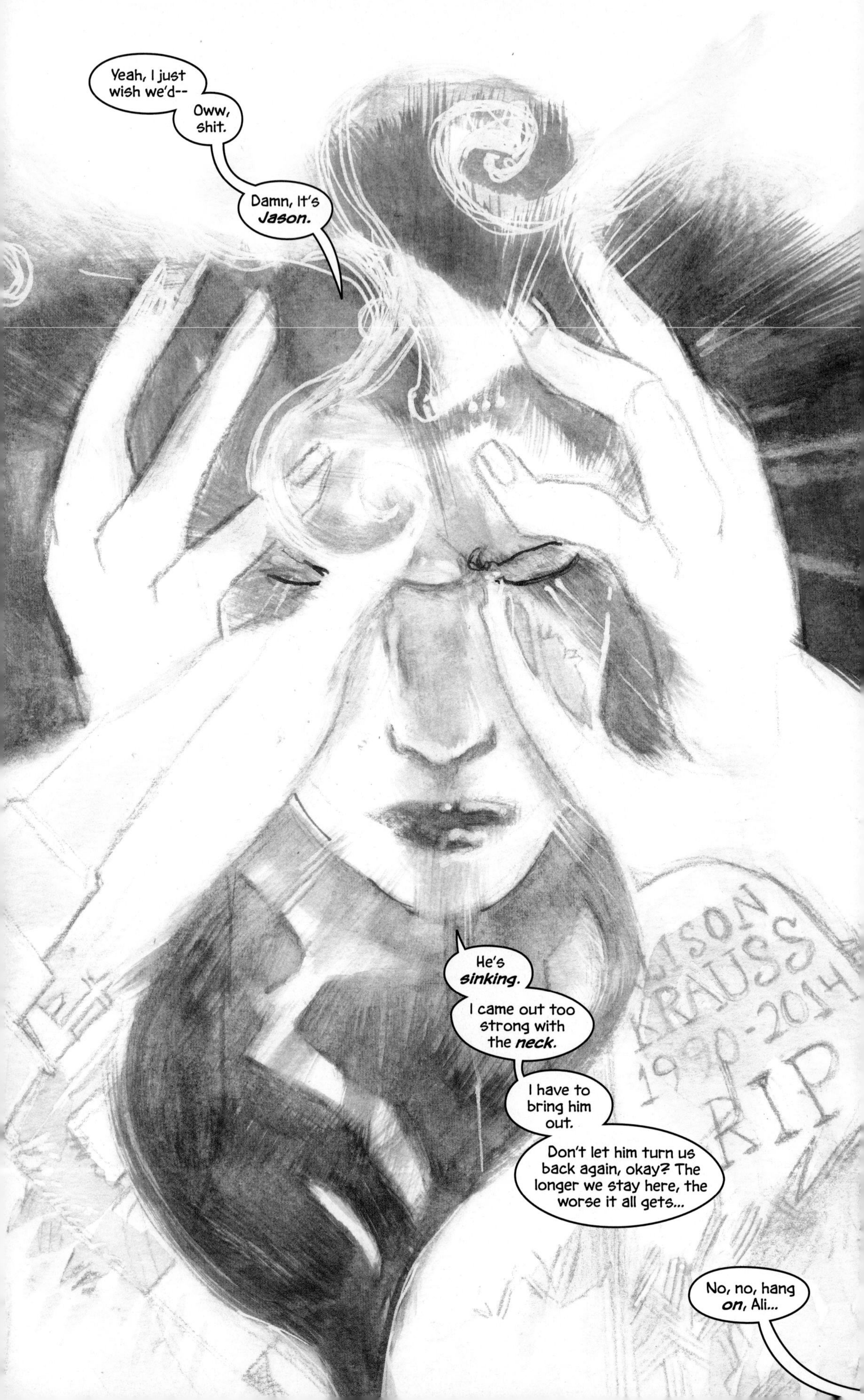
Yeah, I just wish we'd--
Oww, shit.
Damn, It's *Jason.*
ALISON KRAUSS 1990-2014 RIP
He's *sinking.*
I came out too strong with the *neck.*
I have to bring him out.
Don't let him turn us back again, okay? The longer we stay here, the worse it all gets...
No, no, hang *on*, Ali...

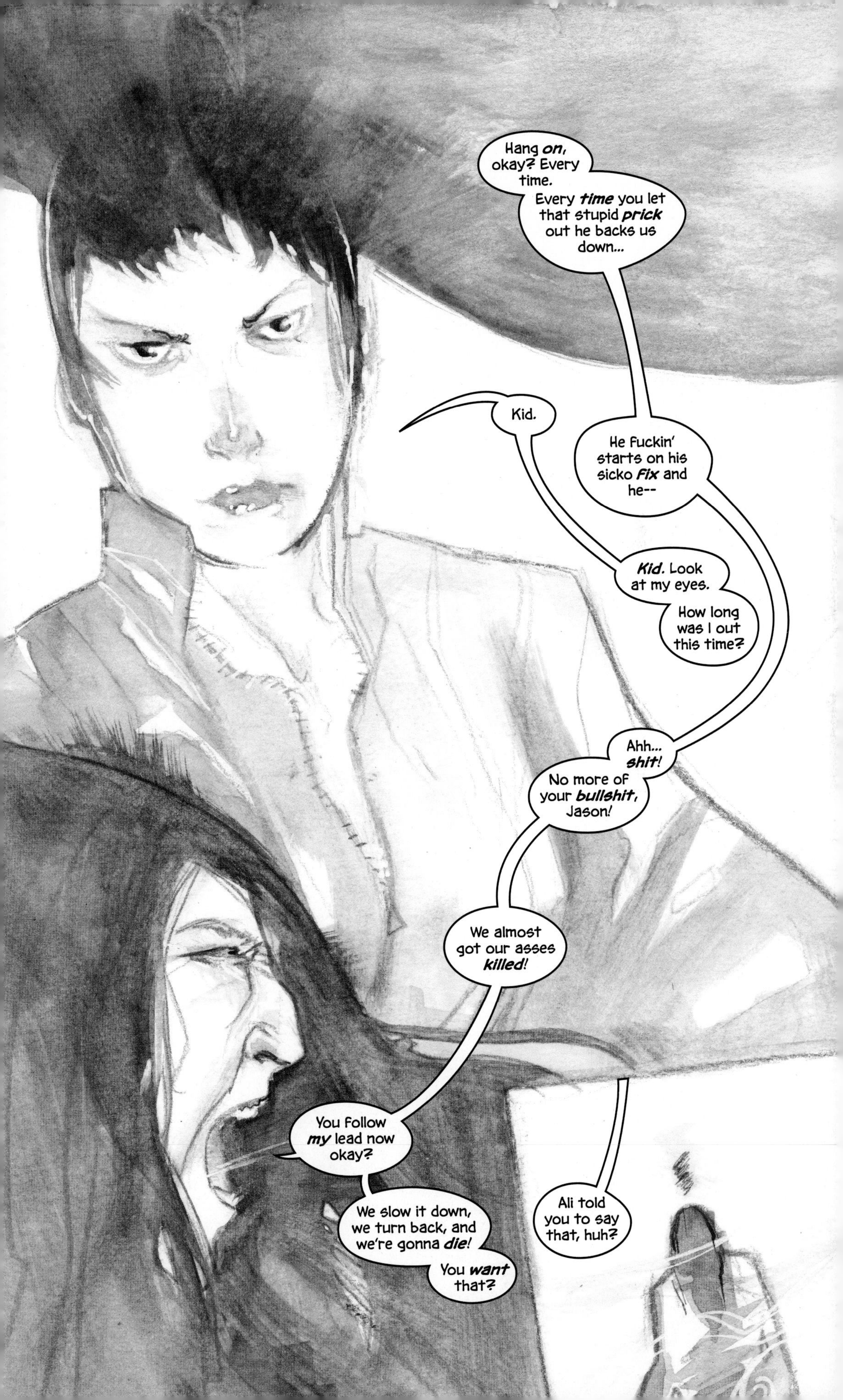
Hang *on*, okay? Every time.
Every *time* you let that stupid *prick* out he backs us down...
He fuckin' starts on his sicko *fix* and he--
Kid.
Kid. Look at my eyes.
How long was I out this time?
Ahh... *shit*!
No more of your *bullshit*, Jason!
We almost got our asses *killed*!
You follow *my* lead now okay?
We slow it down, we turn back, and we're gonna *die*!
You *want* that?
Ali told you to say that, huh?

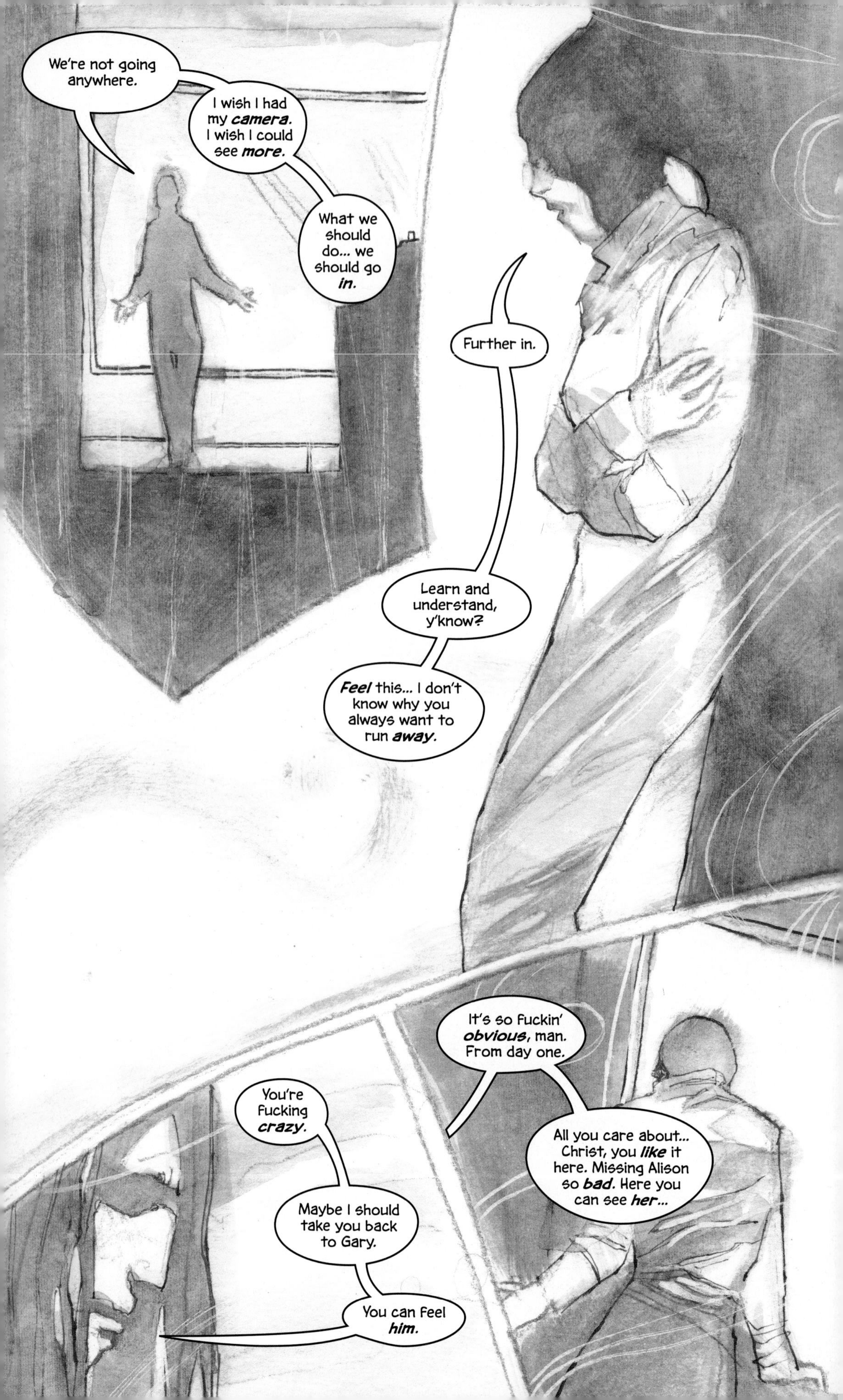
We're not going anywhere.
I wish I had my *camera*. I wish I could see *more*.
What we should do... we should go *in*.
Further in.
Learn and understand, y'know?
Feel this... I don't know why you always want to run *away*.
It's so fuckin' *obvious*, man. From day one.
You're fucking *crazy*.
All you care about... Christ, you *like* it here. Missing Alison so *bad*. Here you can see *her*...
Maybe I should take you back to Gary.
You can feel *him*.

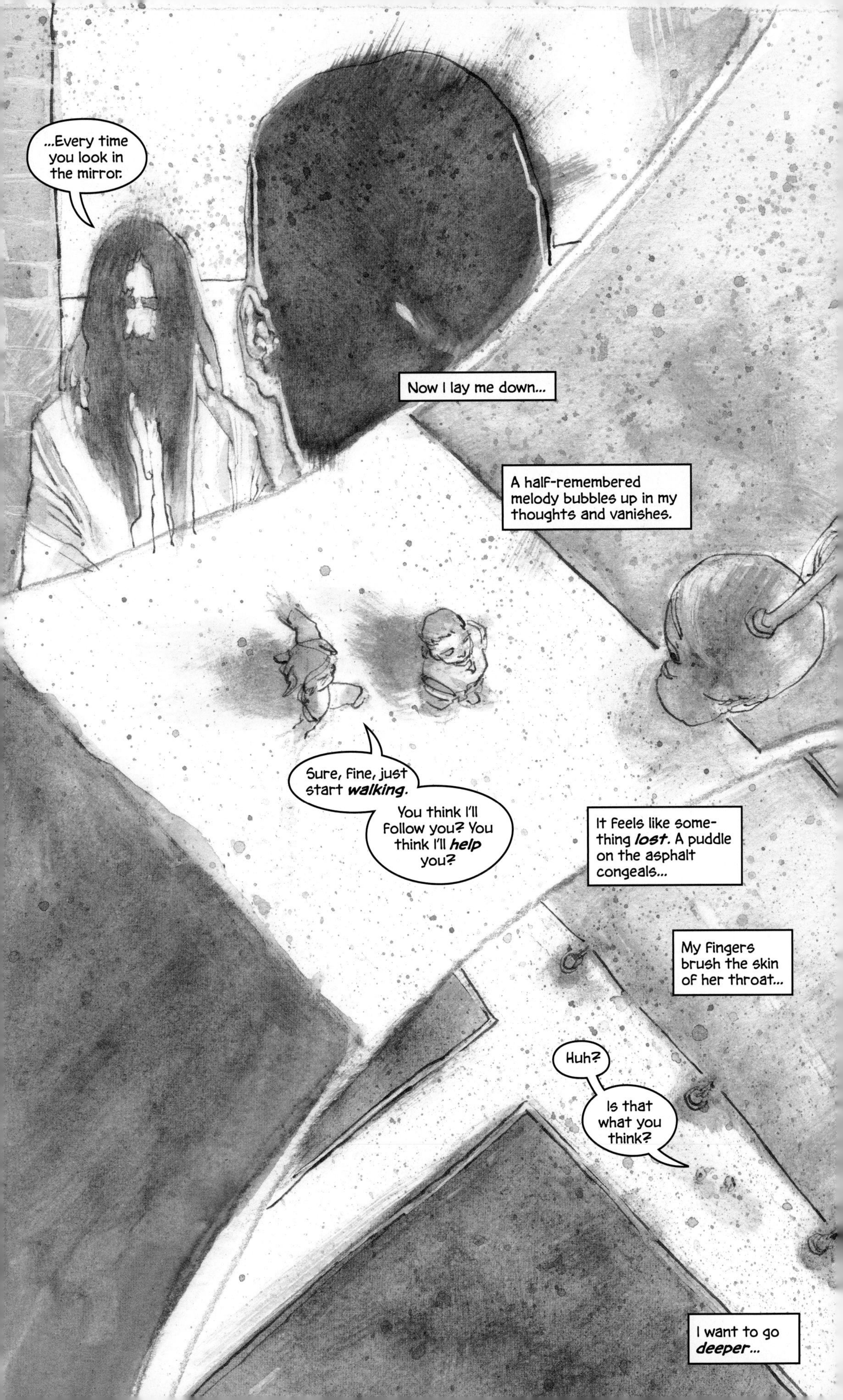
...Every time you look in the mirror.
Now I lay me down...
A half-remembered melody bubbles up in my thoughts and vanishes.
Sure, fine, just start *walking*.
You think I'll follow you? You think I'll *help* you?
It feels like something *lost*. A puddle on the asphalt congeals...
My fingers brush the skin of her throat...
Huh?
Is that what you think?
I want to go *deeper*...

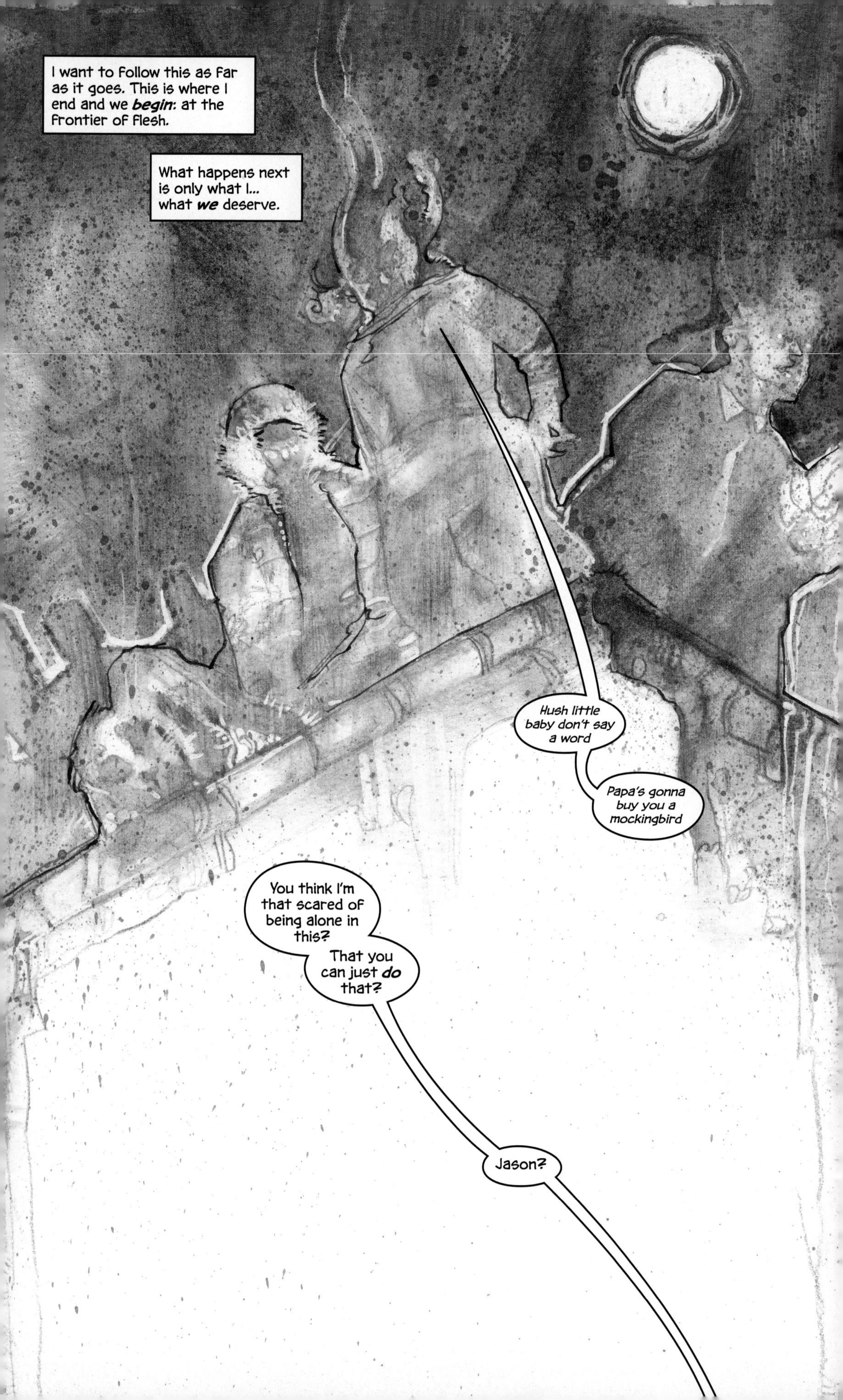
I want to follow this as far as it goes. This is where I end and we *begin*: at the frontier of flesh.
What happens next is only what I... what *we* deserve.
Hush little baby don't say a word
Papa's gonna buy you a mockingbird
You think I'm that scared of being alone in this?
That you can just *do* that?
Jason?

Part Two

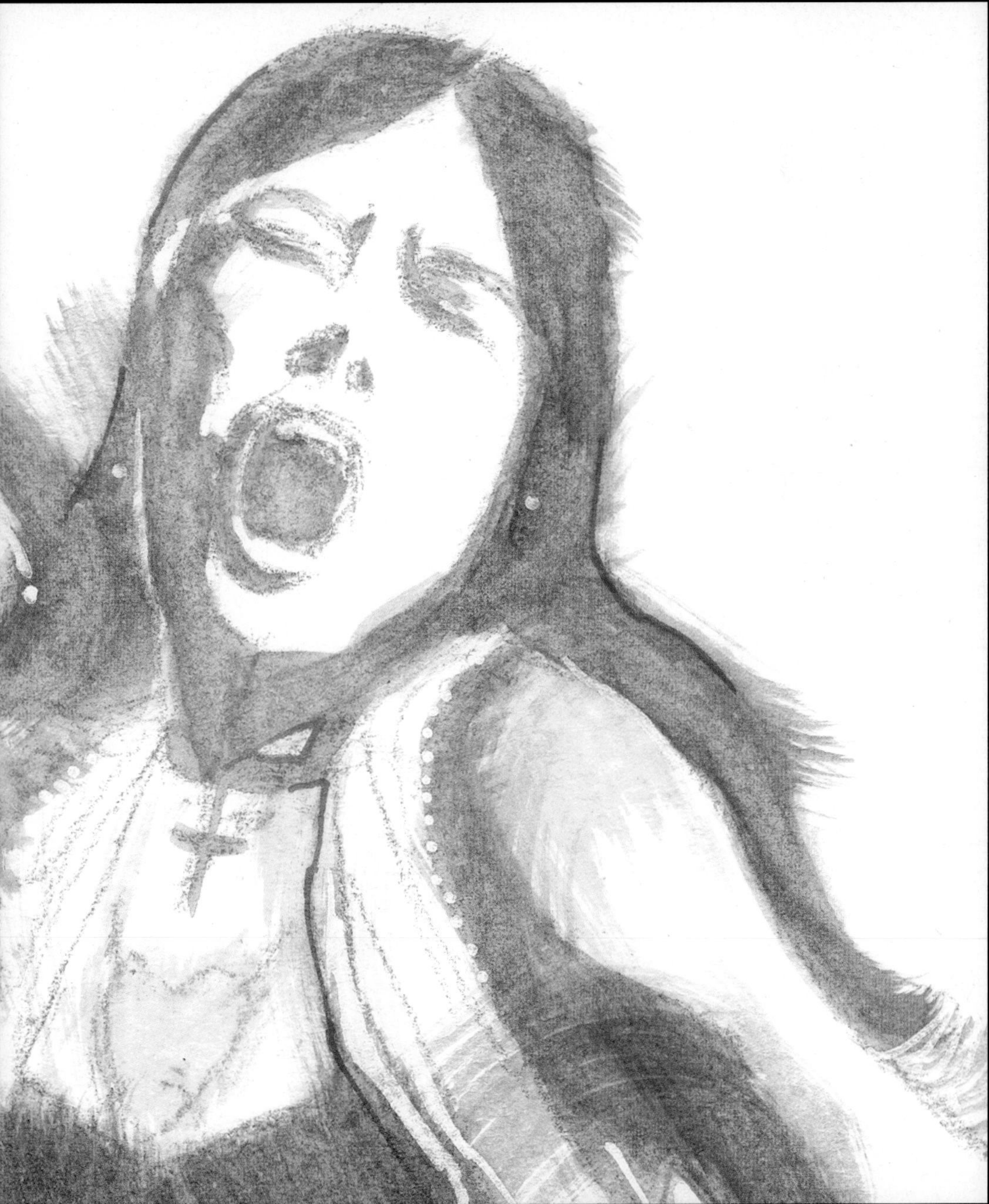

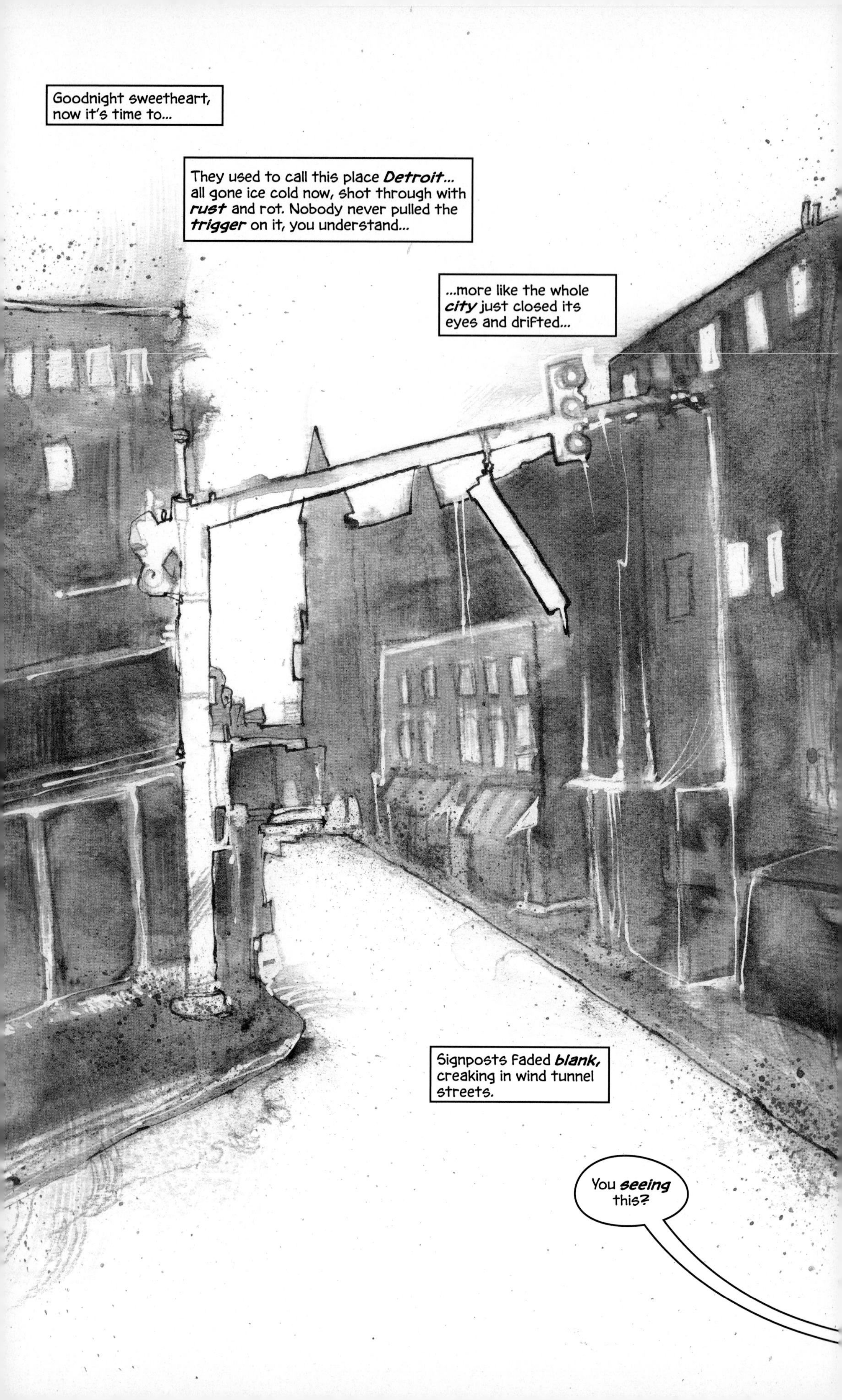

Goodnight sweetheart, now it's time to...
They used to call this place *Detroit*... all gone ice cold now, shot through with *rust* and rot. Nobody never pulled the *trigger* on it, you understand...
...more like the whole *city* just closed its eyes and drifted...
Signposts faded *blank,* creaking in wind tunnel streets.
You *seeing* this?

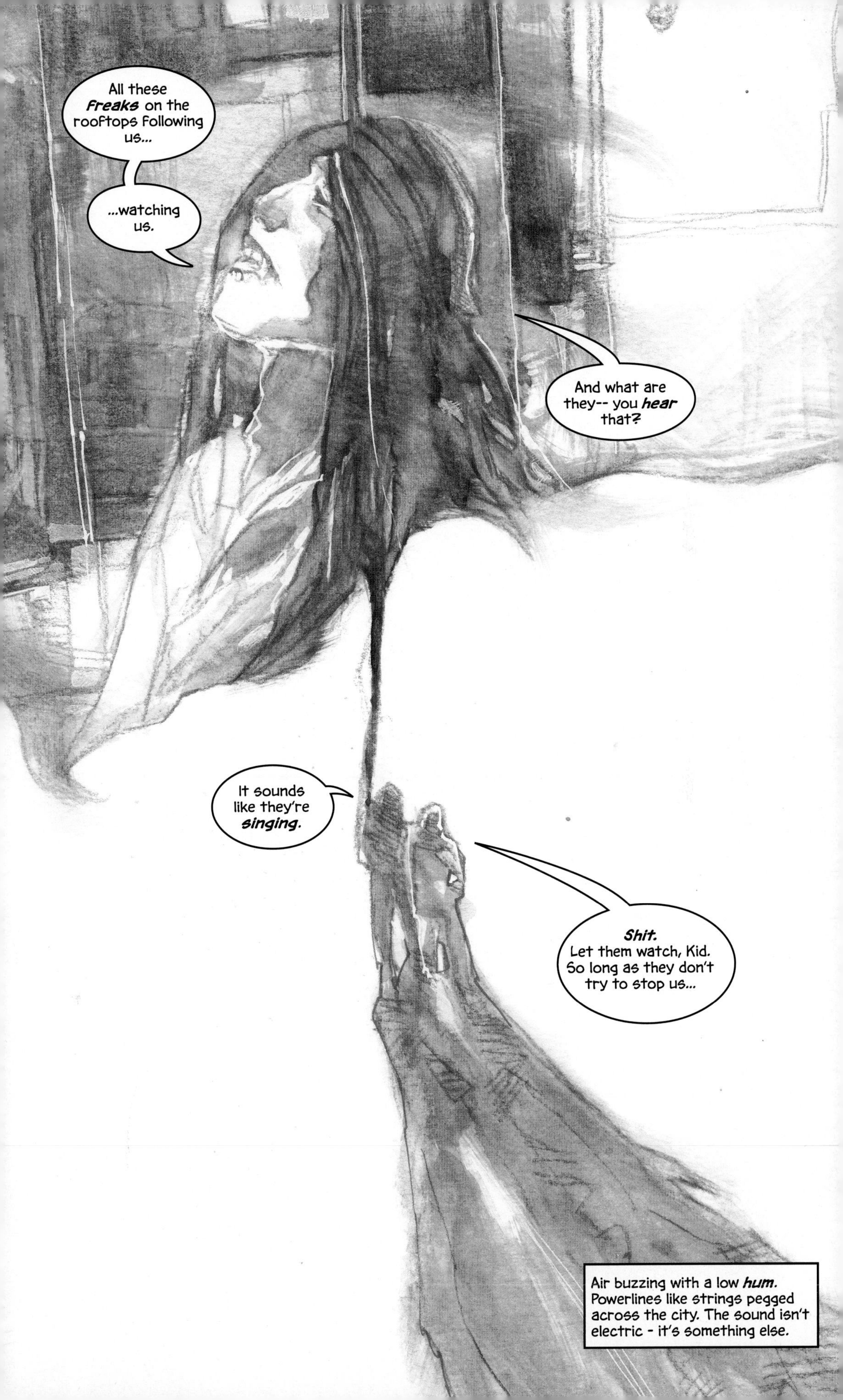
All these *freaks* on the rooftops following us...
...watching us.
And what are they-- you *hear* that?
It sounds like they're *singing*.
Shit. Let them watch, Kid. So long as they don't try to stop us...
Air buzzing with a low *hum*. Powerlines like strings pegged across the city. The sound isn't electric - it's something else.

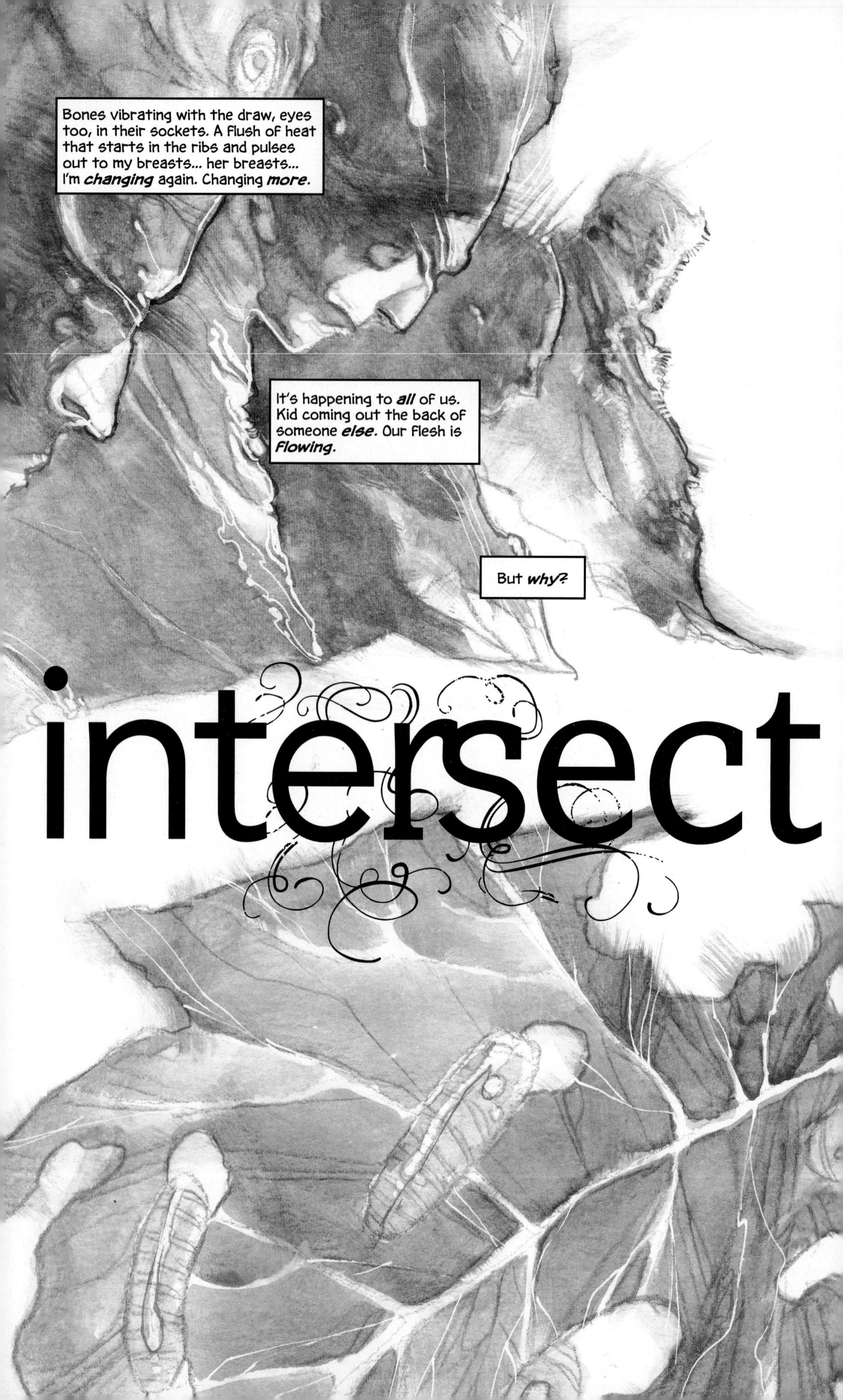
Bones vibrating with the draw, eyes too, in their sockets. A flush of heat that starts in the ribs and pulses out to my breasts... her breasts... I'm *changing* again. Changing *more*.
It's happening to *all* of us. Kid coming out the back of someone *else*. Our flesh is *flowing*.
But *why*?
intersect

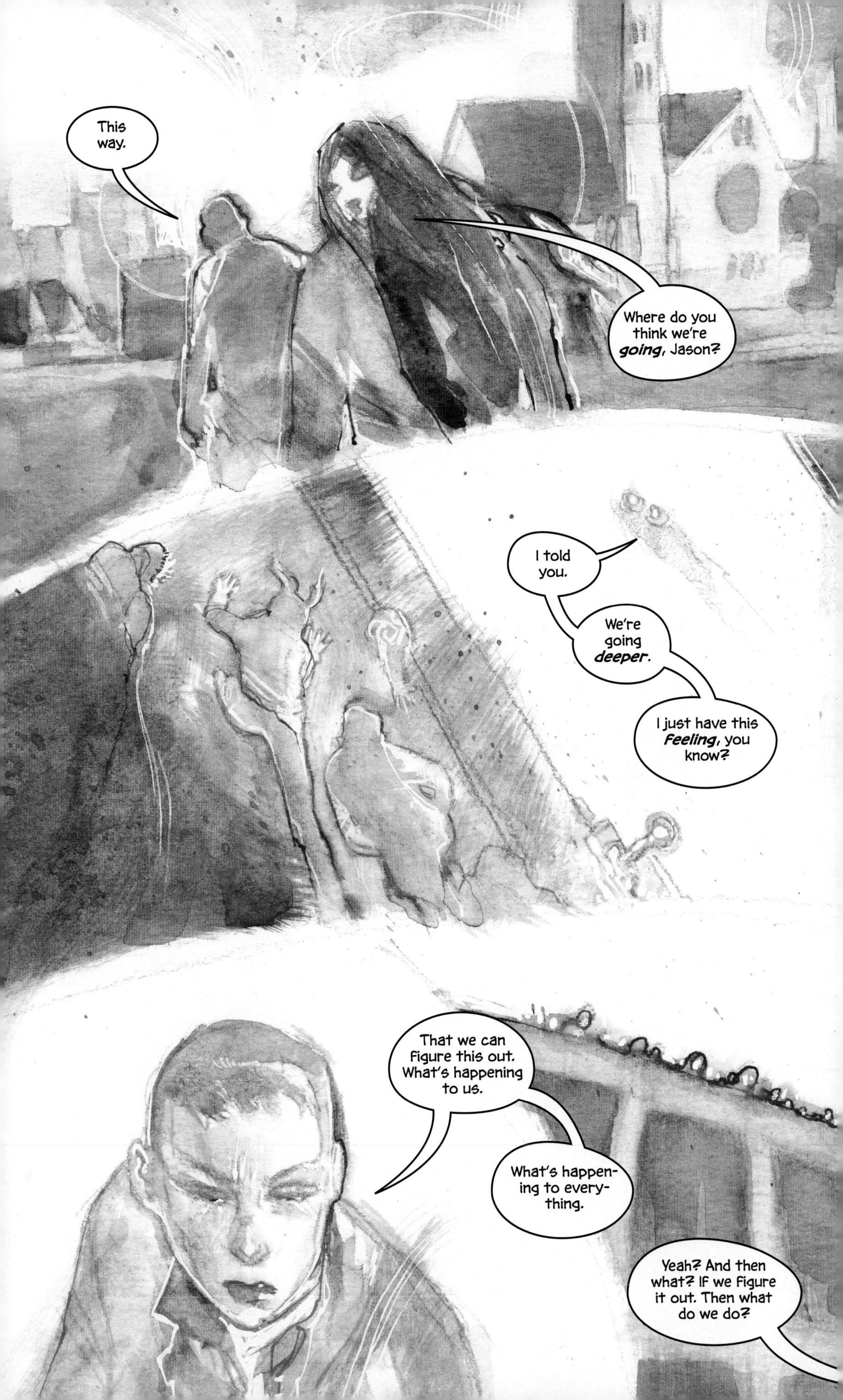
This way.
Where do you think we're *going*, Jason?
I told you.
We're going *deeper*.
I just have this *Feeling*, you know?
That we can figure this out. What's happening to us.
What's happen-ing to every-thing.
Yeah? And then what? If we figure it out. Then what do we do?

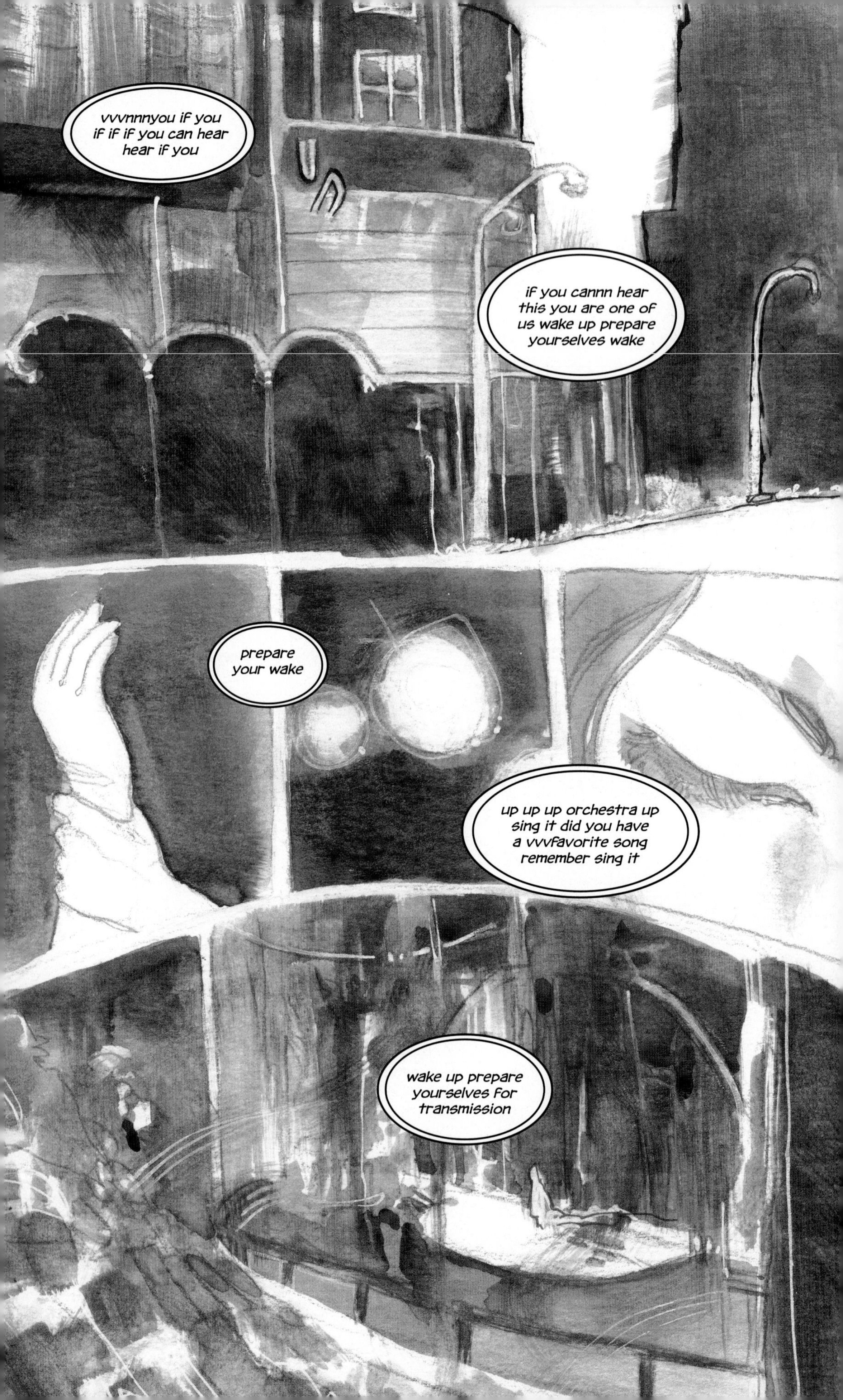

vvvnnnyou if you if if if you can hear hear if you
if you cannn hear this you are one of us wake up prepare yourselves wake
prepare your wake
up up up orchestra up sing it did you have a vvvfavorite song remember sing it
wake up prepare yourselves for transmission

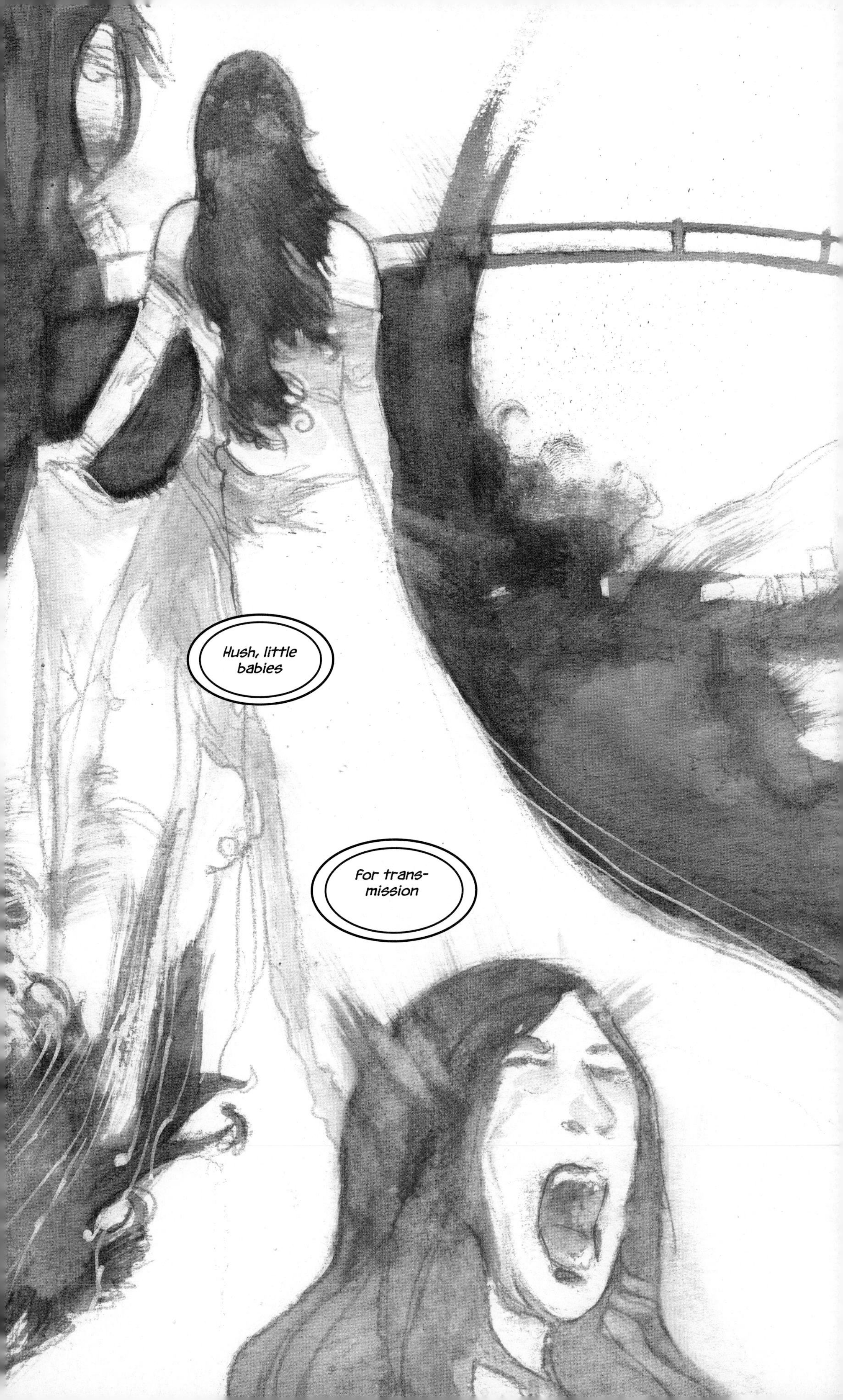
Hush, little babies
For trans-mission

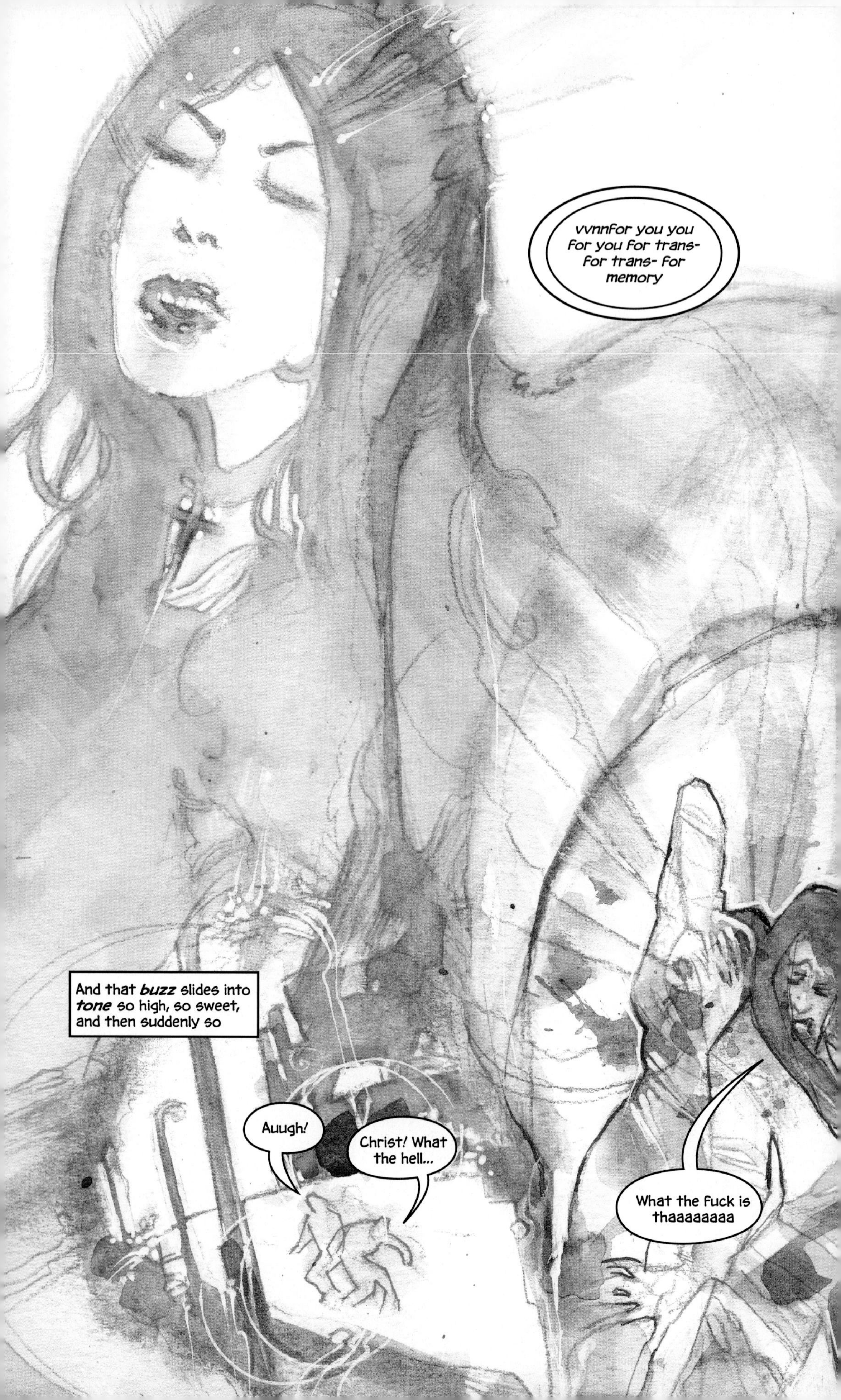
vvnnfor you you for you for trans- for trans- for memory
And that **buzz** slides into ***tone*** so high, so sweet, and then suddenly so
Auugh!
Christ! What the hell...
What the fuck is thaaaaaaaa

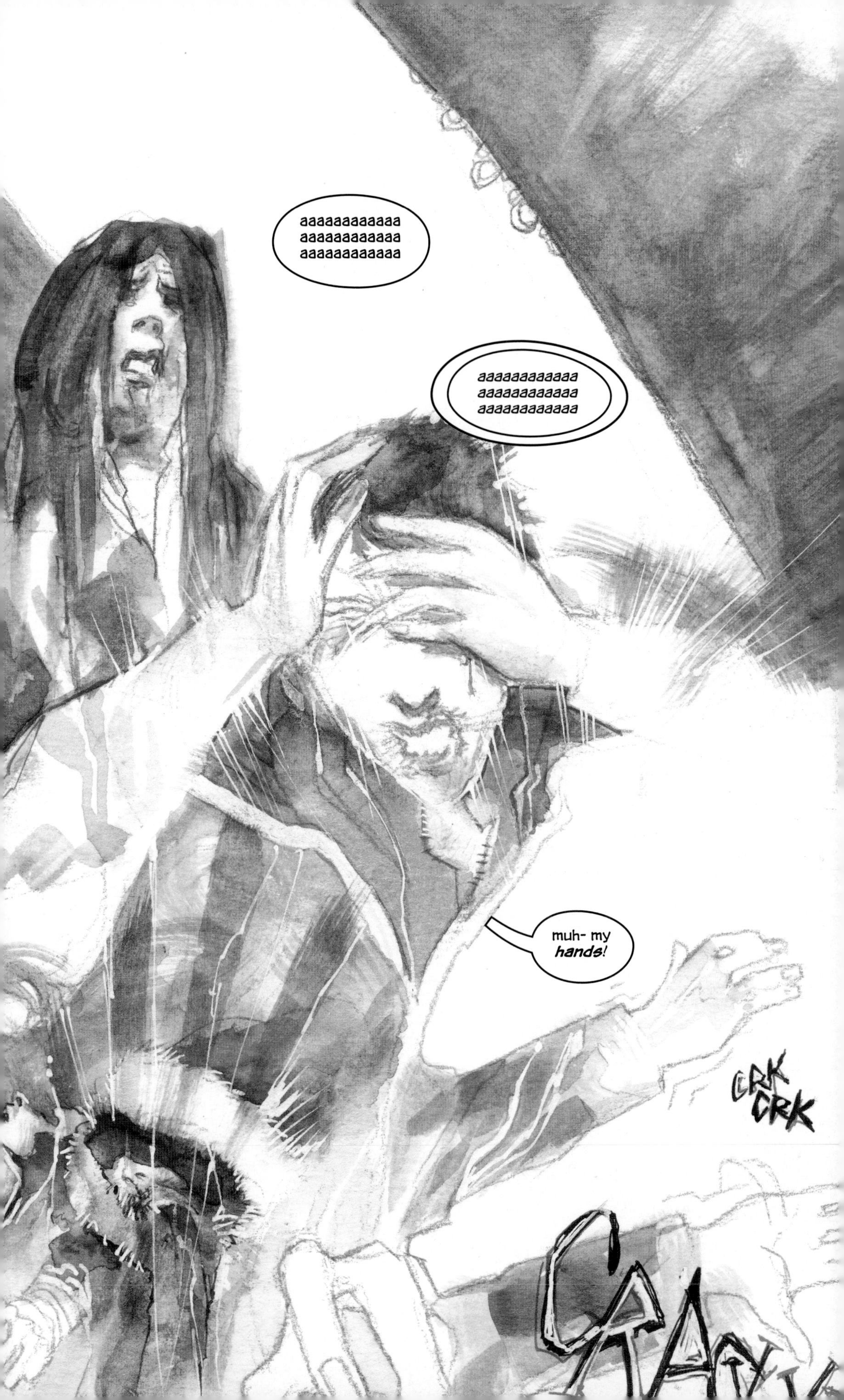
aaaaaaaaaaaa
aaaaaaaaaaaa
aaaaaaaaaaaa
aaaaaaaaaaaa
aaaaaaaaaaaa
aaaaaaaaaaaa
muh- my *hands*!
CRK CRK

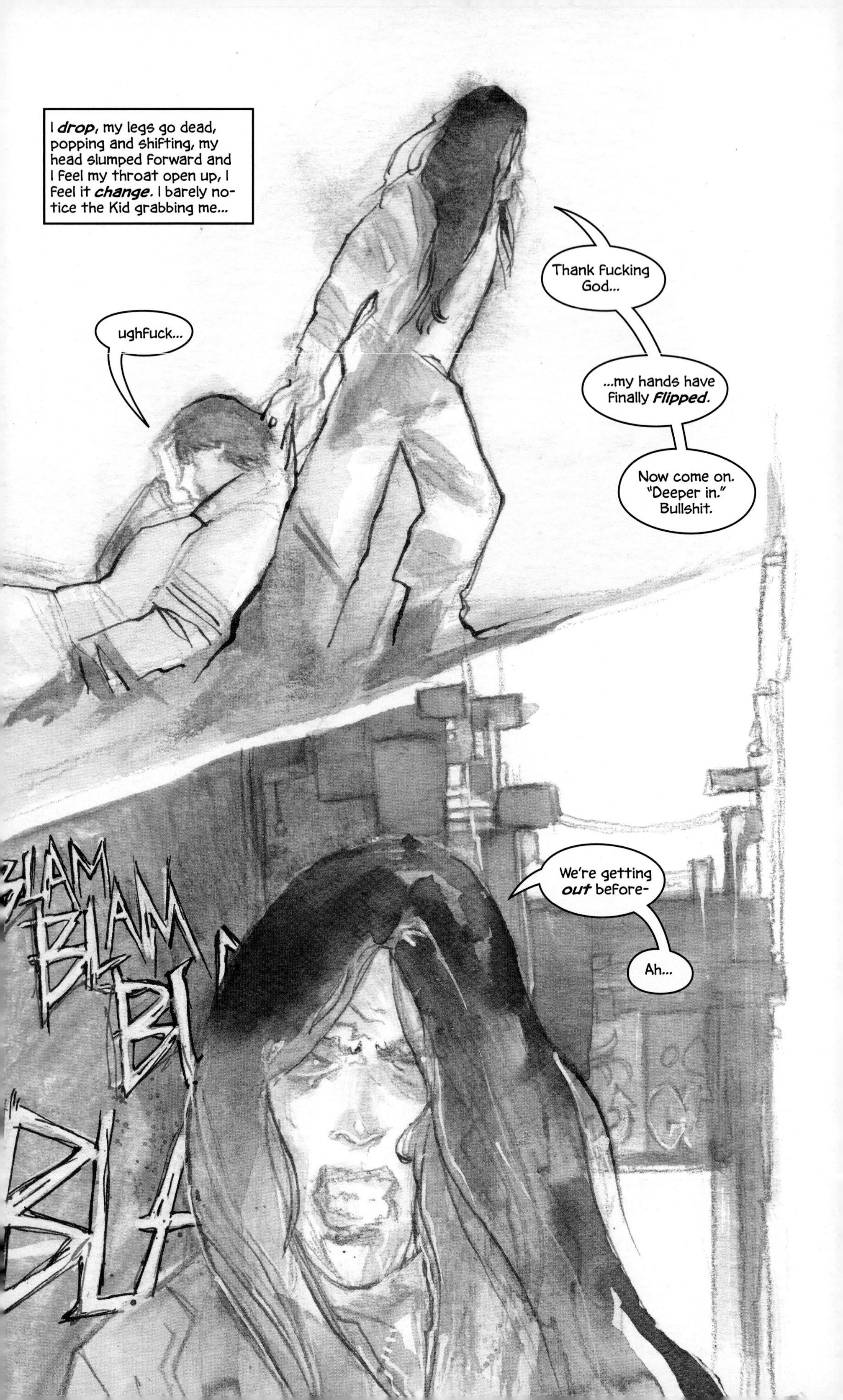
I *drop*, my legs go dead, popping and shifting, my head slumped forward and I feel my throat open up, I feel it *change*. I barely notice the Kid grabbing me...
ughfuck...
Thank fucking God...
...my hands have finally *flipped*.
Now come on. "Deeper in." Bullshit.
BLAM BLAM BLAM
We're getting *out* before-
Ah...

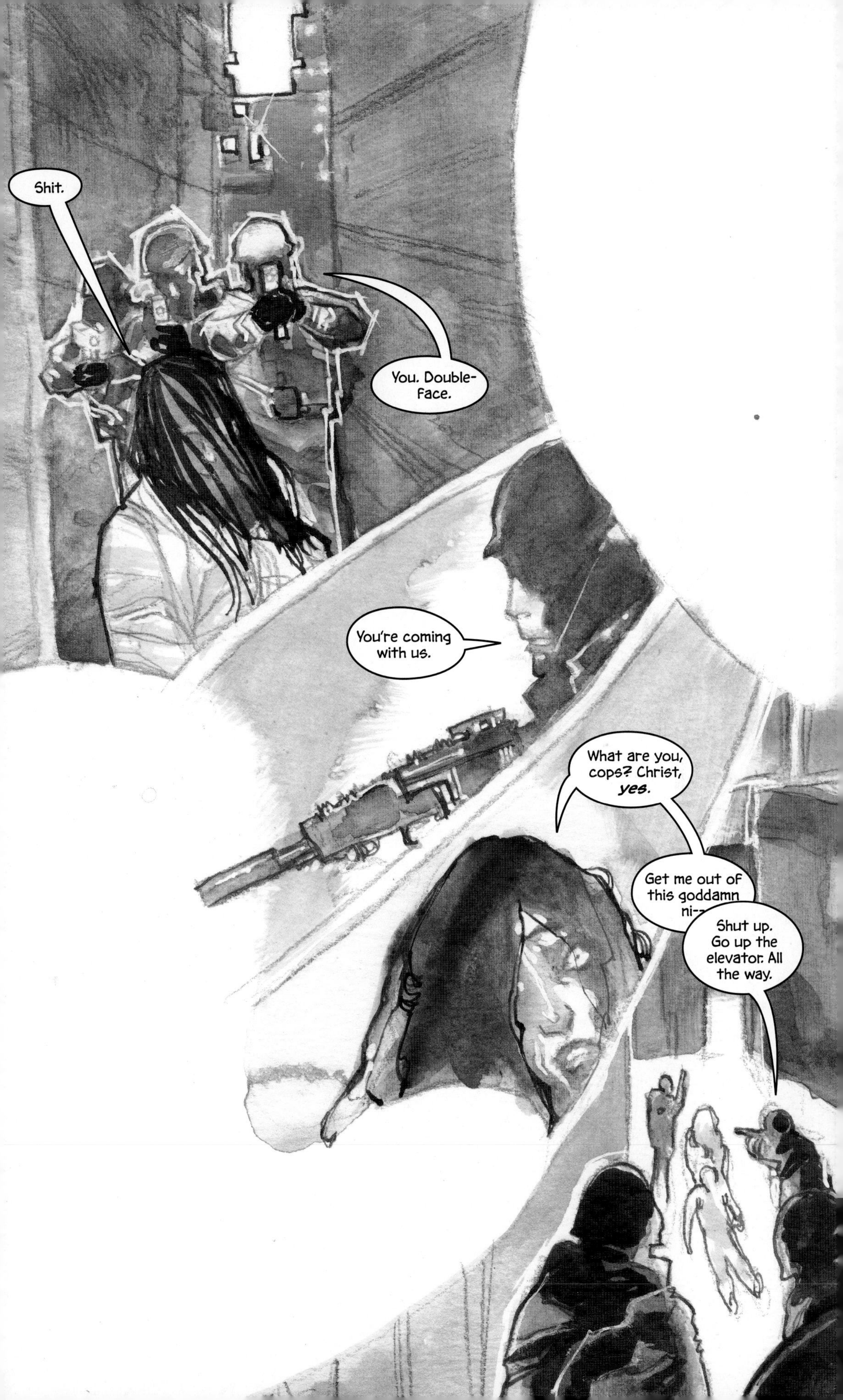
Shit.
You. Double-face.
You're coming with us.
What are you, cops? Christ, *yes.*
Get me out of this goddamn ni--
Shut up. Go up the elevator. All the way.

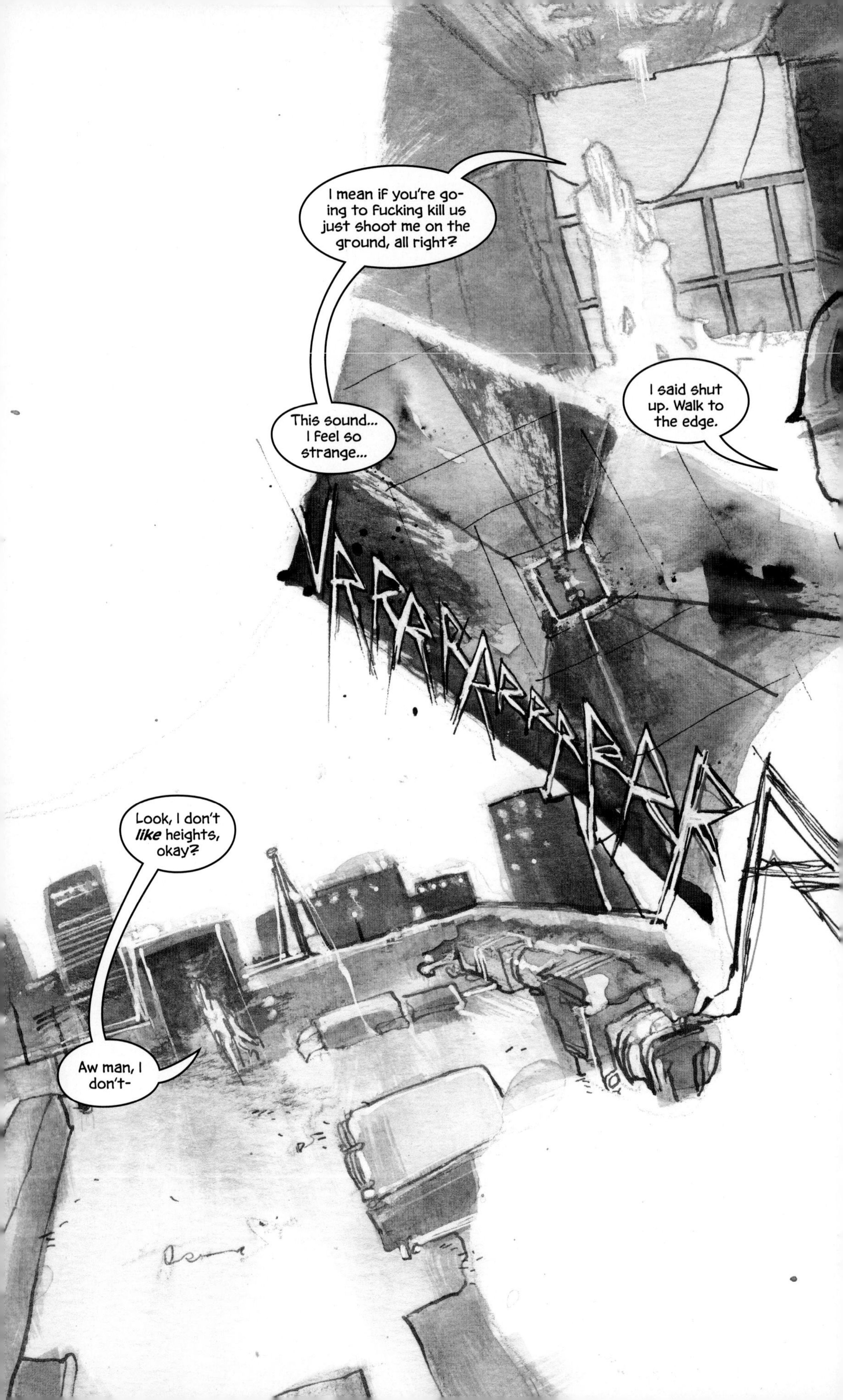
I mean if you're going to fucking kill us just shoot me on the ground, all right?
This sound... I feel so strange...
I said shut up. Walk to the edge.
Look, I don't *like* heights, okay?
Aw man, I don't-

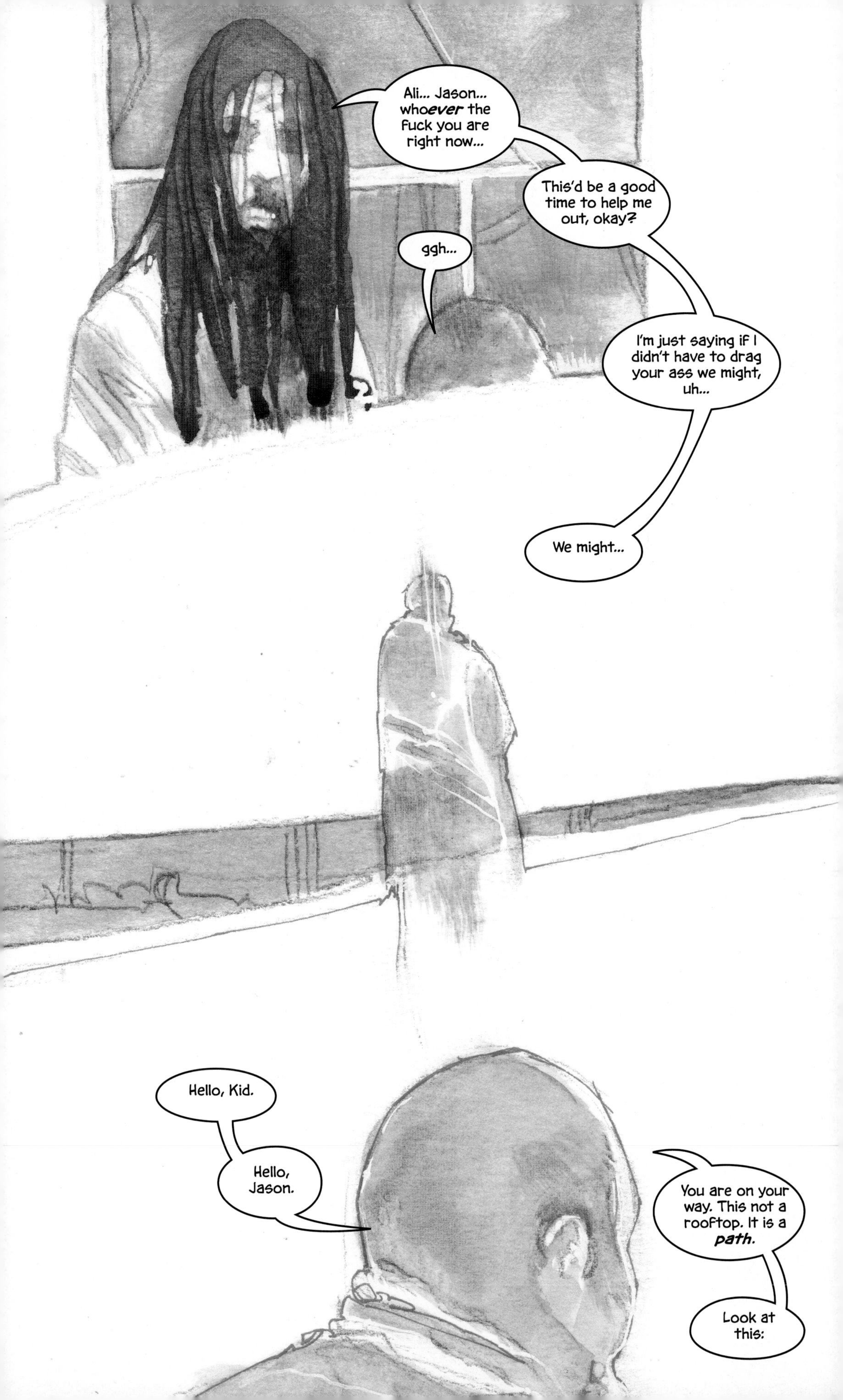
Ali... Jason... whoever the fuck you are right now...
This'd be a good time to help me out, okay?
ggh...
I'm just saying if I didn't have to drag your ass we might, uh...
We might...
Hello, Kid.
Hello, Jason.
You are on your way. This not a rooftop. It is a path.
Look at this:

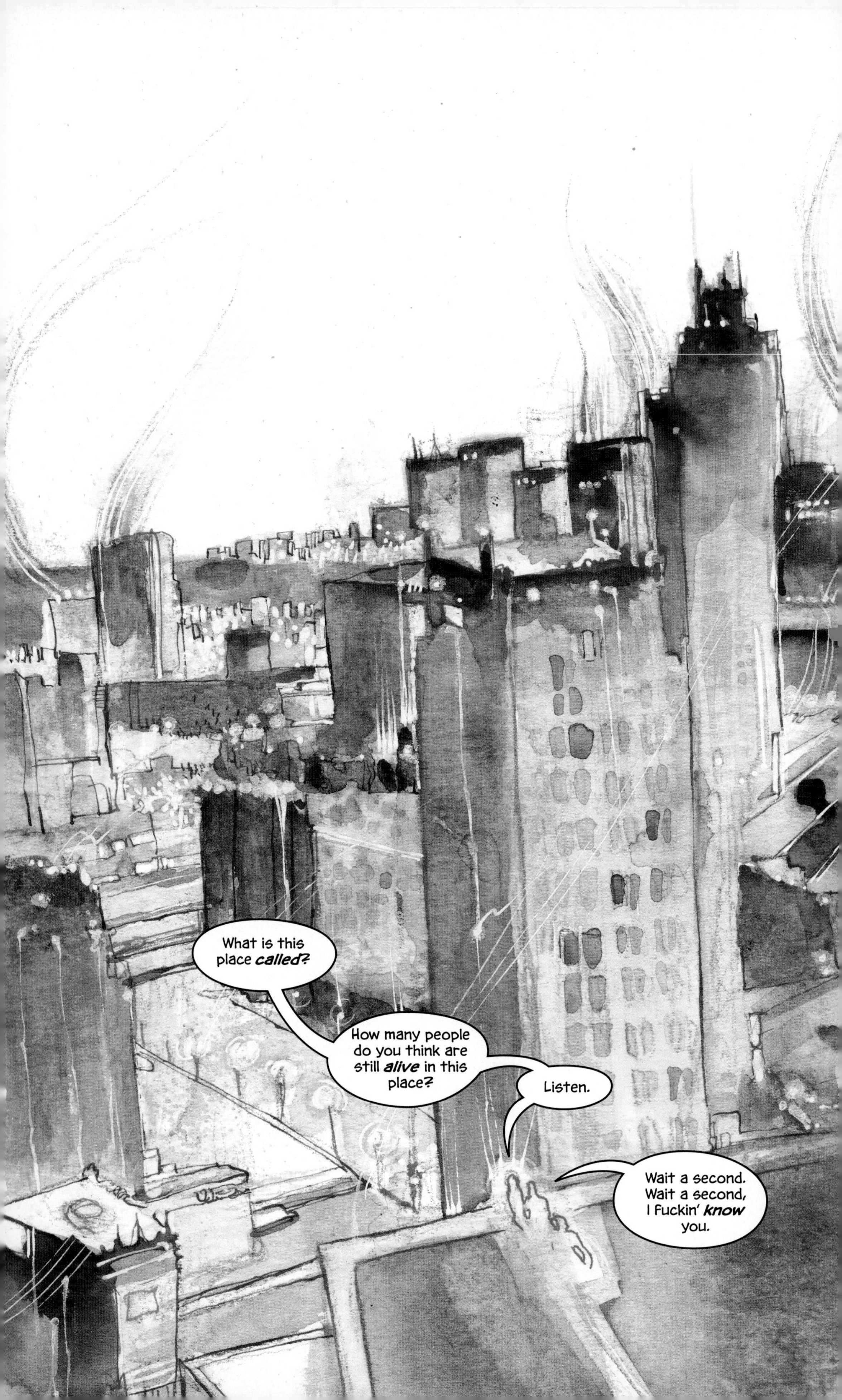
What is this place *called*?
How many people do you think are still *alive* in this place?
Listen.
Wait a second. Wait a second, I fuckin' *know* you.

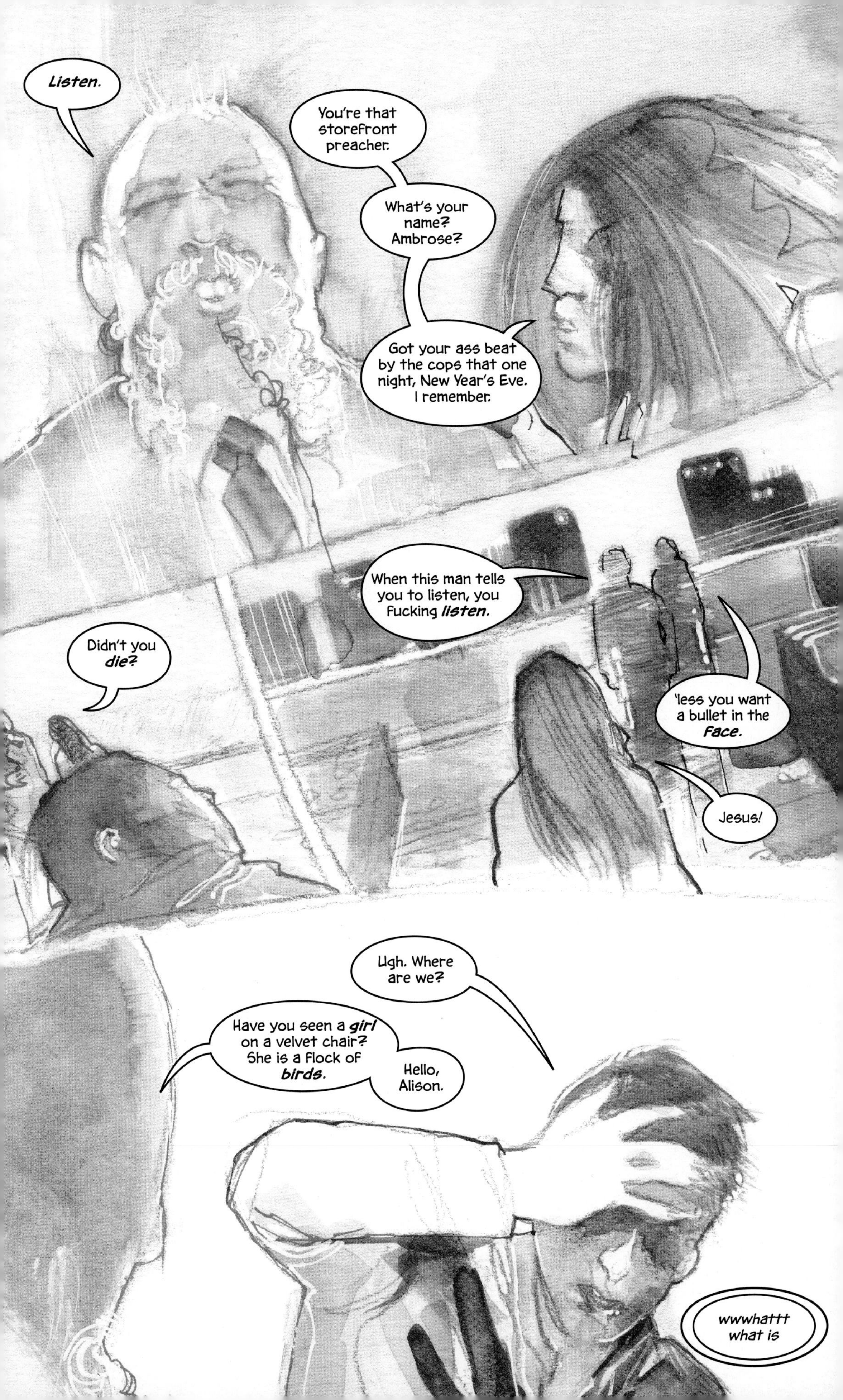
Listen.
You're that storefront preacher.
What's your name? Ambrose?
Got your ass beat by the cops that one night, New Year's Eve. I remember.
When this man tells you to listen, you fucking listen.
Didn't you die?
'less you want a bullet in the face.
Jesus!
Ugh. Where are we?
Have you seen a girl on a velvet chair? She is a flock of birds.
Hello, Alison.
wwwhattt what is

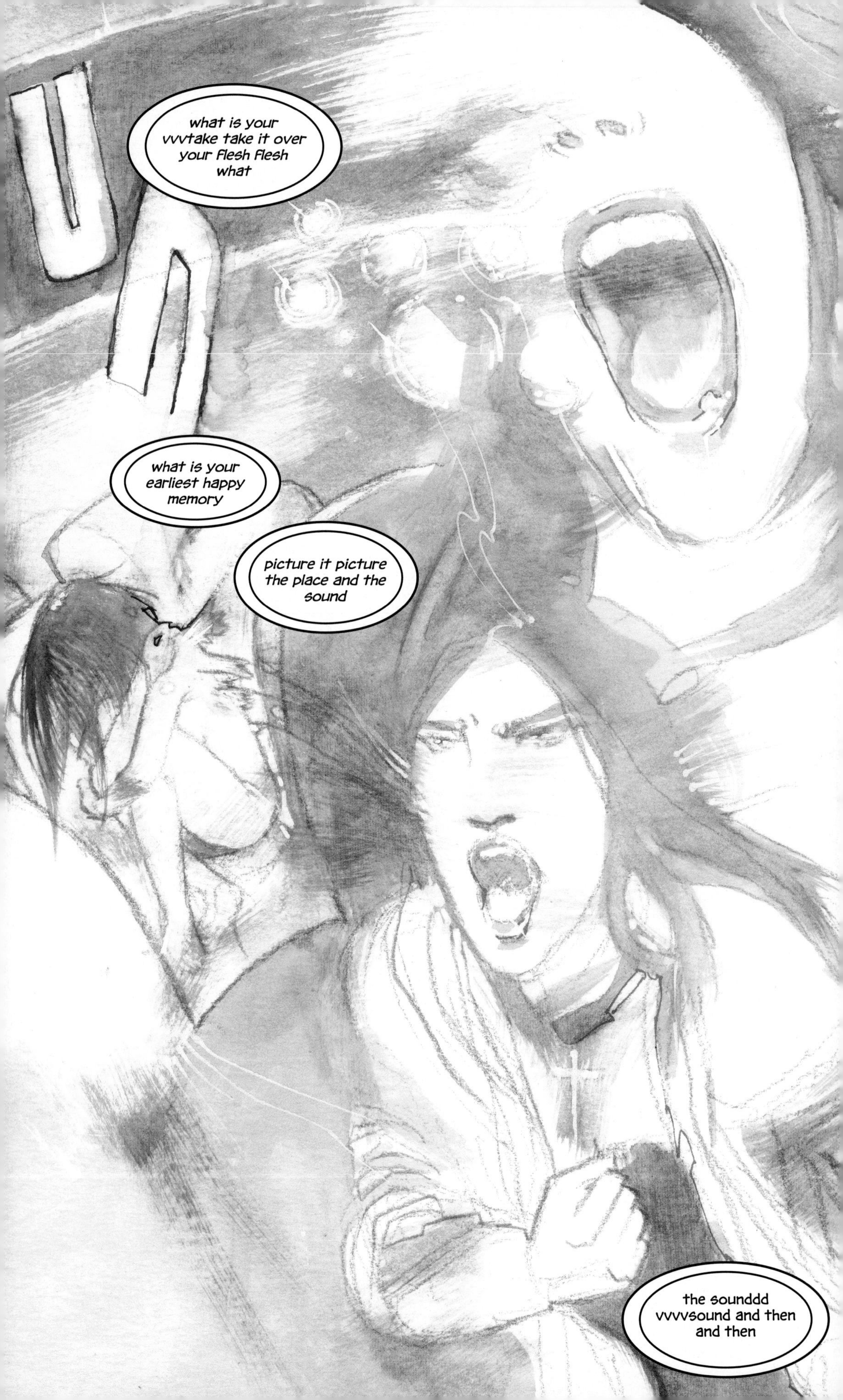
what is your vvvtake take it over your flesh flesh what
what is your earliest happy memory
picture it picture the place and the sound
the sounddd vvvvsound and then and then

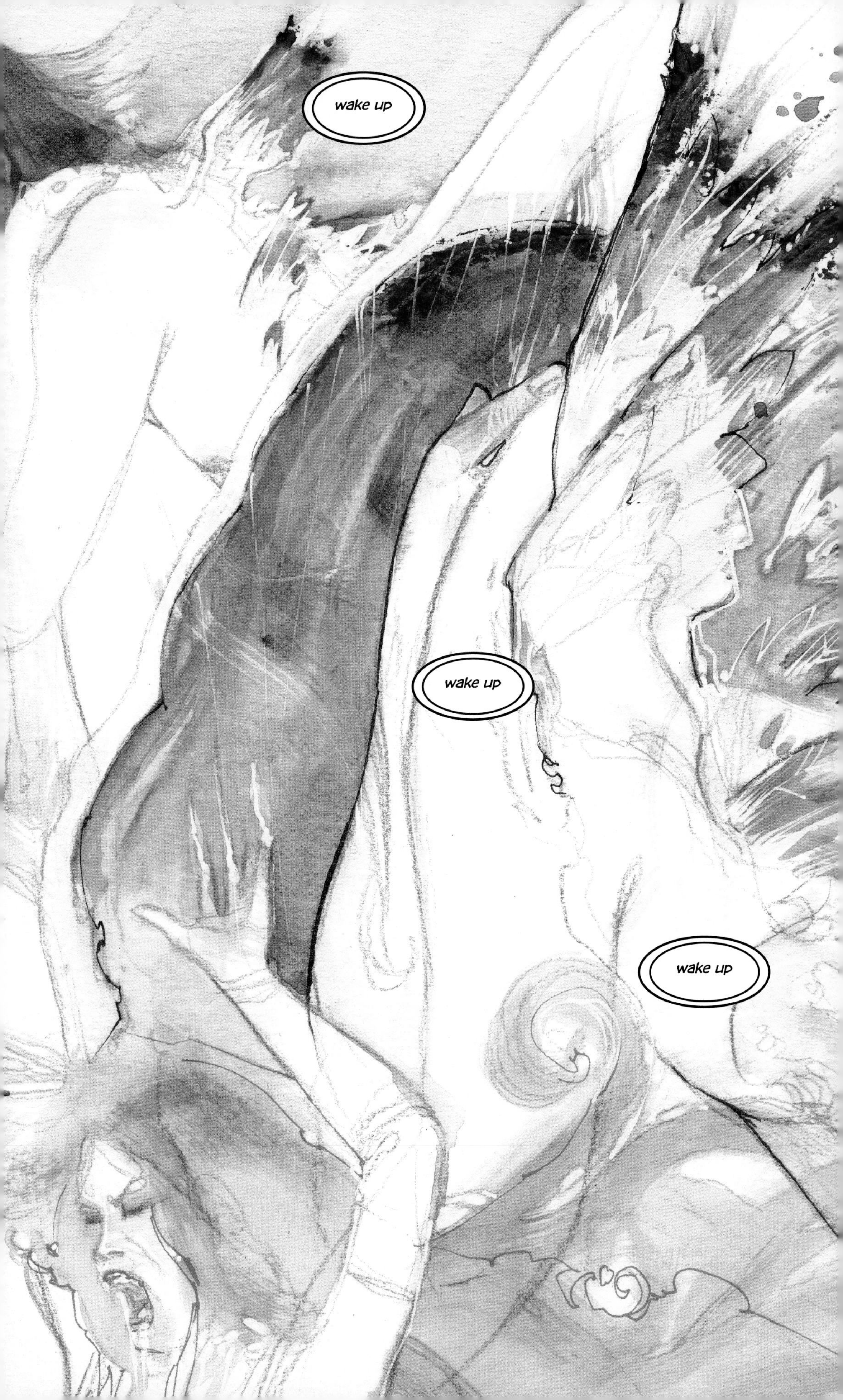
wake up
wake up
wake up

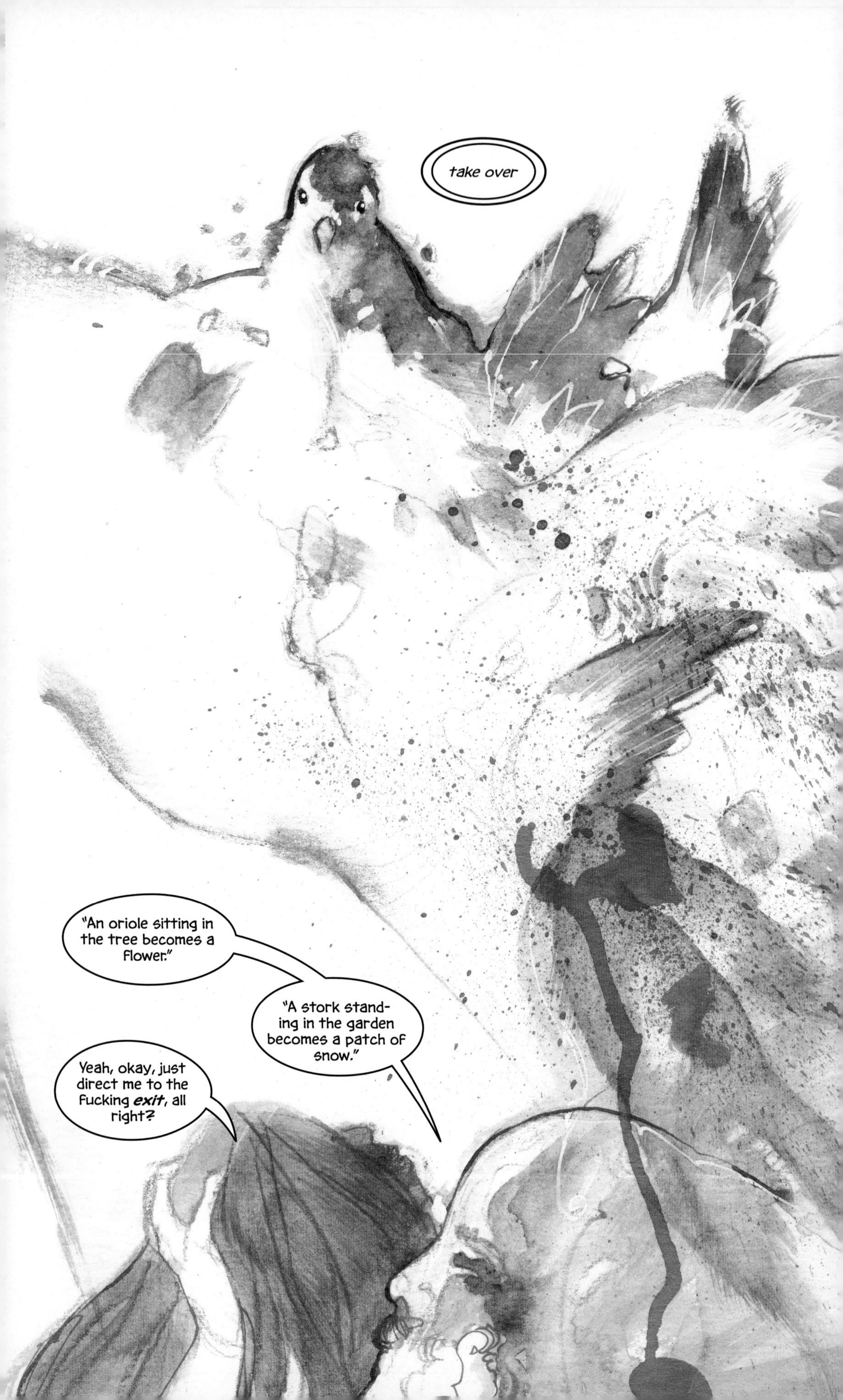
take over
"An oriole sitting in the tree becomes a flower."
"A stork standing in the garden becomes a patch of snow."
Yeah, okay, just direct me to the fucking *exit*, all right?

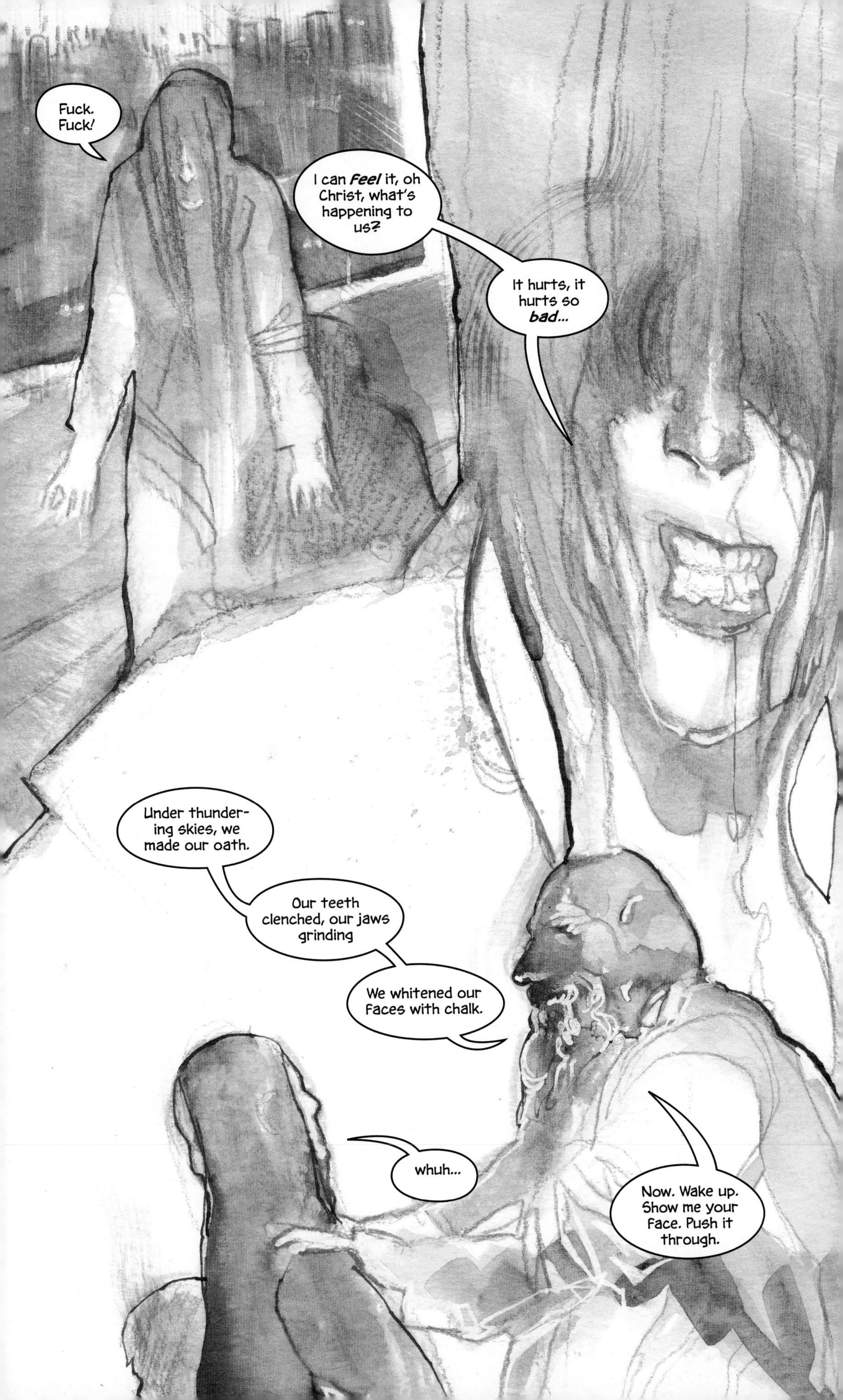
Fuck. Fuck!
I can *Feel* it, oh Christ, what's happening to us?
It hurts, it hurts so ***bad***...
Under thunder-ing skies, we made our oath.
Our teeth clenched, our jaws grinding
We whitened our faces with chalk.
whuh...
Now. Wake up. Show me your face. Push it through.

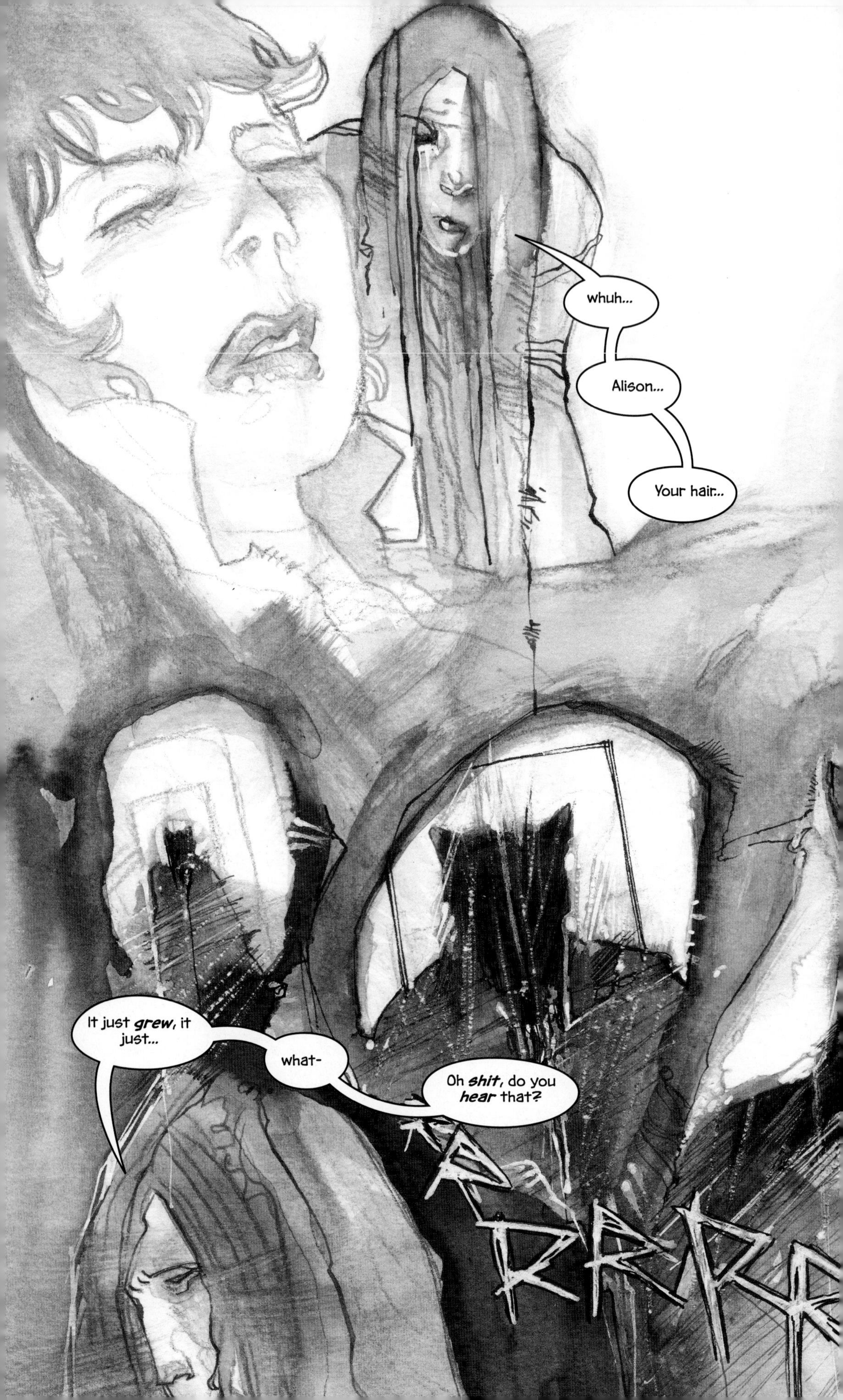
whuh...
Alison...
Your hair...
It just *grew*, it just...
what-
Oh *shit*, do you *hear* that?
RRRRR

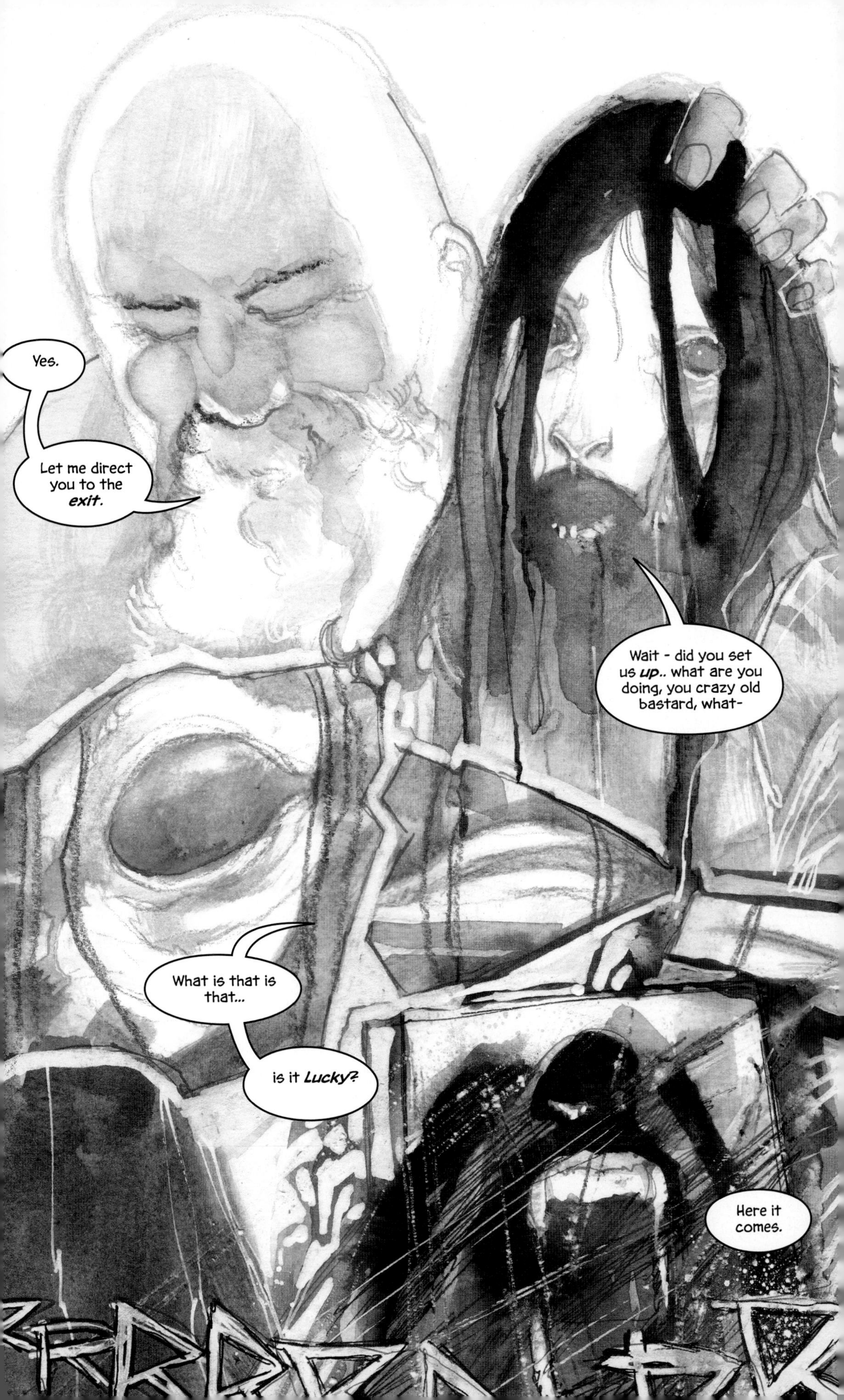
Yes.
Let me direct you to the *exit*.
Wait - did you set us *up*.. what are you doing, you crazy old bastard, what-
What is that is that...
is it *Lucky*?
Here it comes.

Part Three

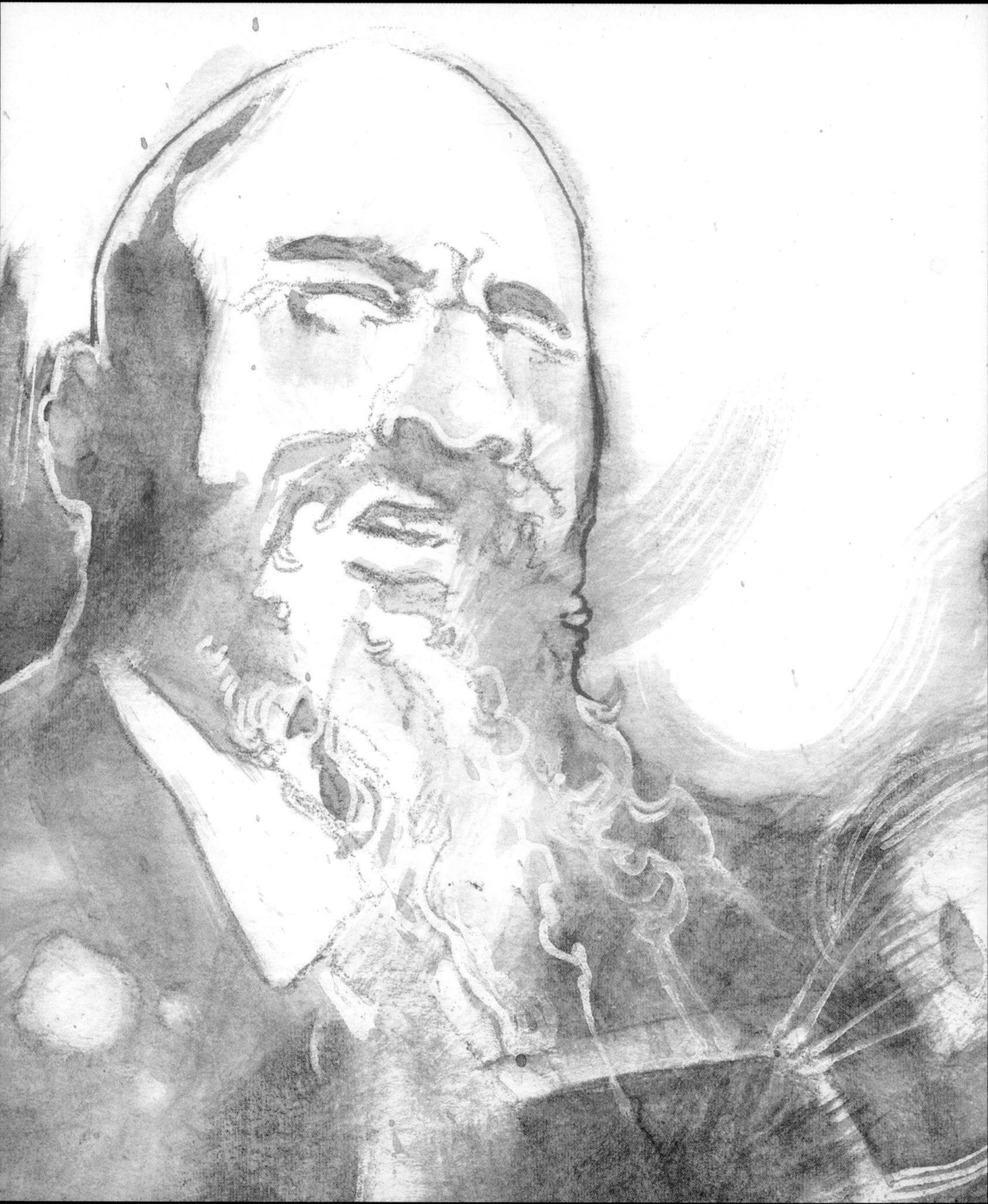

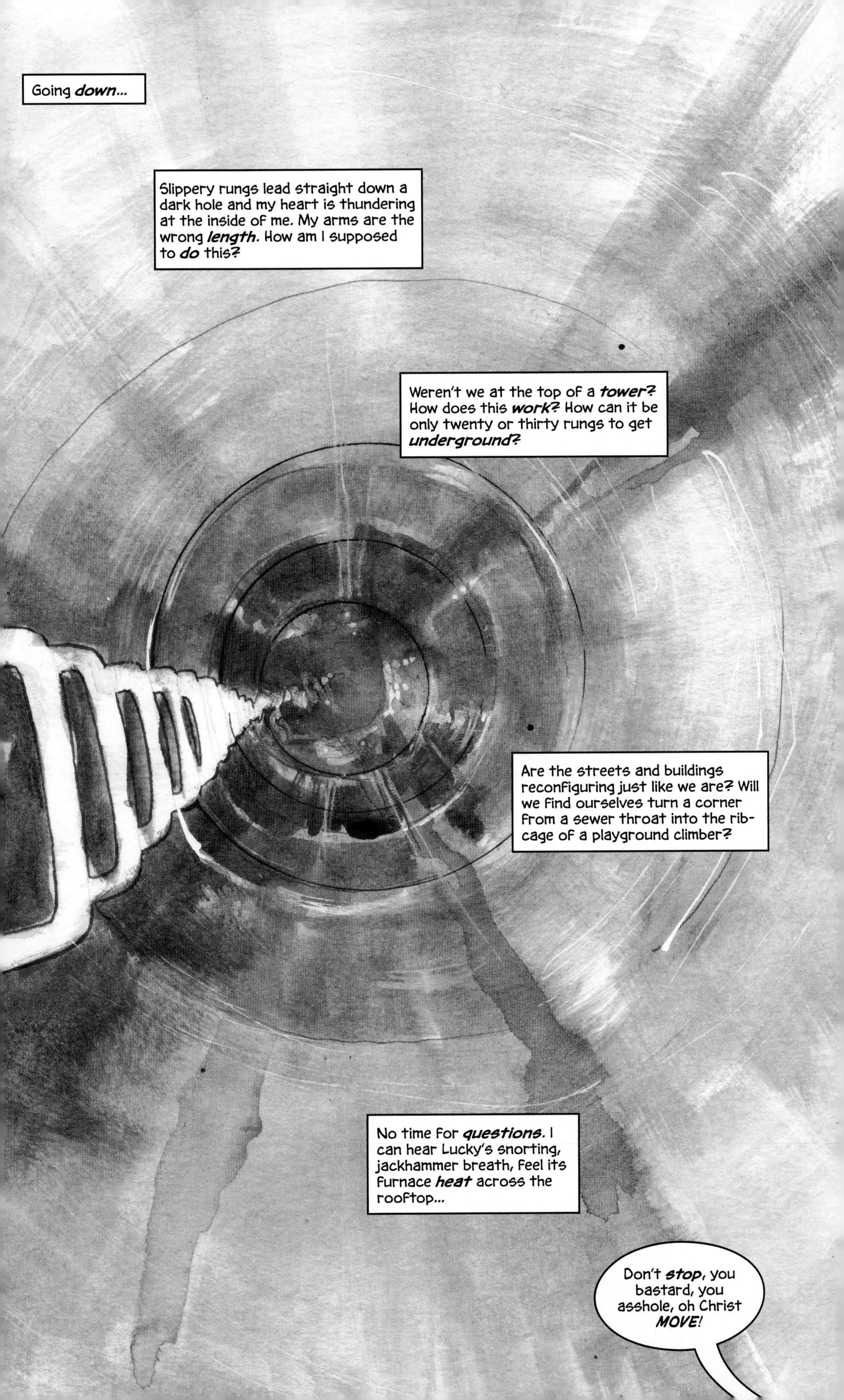

Going *down*...
Slippery rungs lead straight down a dark hole and my heart is thundering at the inside of me. My arms are the wrong *length*. How am I supposed to *do* this?
Weren't we at the top of a *tower*? How does this *work*? How can it be only twenty or thirty rungs to get *underground*?
Are the streets and buildings reconfiguring just like we are? Will we find ourselves turn a corner from a sewer throat into the rib-cage of a playground climber?
No time for *questions*. I can hear Lucky's snorting, jackhammer breath, feel its furnace *heat* across the rooftop...
Don't *stop*, you bastard, you asshole, oh Christ *MOVE*!

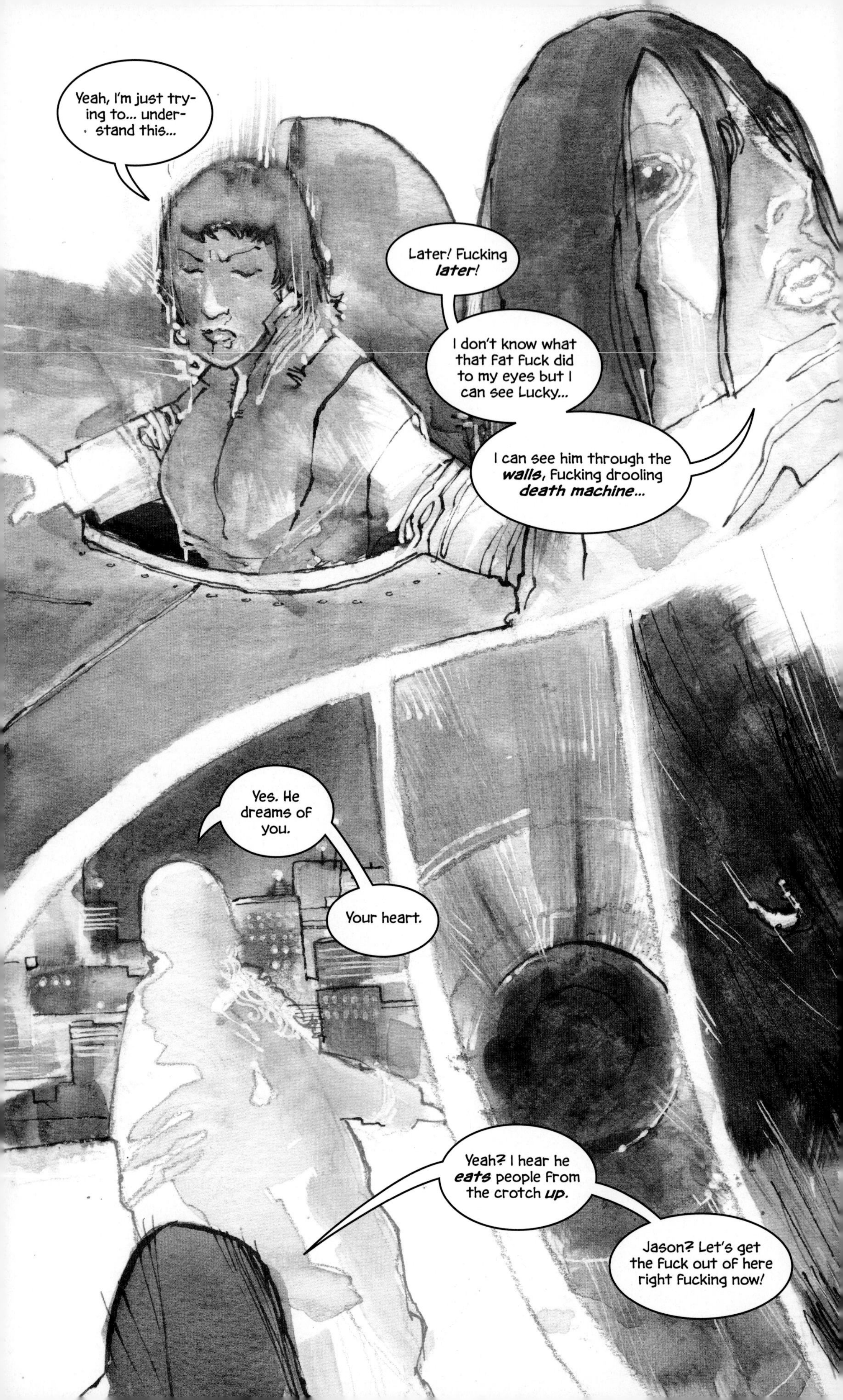
Yeah, I'm just try-ing to... under-stand this...
Later! Fucking *later!*
I don't know what that fat fuck did to my eyes but I can see Lucky...
I can see him through the *walls*, fucking drooling *death machine*...
Yes. He dreams of you.
Your heart.
Yeah? I hear he *eats* people from the crotch *up*.
Jason? Let's get the fuck out of here right fucking now!

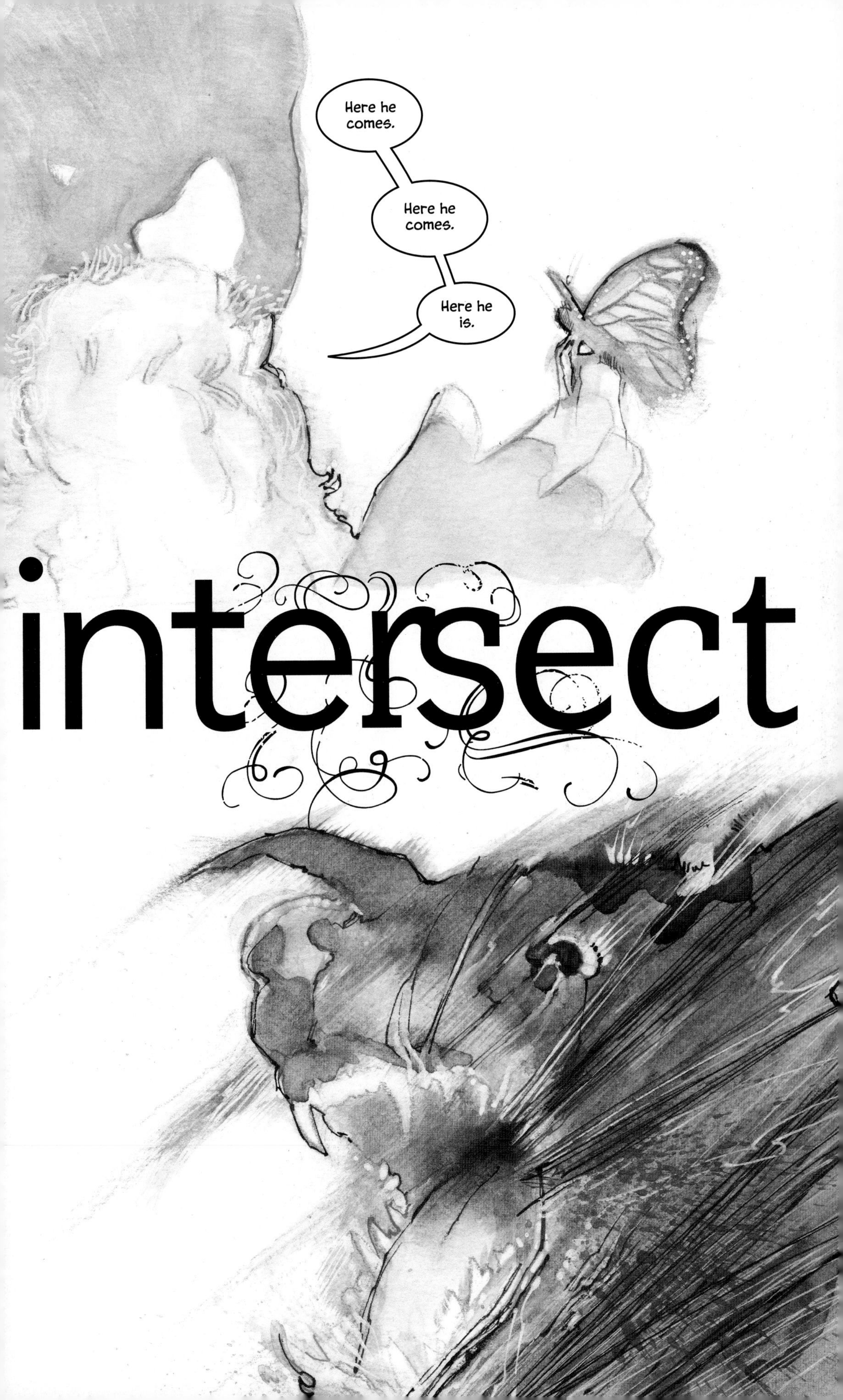
Here he comes.
Here he comes.
Here he is.
intersect

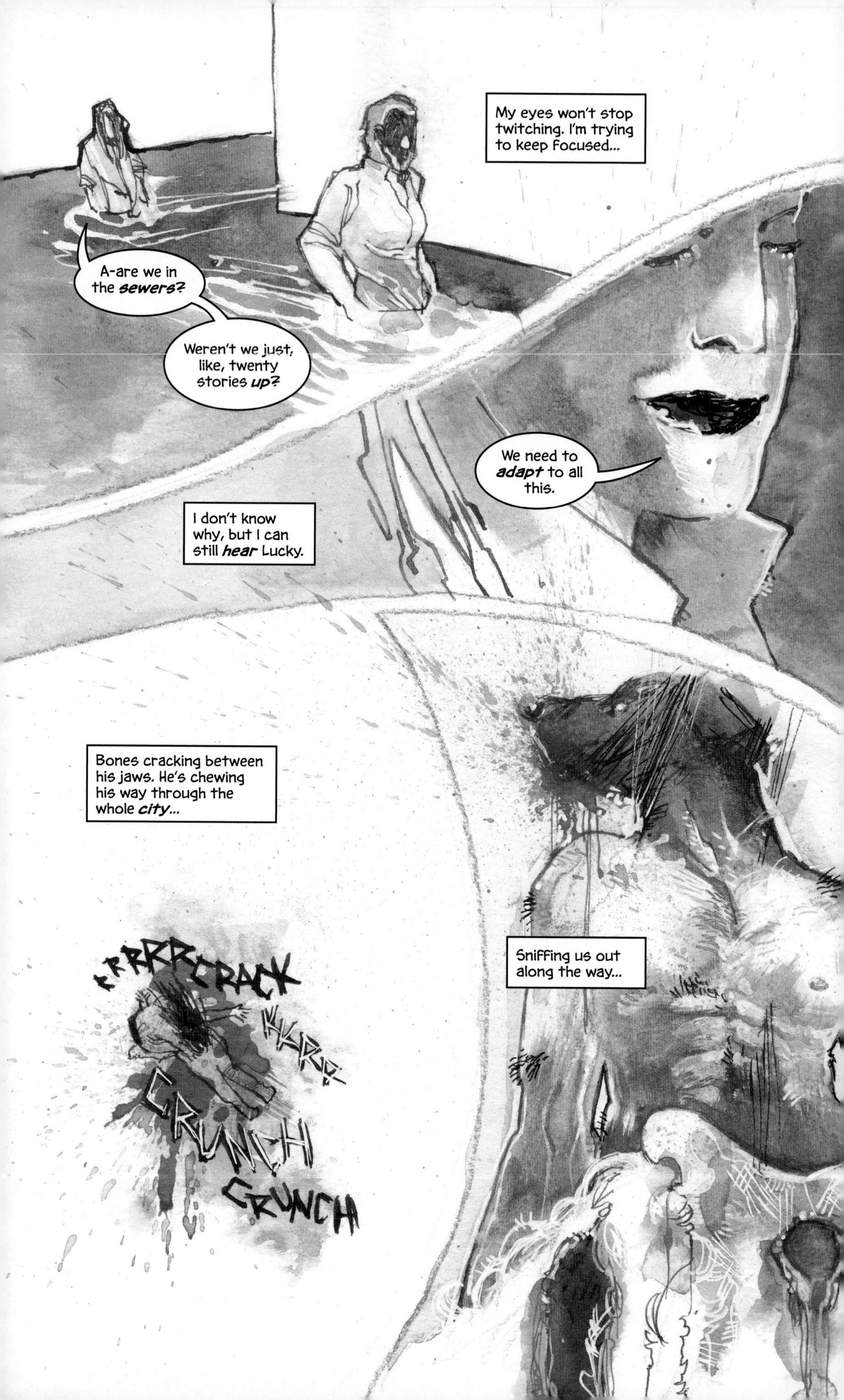
My eyes won't stop twitching. I'm trying to keep focused...
A-are we in the *sewers?*
Weren't we just, like, twenty stories *up?*
We need to *adapt* to all this.
I don't know why, but I can still *hear* Lucky.
Bones cracking between his jaws. He's chewing his way through the whole *city*...
Sniffing us out along the way...
RRRRCRACK
CRUNCH
CRUNCH

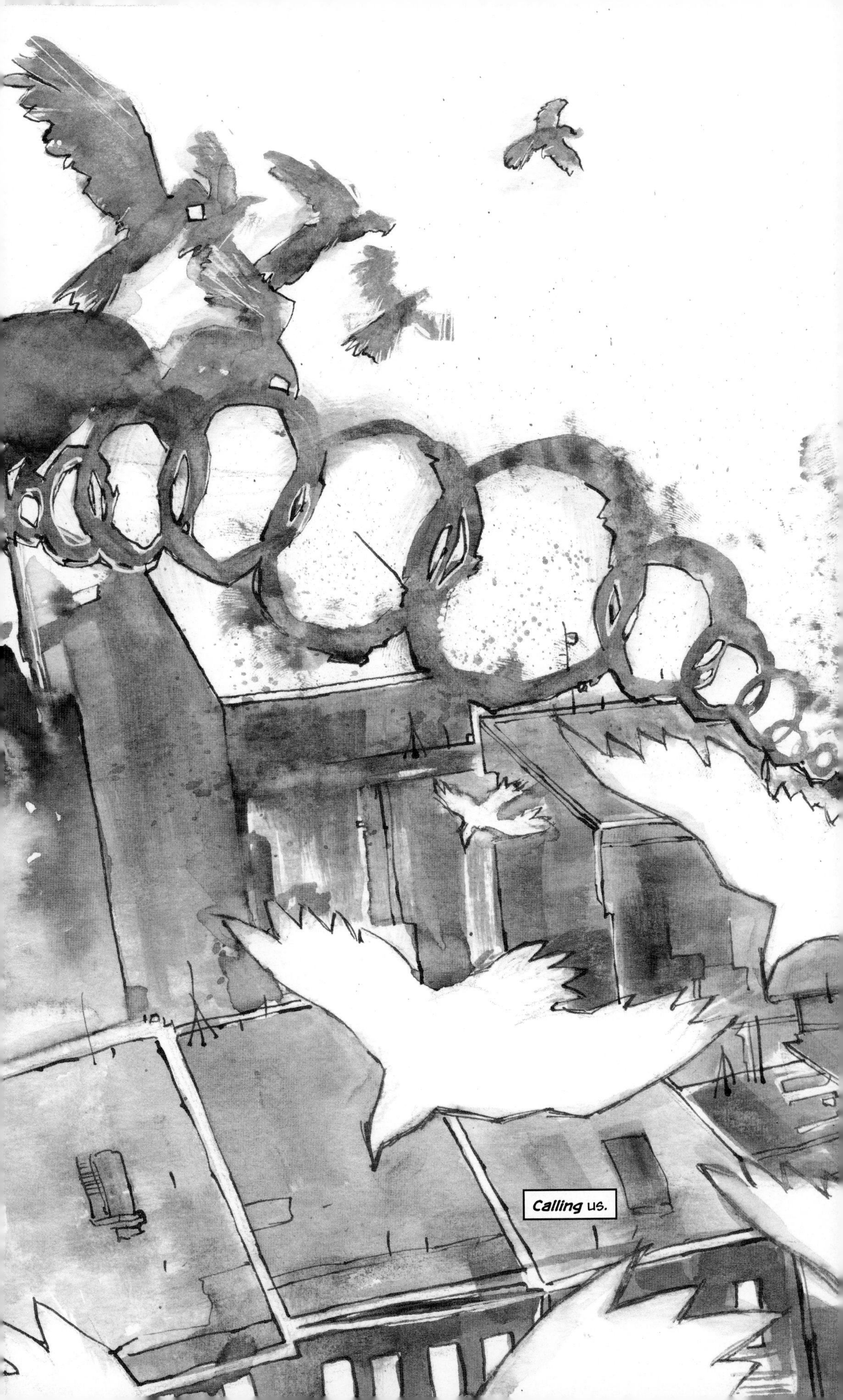
Calling us.

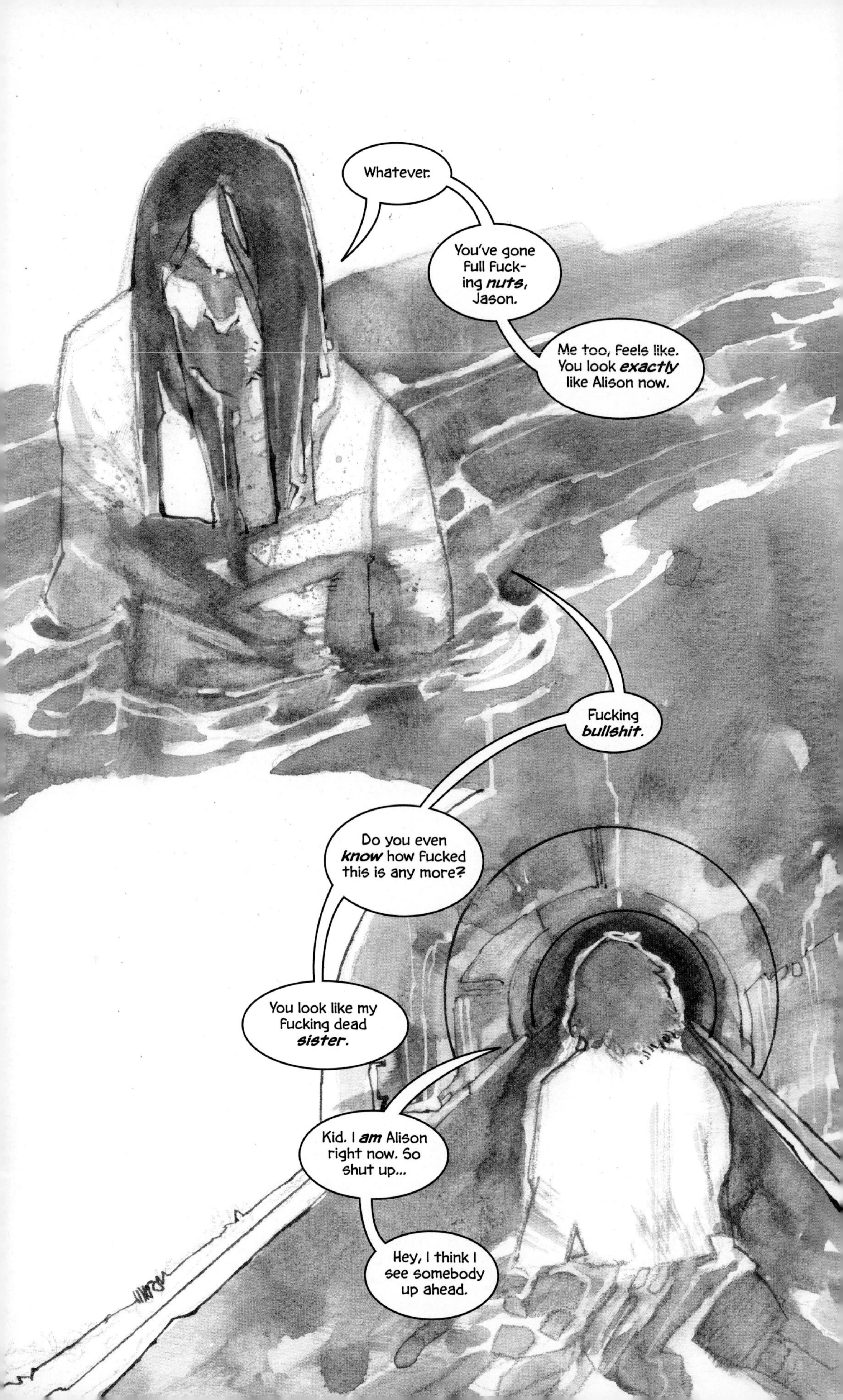
Whatever.
You've gone full fucking *nuts*, Jason.
Me too, Feels like. You look *exactly* like Alison now.
Fucking *bullshit*.
Do you even *know* how fucked this is any more?
You look like my fucking dead *sister*.
Kid. I *am* Alison right now. So shut up...
Hey, I think I see somebody up ahead.

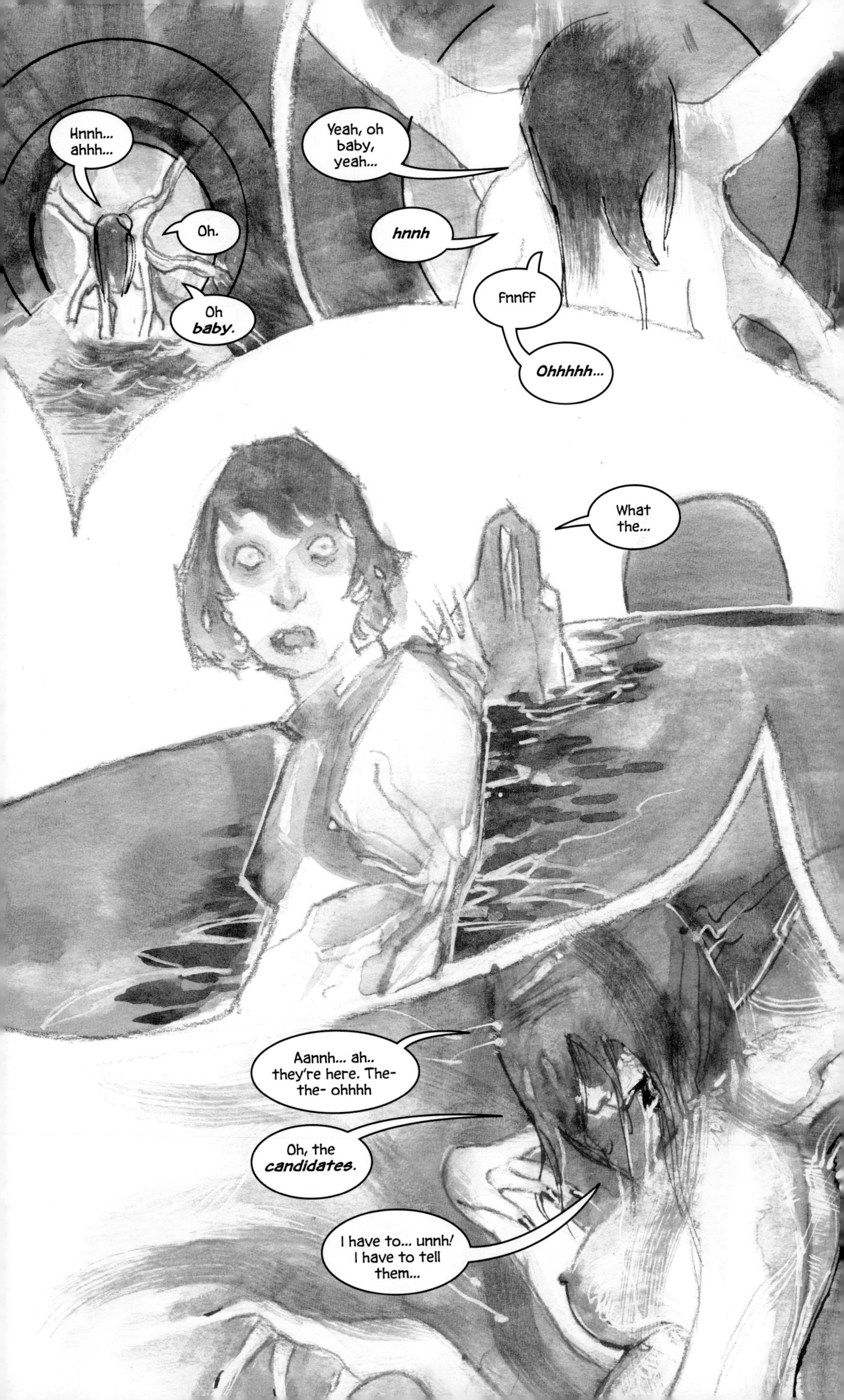
Hnnh... ahhh...
Oh.
Oh baby.
Yeah, oh baby, yeah...
hnnh
fnnff
Ohhhhh...
What the...
Aannh... ah.. they're here. The- the- ohhhh
Oh, the candidates.
I have to... unnh! I have to tell them...

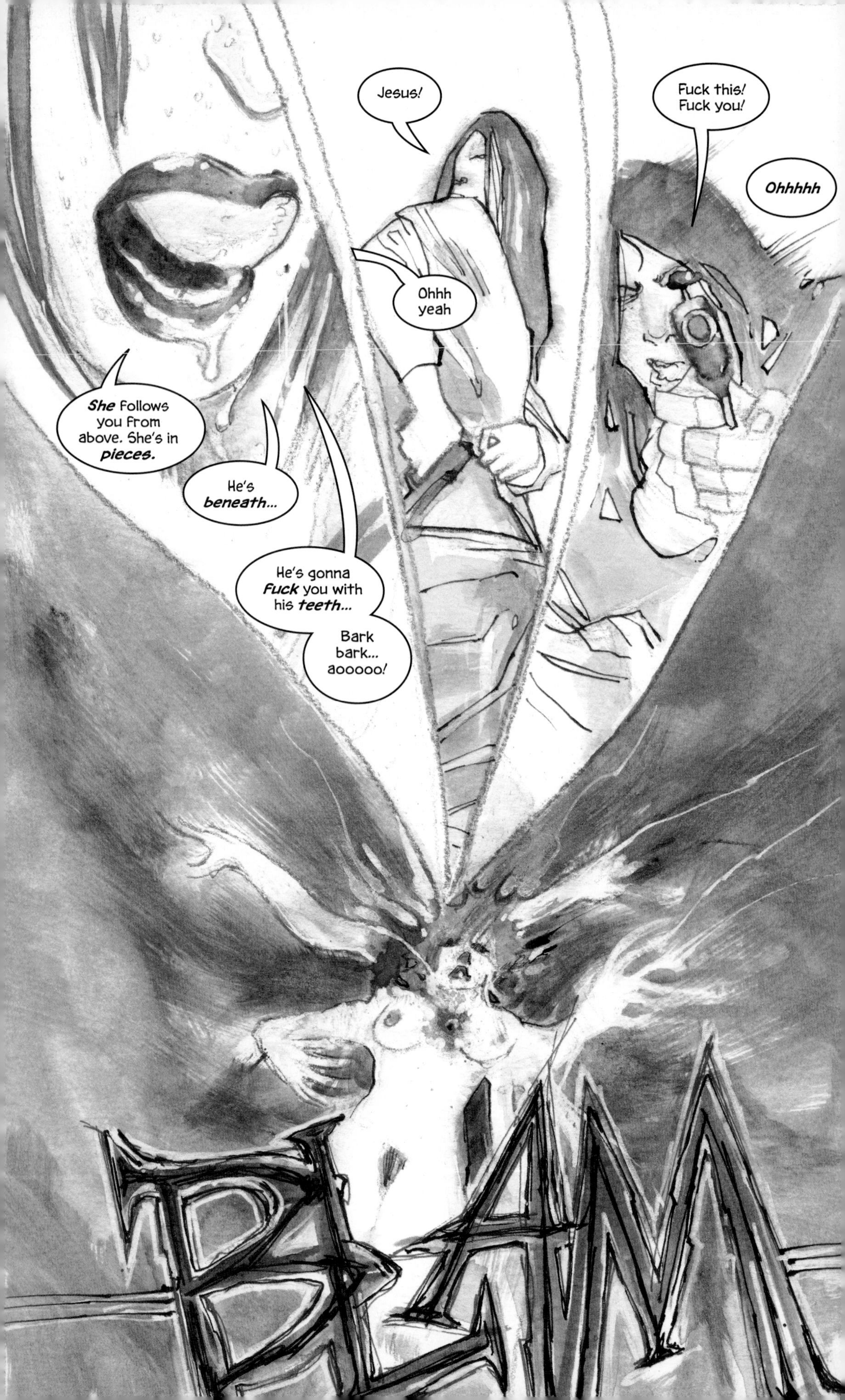
She follows you from above. She's in pieces.
He's beneath...
He's gonna Fuck you with his teeth...
Bark bark... aooooo!
Jesus!
Ohhh yeah
Fuck this! Fuck you!
Ohhhhh
BLAM

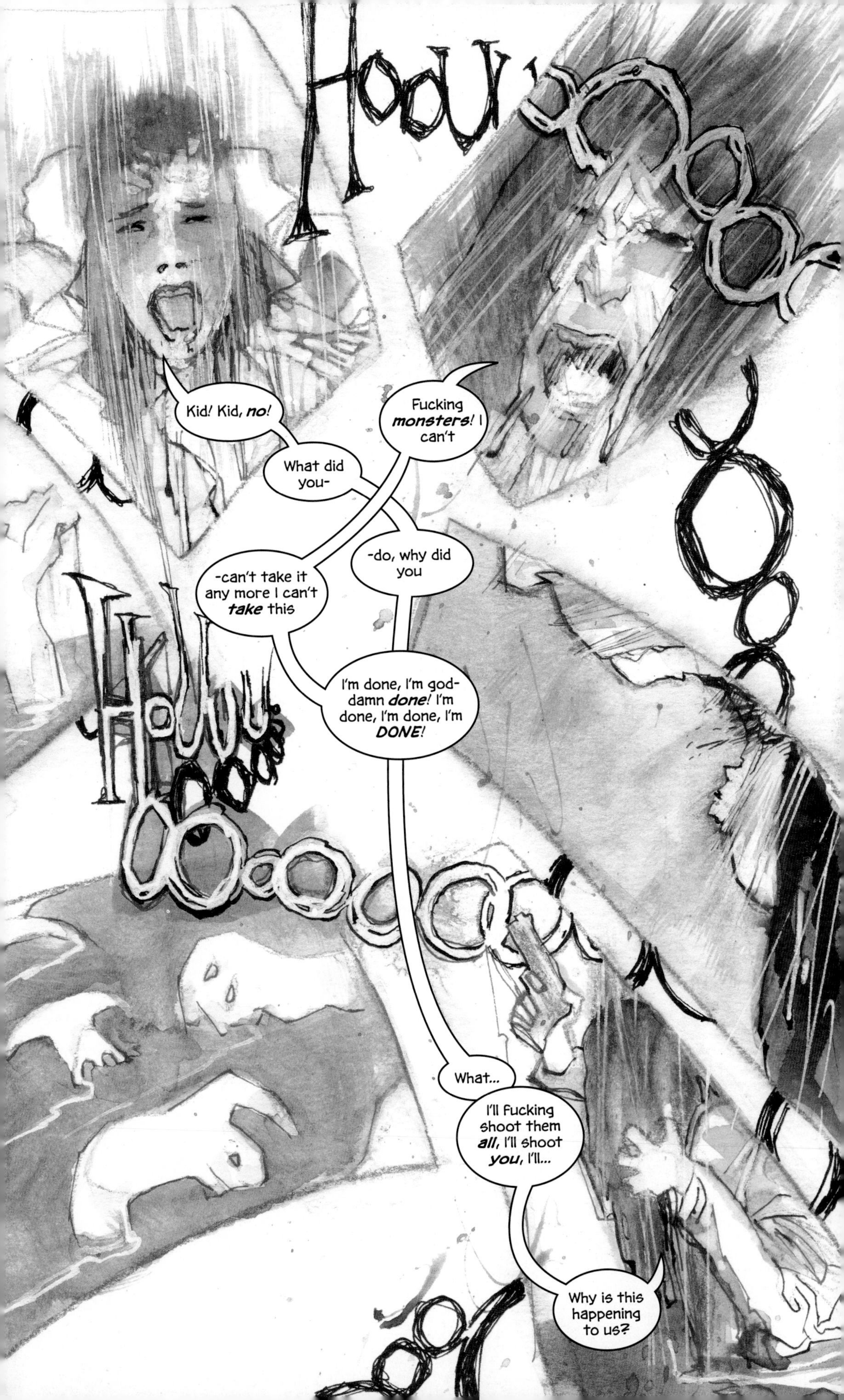
HOOUUOOOOOO
Kid! Kid, *no*!
What did you-
Fucking *monsters*! I can't
-can't take it any more I can't *take* this
-do, why did you
HOUUUOOOOOOO
I'm done, I'm god-damn *done*! I'm done, I'm done, I'm *DONE*!
What...
I'll fucking shoot them *all*, I'll shoot *you*, I'll...
Why is this happening to us?

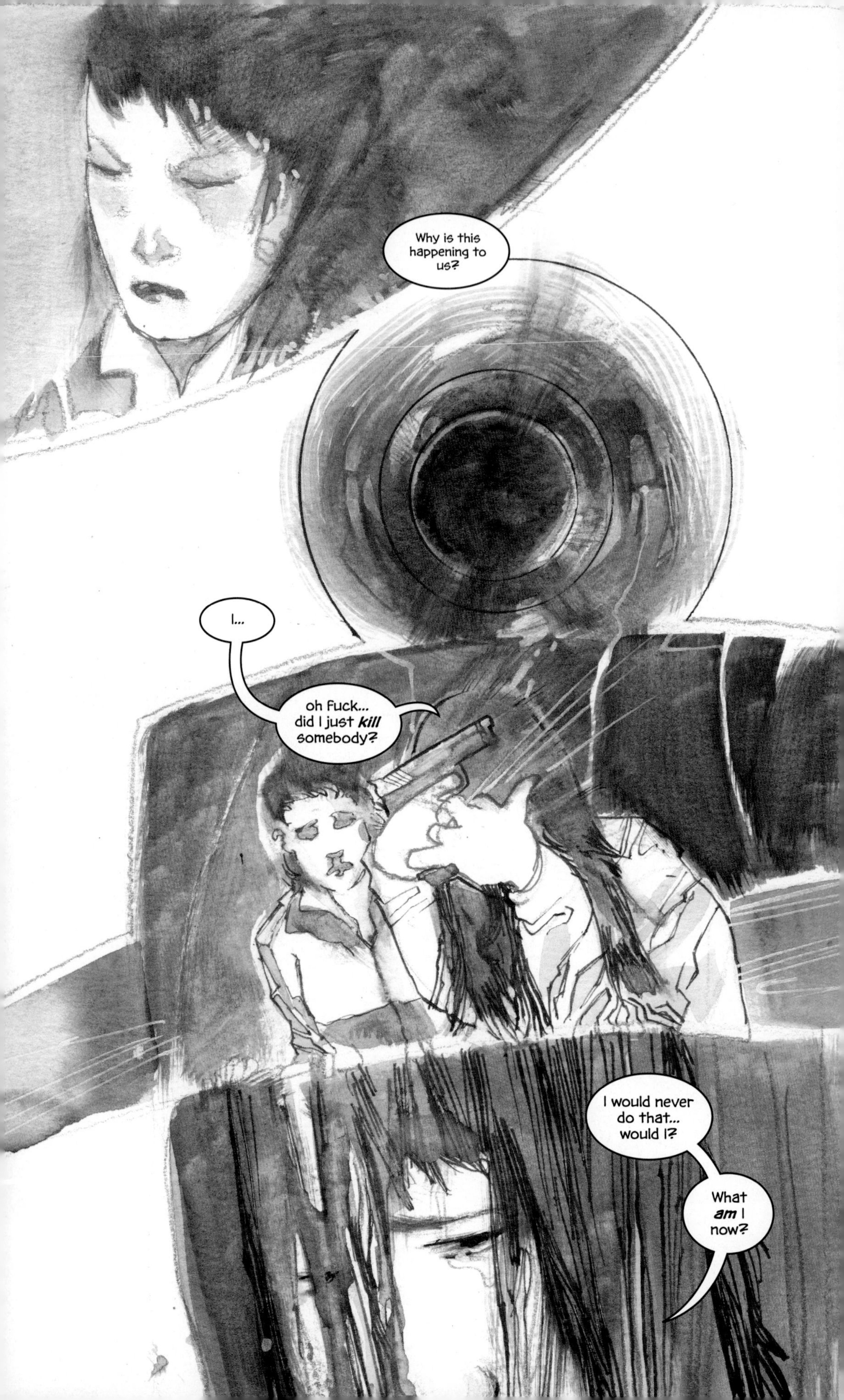
Why is this happening to us?
I...
oh fuck... did I just kill somebody?
I would never do that... would I?
What am I now?

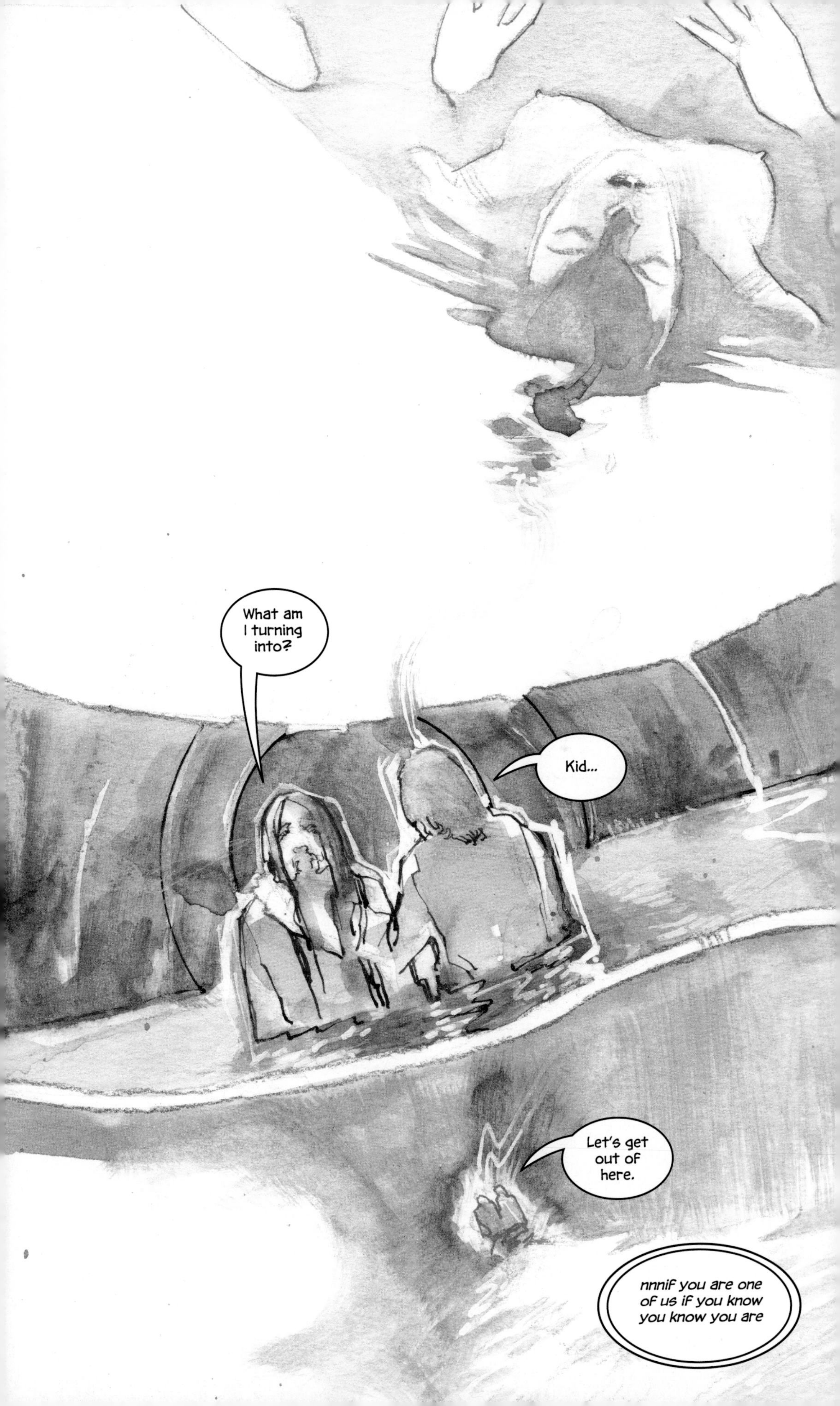
What am I turning into?
Kid...
Let's get out of here.
nnnif you are one of us if you know you know you are

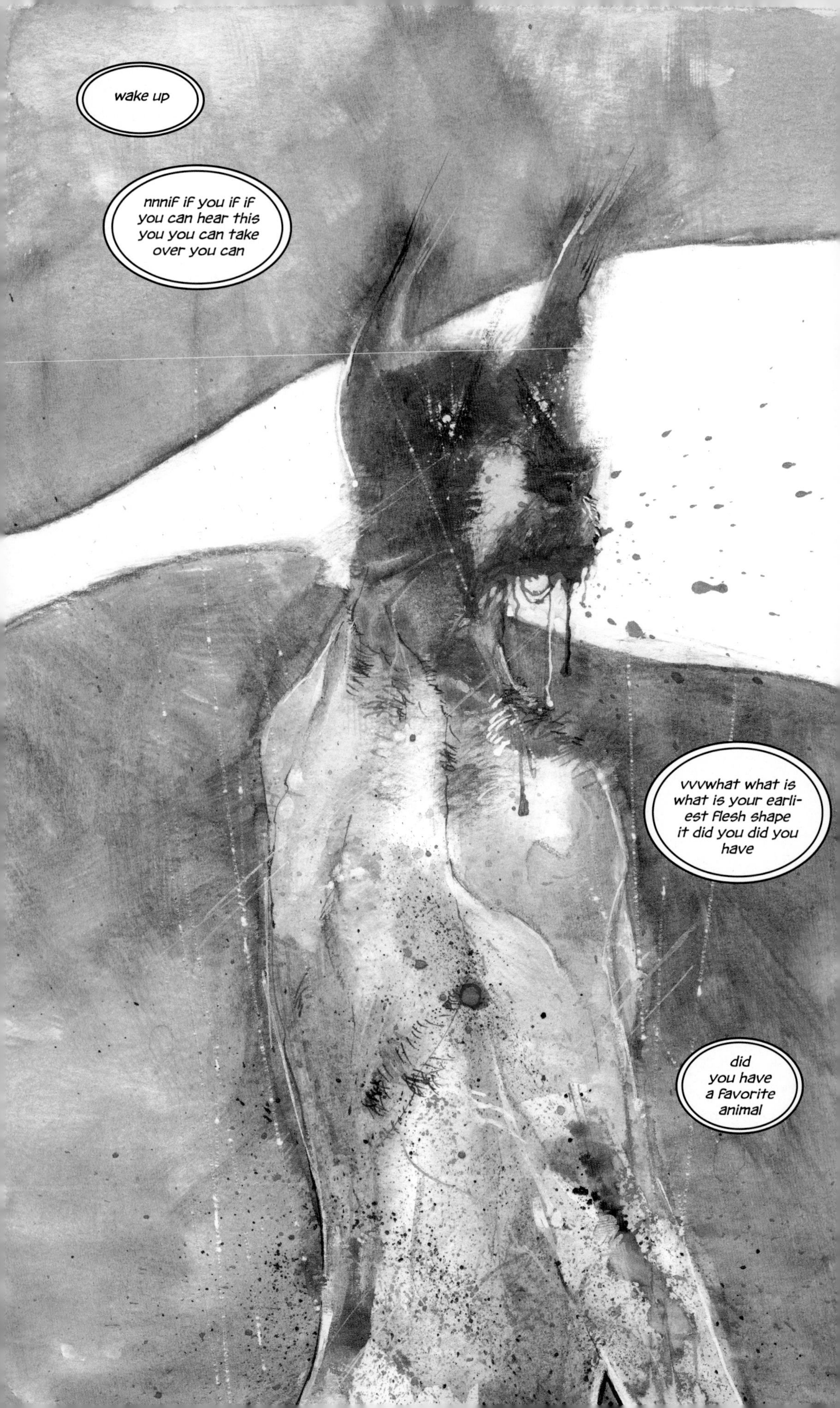
wake up
nnnif if you if if you can hear this you you can take over you can
vvvwhat what is what is your earli- est flesh shape it did you did you have
did you have a favorite animal

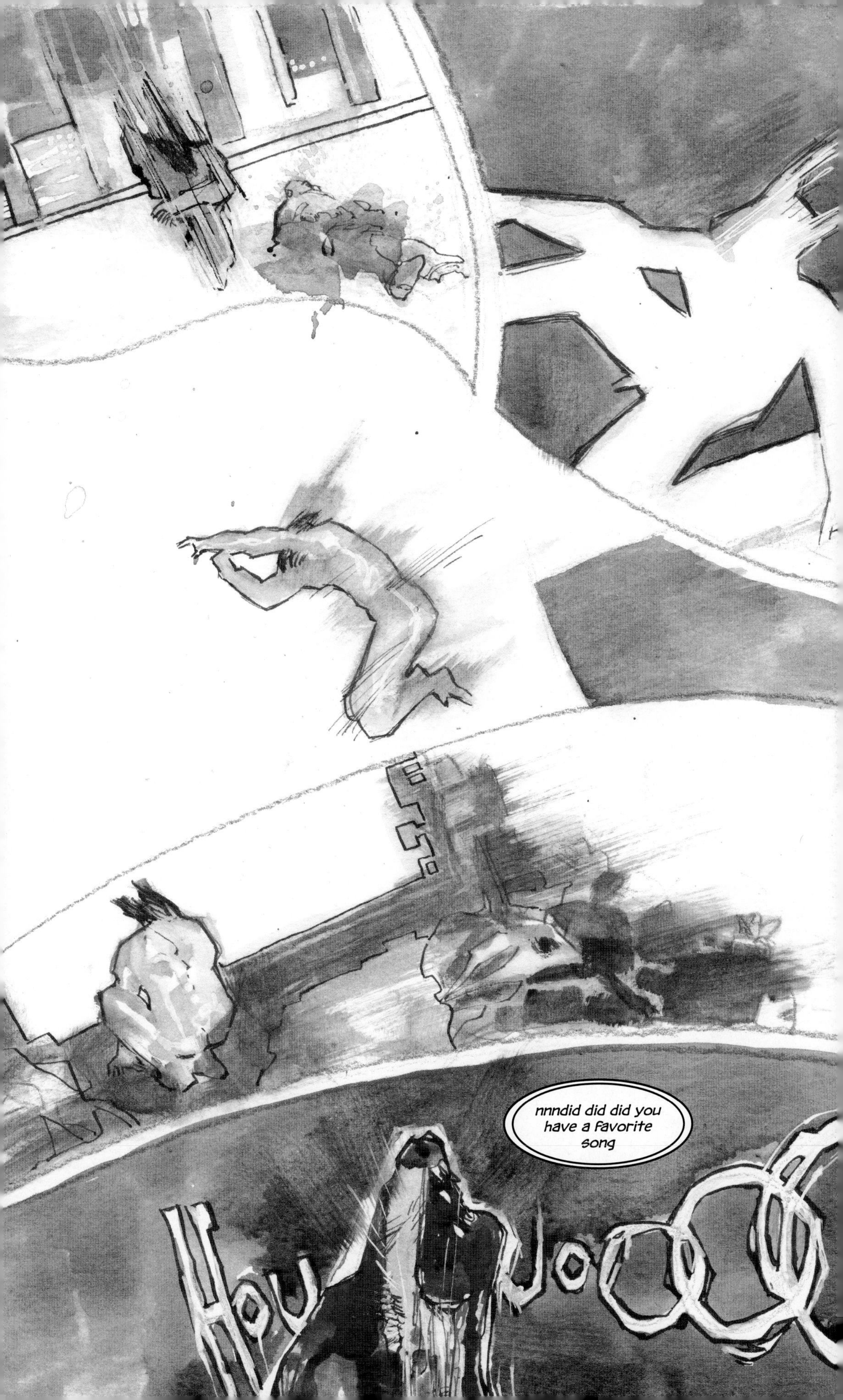
nnndid did did you have a favorite song
Hou Joooo

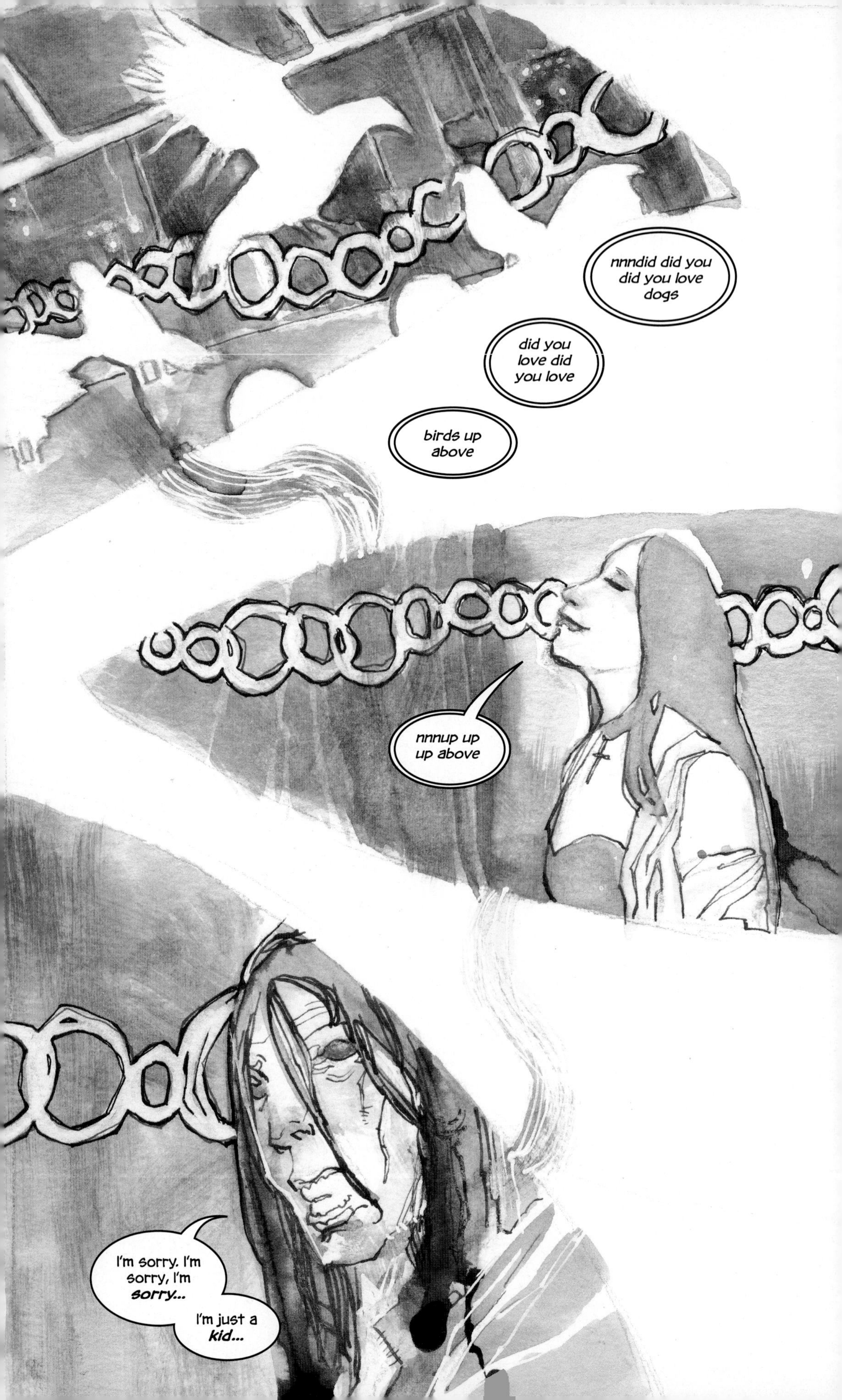
nnndid did you did you love dogs
did you love did you love
birds up above
nnnup up up above
I'm sorry. I'm sorry, I'm *sorry...*
I'm just a *kid...*

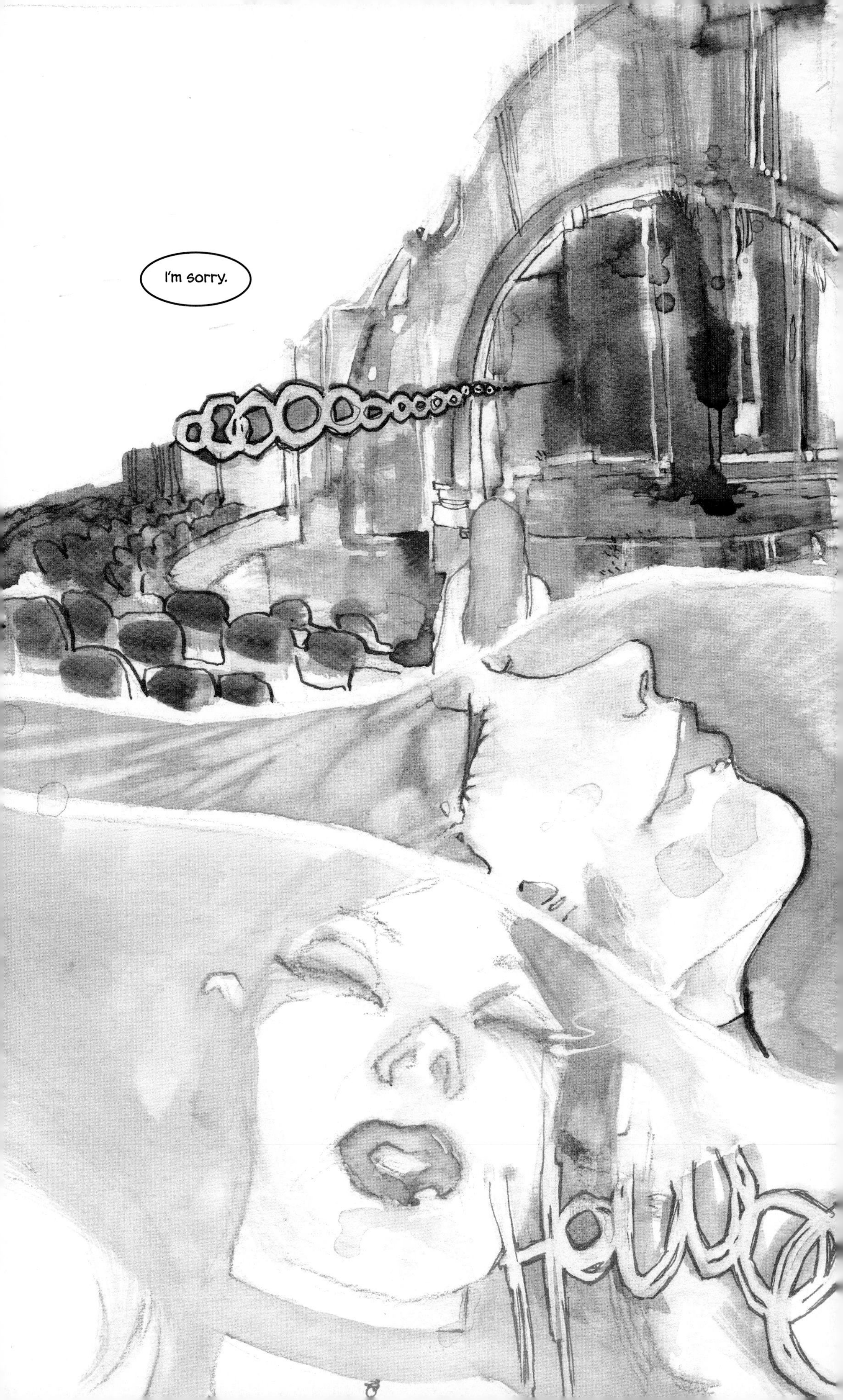
I'm sorry.

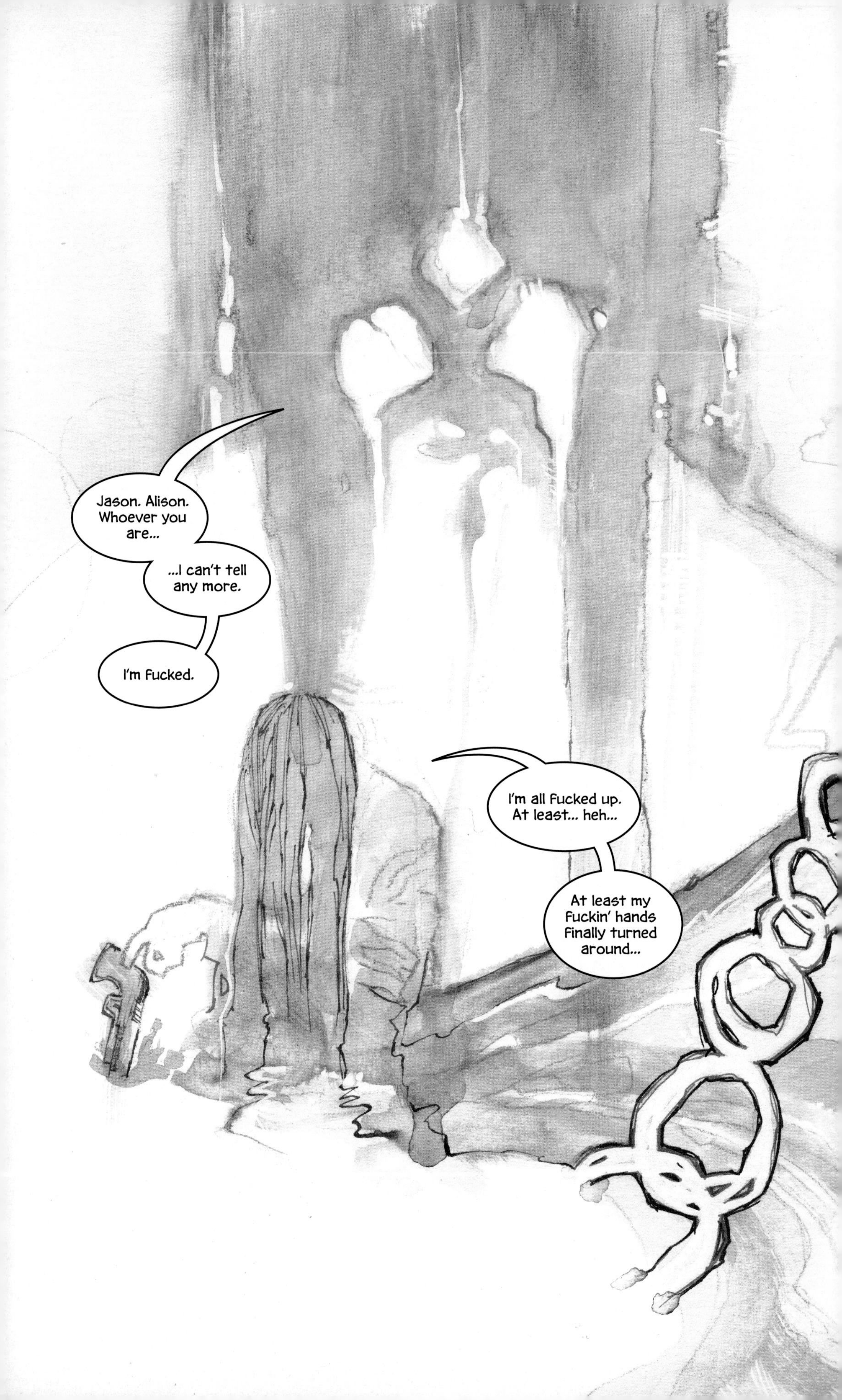
Jason. Alison. Whoever you are...
...I can't tell any more.
I'm fucked.
I'm all fucked up. At least... heh...
At least my fuckin' hands finally turned around...

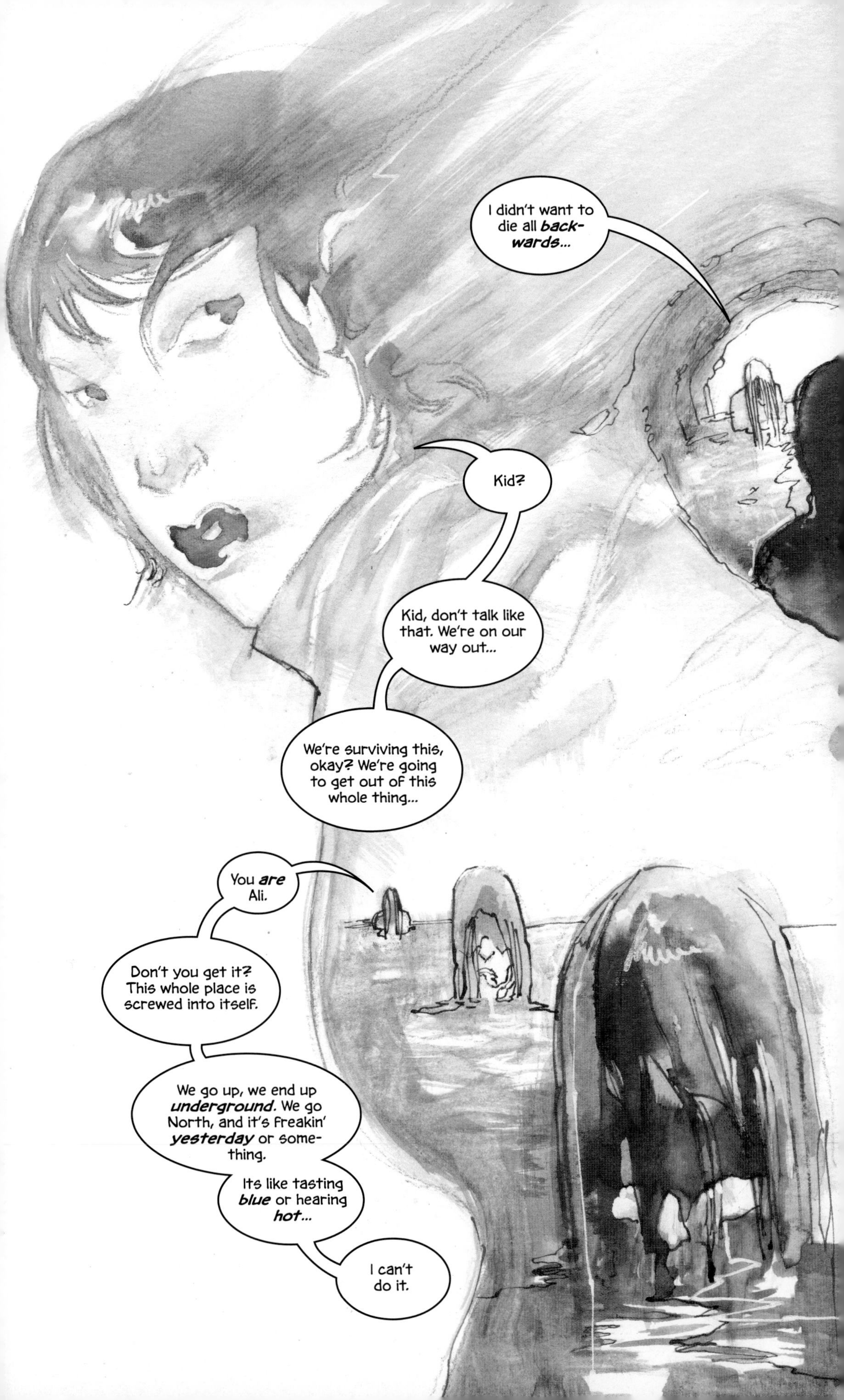
I didn't want to die all *backwards*...
Kid?
Kid, don't talk like that. We're on our way out...
We're surviving this, okay? We're going to get out of this whole thing...
You *are* Ali.
Don't you get it? This whole place is screwed into itself.
We go up, we end up *underground*. We go North, and it's freakin' *yesterday* or something.
Its like tasting *blue* or hearing *hot*...
I can't do it.

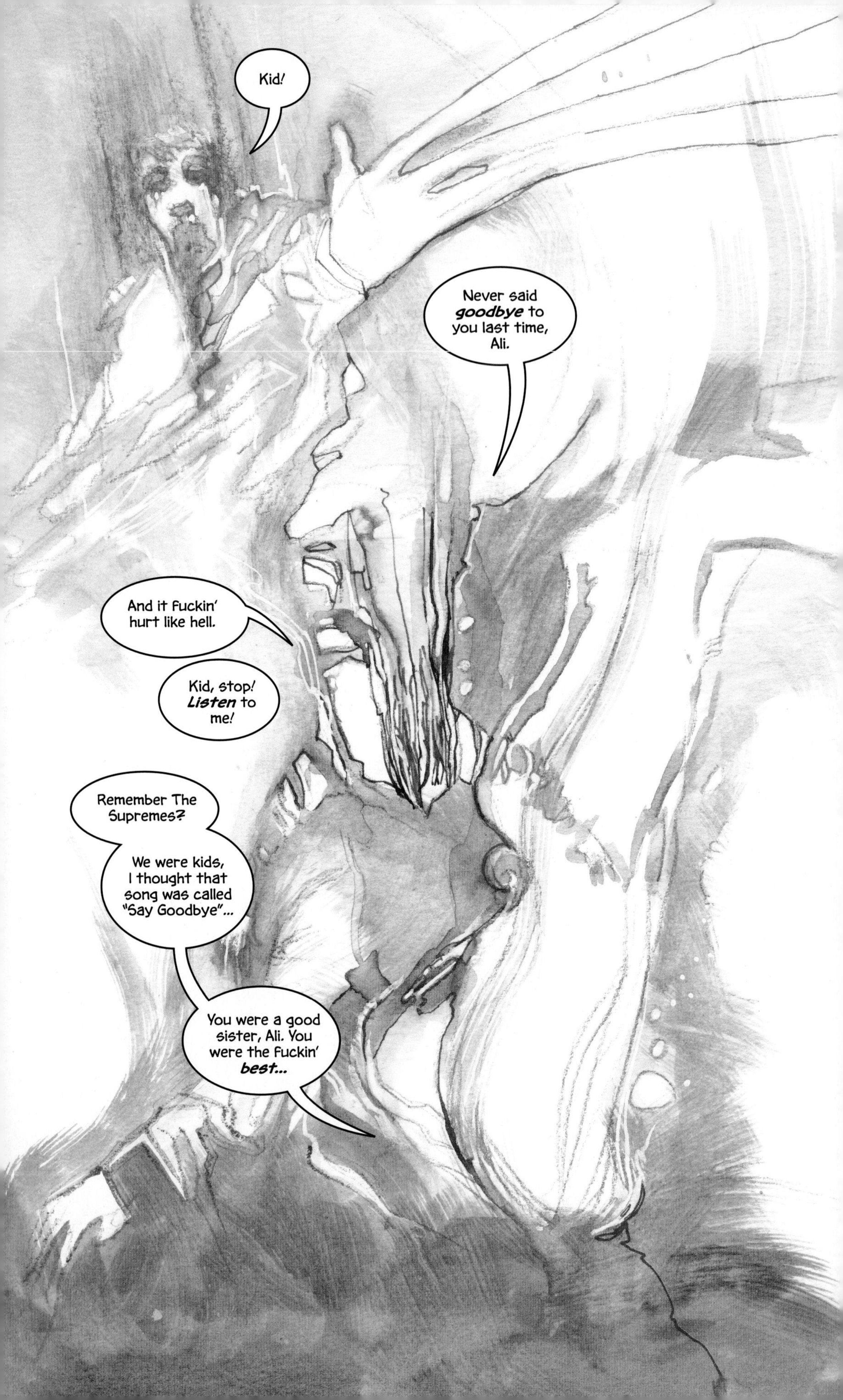
Kid!
Never said *goodbye* to you last time, Ali.
And it fuckin' hurt like hell.
Kid, stop! *Listen* to me!
Remember The Supremes?
We were kids, I thought that song was called "Say Goodbye"...
You were a good sister, Ali. You were the fuckin' *best...*

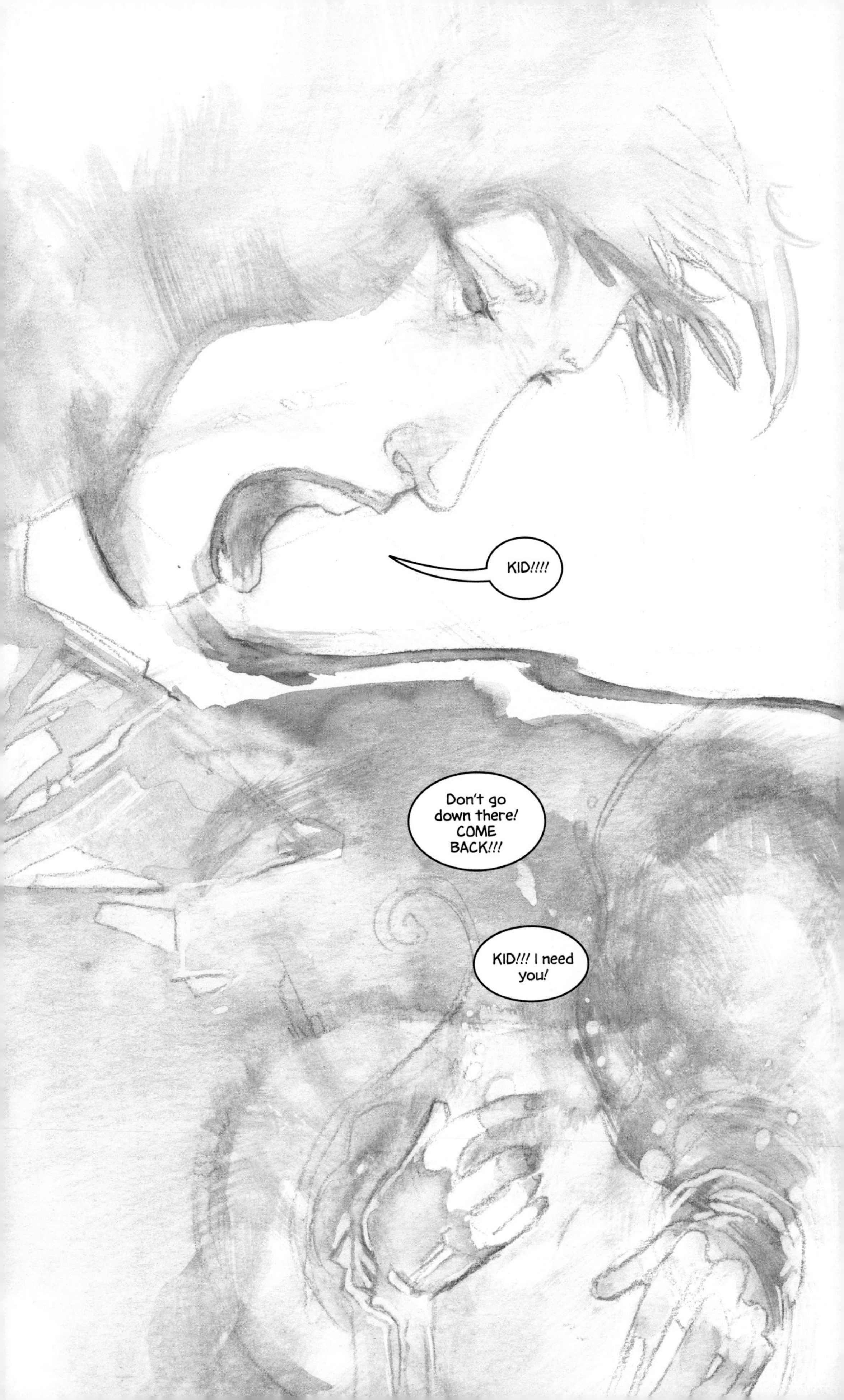
KID!!!!
Don't go down there! COME BACK!!!
KID!!! I need you!

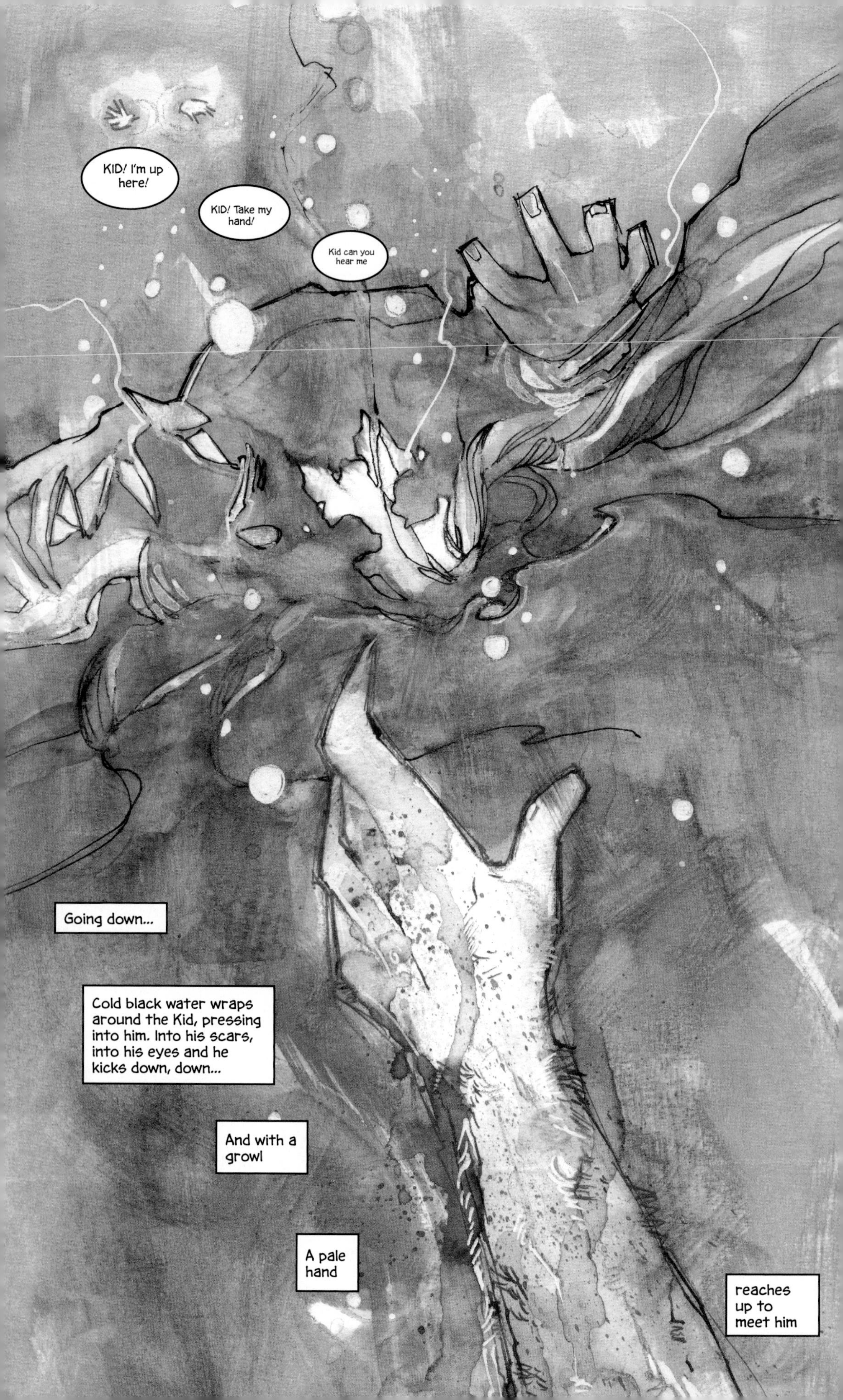
KID! I'm up here!
KID! Take my hand!
Kid can you hear me
Going down...
Cold black water wraps around the Kid, pressing into him. Into his scars, into his eyes and he kicks down, down...
And with a growl
A pale hand
reaches up to meet him

Part Four

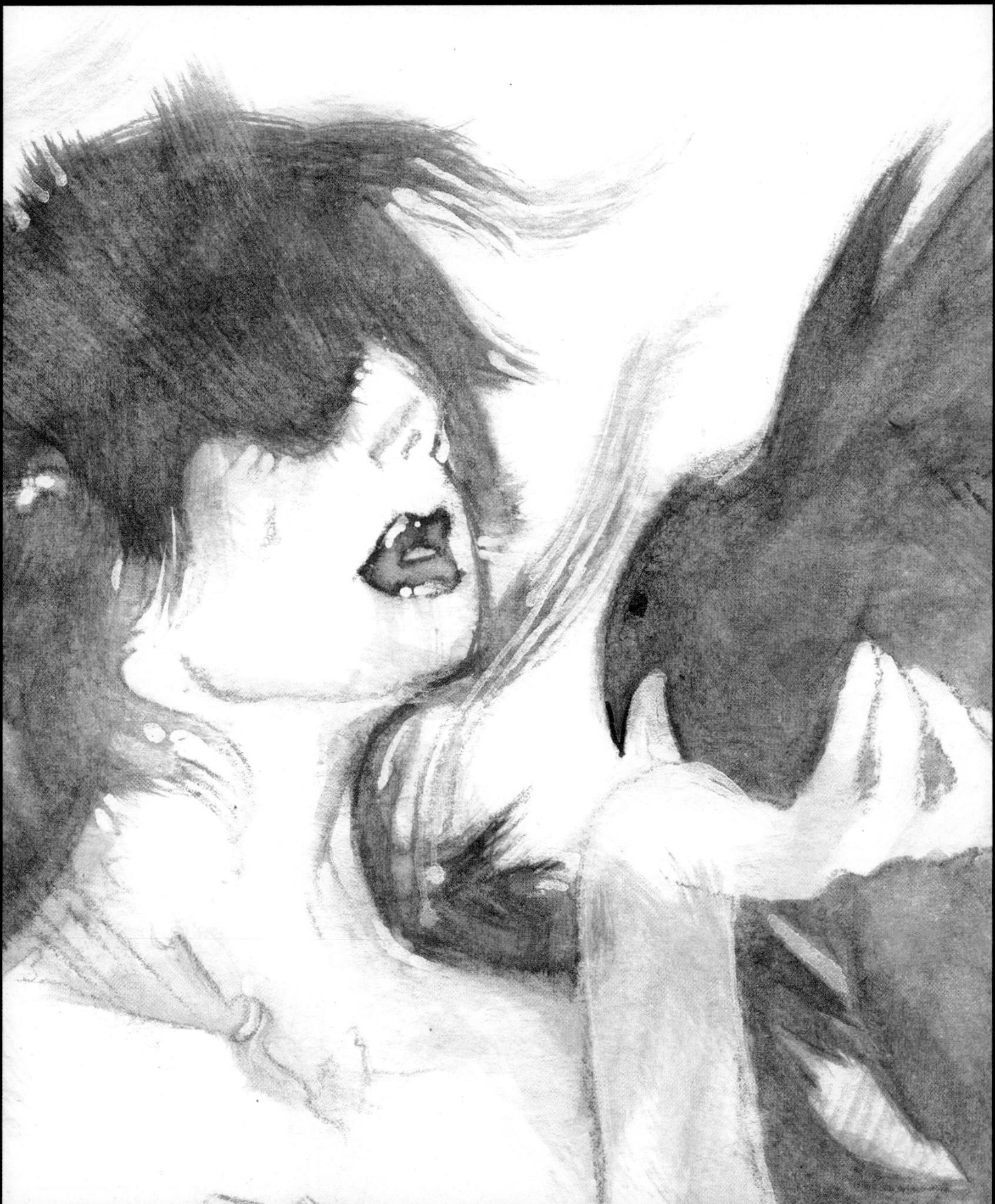

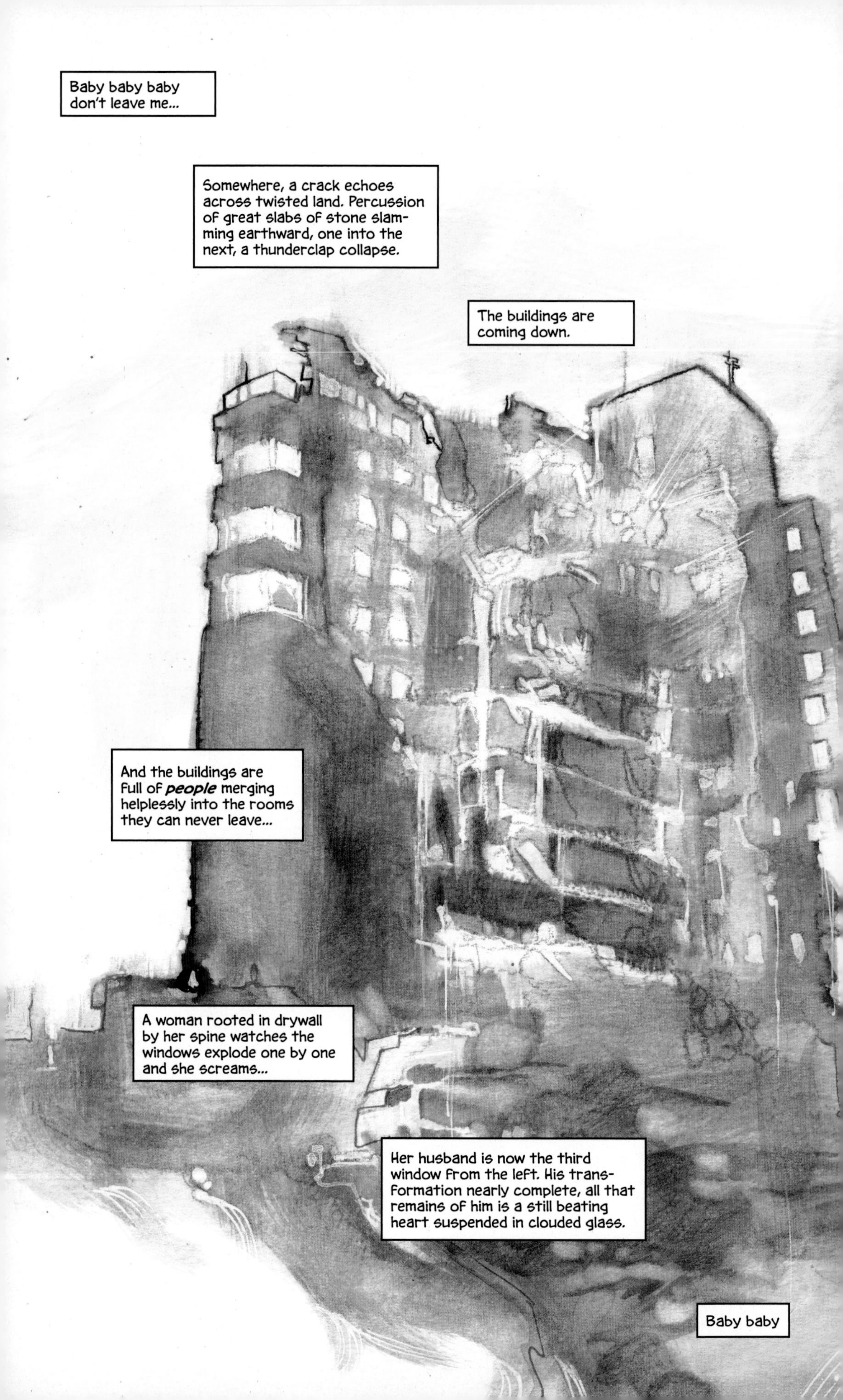
Baby baby baby don't leave me...
Somewhere, a crack echoes across twisted land. Percussion of great slabs of stone slamming earthward, one into the next, a thunderclap collapse.
The buildings are coming down.
And the buildings are full of *people* merging helplessly into the rooms they can never leave...
A woman rooted in drywall by her spine watches the windows explode one by one and she screams...
Her husband is now the third window from the left. His transformation nearly complete, all that remains of him is a still beating heart suspended in clouded glass.
Baby baby

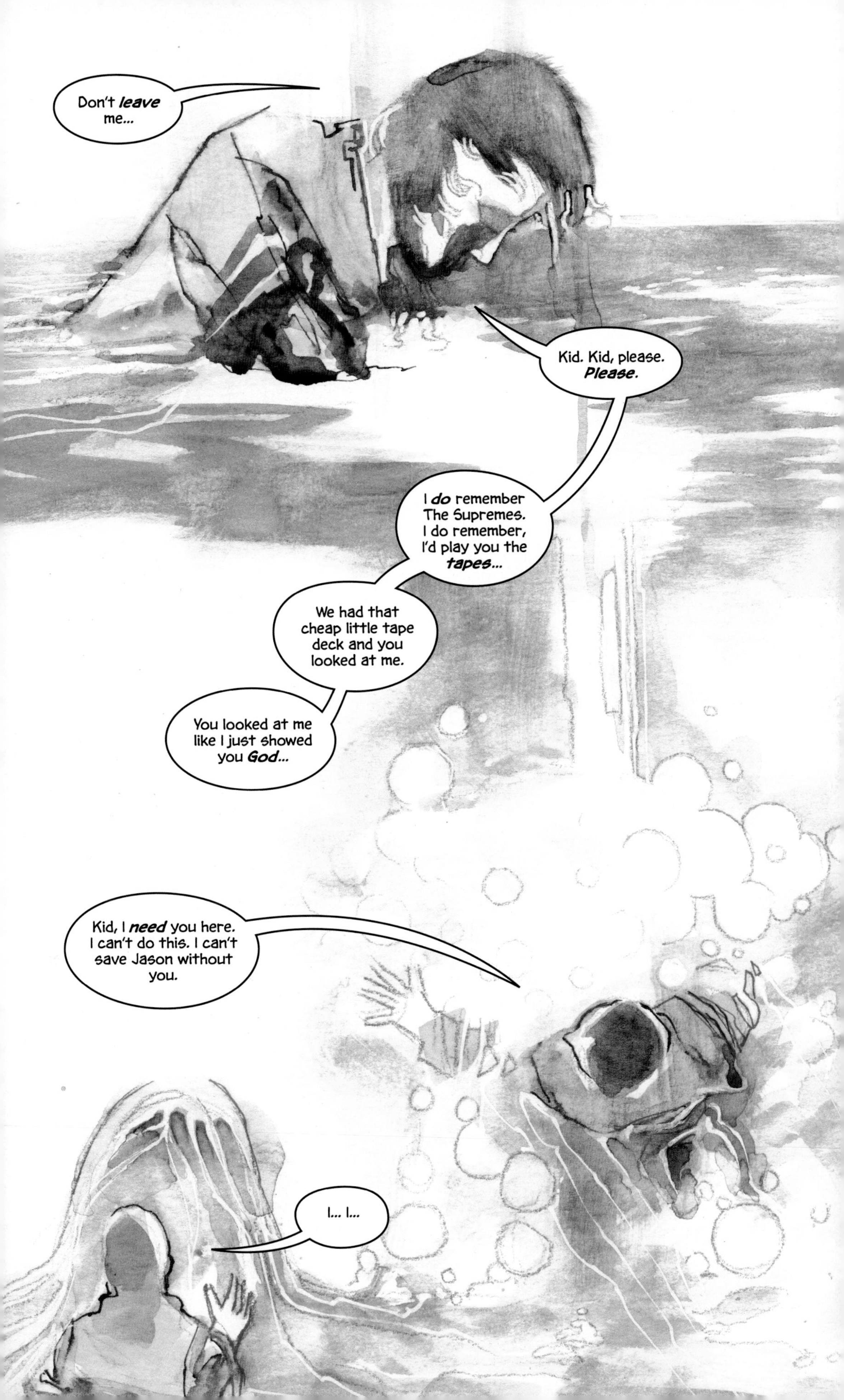
Don't *leave* me...
Kid. Kid, please. ***Please.***
I *do* remember The Supremes. I do remember, I'd play you the *tapes*...
We had that cheap little tape deck and you looked at me.
You looked at me like I just showed you *God*...
Kid, I *need* you here. I can't do this. I can't save Jason without you.
I... I...

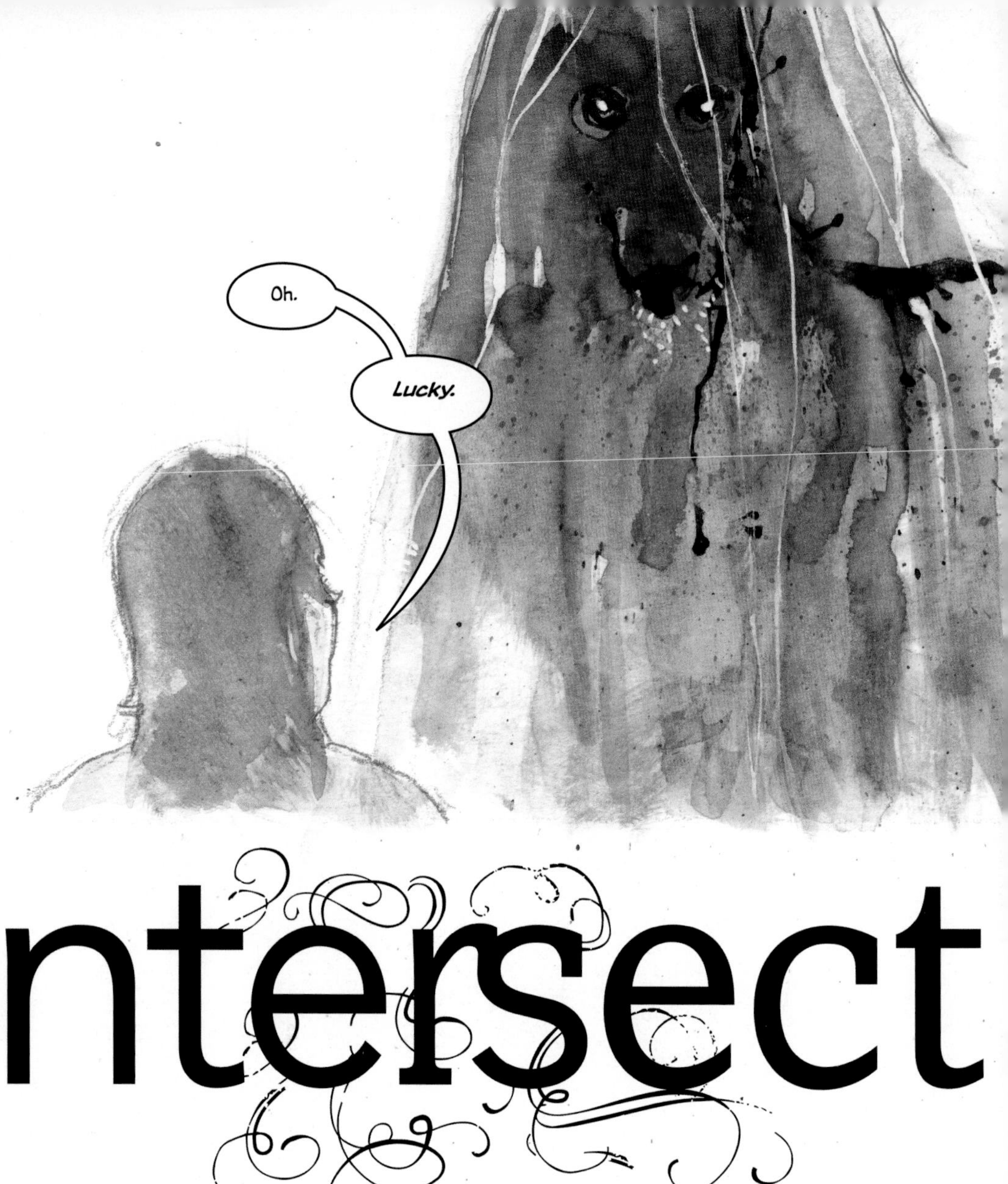
Oh.
Lucky.

intersect

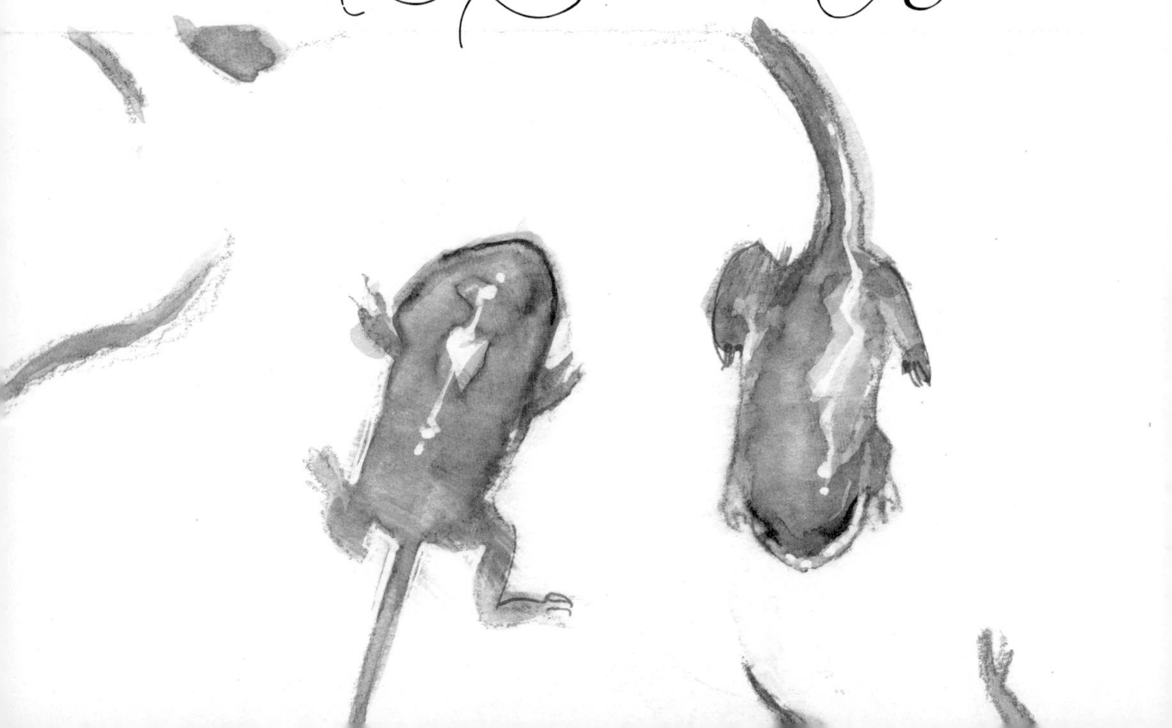

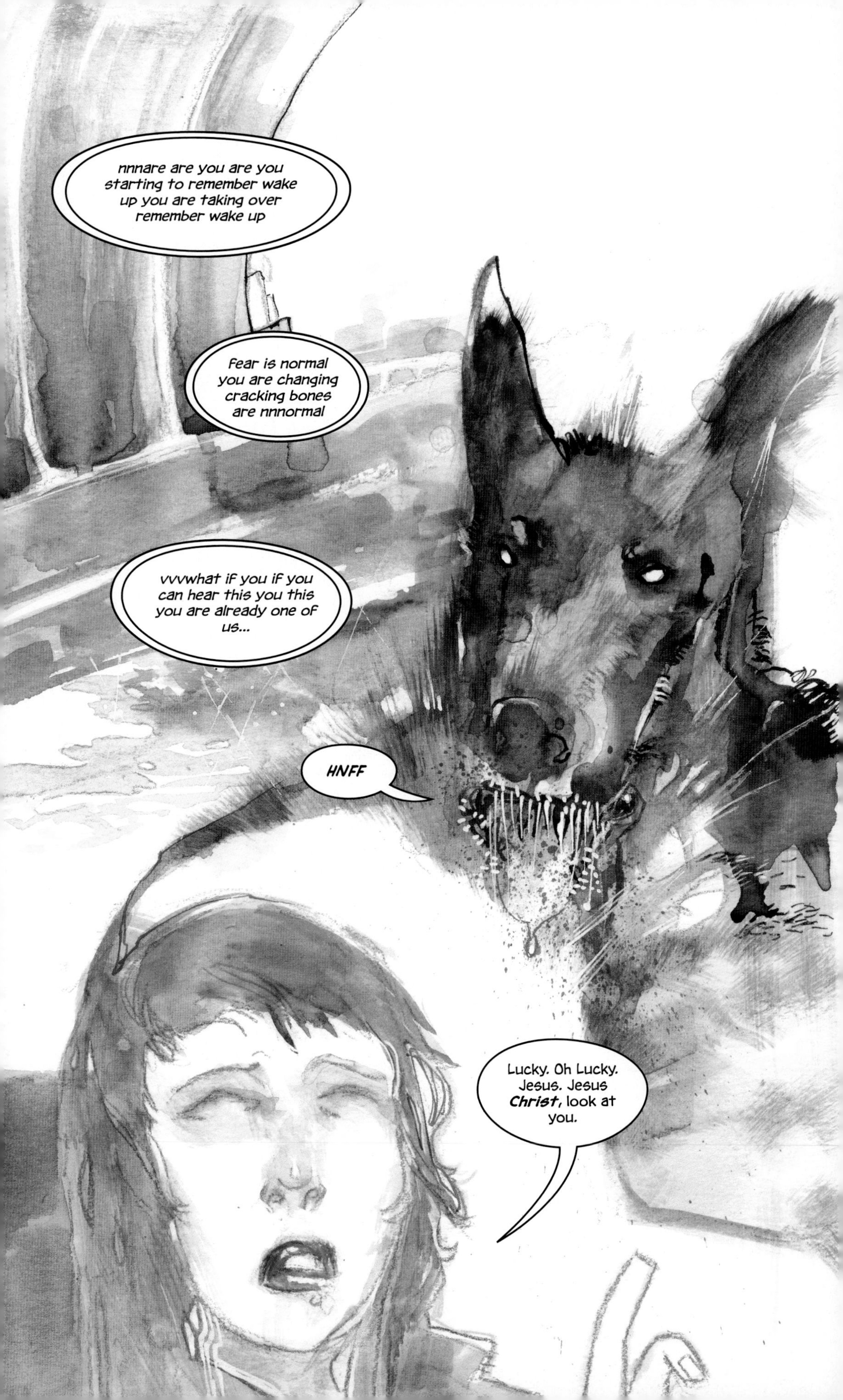
nnnare are you are you starting to remember wake up you are taking over remember wake up
Fear is normal you are changing cracking bones are nnnormal
vvvwhat if you if you can hear this you this you are already one of us...
HNFF
Lucky. Oh Lucky. Jesus. Jesus *Christ*, look at you.

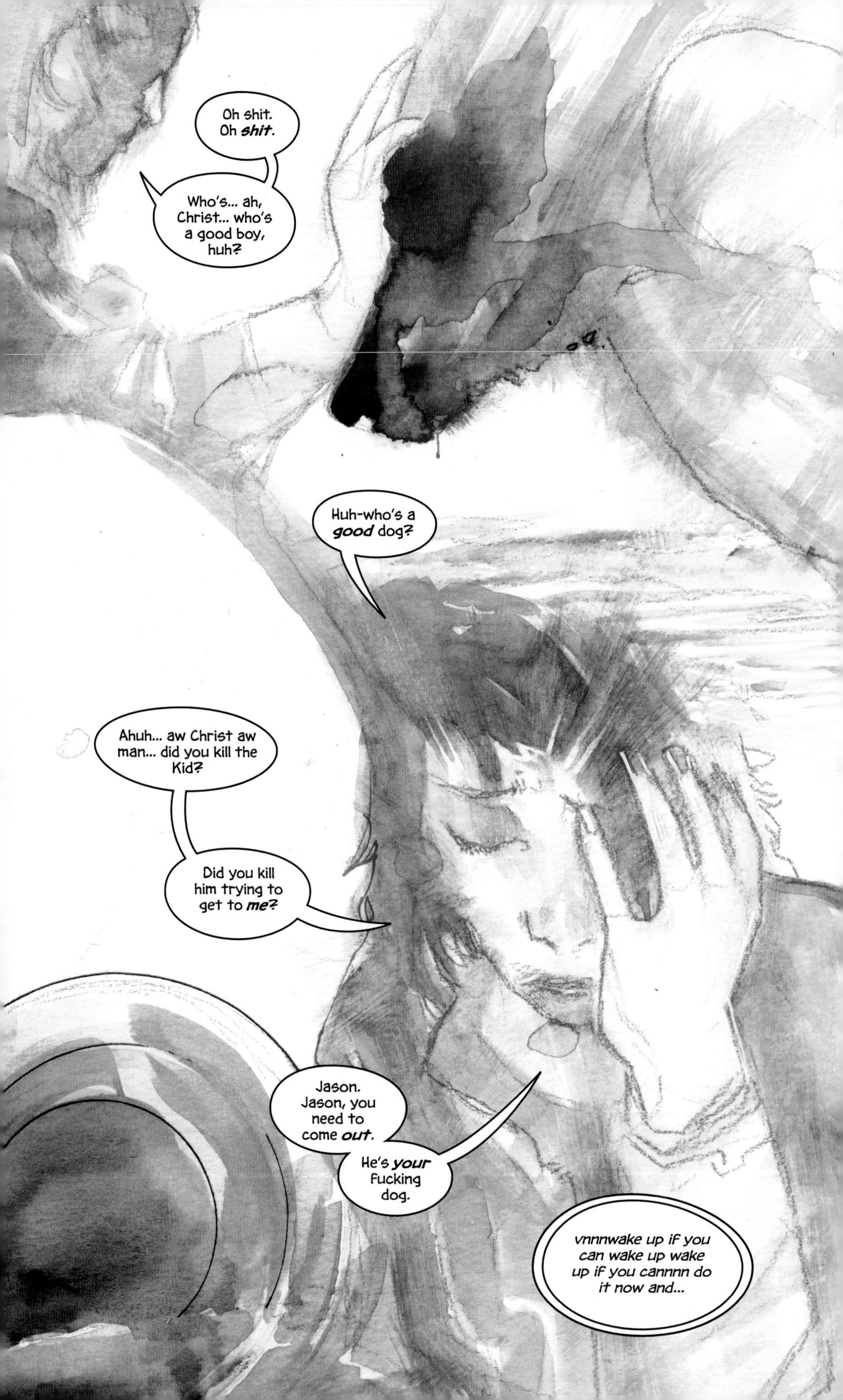
Oh shit. Oh *shit*.
Who's... ah, Christ... who's a good boy, huh?
Huh-who's a *good* dog?
Ahuh... aw Christ aw man... did you kill the Kid?
Did you kill him trying to get to *me*?
Jason. Jason, you need to come *out*.
He's *your* fucking dog.
vnnnwake up if you can wake up wake up if you cannnn do it now and...

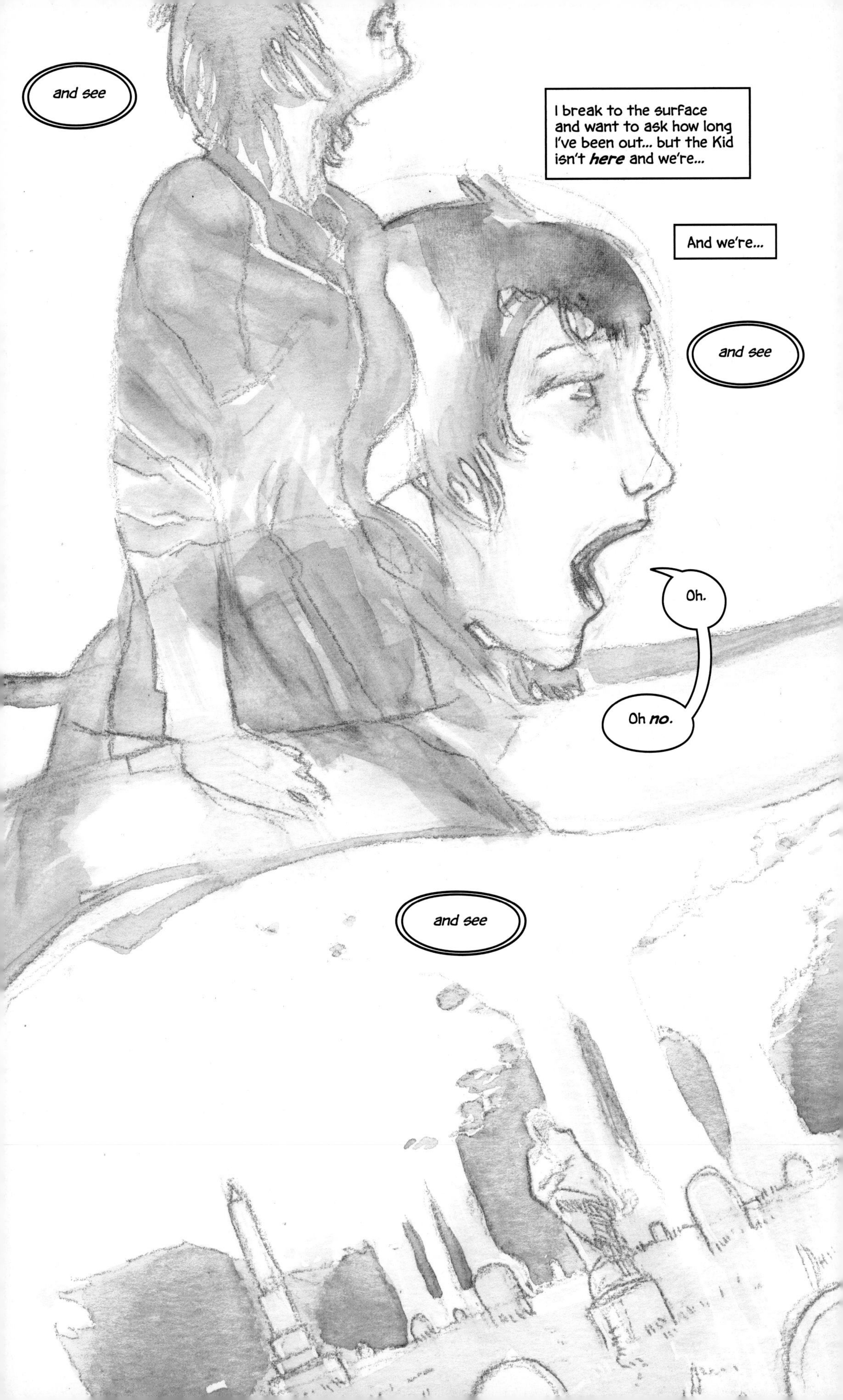
and see
I break to the surface and want to ask how long I've been out... but the Kid isn't *here* and we're...
And we're...
and see
Oh.
Oh *no.*
and see

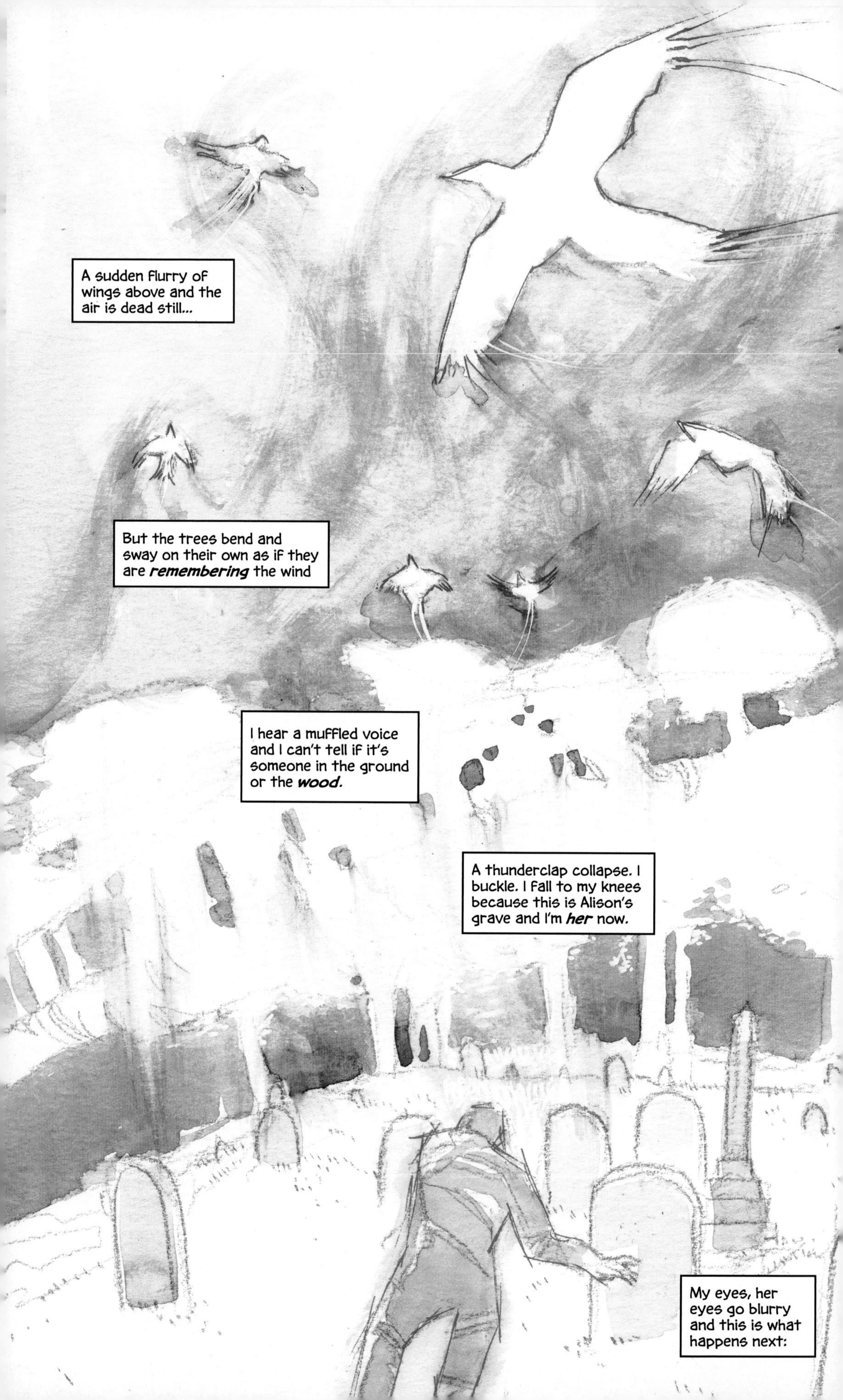
A sudden flurry of wings above and the air is dead still...
But the trees bend and sway on their own as if they are *remembering* the wind
I hear a muffled voice and I can't tell if it's someone in the ground or the *wood.*
A thunderclap collapse. I buckle. I fall to my knees because this is Alison's grave and I'm *her* now.
My eyes, her eyes go blurry and this is what happens next:

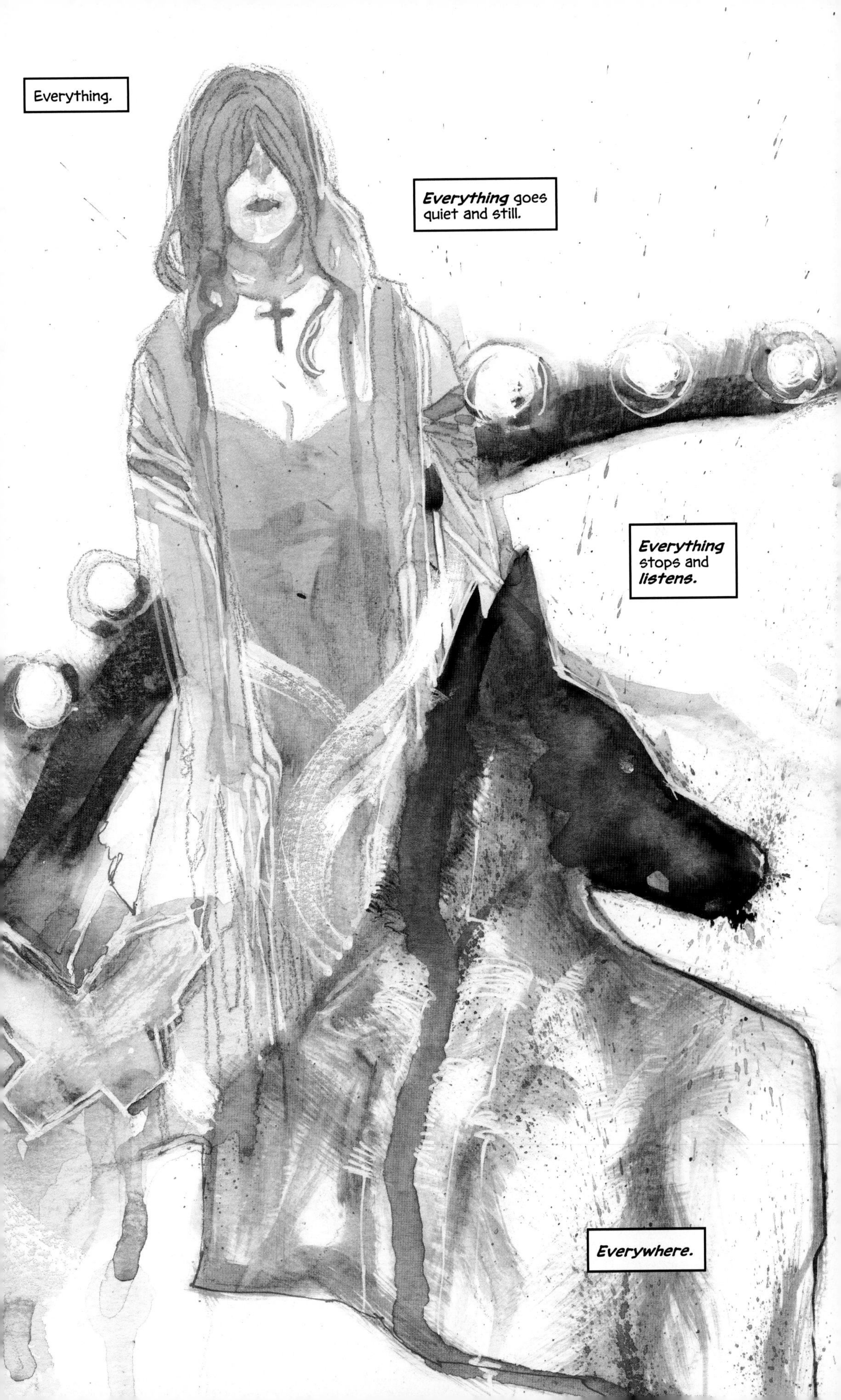
Everything.
Everything goes quiet and still.
Everything stops and ***listens.***
Everywhere.

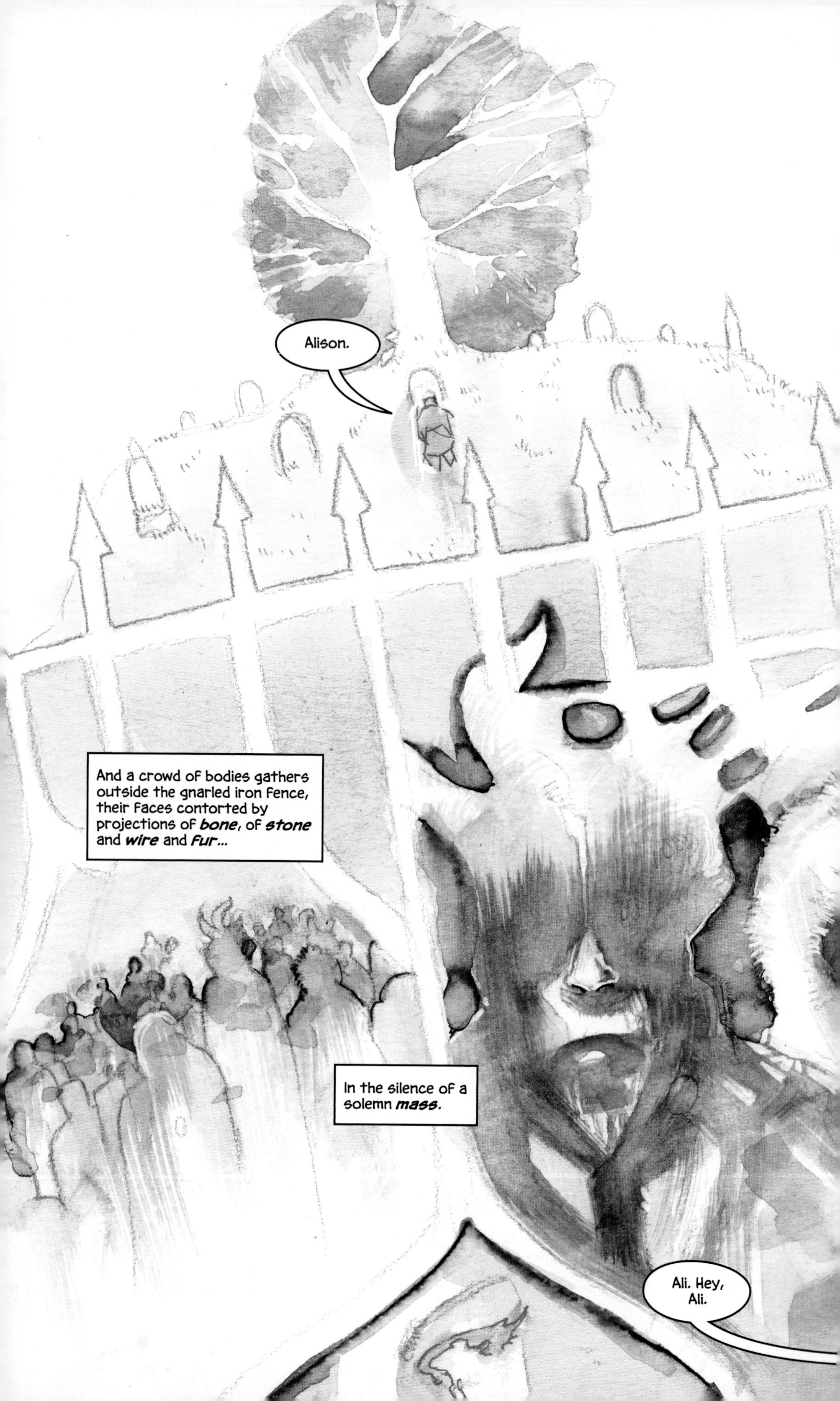

Alison.
And a crowd of bodies gathers outside the gnarled iron fence, their faces contorted by projections of *bone*, of *stone* and *wire* and *fur*...
In the silence of a solemn *mass*.
Ali. Hey, Ali.

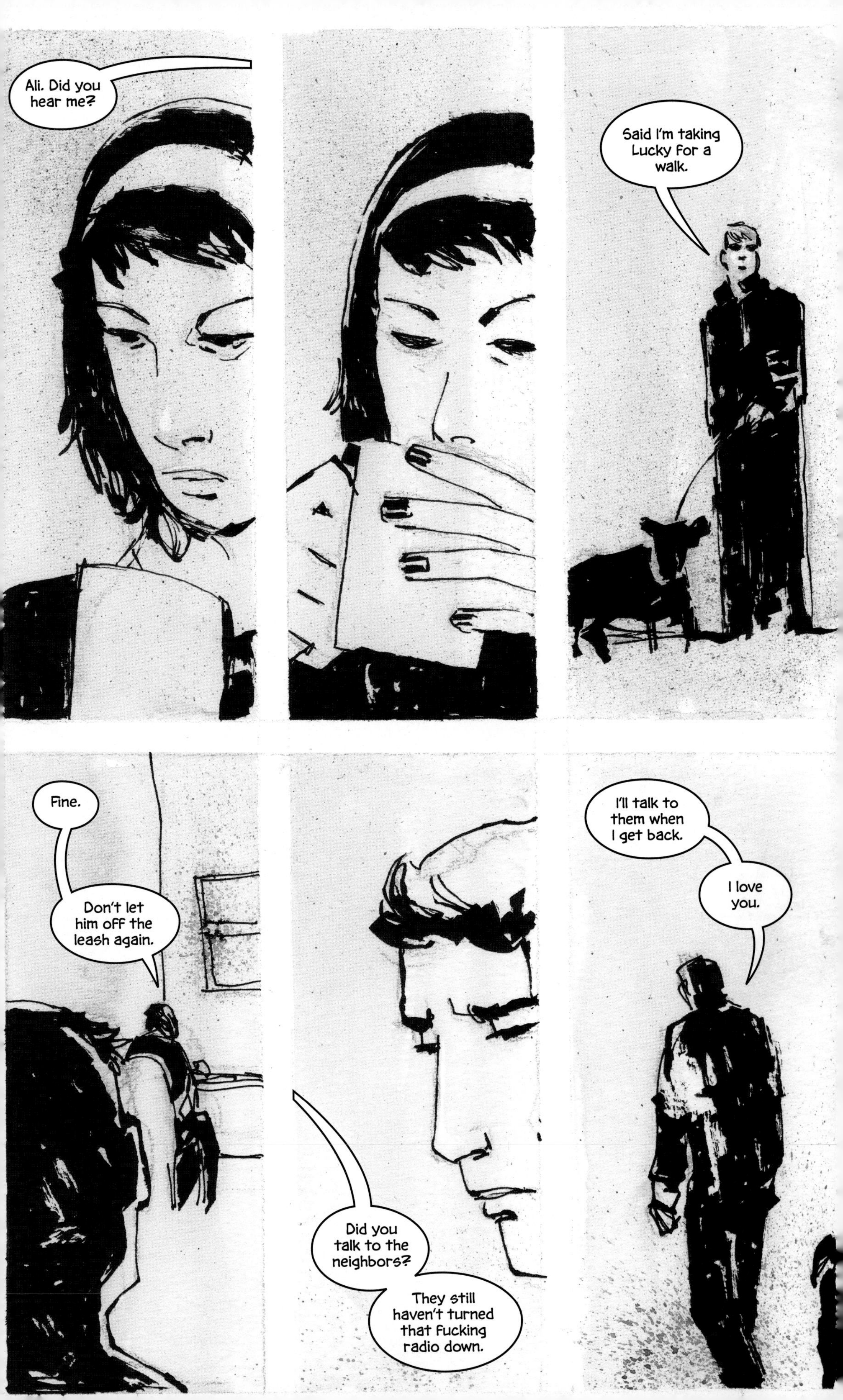
Ali. Did you hear me?
Said I'm taking Lucky for a walk.
Fine.
Don't let him off the leash again.
Did you talk to the neighbors?
They still haven't turned that fucking radio down.
I'll talk to them when I get back.
I love you.

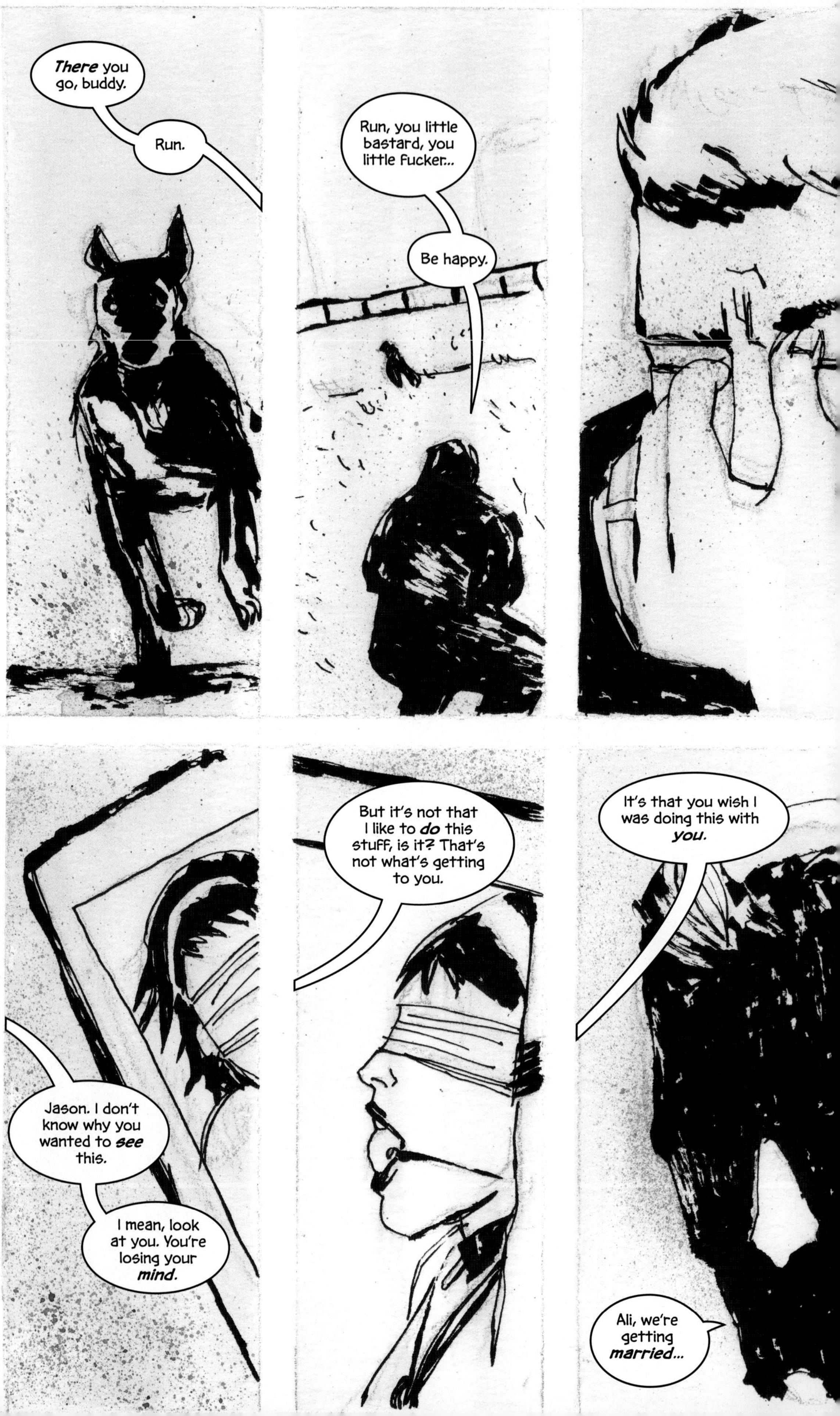
There you go, buddy.
Run.
Run, you little bastard, you little fucker...
Be happy.
Jason. I don't know why you wanted to *see* this.
I mean, look at you. You're losing your *mind*.
But it's not that I like to *do* this stuff, is it? That's not what's getting to you.
It's that you wish I was doing this with *you*.
Ali, we're getting *married*...

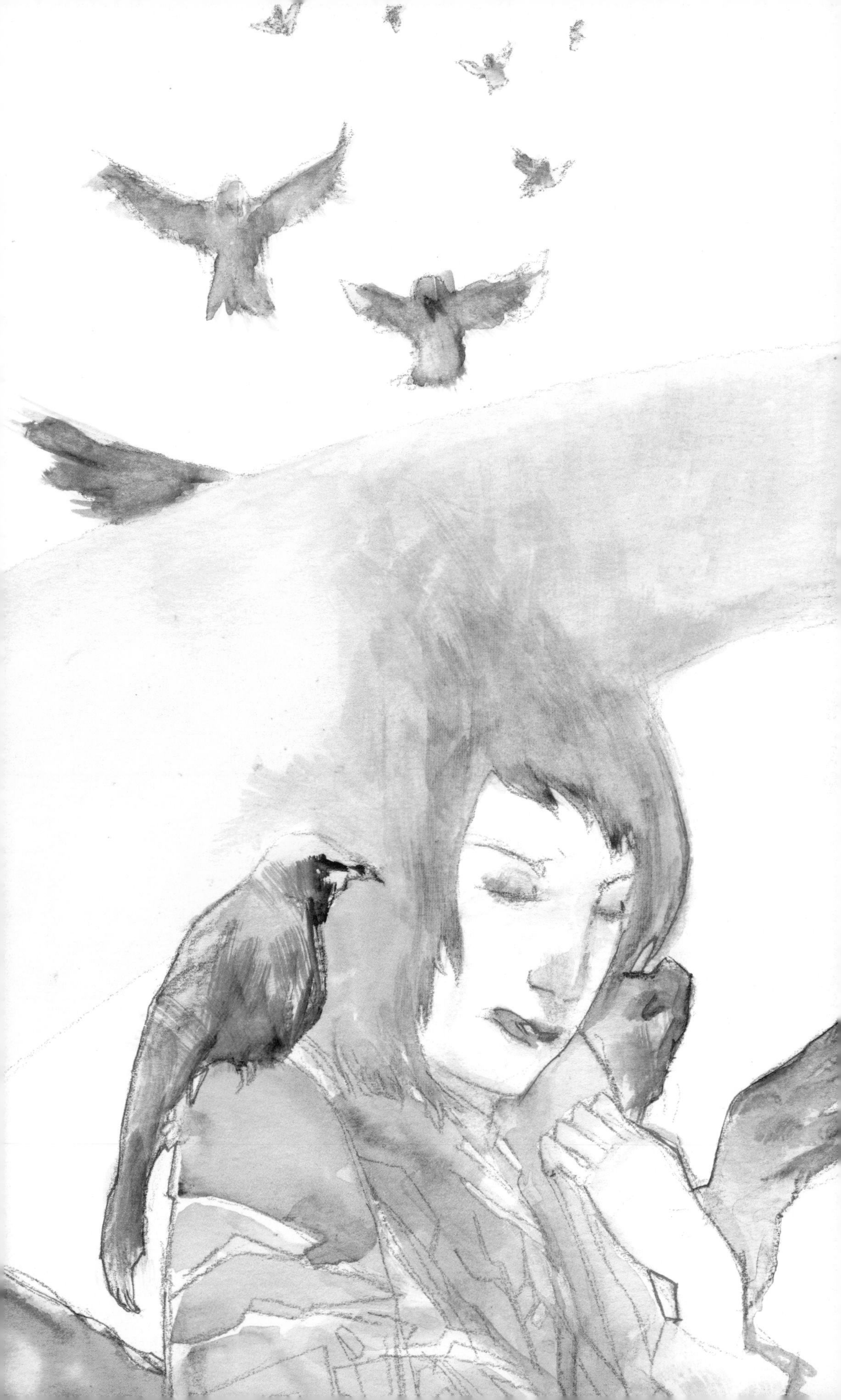

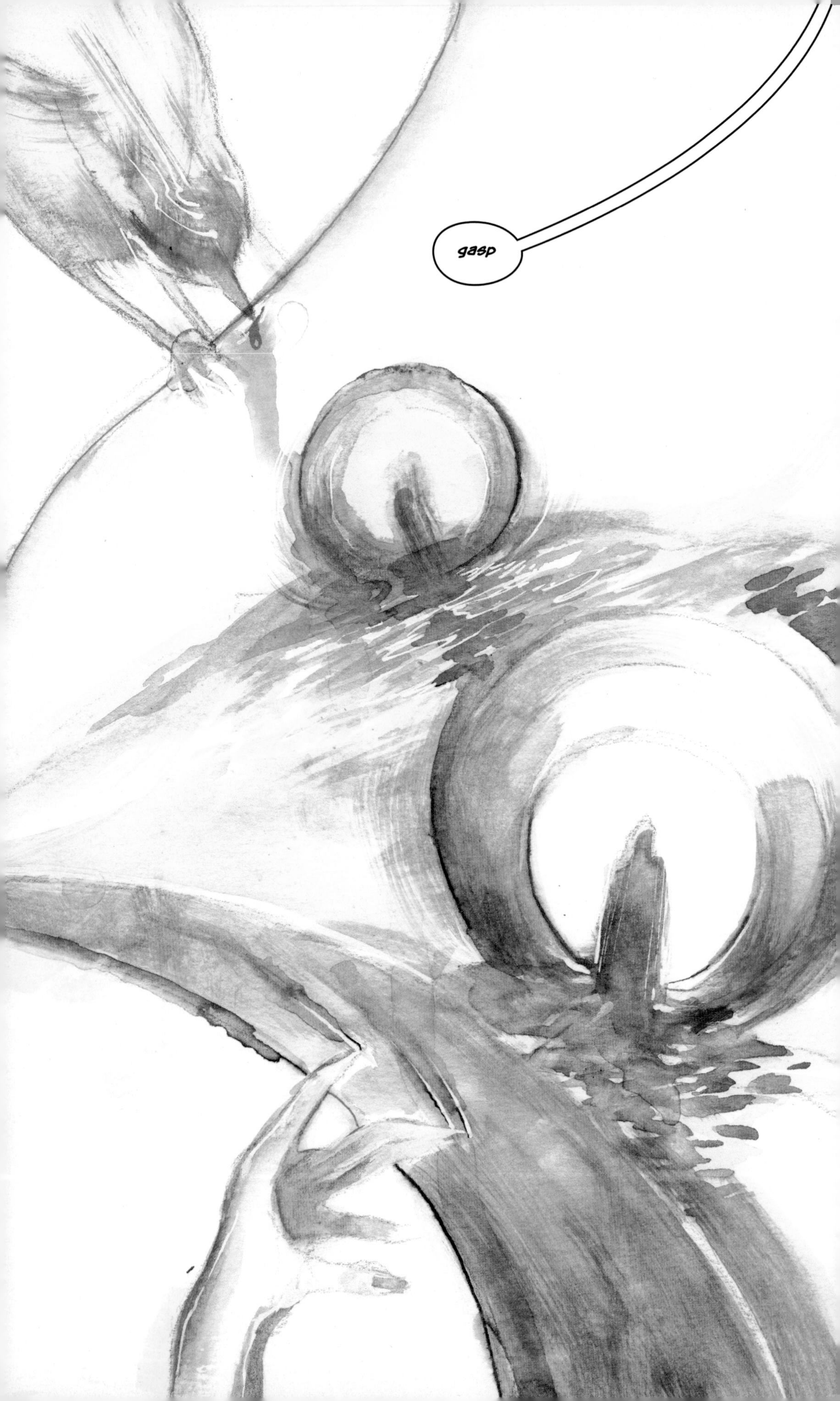
gasp

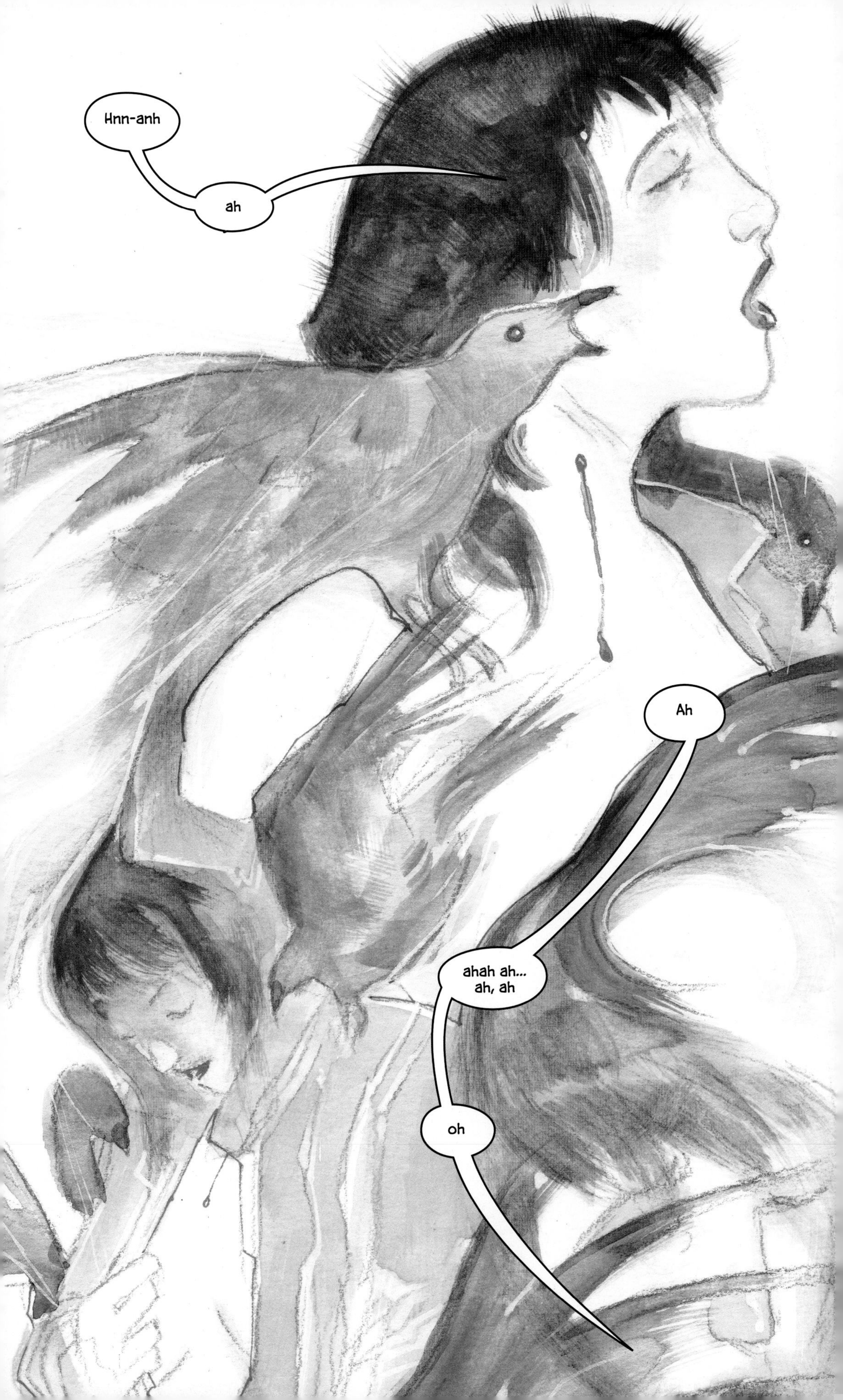
Hnn-anh
ah
Ah
ahah ah... ah, ah
oh

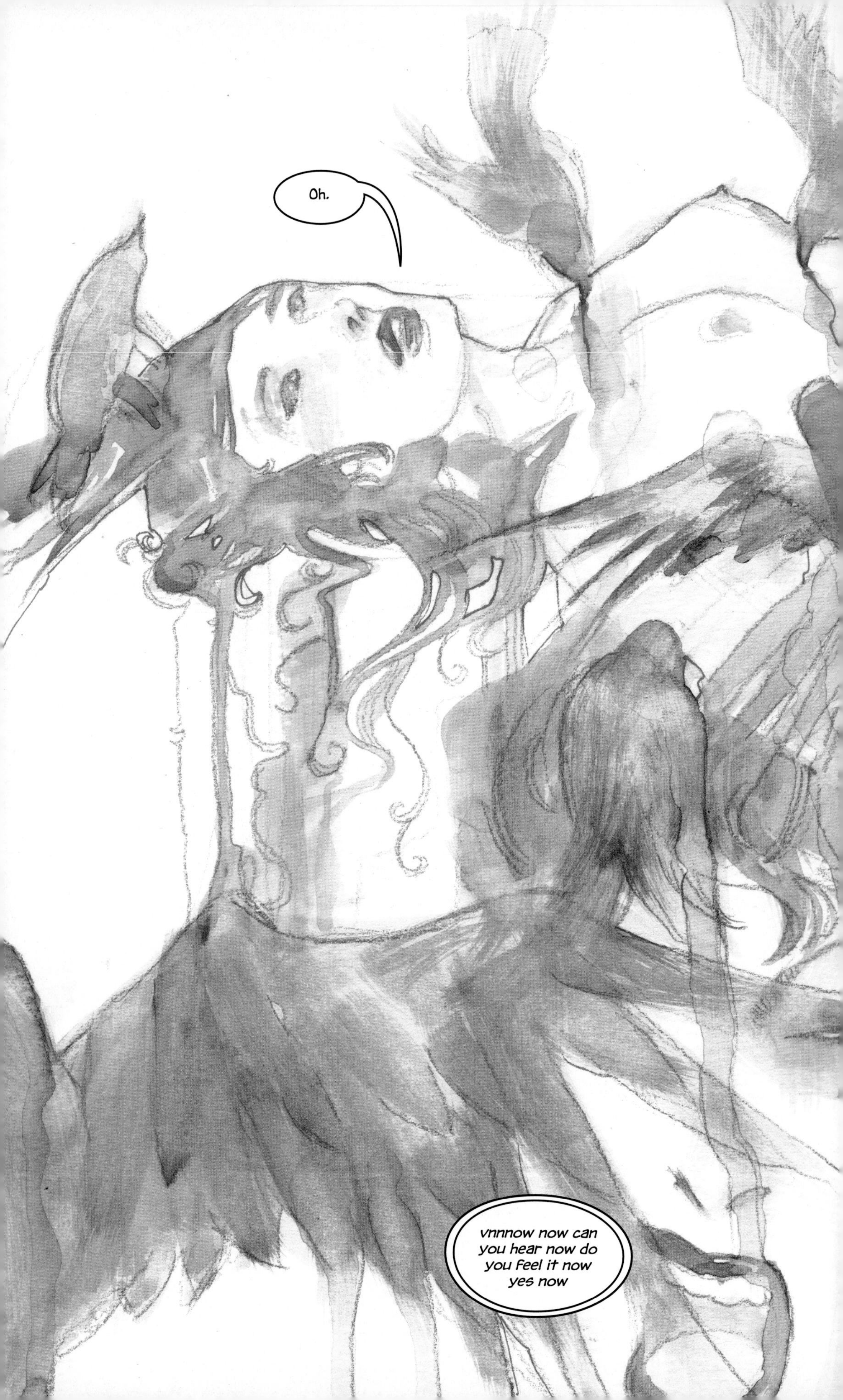
Oh.
vnnnow now can you hear now do you feel it now yes now

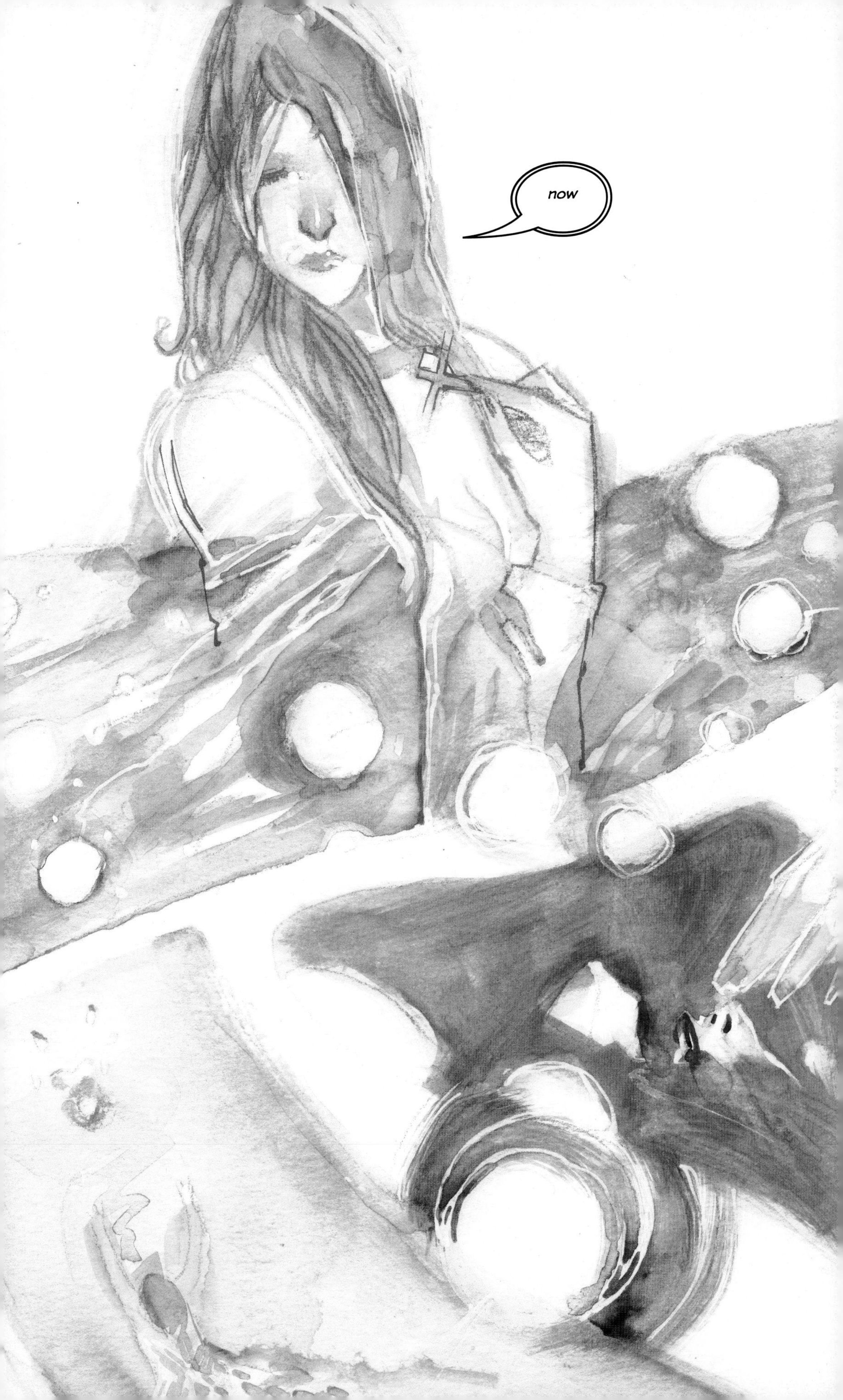
now

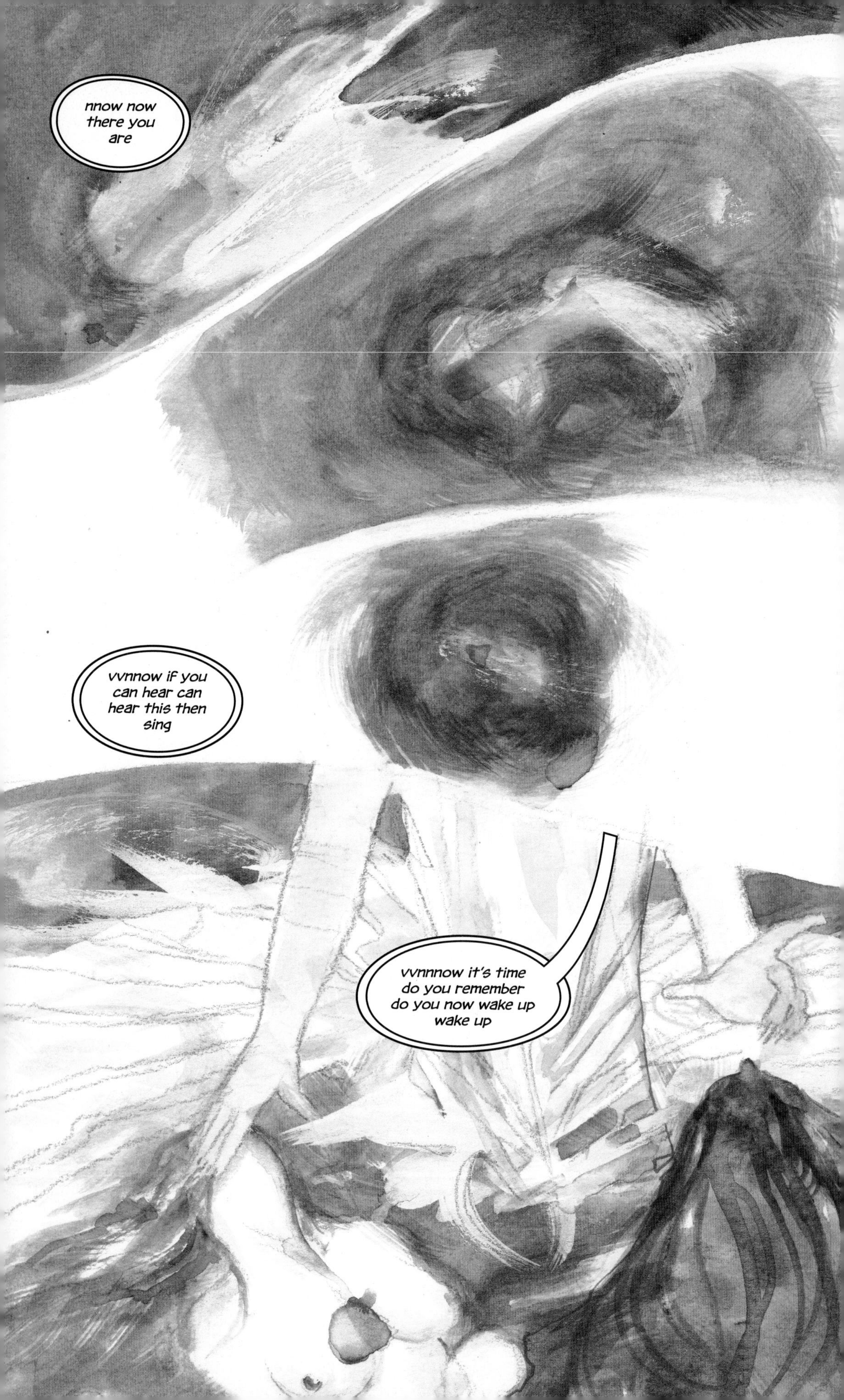
nnow now there you are
vvnnow if you can hear can hear this then sing
vvnnnow it's time do you remember do you now wake up wake up

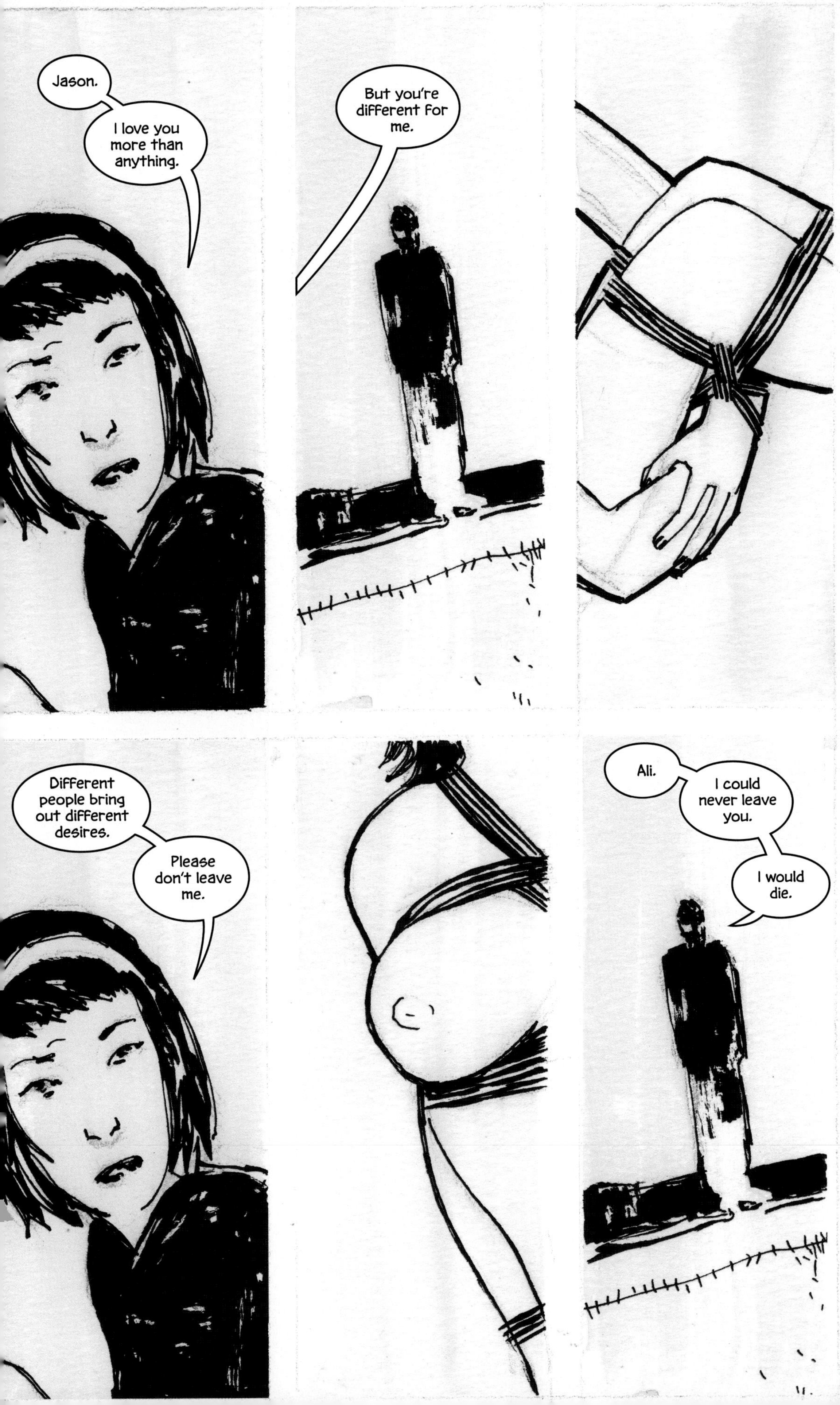
Jason.
I love you more than anything.
But you're different for me.
Different people bring out different desires.
Please don't leave me.
Ali.
I could never leave you.
I would die.

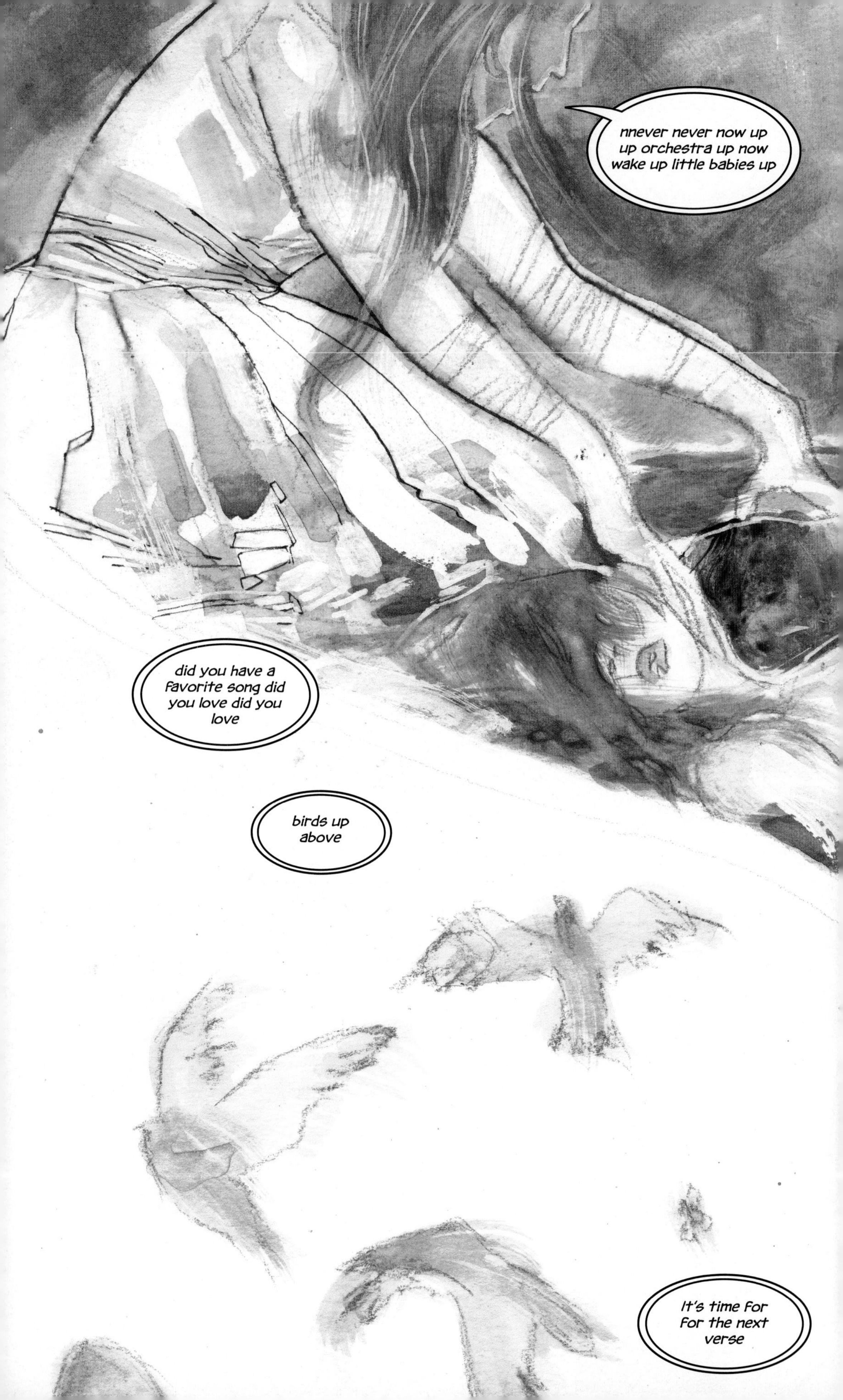
nnever never now up up orchestra up now wake up little babies up
did you have a favorite song did you love did you love
birds up above
It's time for for the next verse

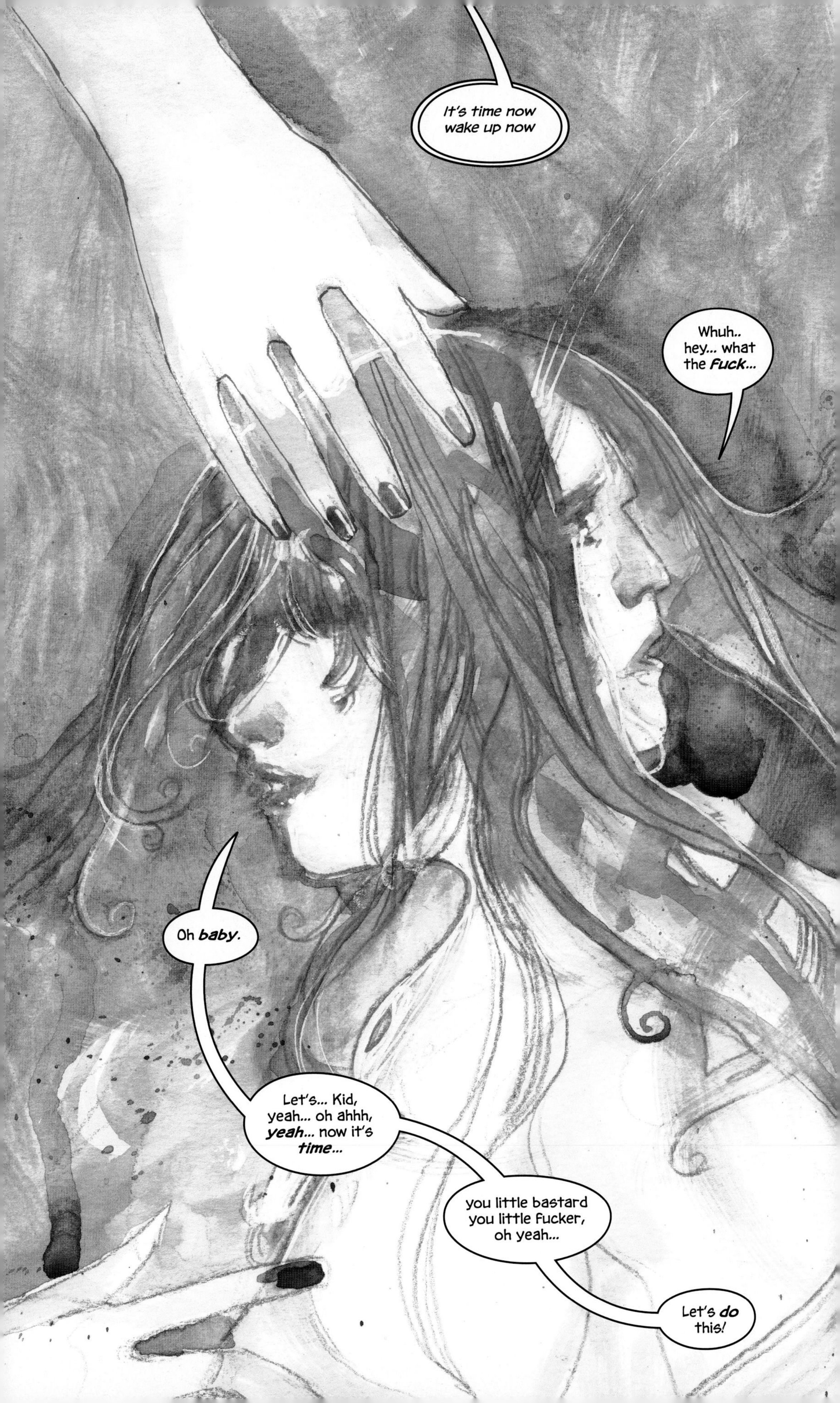
It's time now wake up now
Whuh.. hey... what the *Fuck*...
Oh *baby*.
Let's... Kid, yeah... oh ahhh, *yeah*... now it's *time*...
you little bastard you little fucker, oh yeah...
Let's *do* this!

Part Five

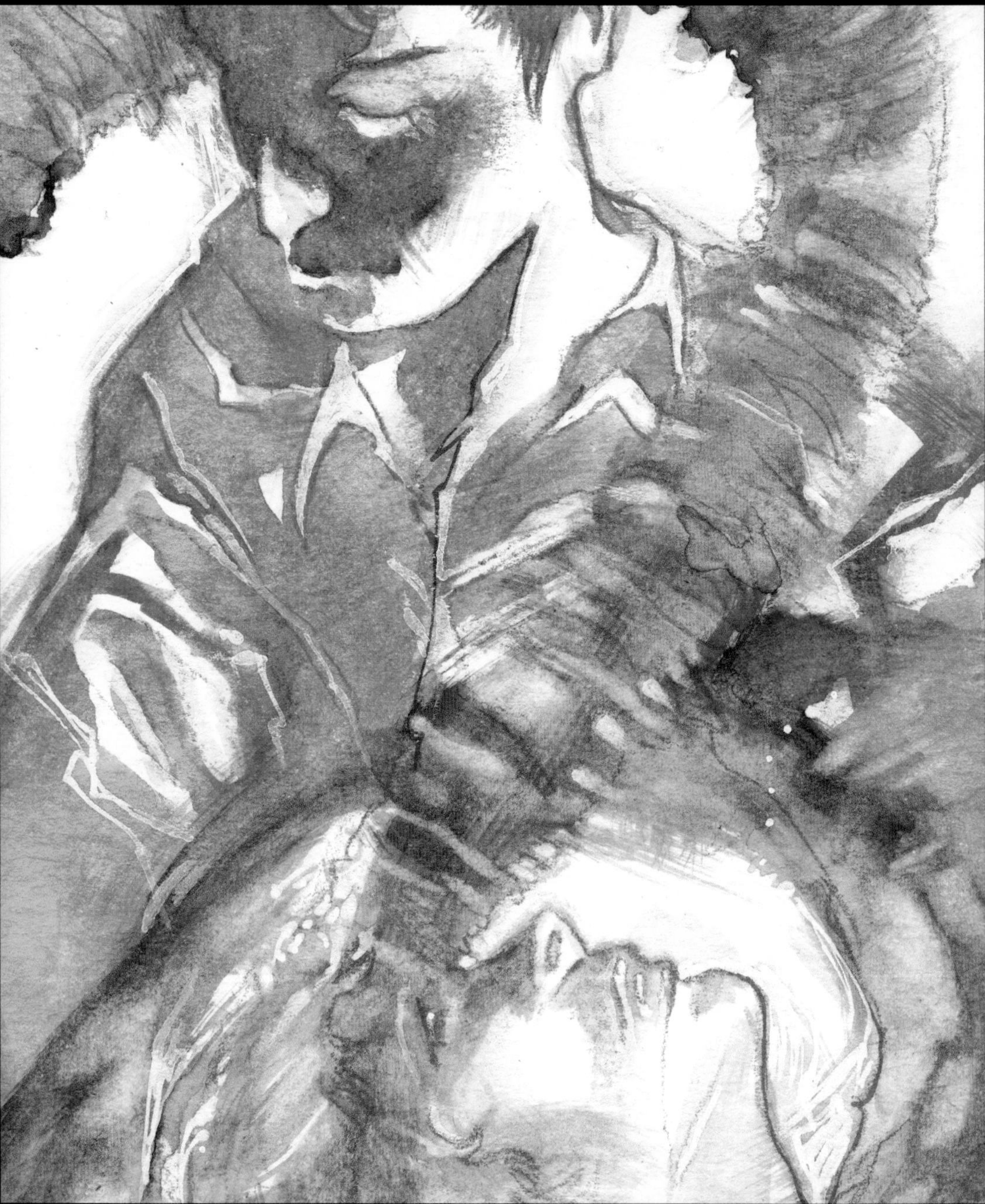

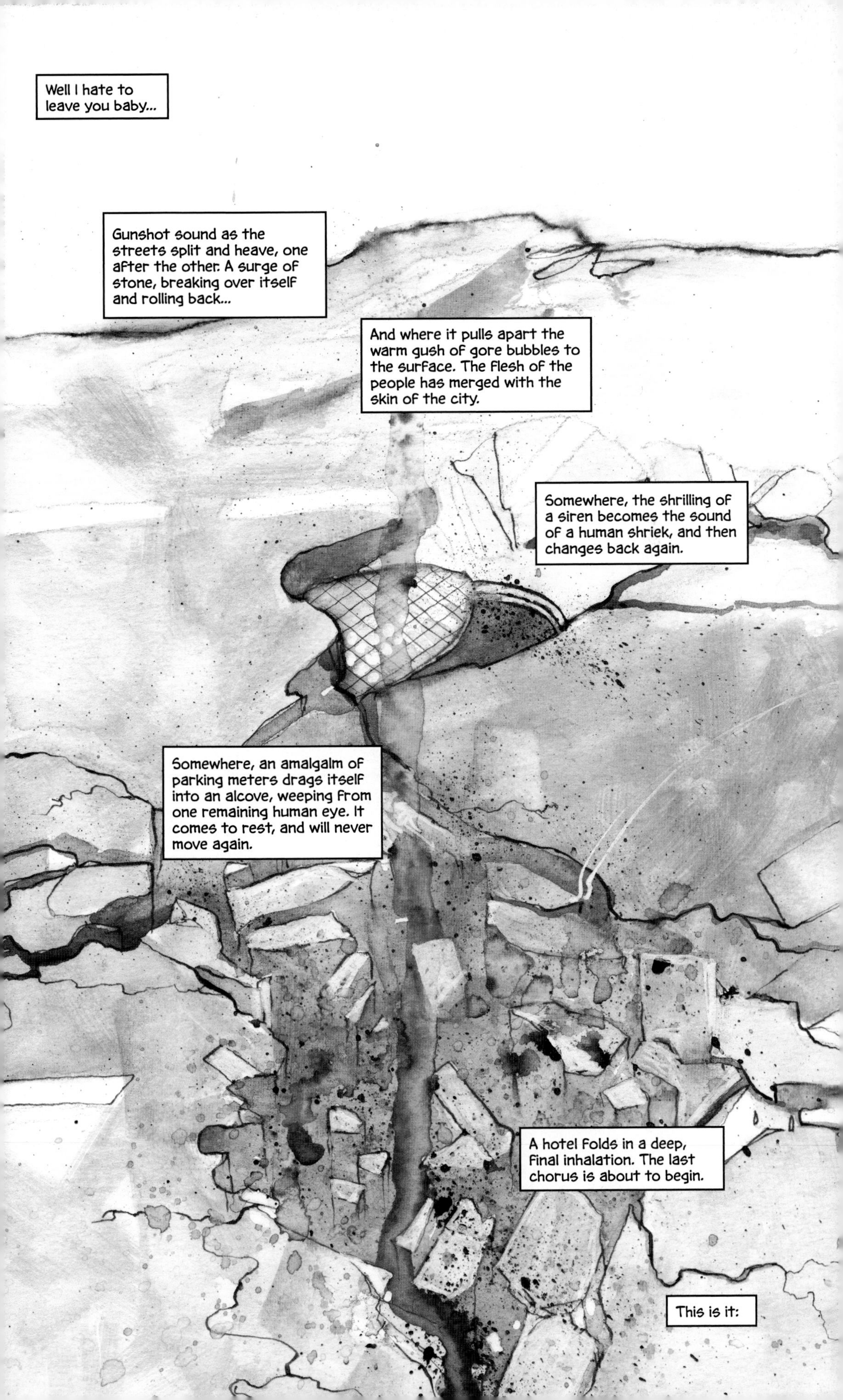
Well I hate to leave you baby...
Gunshot sound as the streets split and heave, one after the other. A surge of stone, breaking over itself and rolling back...
And where it pulls apart the warm gush of gore bubbles to the surface. The flesh of the people has merged with the skin of the city.
Somewhere, the shrilling of a siren becomes the sound of a human shriek, and then changes back again.
Somewhere, an amalgalm of parking meters drags itself into an alcove, weeping from one remaining human eye. It comes to rest, and will never move again.
A hotel folds in a deep, final inhalation. The last chorus is about to begin.
This is it:

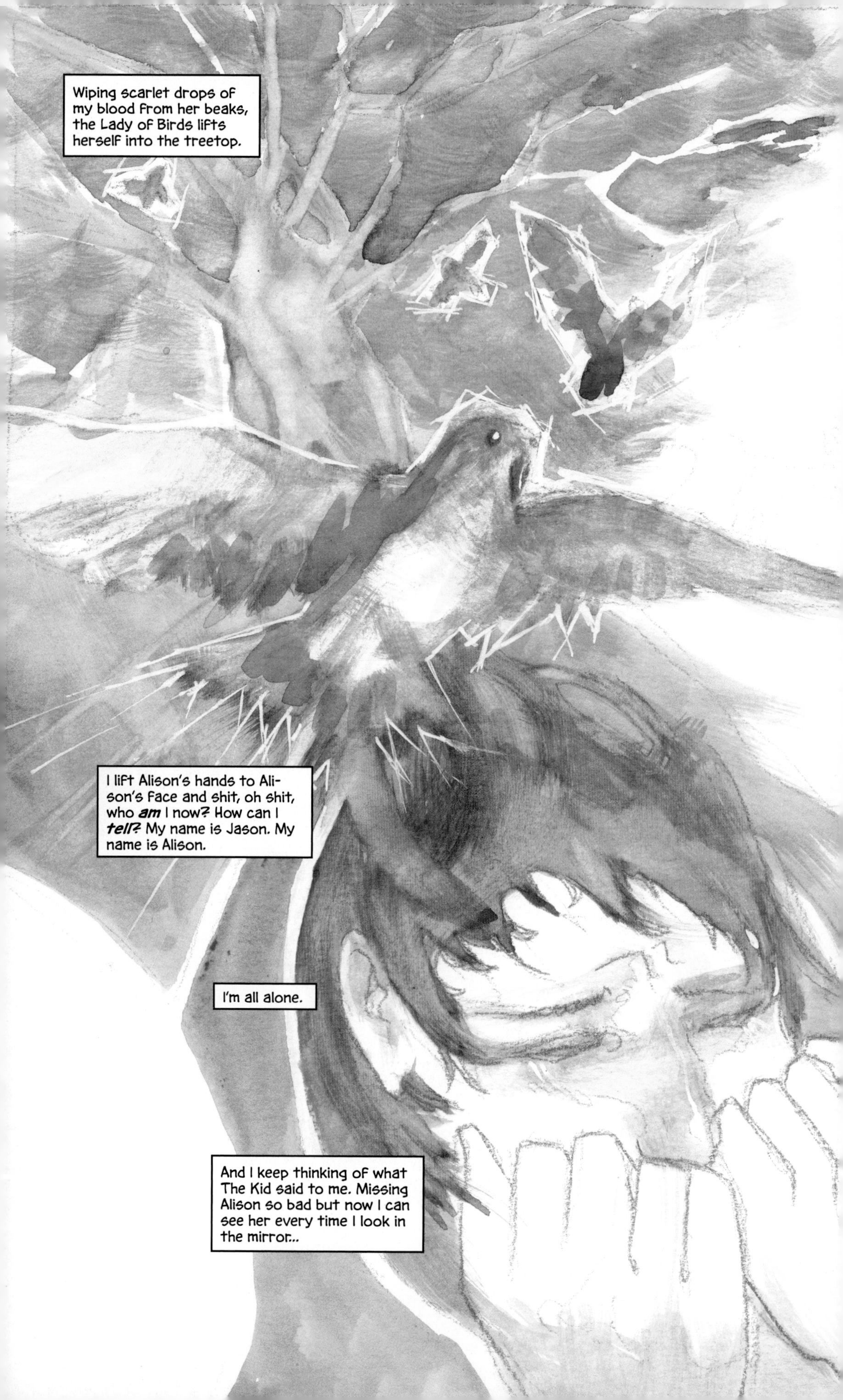
Wiping scarlet drops of my blood from her beaks, the Lady of Birds lifts herself into the treetop.
I lift Alison's hands to Alison's face and shit, oh shit, who *am* I now? How can I *tell?* My name is Jason. My name is Alison.
I'm all alone.
And I keep thinking of what The Kid said to me. Missing Alison so bad but now I can see her every time I look in the mirror...

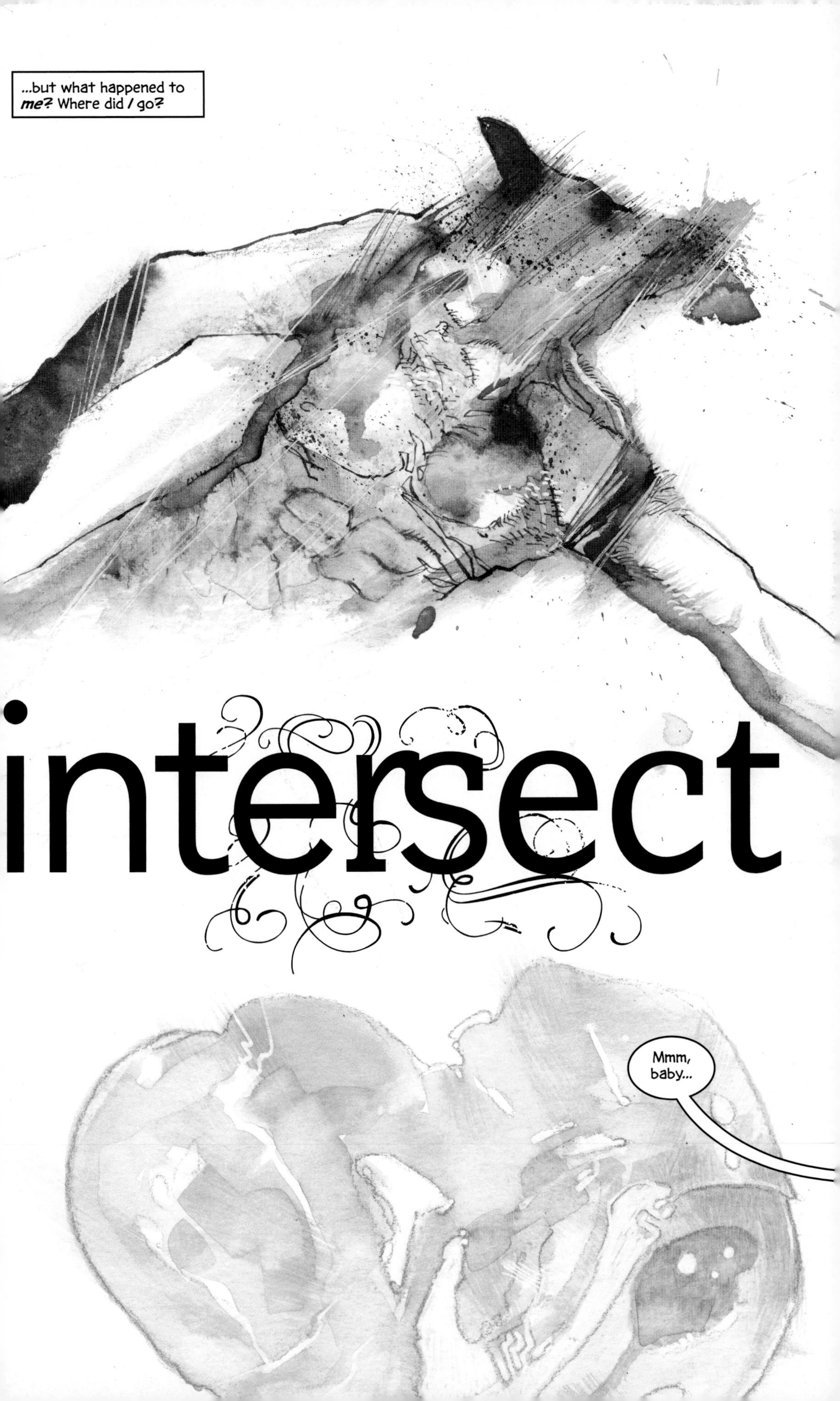
...but what happened to *me?* Where did *I* go?
intersect
Mmm, baby...

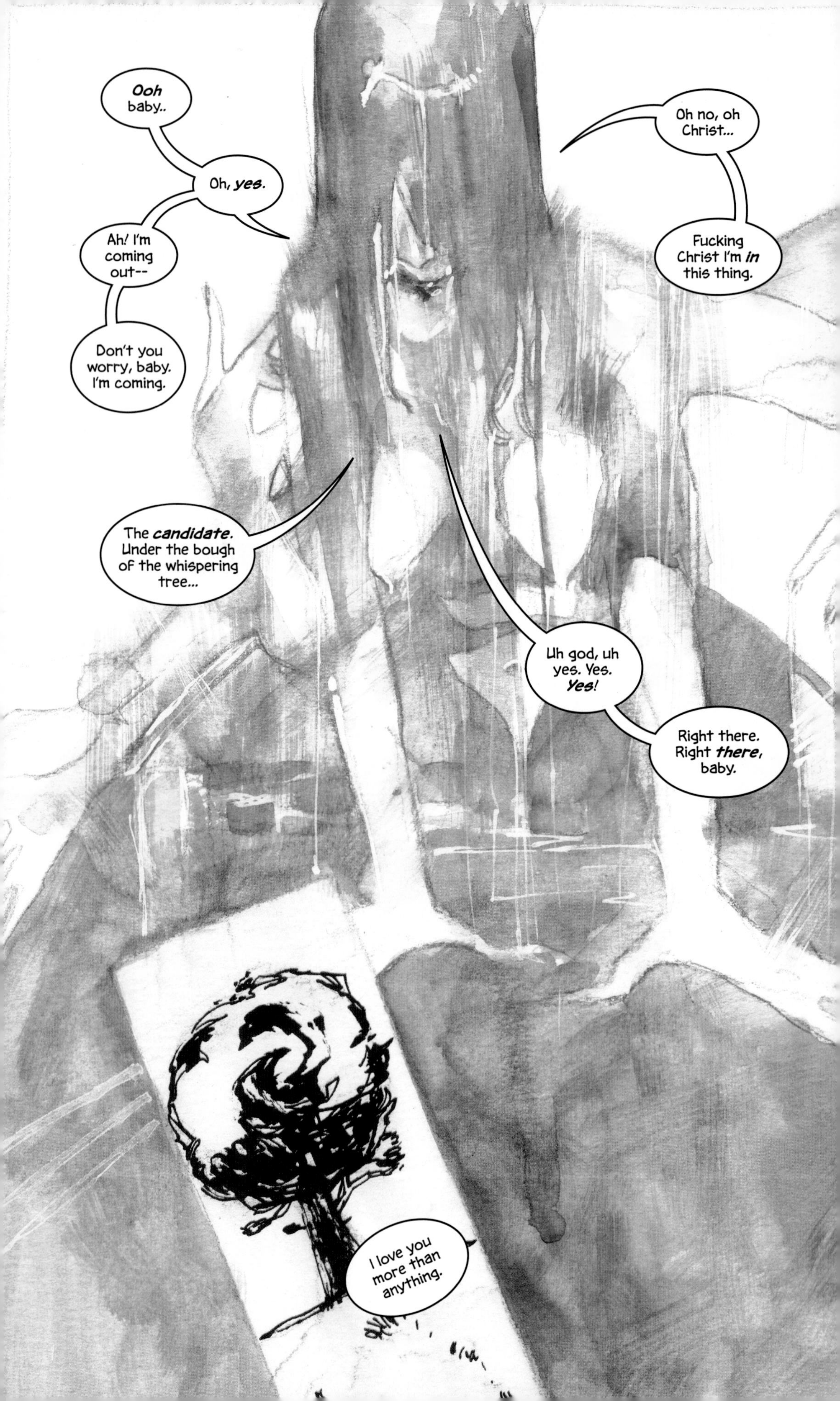

Ooh baby..
Oh, yes.
Ah! I'm coming out--
Don't you worry, baby. I'm coming.
Oh no, oh Christ...
Fucking Christ I'm in this thing.
The candidate. Under the bough of the whispering tree...
Uh god, uh yes. Yes. Yes!
Right there. Right there, baby.
I love you more than anything.

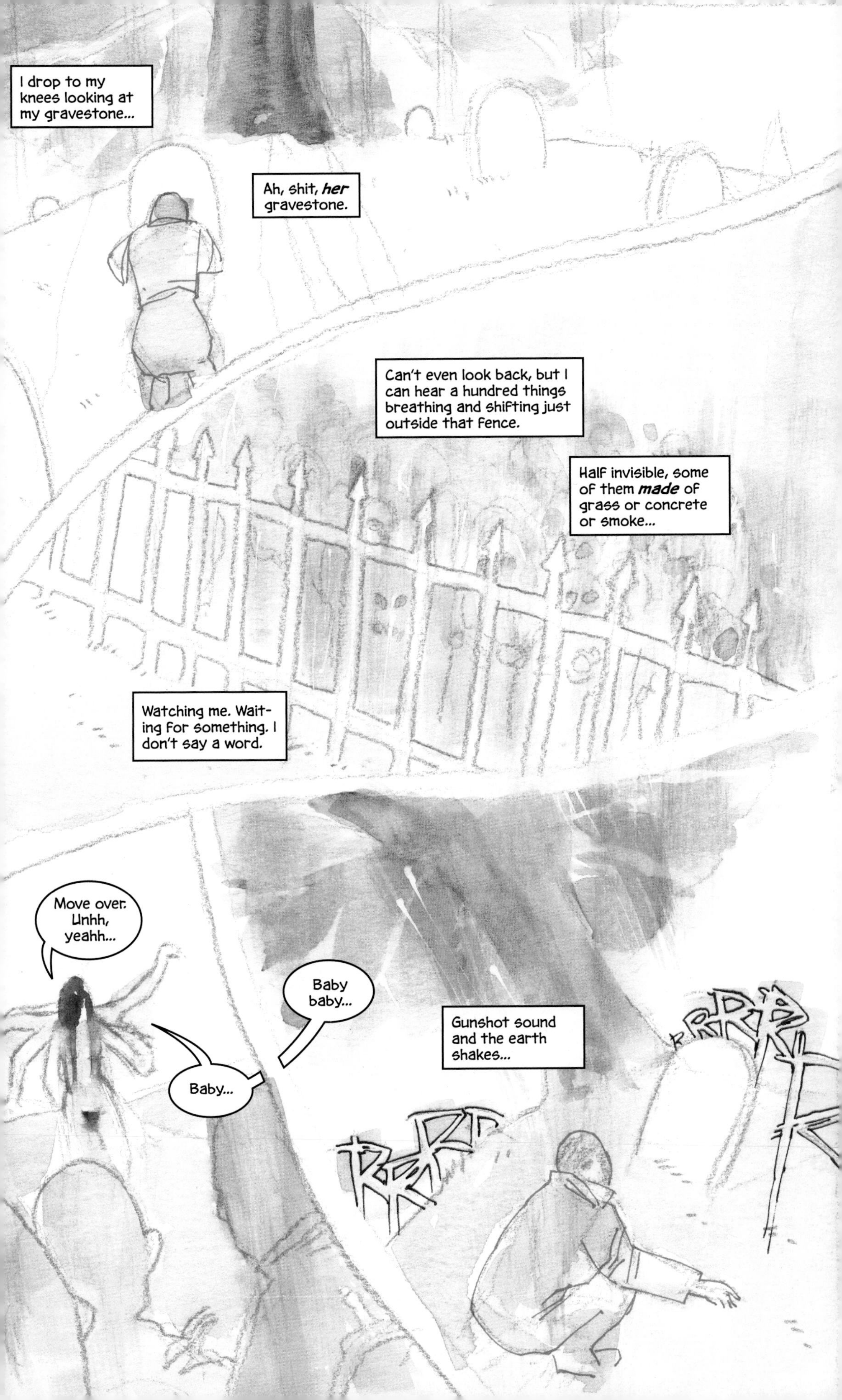
I drop to my knees looking at my gravestone...
Ah, shit, ***her*** gravestone.
Can't even look back, but I can hear a hundred things breathing and shifting just outside that fence.
Half invisible, some of them ***made*** of grass or concrete or smoke...
Watching me. Waiting for something. I don't say a word.
Move over. Unhh, yeahh...
Baby...
Baby baby...
Gunshot sound and the earth shakes...

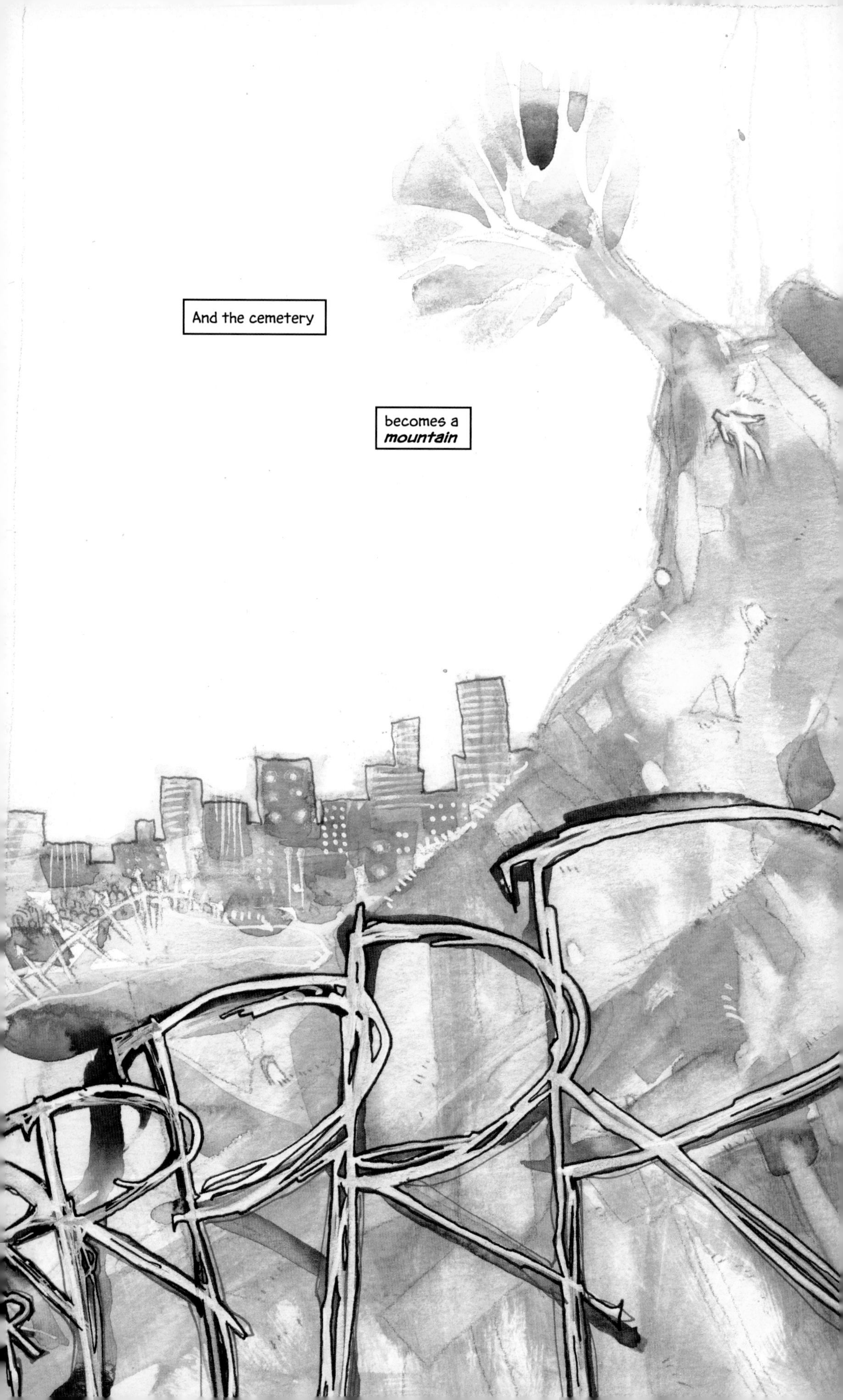
And the cemetery
becomes a *mountain*

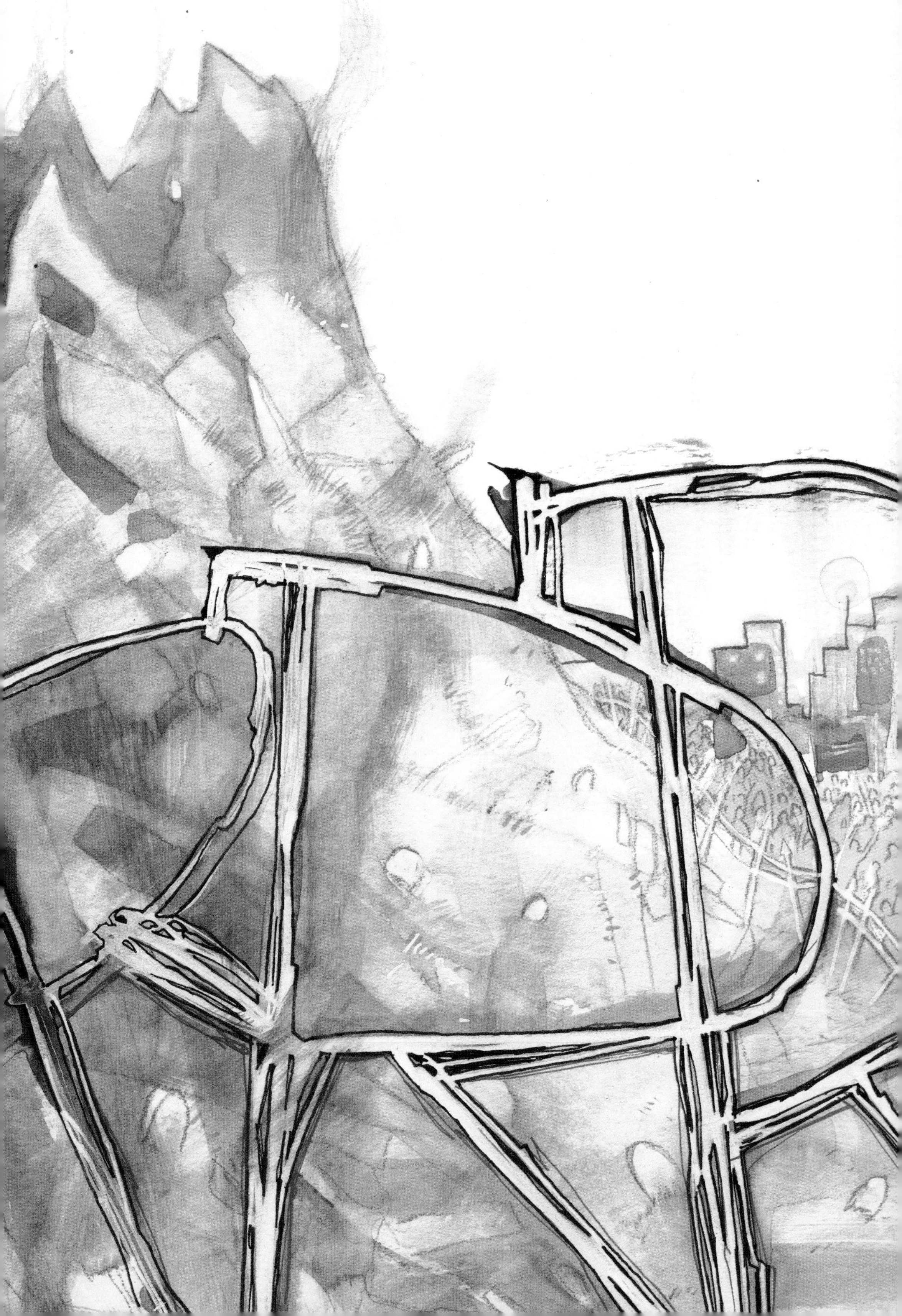

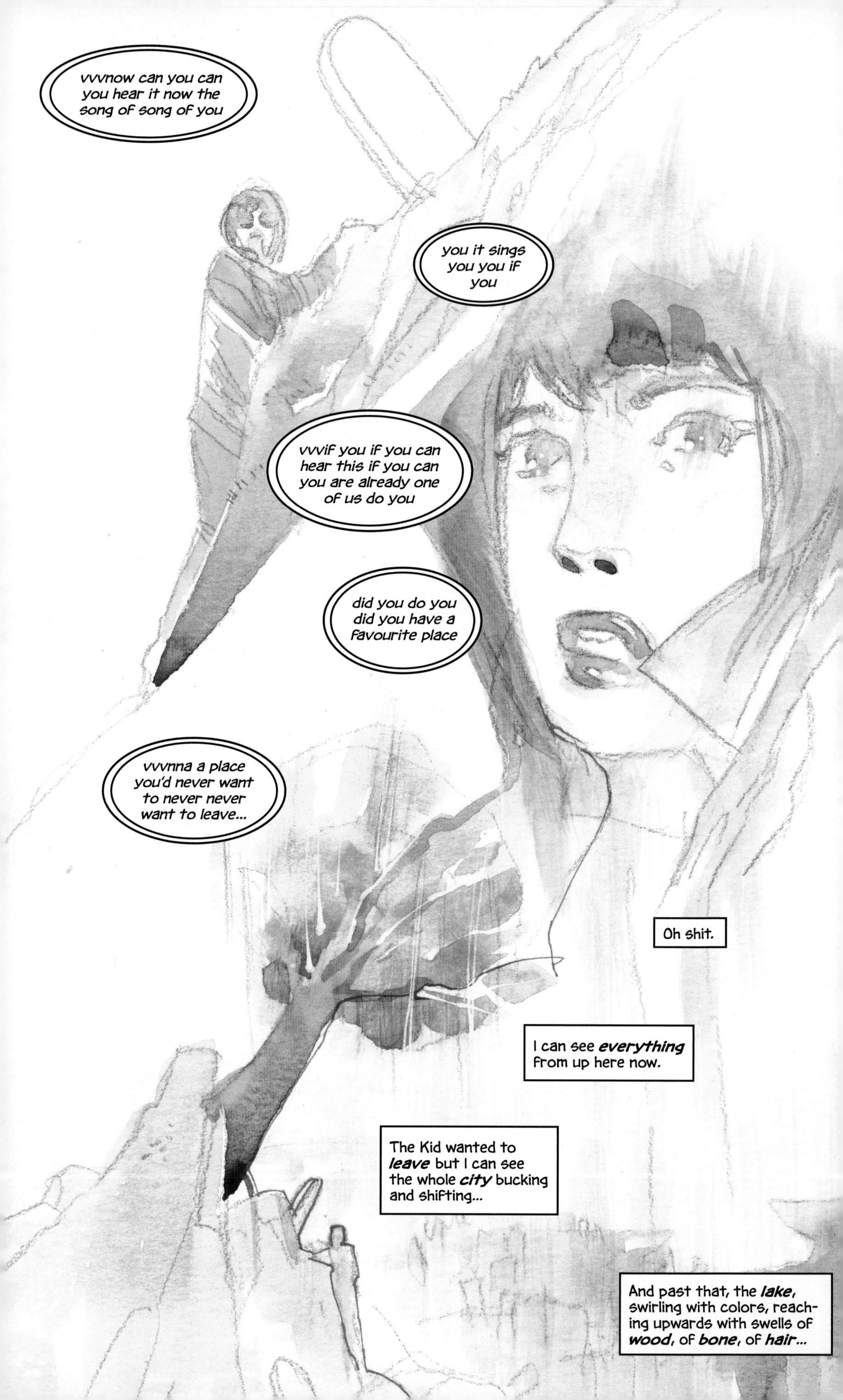
vvvnow can you can you hear it now the song of song of you
you it sings you you if you
vvvif you if you can hear this if you can you are already one of us do you
did you do you did you have a favourite place
vvvnna a place you'd never want to never never want to leave...
Oh shit.
I can see *everything* from up here now.
The Kid wanted to *leave* but I can see the whole *city* bucking and shifting...
And past that, the *lake*, swirling with colors, reaching upwards with swells of ***wood***, of ***bone***, of ***hair***...

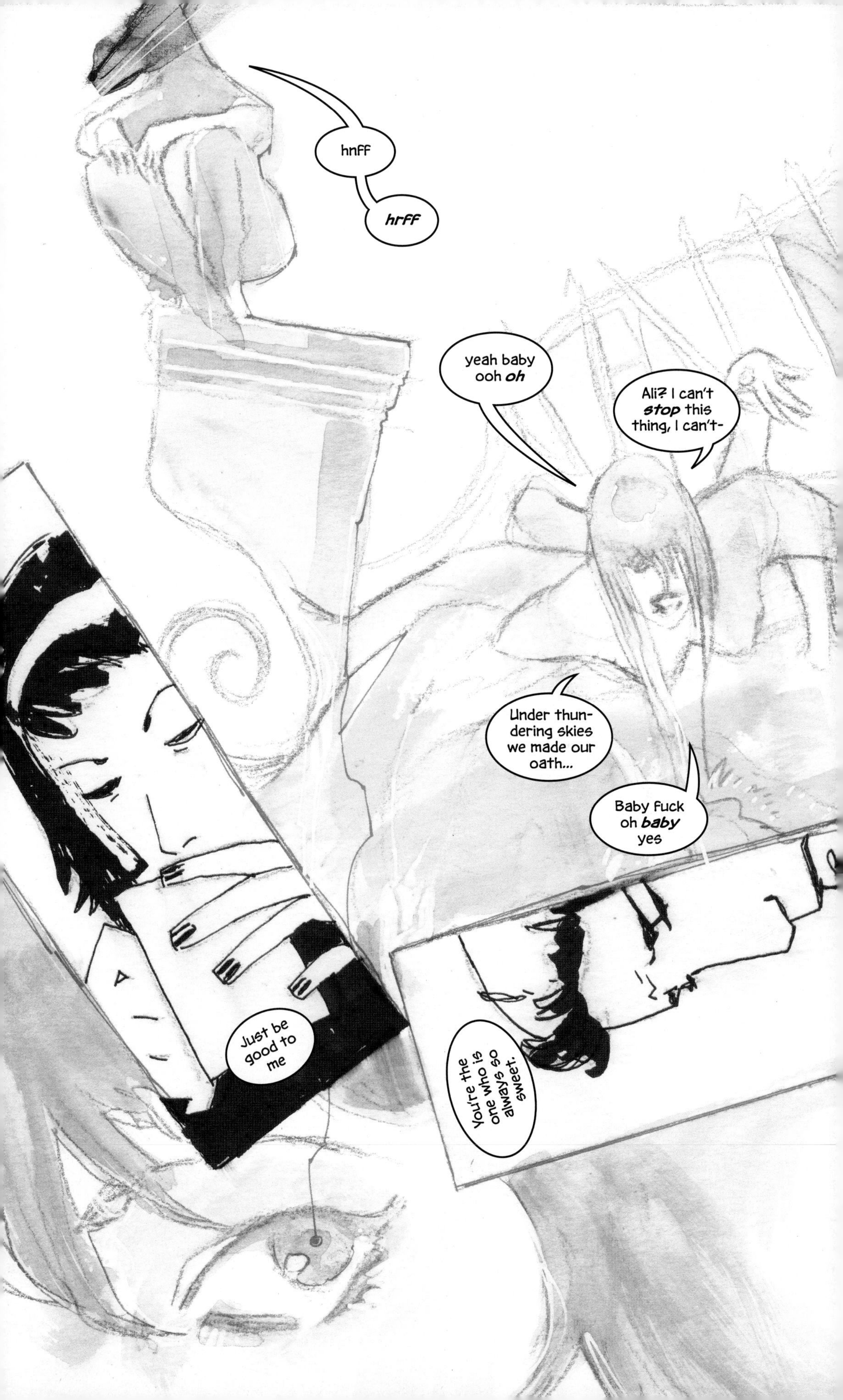
hnff
hrff
yeah baby ooh oh
Ali? I can't stop this thing, I can't-
Under thundering skies we made our oath...
Baby fuck oh baby yes
Just be good to me
You're the one who is always so sweet.

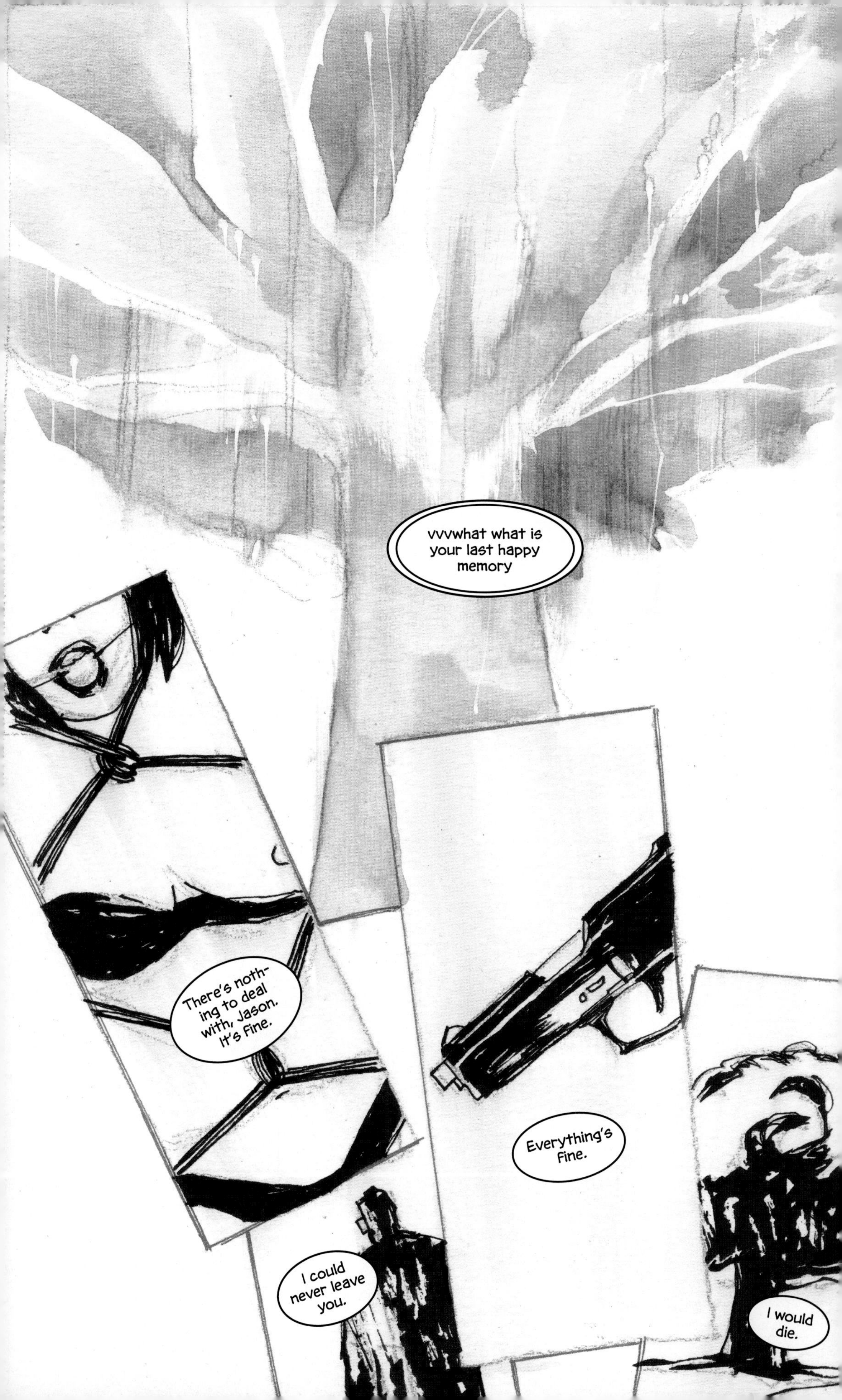
vvvwhat what is your last happy memory
There's noth-ing to deal with, Jason. It's fine.
Everything's fine.
I could never leave you.
I would die.

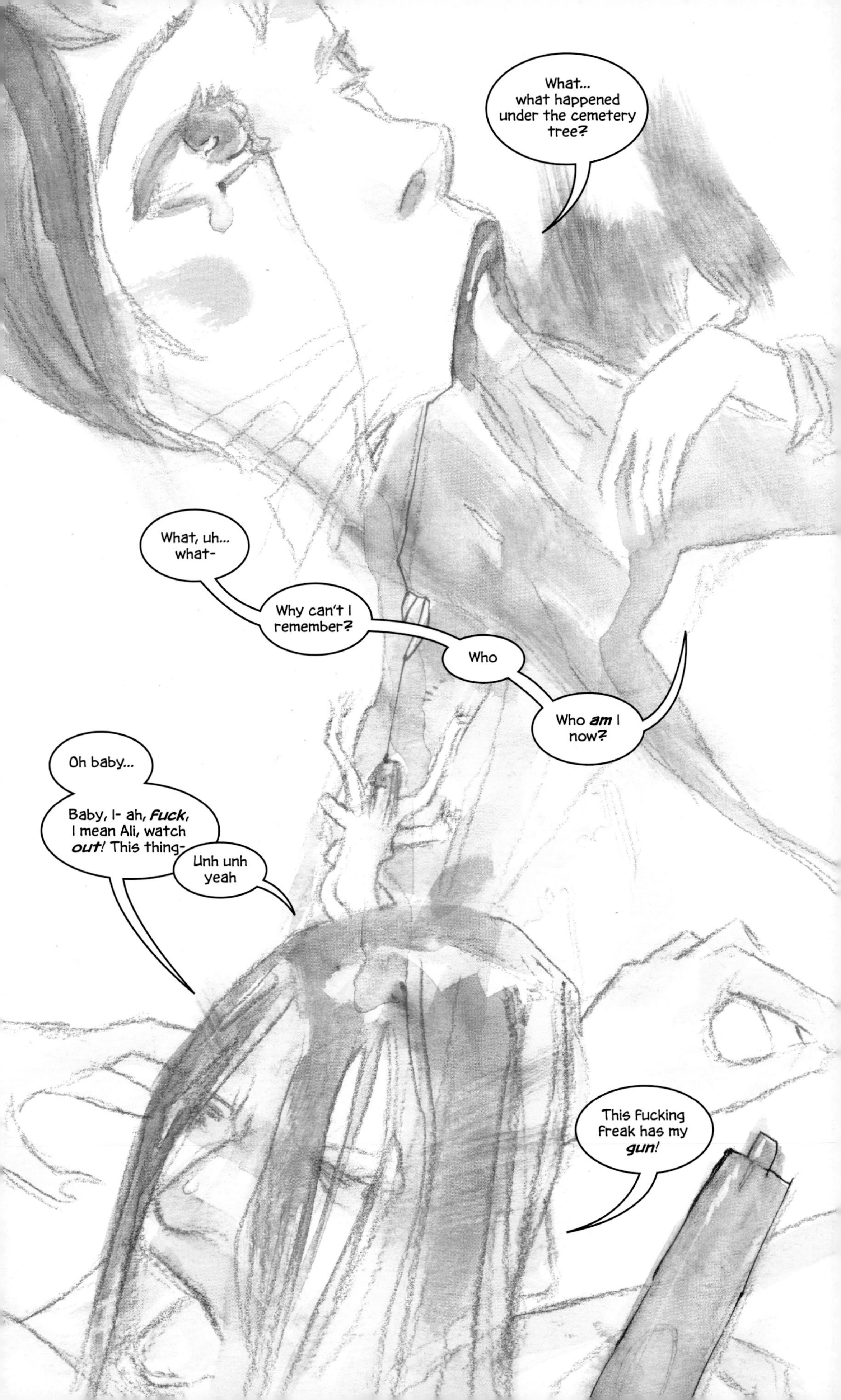
What... what happened under the cemetery tree?
What, uh... what-
Why can't I remember?
Who
Who *am* I now?
Oh baby...
Baby, I- ah, *Fuck*, I mean Ali, watch *out*! This thing-
Unh unh yeah
This fucking freak has my *gun*!

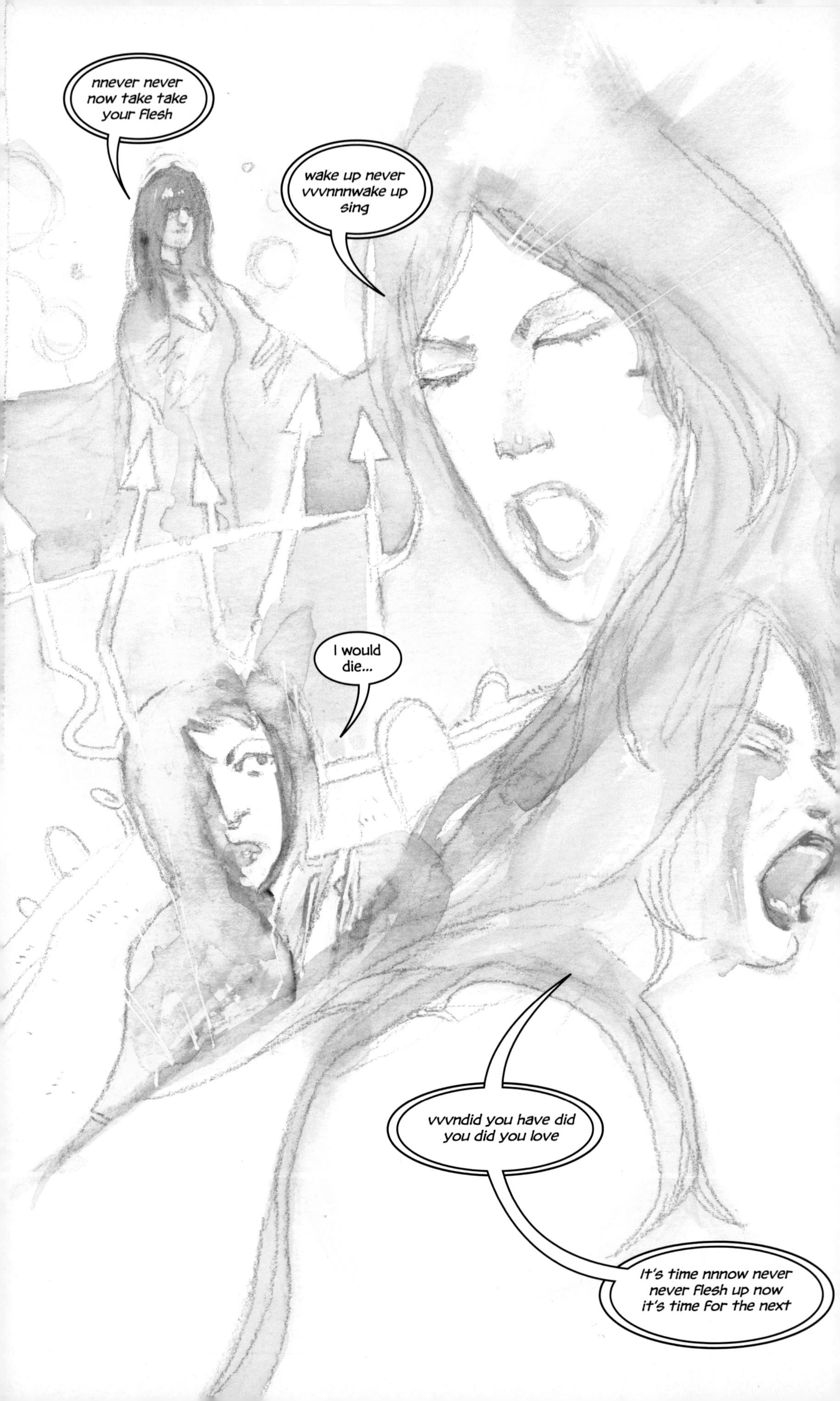
nnever never now take take your flesh
wake up never vvvnnnwake up sing
I would die...
vvvndid you have did you did you love
It's time nnnow never never flesh up now it's time for the next

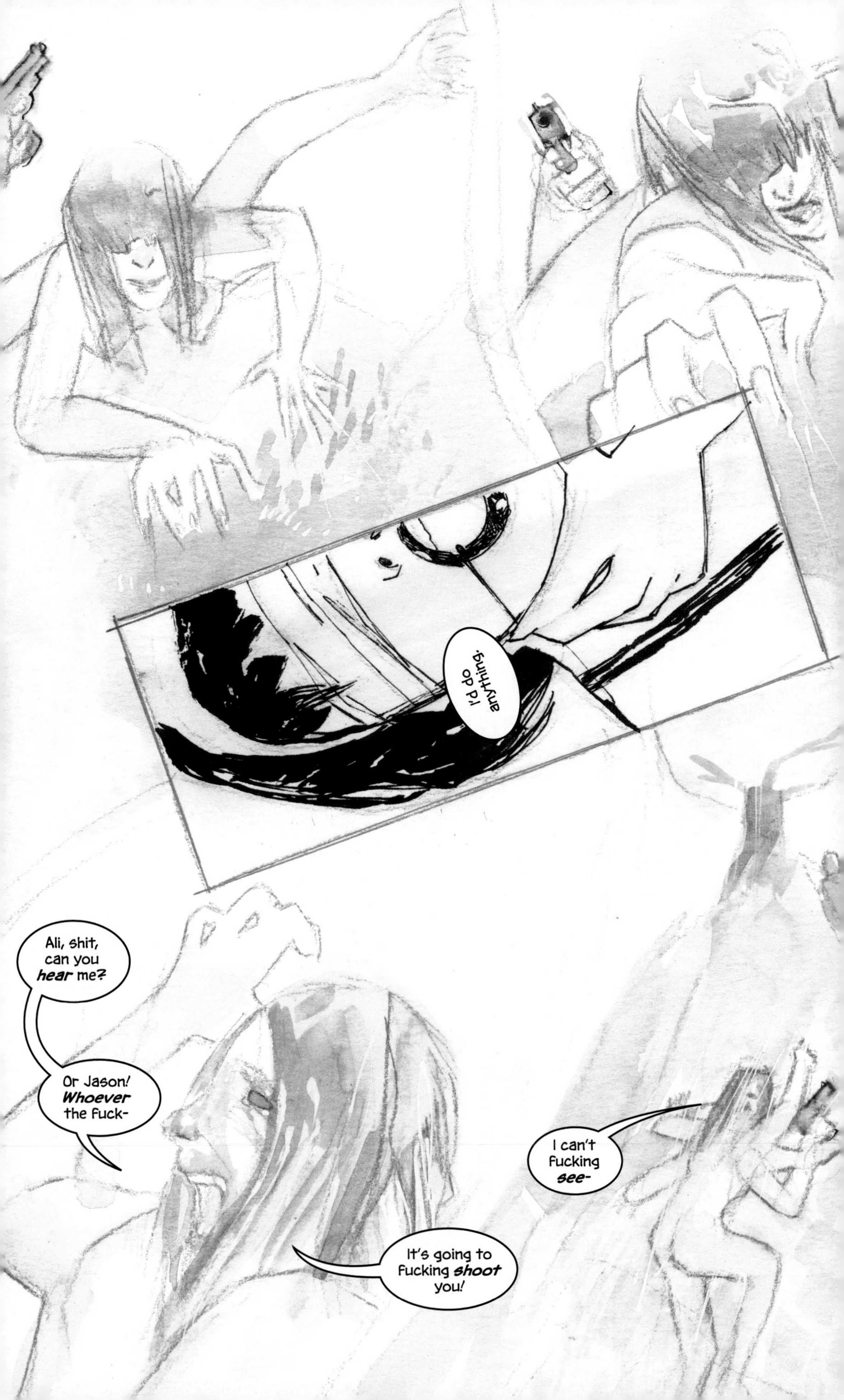
I'd do anything.
Ali, shit, can you *hear* me?
Or Jason! *Whoever* the fuck-
I can't fucking *see*-
It's going to fucking *shoot* you!

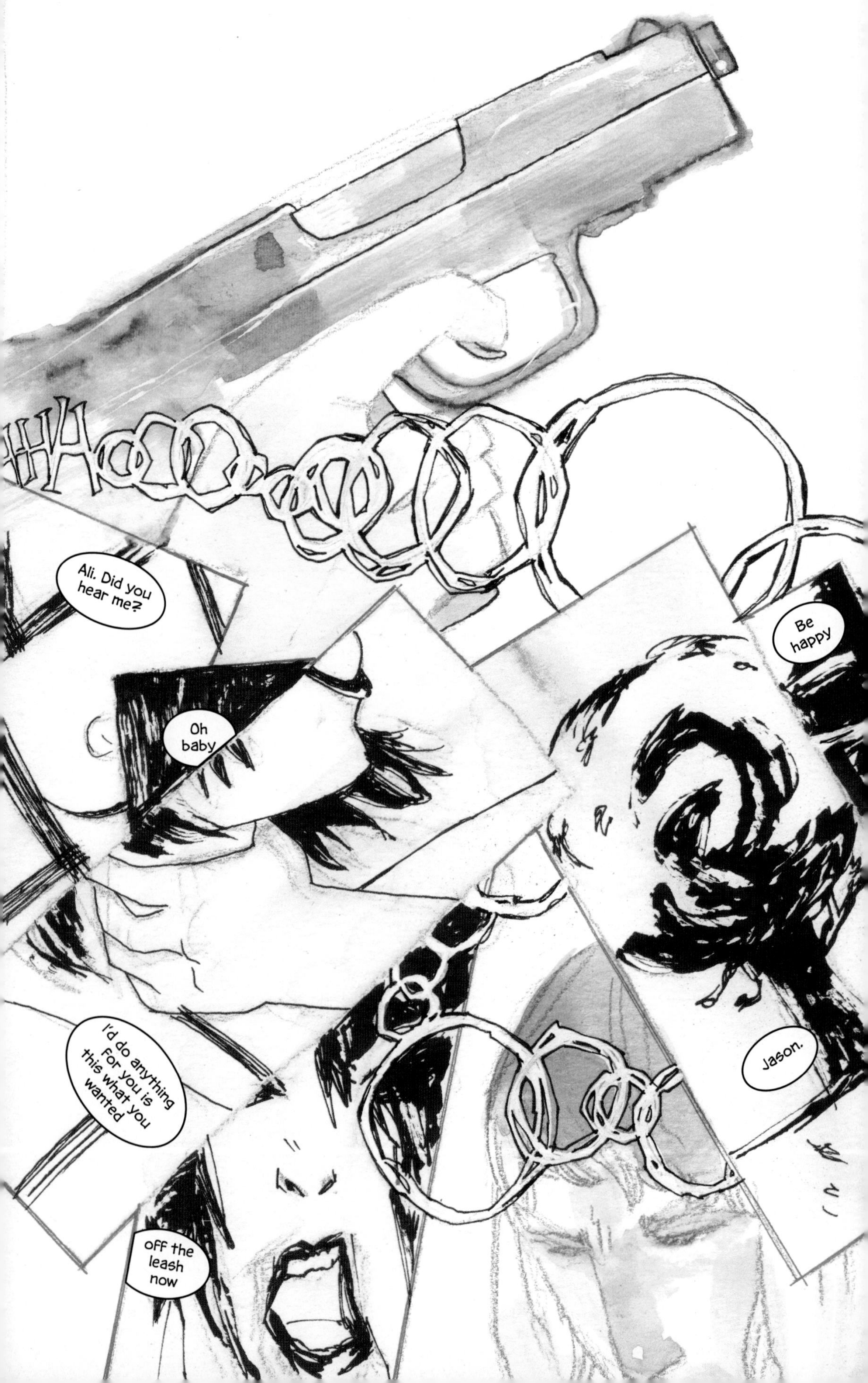
HHAOOOOOOOOOO
Ali. Did you hear me?
Oh baby
Be happy
Jason.
I'd do anything for you is this what you wanted
off the leash now

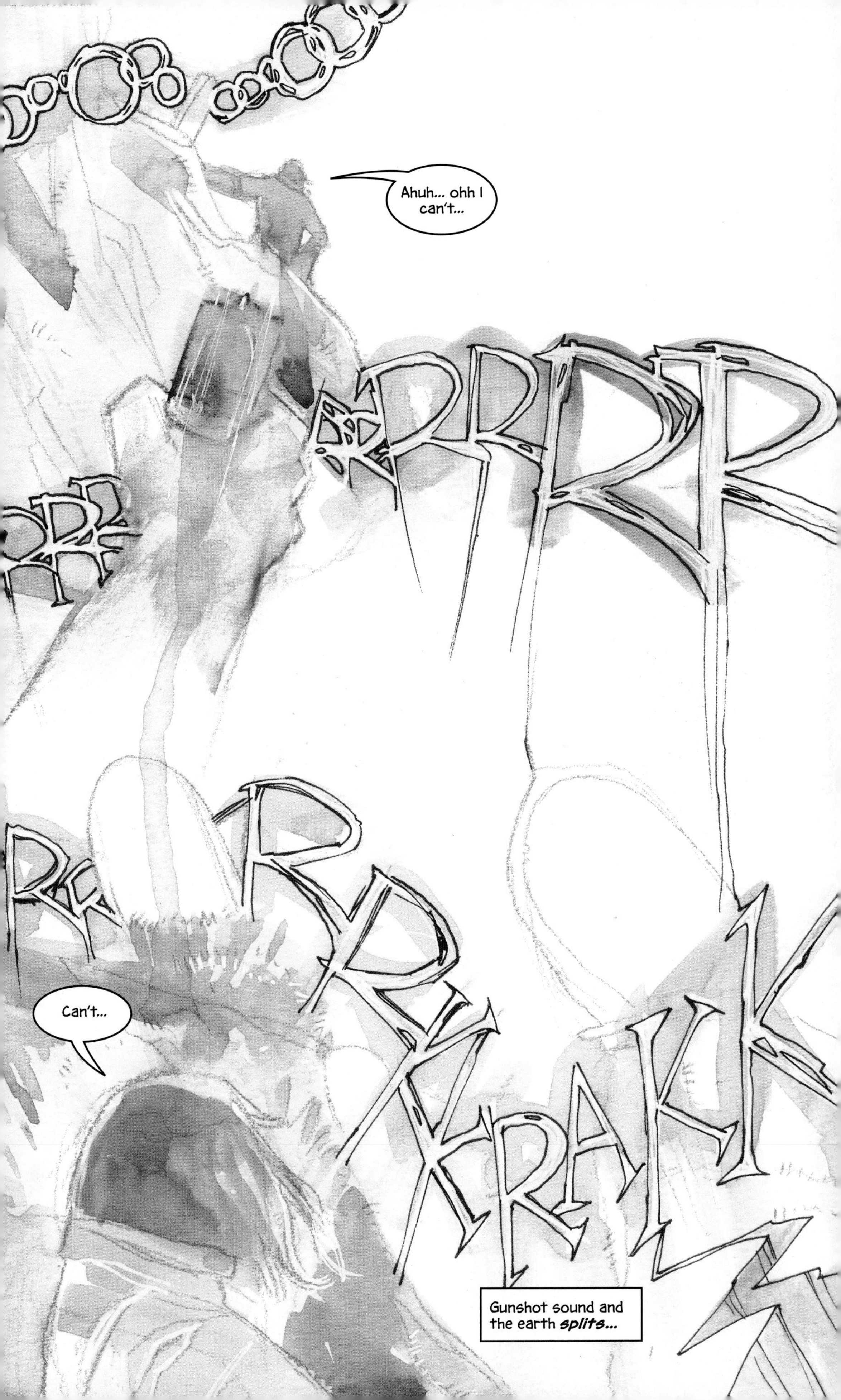
Ahuh... ohh I can't...
RRRRR
RRRRR
Can't...
KRAKK
Gunshot sound and the earth *splits...*

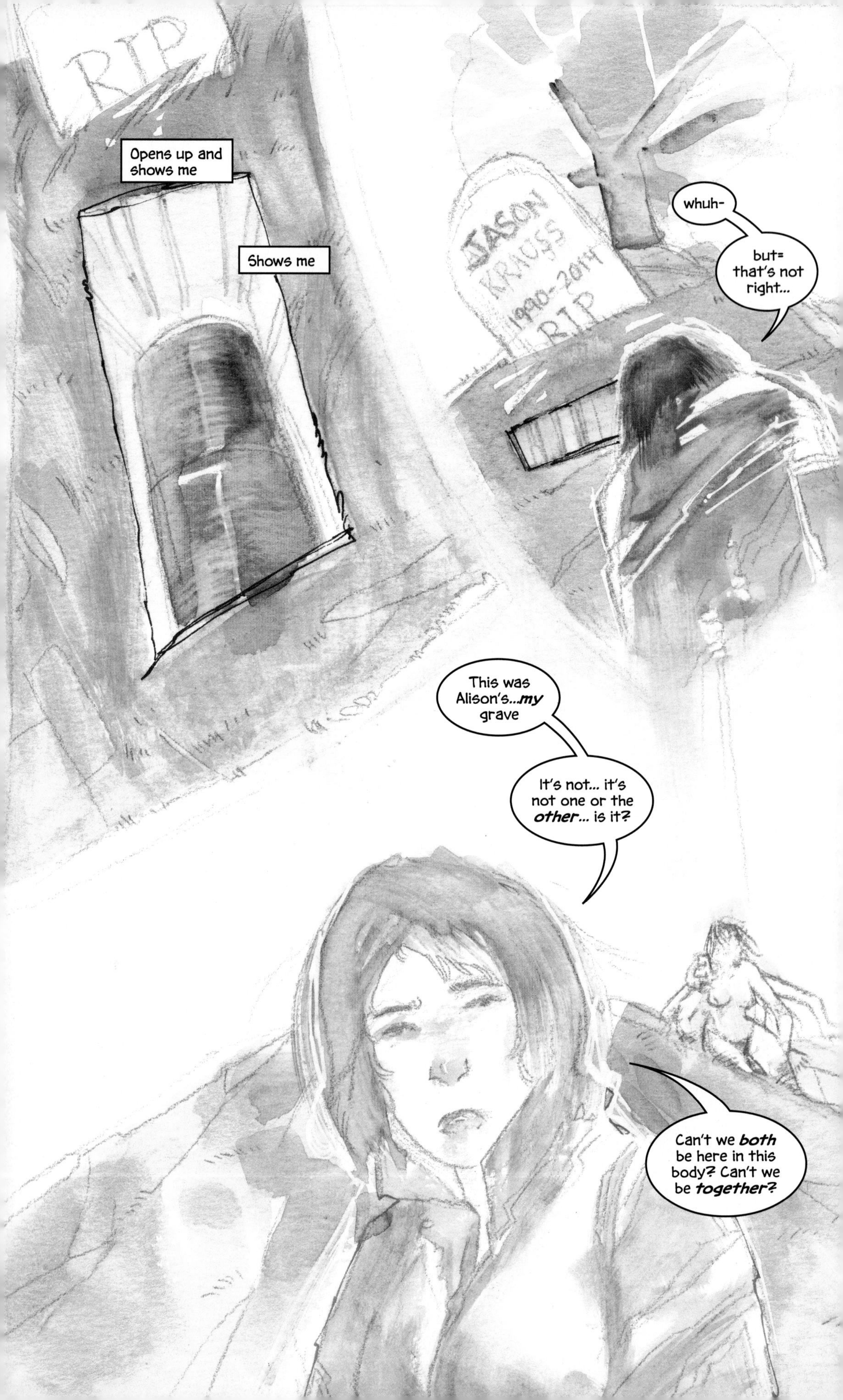
RIP
Opens up and shows me
Shows me
JASON KRAUSS 1990-2014 RIP
whuh-
but= that's not right...
This was Alison's...*my* grave
It's not... it's not one or the *other*... is it?
Can't we *both* be here in this body? Can't we be *together*?

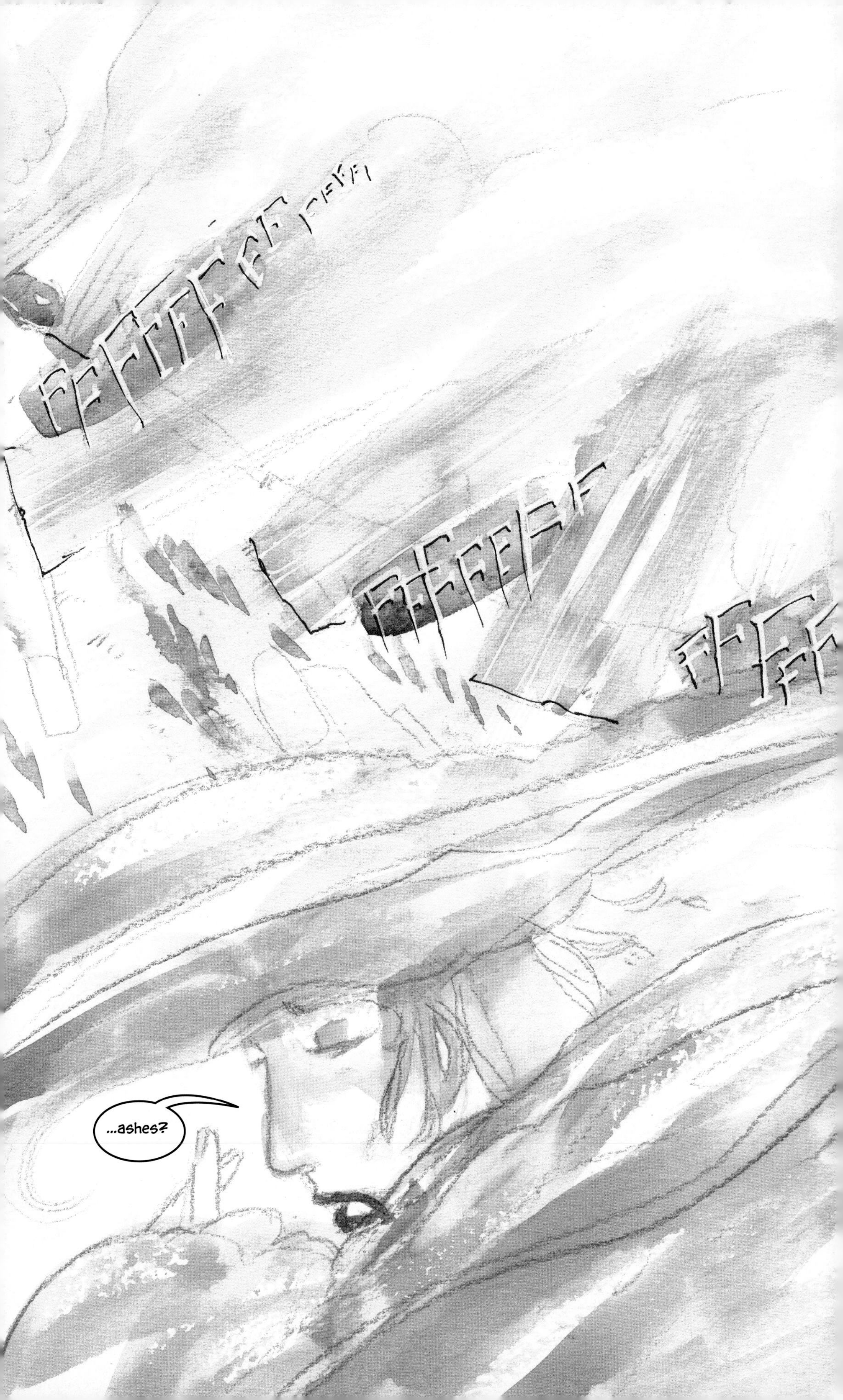
...ashes?

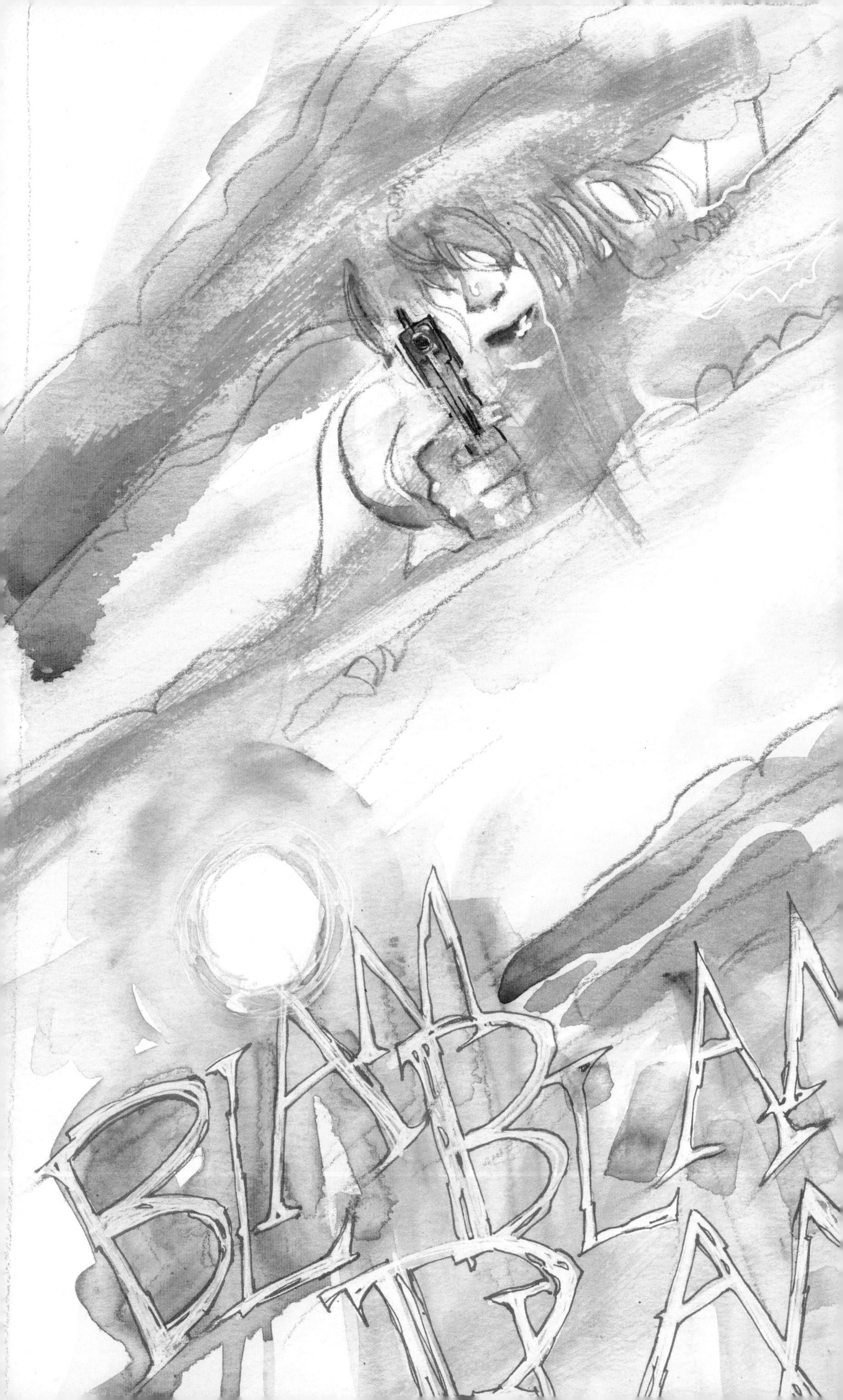
BLAM BLAM BLAM

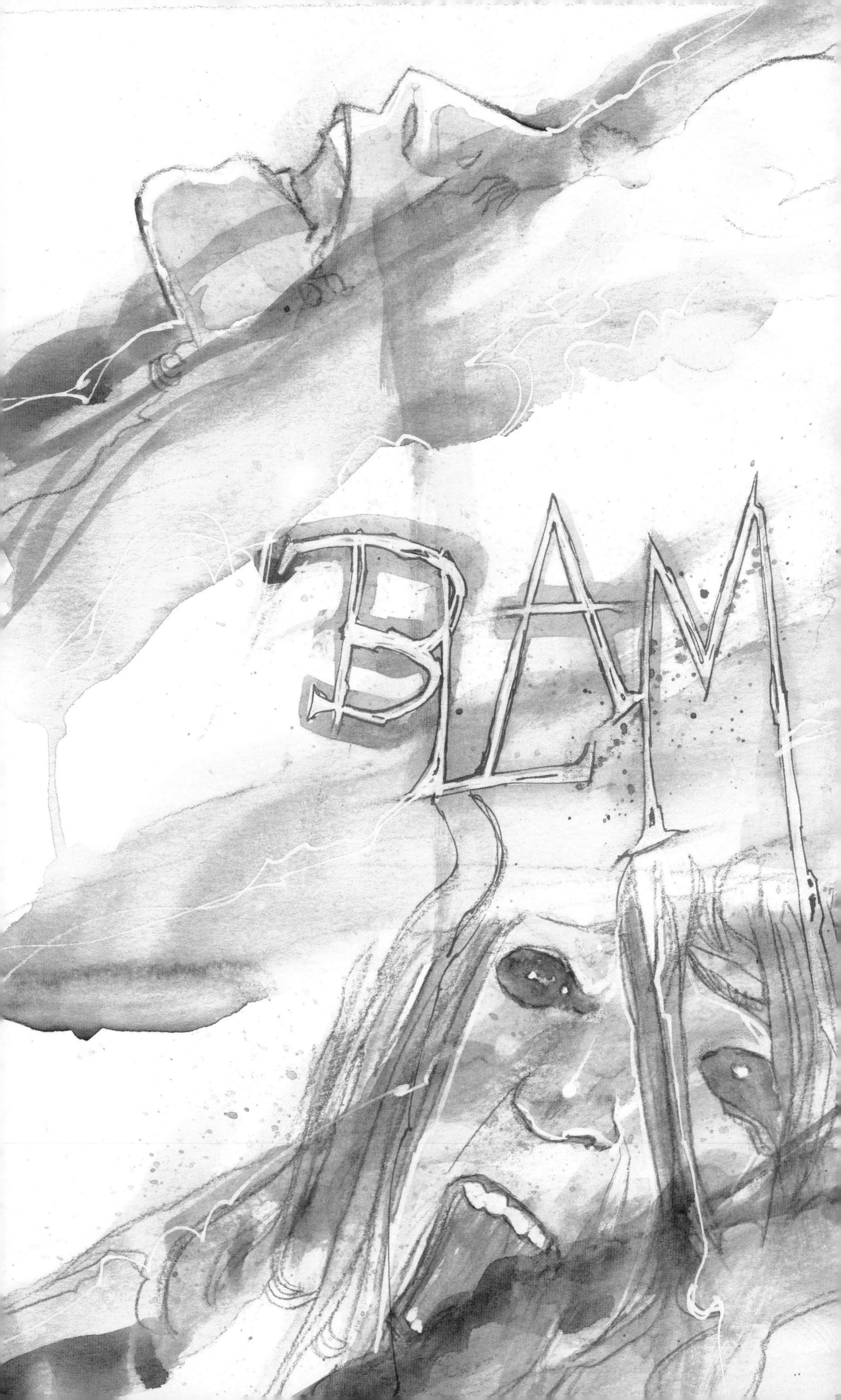
BLAM

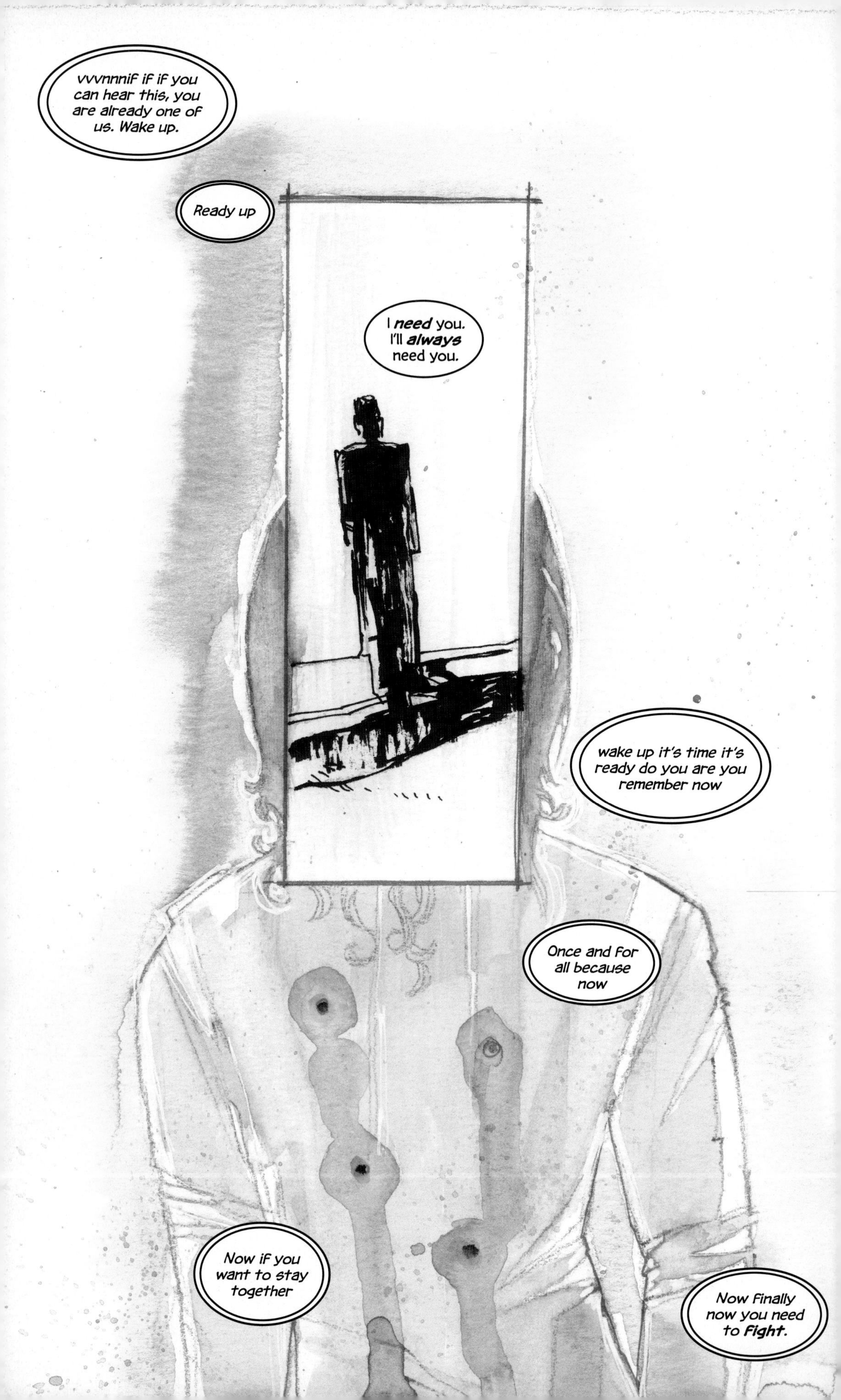
vvvnnnif if if you can hear this, you are already one of us. Wake up.
Ready up
I **need** you. I'll **always** need you.
wake up it's time it's ready do you are you remember now
Once and for all because now
Now if you want to stay together
Now finally now you need to **fight**.

Part Six

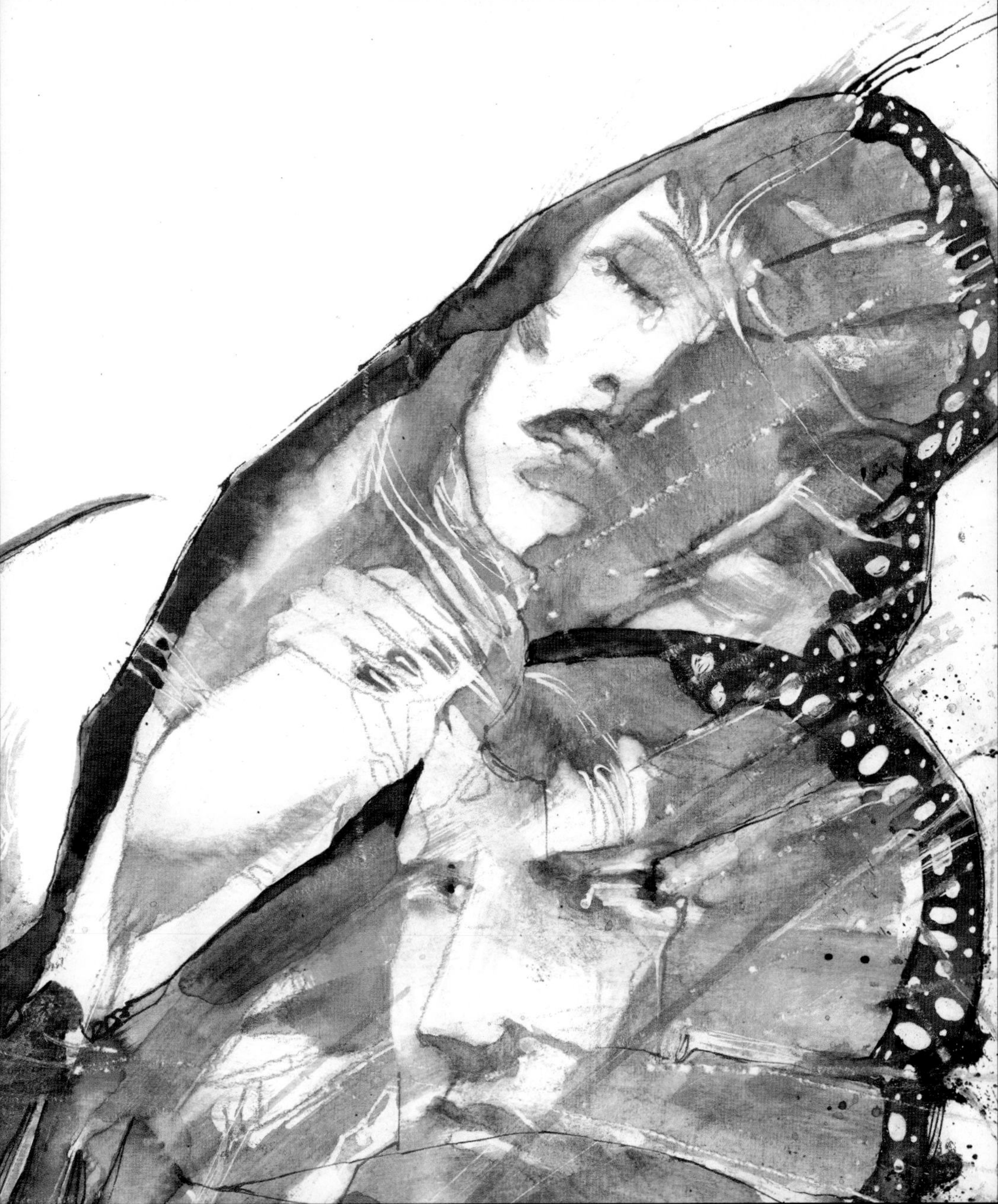

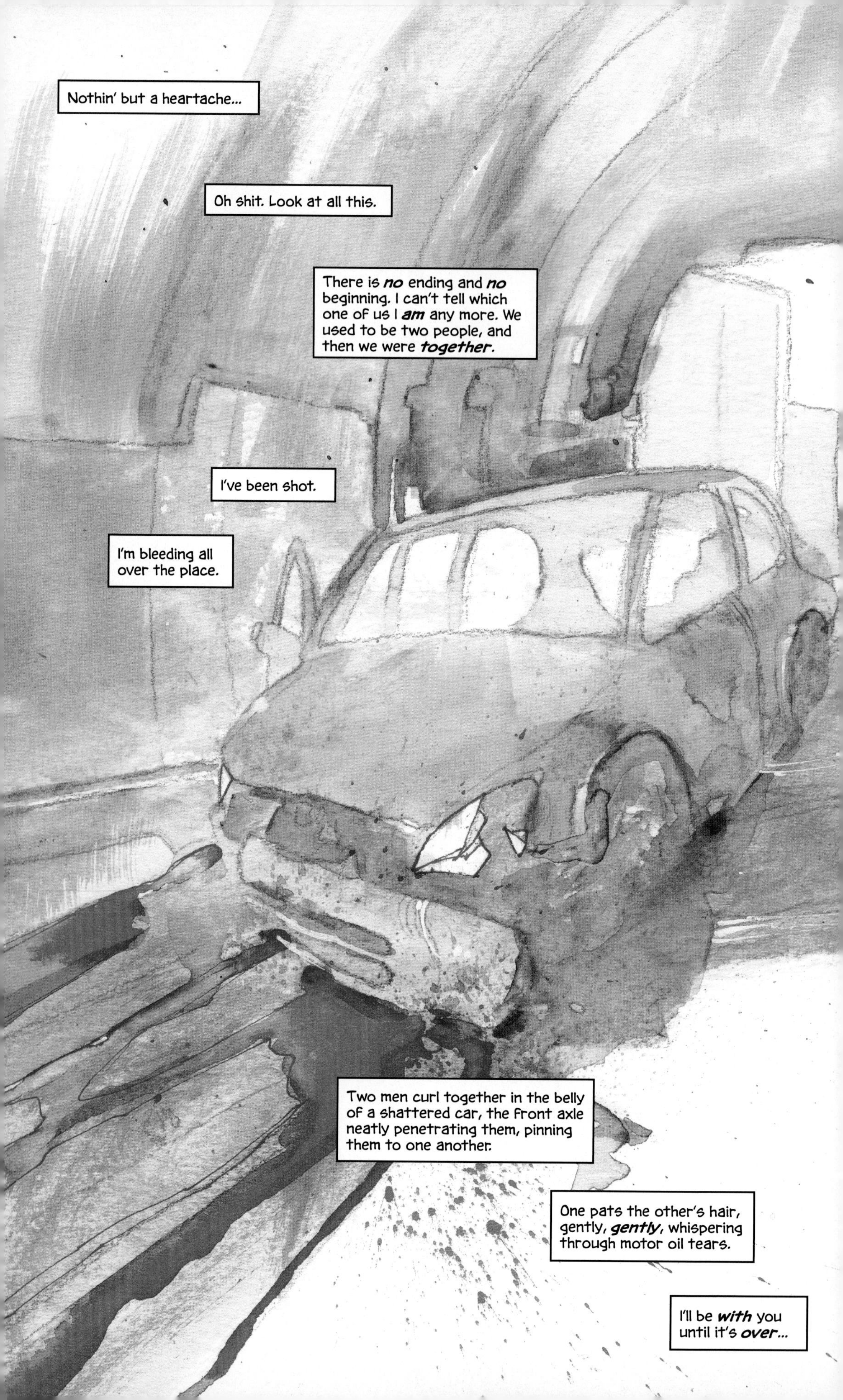
Nothin' but a heartache...
Oh shit. Look at all this.
There is **no** ending and **no** beginning. I can't tell which one of us I **am** any more. We used to be two people, and then we were **together**.
I've been shot.
I'm bleeding all over the place.
Two men curl together in the belly of a shattered car, the front axle neatly penetrating them, pinning them to one another.
One pats the other's hair, gently, **gently**, whispering through motor oil tears.
I'll be **with** you until it's **over**...

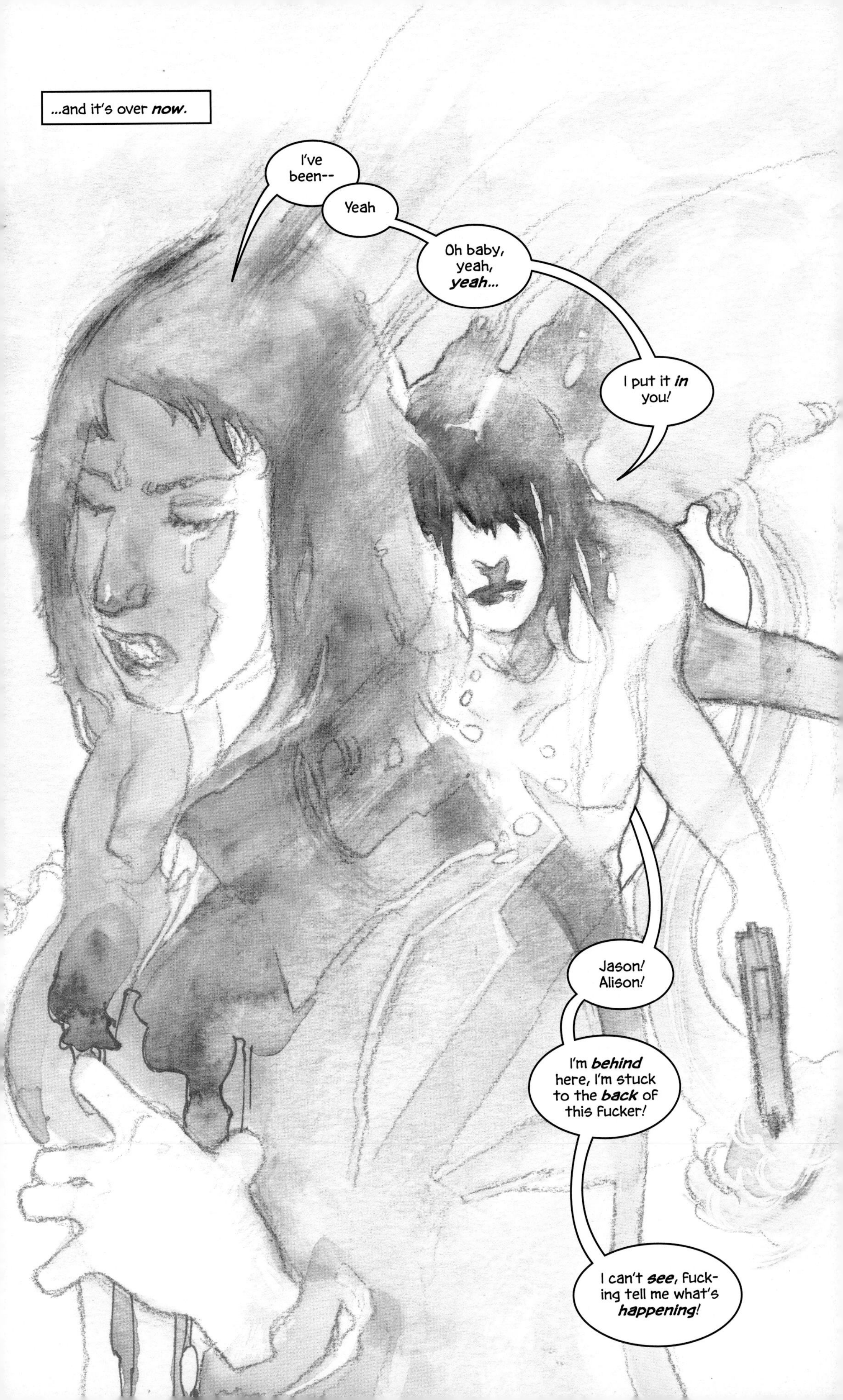
...and it's over *now.*
I've been--
Yeah
Oh baby, yeah, *yeah...*
I put it *in* you!
Jason! Alison!
I'm *behind* here, I'm stuck to the *back* of this fucker!
I can't *see*, fucking tell me what's *happening*!

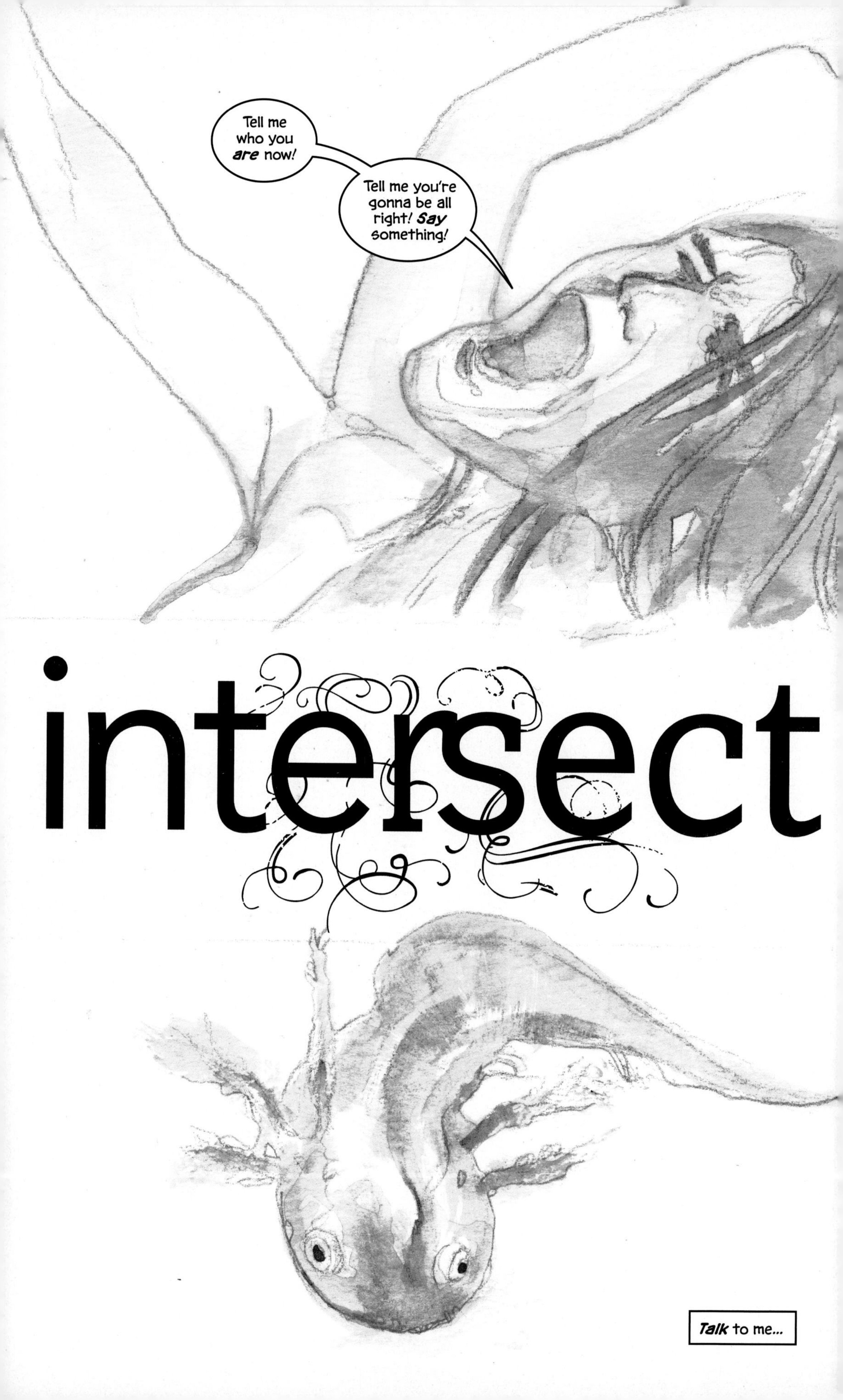
Tell me who you *are* now!
Tell me you're gonna be all right! *Say* something!
intersect
Talk to me...

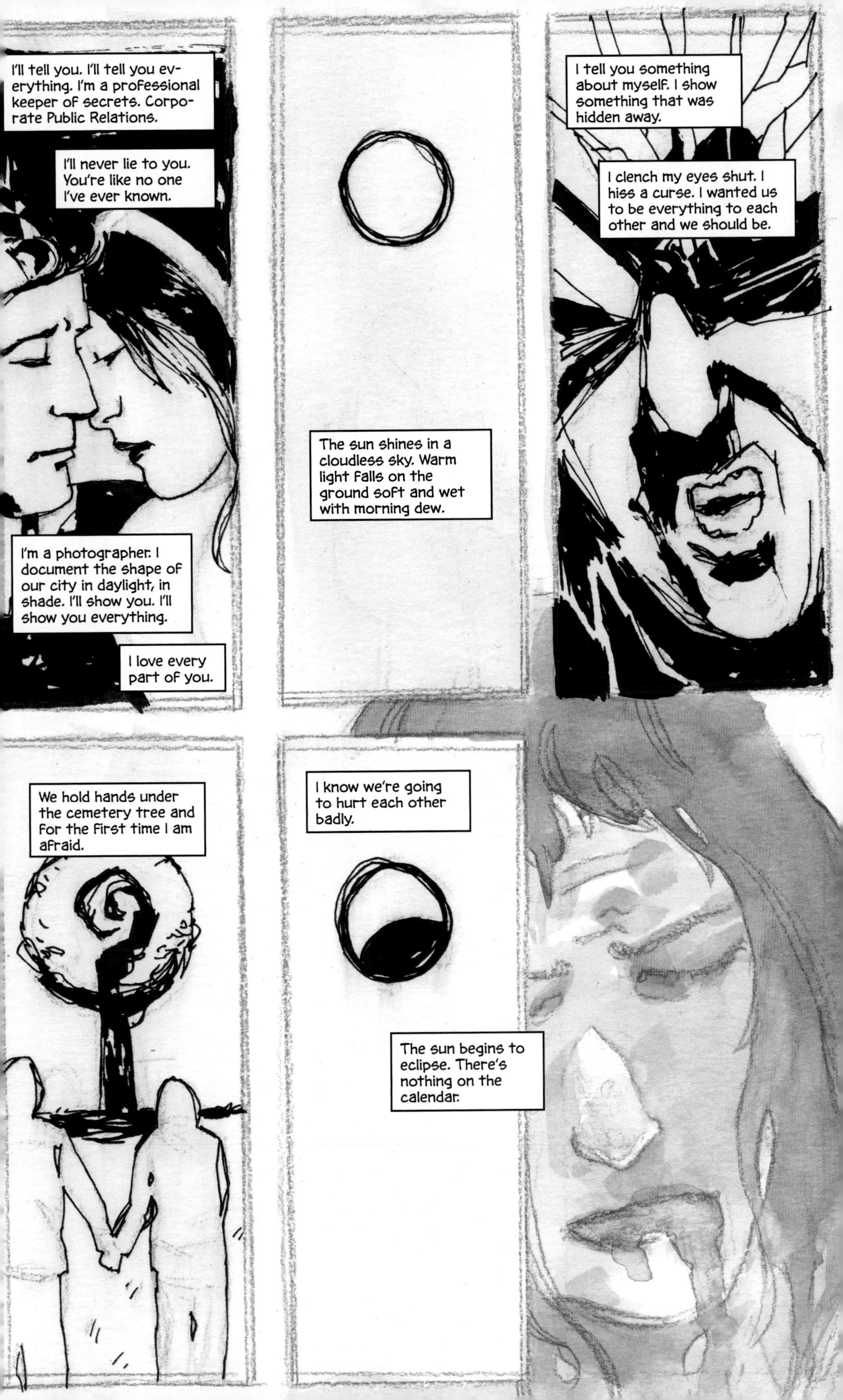
I'll tell you. I'll tell you everything. I'm a professional keeper of secrets. Corporate Public Relations.
I'll never lie to you. You're like no one I've ever known.
I'm a photographer. I document the shape of our city in daylight, in shade. I'll show you. I'll show you everything.
I love every part of you.
The sun shines in a cloudless sky. Warm light falls on the ground soft and wet with morning dew.
I tell you something about myself. I show something that was hidden away.
I clench my eyes shut. I hiss a curse. I wanted us to be everything to each other and we should be.
We hold hands under the cemetery tree and for the first time I am afraid.
I know we're going to hurt each other badly.
The sun begins to eclipse. There's nothing on the calendar.

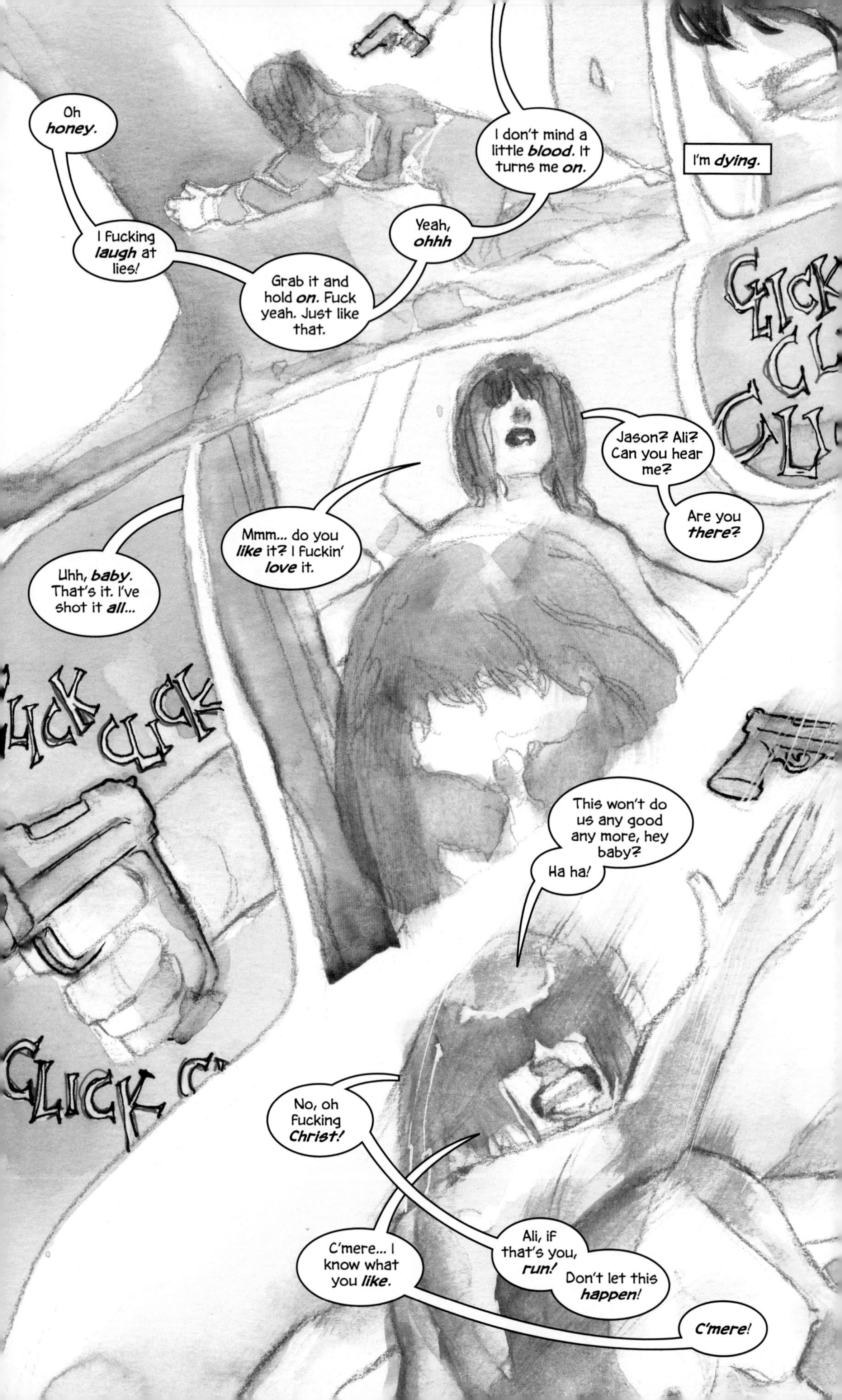
Oh honey.
I fucking laugh at lies!
Grab it and hold on. Fuck yeah. Just like that.
Yeah, ohhh
I don't mind a little blood. It turns me on.
I'm dying.
CLICK
Jason? Ali? Can you hear me?
Are you there?
Mmm... do you like it? I fuckin' love it.
Uhh, baby. That's it. I've shot it all...
CLICK
This won't do us any good any more, hey baby?
Ha ha!
CLICK
No, oh fucking Christ!
Ali, if that's you, run!
Don't let this happen!
C'mere... I know what you like.
C'mere!

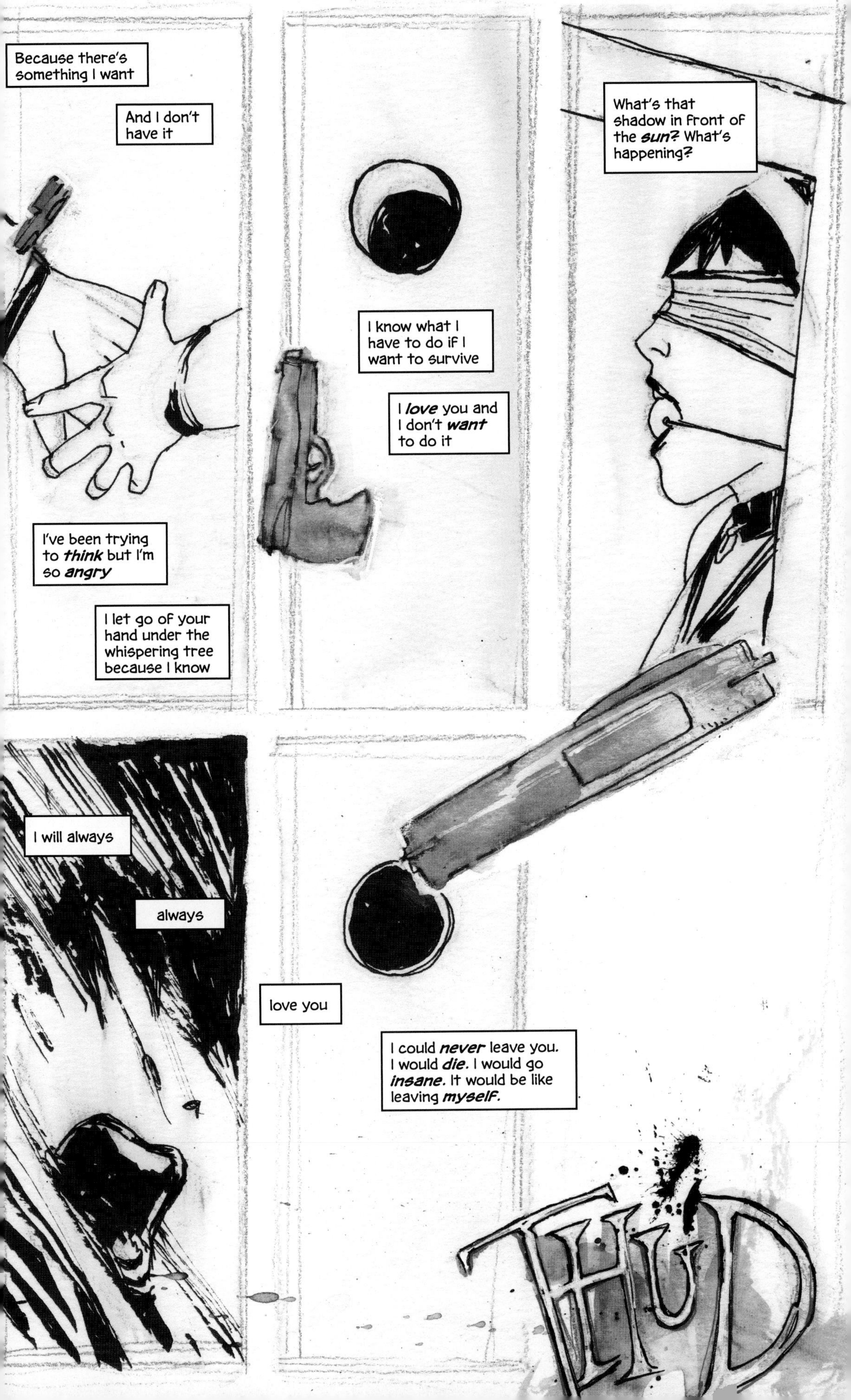

Because there's something I want
And I don't have it
I've been trying to *think* but I'm so *angry*
I let go of your hand under the whispering tree because I know
I know what I have to do if I want to survive
I *love* you and I don't *want* to do it
What's that shadow in front of the *sun*? What's happening?
I will always
always
love you
I could *never* leave you. I would *die*. I would go *insane*. It would be like leaving *myself*.
THUD

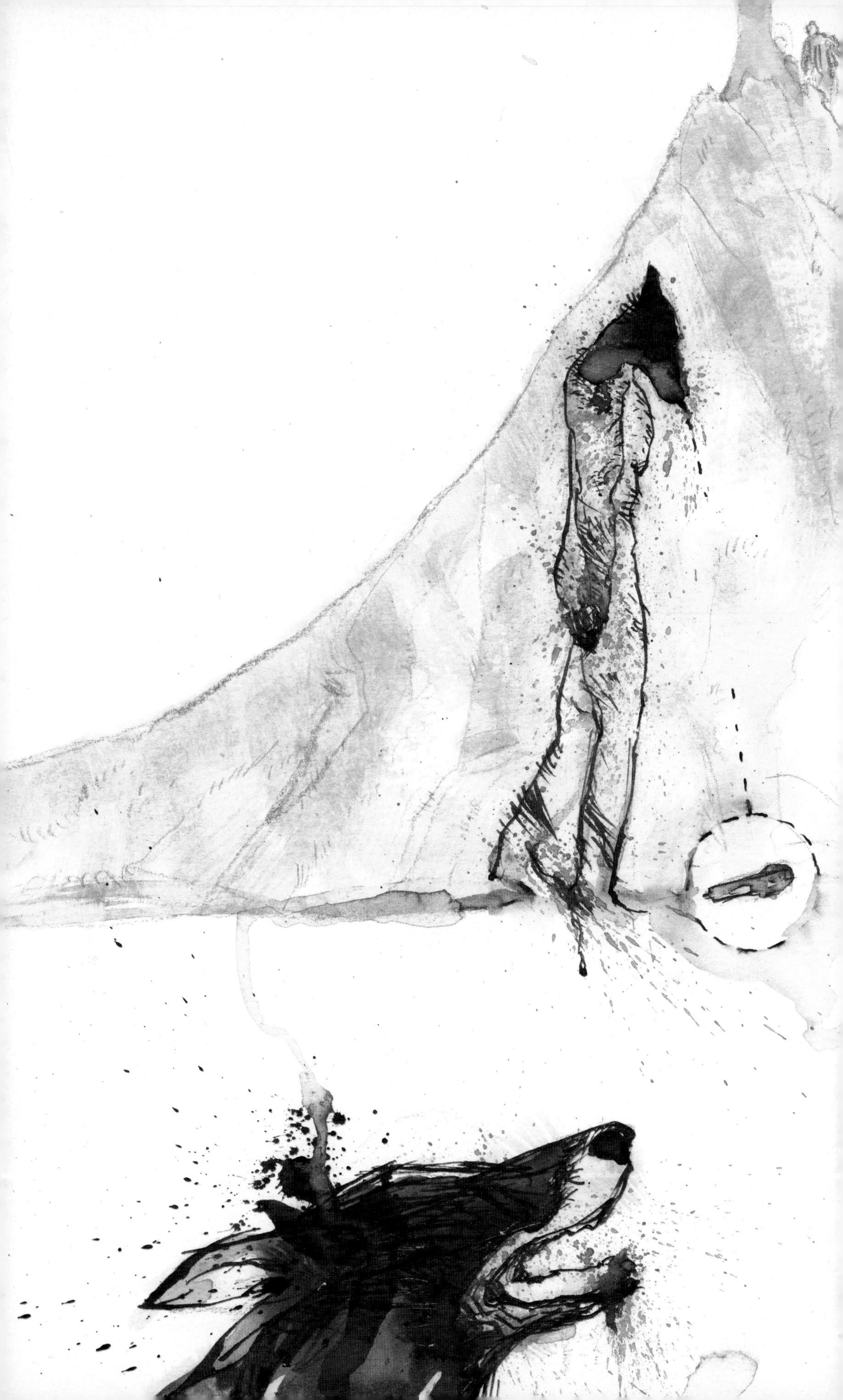

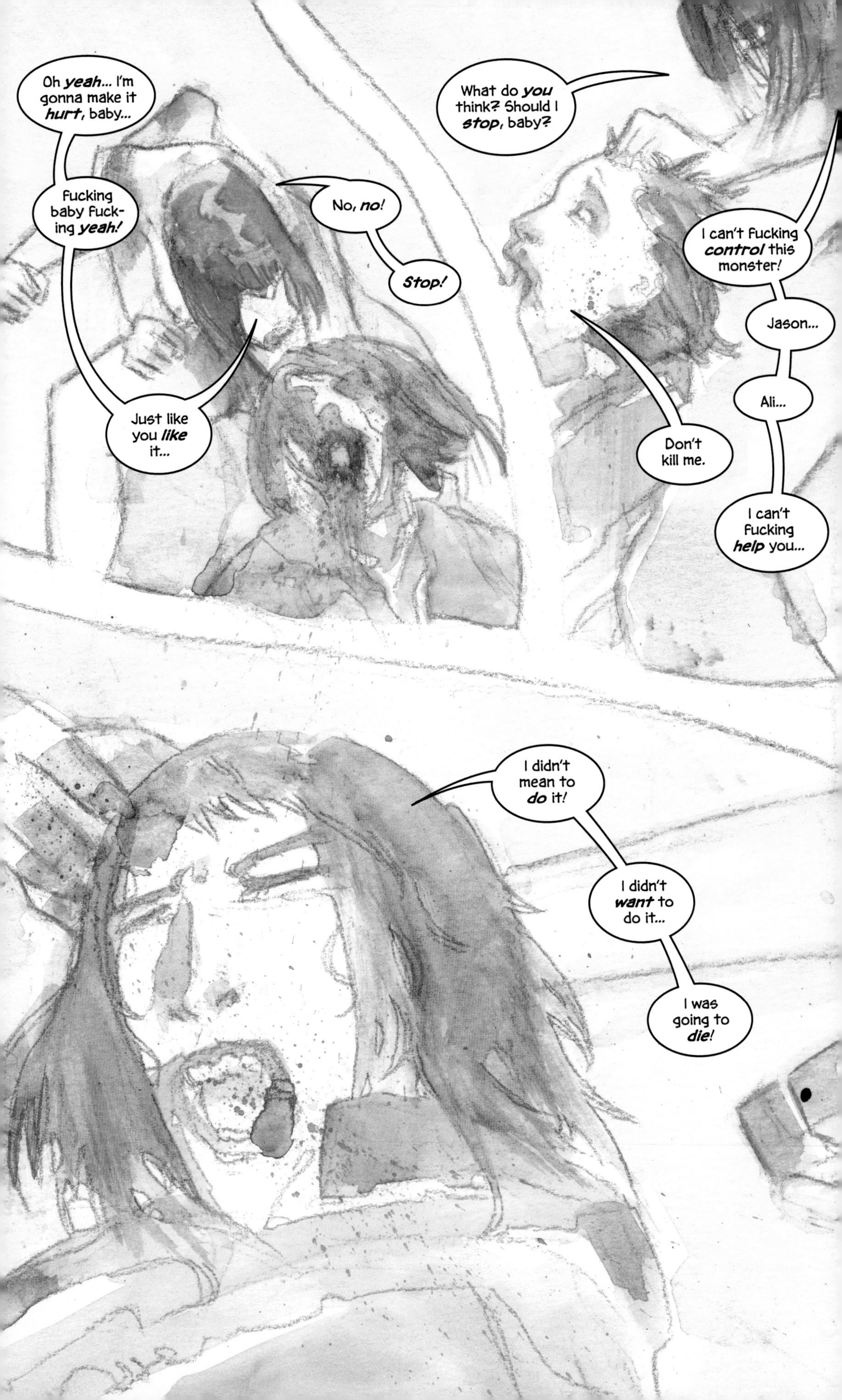
Oh *yeah*... I'm gonna make it *hurt*, baby...
Fucking baby Fuck-ing *yeah!*
Just like you *like* it...
No, *no!*
Stop!
What do *you* think? Should I *stop*, baby?
Don't kill me.
I can't Fucking *control* this monster!
Jason...
Ali...
I can't Fucking *help* you...
I didn't mean to *do* it!
I didn't *want* to do it...
I was going to *die!*

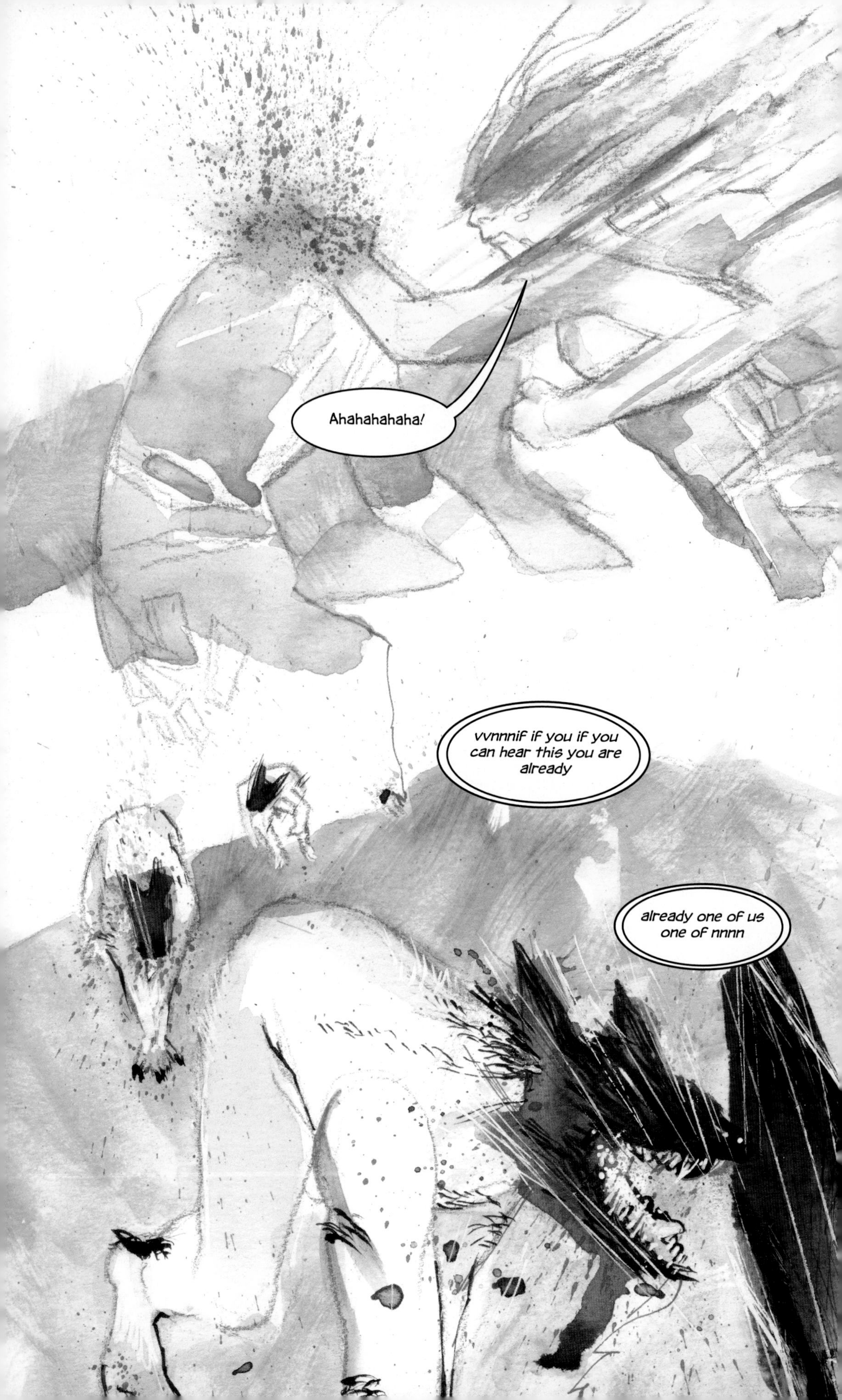

Ahahahahaha!
vvnnnif if you if you can hear this you are already
already one of us one of nnnn

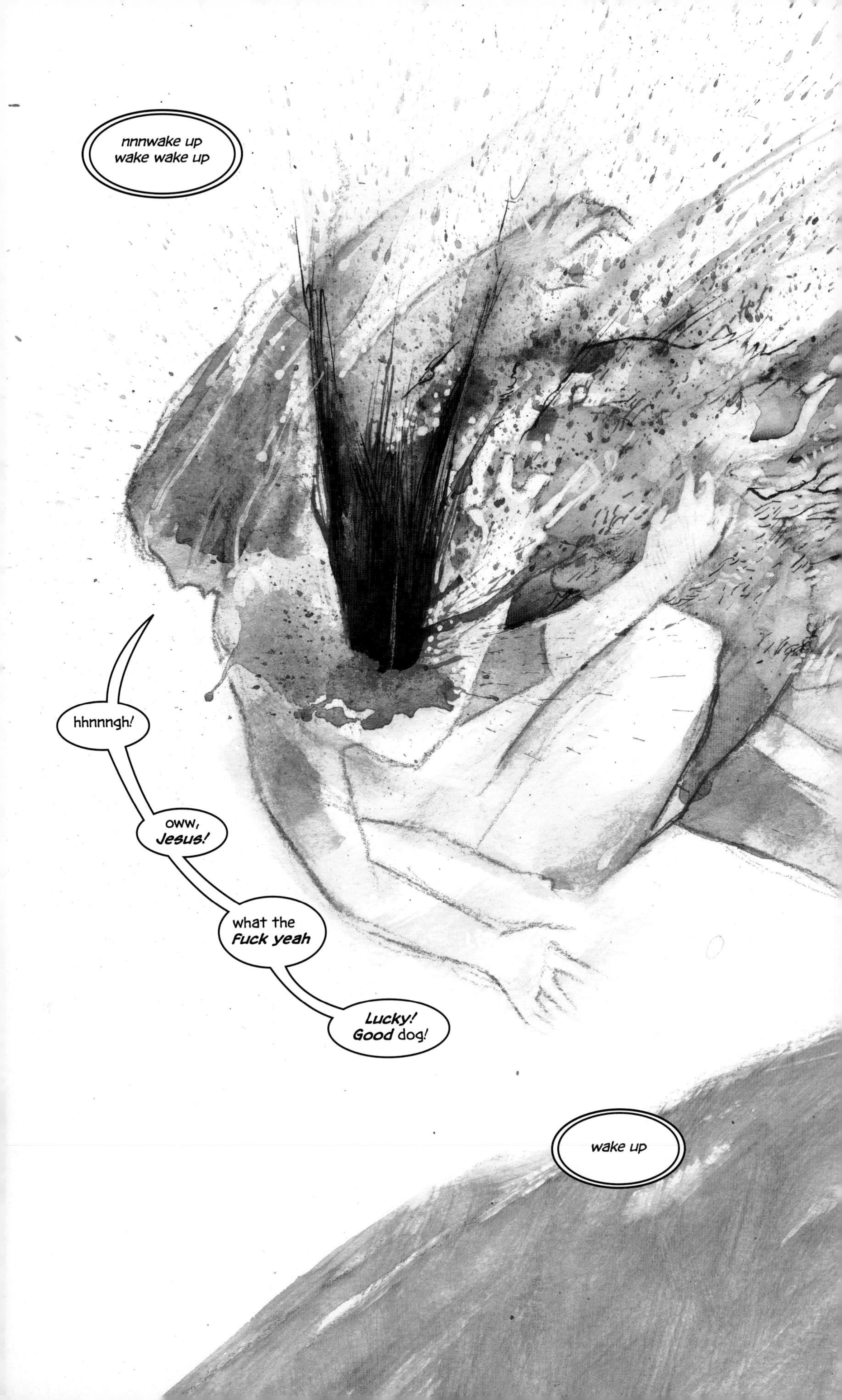
nnnwake up
wake wake up
hhnnngh!
oww, Jesus!
what the Fuck yeah
Lucky! Good dog!
wake up

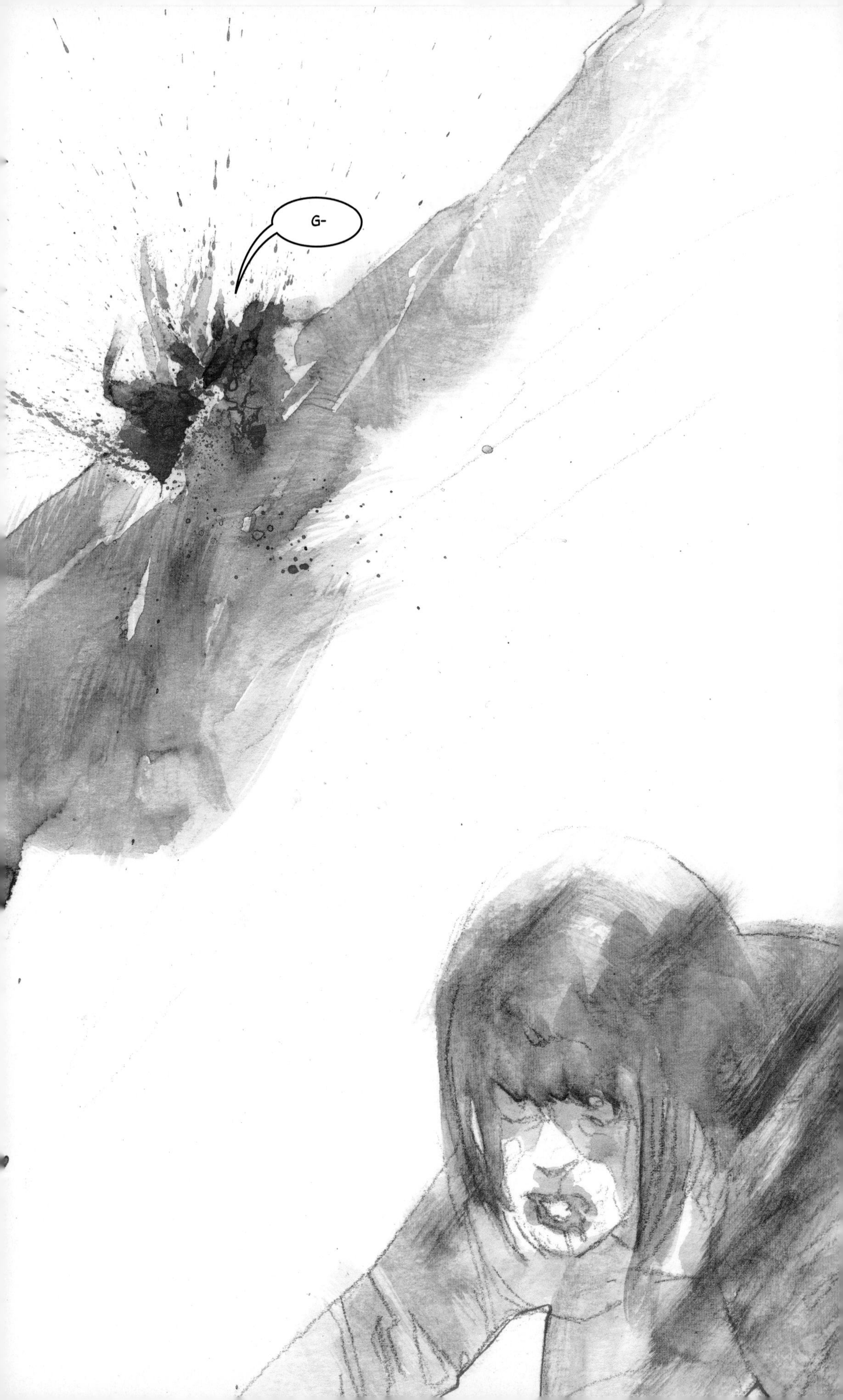
G-

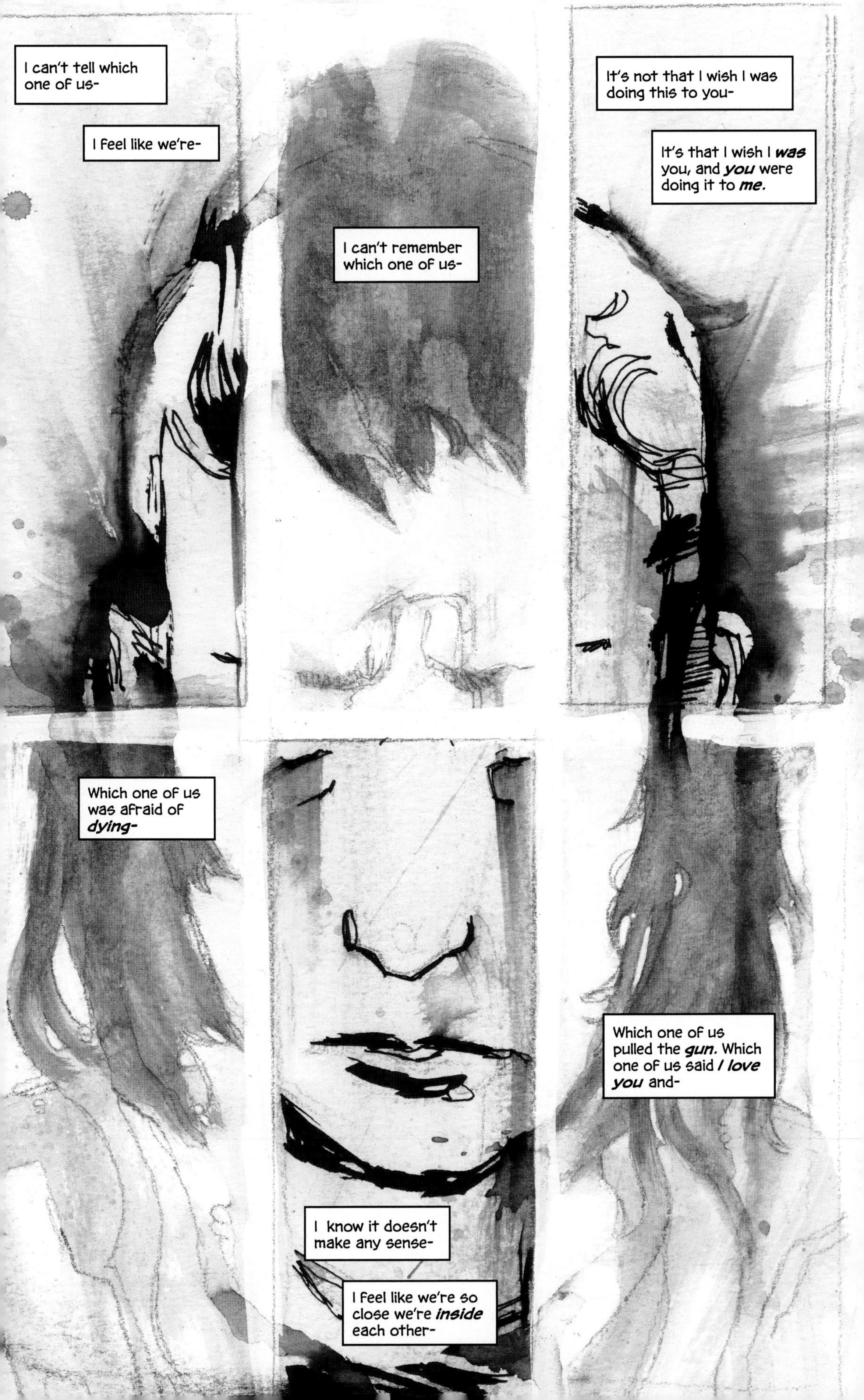
I can't tell which one of us-
I feel like we're-
I can't remember which one of us-
It's not that I wish I was doing this to you-
It's that I wish I *was* you, and *you* were doing it to *me.*
Which one of us was afraid of *dying-*
Which one of us pulled the *gun*. Which one of us said *I love you* and-
I know it doesn't make any sense-
I feel like we're so close we're *inside* each other-

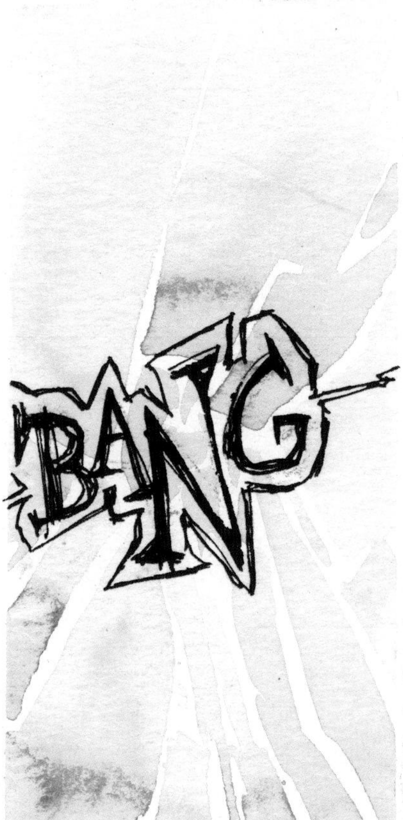
BANG

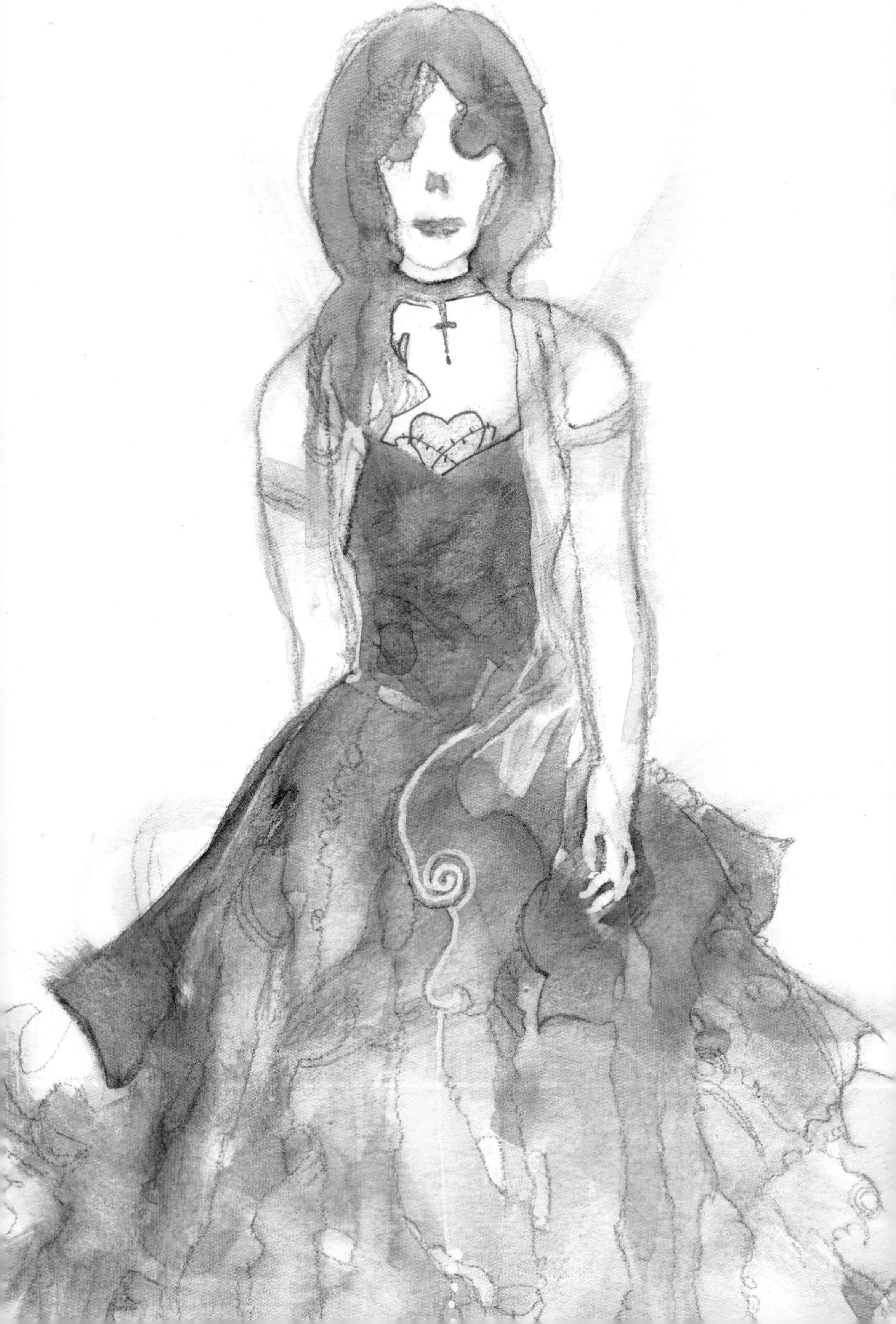

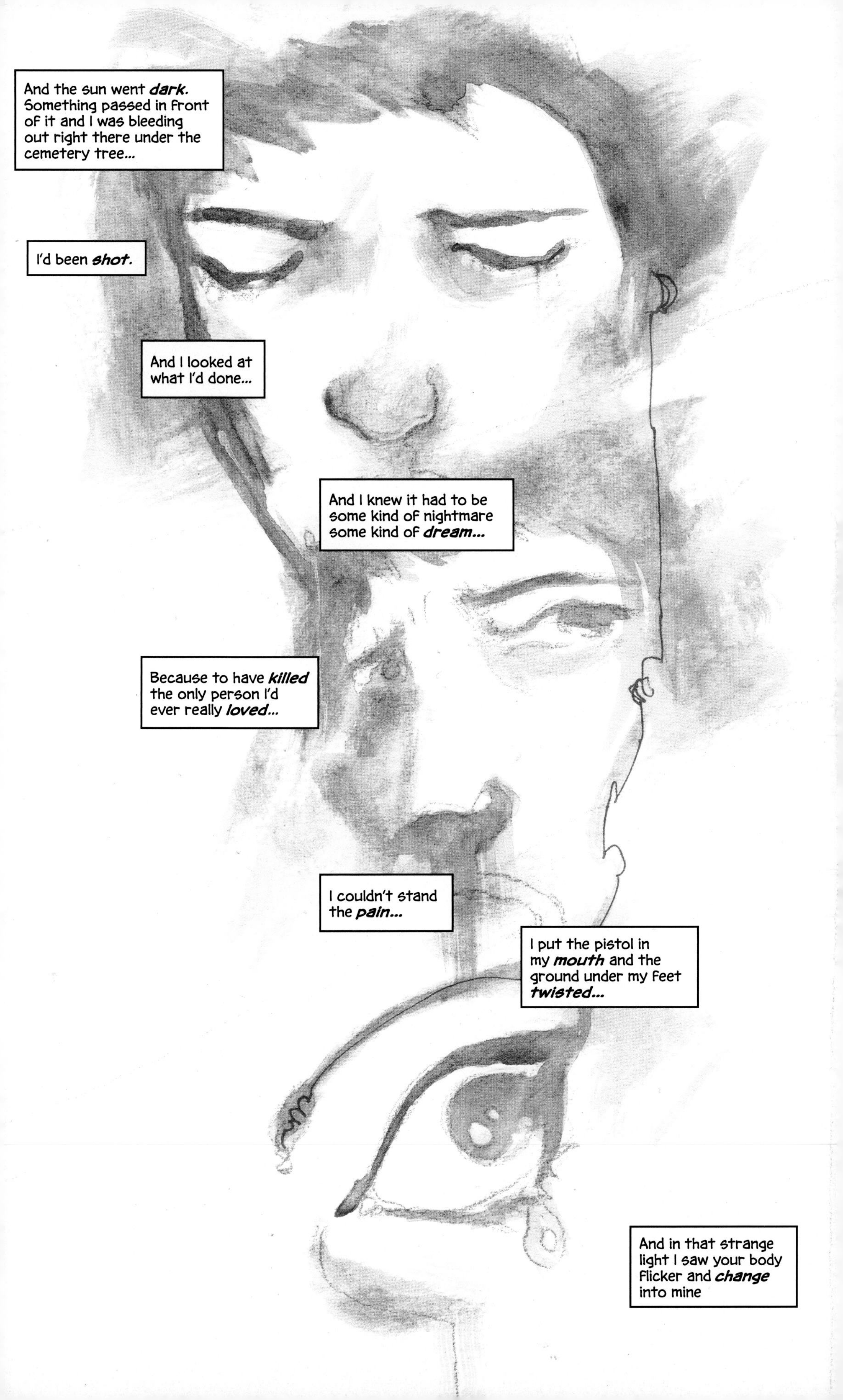
And the sun went *dark*. Something passed in front of it and I was bleeding out right there under the cemetery tree...
I'd been *shot*.
And I looked at what I'd done...
And I knew it had to be some kind of nightmare some kind of *dream*...
Because to have *killed* the only person I'd ever really *loved*...
I couldn't stand the *pain*...
I put the pistol in my *mouth* and the ground under my feet *twisted*...
And in that strange light I saw your body flicker and *change* into mine

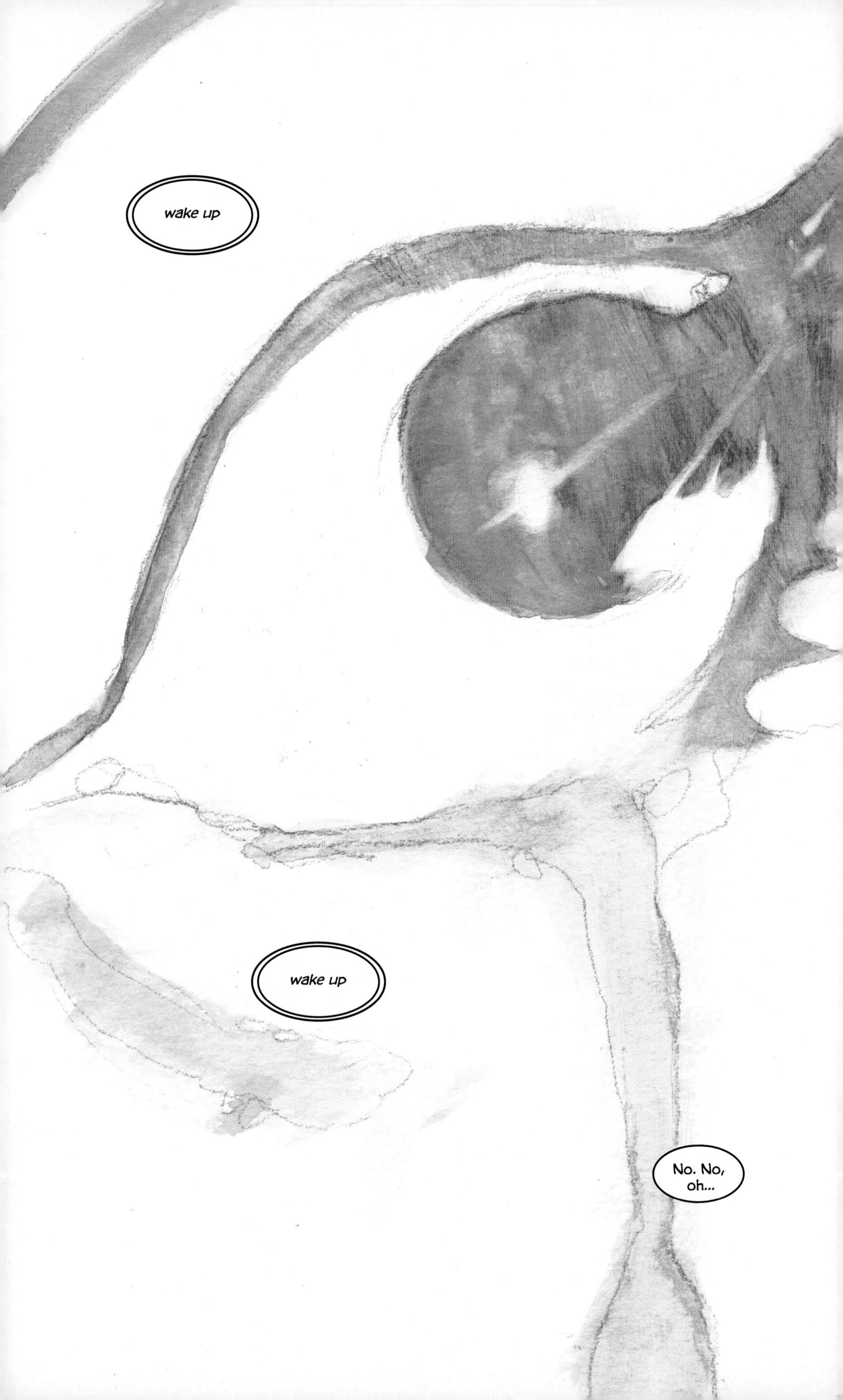
wake up
wake up
No. No,
oh...

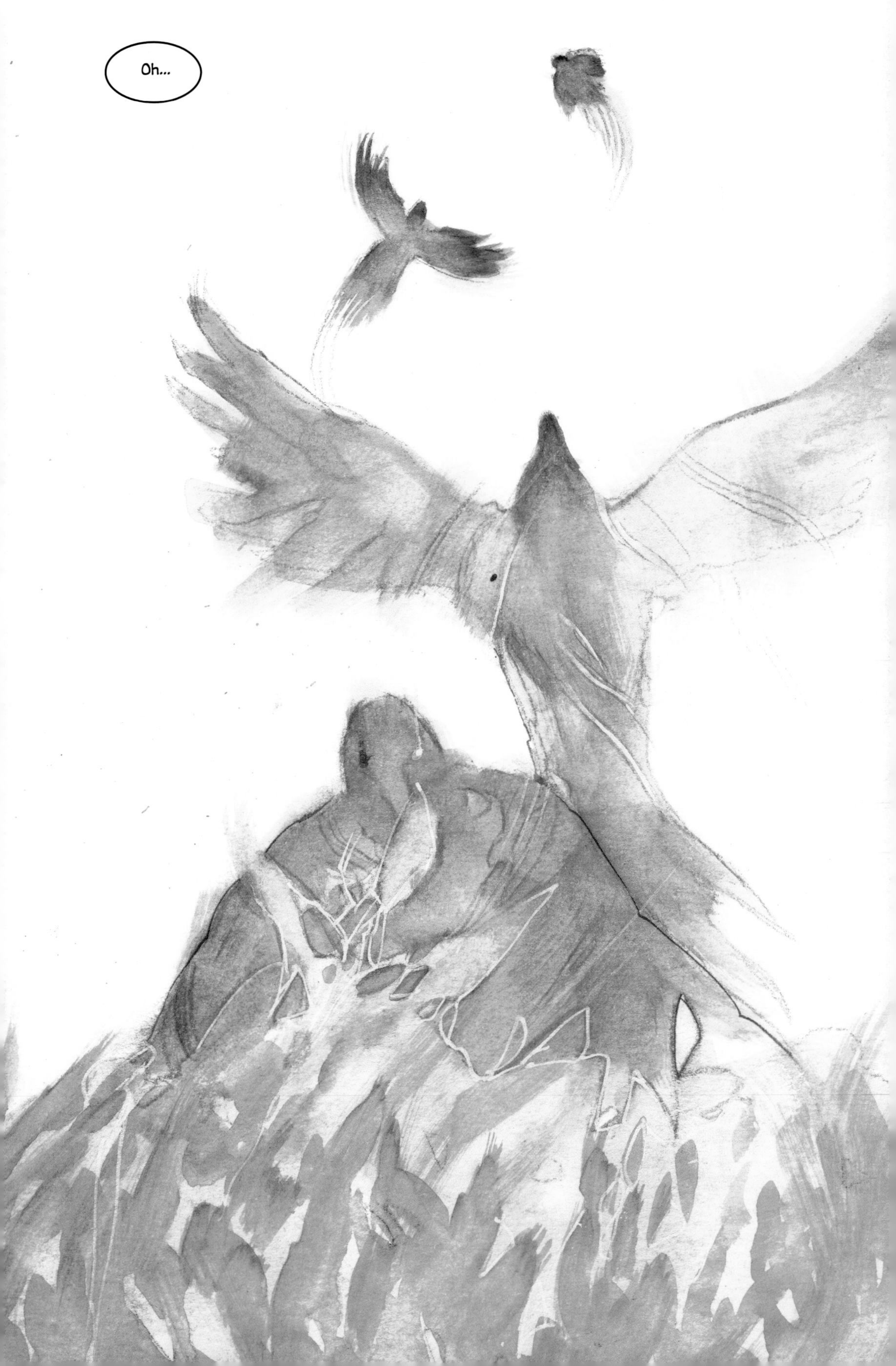
Oh...

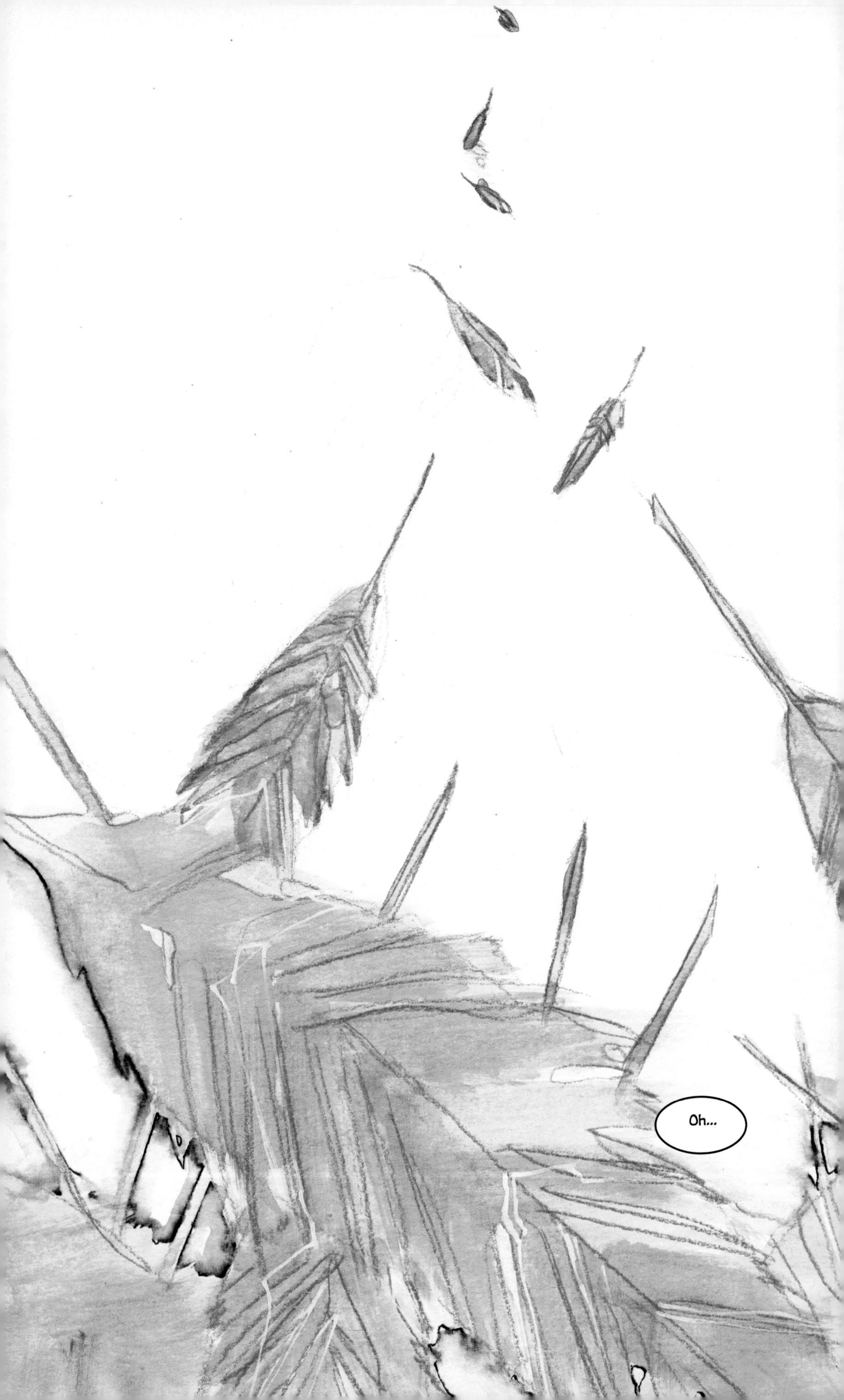
Oh...

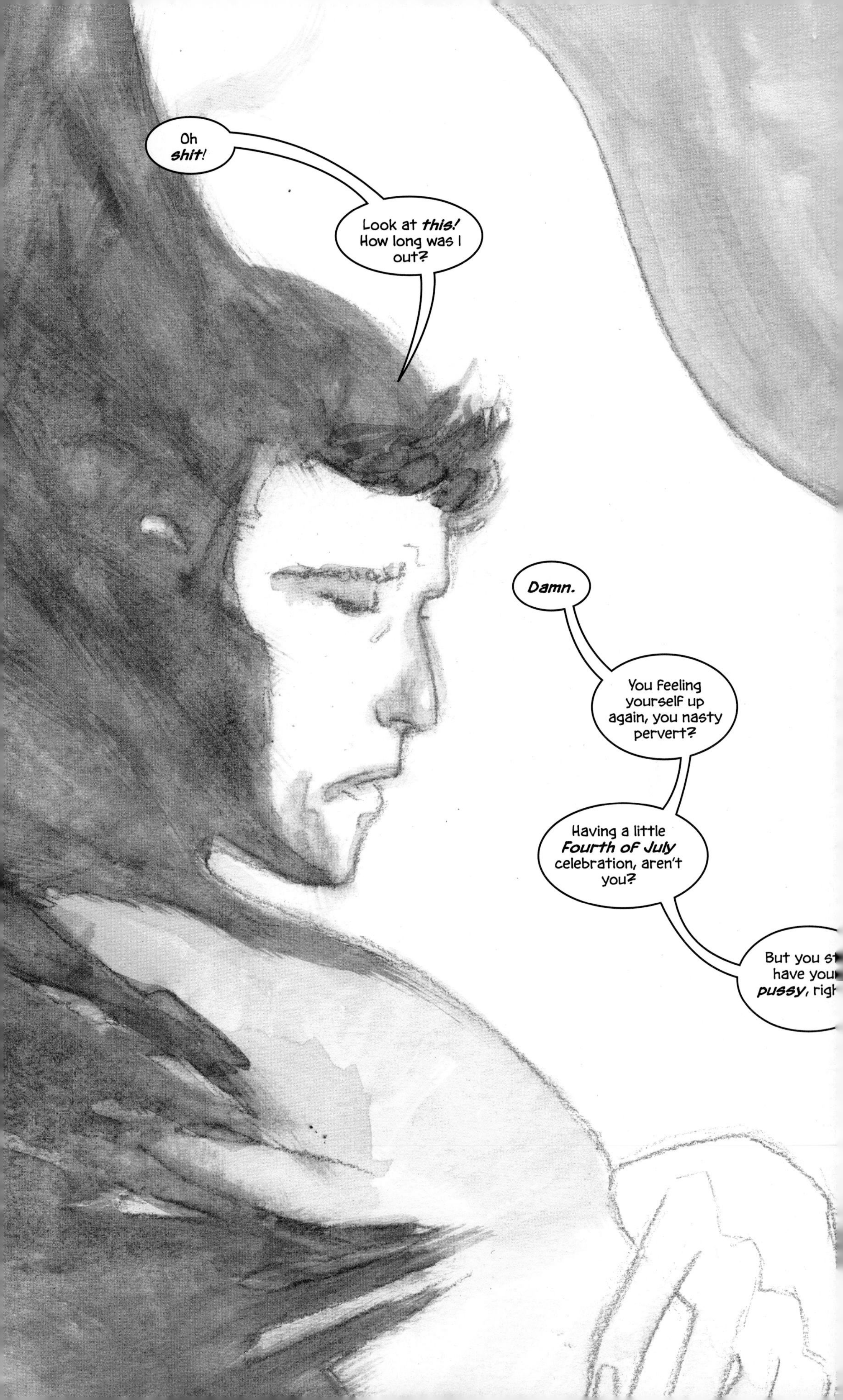
Oh *shit!*
Look at *this!* How long was I out?
Damn.
You feeling yourself up again, you nasty pervert?
Having a little *Fourth of July* celebration, aren't you?
But you st have your *pussy*, righ

About the Author

Ray Fawkes is a Toronto-based author and illustrator. He is an Eisner, Harvey, Shuster, and Doug Wright Award nominee for his work on various graphic novels and comic book titles, and is a YALSA award winner for his "Possessions" series. His work for DC and Marvel comics includes such titles as Batman:Eternal, Constantine, Justice League Dark, and Wolverines, and he is the creator of the critically acclaimed graphic novels ONE SOUL and THE PEOPLE INSIDE.